THE OCEAN LINER

ALSO BY MARIUS GABRIEL

The Designer
Wish Me Luck as You Wave Me Goodbye
Take Me to Your Heart Again
The Original Sin
The Mask of Time
A House of Many Rooms
The Seventh Moon

THE OCEAN LINER

MARIUS GABRIEL

LAKE UNION
PUBLISHING

This is a work of fiction. Names, characters, organizations, places, events, and incidents are either products of the author's imagination or are used fictitiously.

Published by Lake Union Publishing, Seattle

www.apub.com

ISBN-13: 9781477805145
ISBN-10: 1477805141

Cover design by Debbie Clement

Cover photography by Raúl Garcia

Printed in the United States of America

For Teddy, Tom, Emma and Sabby

Le Havre, 1939

'He's a very ugly man,' Rachel said. 'Even uglier than his photographs.'

'But look at his eyes,' Masha replied. 'They burn like coals.'

'Well, I don't find him impressive. And as for his music—'

'You don't like his music?'

'Not in the slightest.' Rachel, who had studied at the music conservatory in Leipzig before the Nazis had ejected her, had firm views on modern music. 'If I wish to be disturbed, I shall go to the zoo and listen to the tigers roar.'

'But that's exactly my point. His music excites one, the way a dangerous animal excites one.' The two girls had been craning over the railing to watch Stravinsky come aboard their ship. They thought of it as 'theirs', this magnificent American liner, even though it had so far carried them only from Bremen to Le Havre. But those five hundred nautical miles had already taken them into a new world.

Stravinsky was making slow progress up the gangplank, helped by a middle-aged woman, evidently his travelling companion. They were met by the charming senior steward, Mr Nightingale, immaculate in his white serge and gold buttons. Mr Nightingale attempted to take the composer's bag, but he refused. 'I'm sure it contains his latest work,' Masha whispered to Rachel, 'too precious to be entrusted to anyone.'

Perhaps sensing that he was being watched, Stravinsky looked up. His eyes met the girls'. They both darted back from the rail and began to walk along the deck swiftly, arm in arm, past the rows of loungers, embarrassed at having been caught staring at the great man.

'I saw *The Rite of Spring* in Berlin, a few years ago,' Rachel said. 'It's about a young girl who dances herself to death. I found it quite horrible.'

'I've seen it too. I was electrified.'

'Hardly a pleasant sensation, I should say. That's how the Americans execute their criminals, isn't it?'

'I felt my heart beating so hard that I thought it was going to jump out of my chest. The Nazi papers said it was degenerate rubbish, of course.'

'Well, one has to bow to the sublime taste of the Nazis. And it's unfortunate that he's a Jew. He is the kind of conceited Jew who gives all us Jews a bad name.'

'As a matter of fact, my dear Rachel, he is Russian Orthodox, and a devout Christian.'

Rachel arched her plucked eyebrows satirically. 'Oh, Masha! Not even a Jew, and you're in love with him?'

'I'm not in love with him – only with his music.'

'I am distressed to see you already whoring after the Gentile,' Rachel replied with a pious sniff.

'You're very naughty to make fun of Rabbi Moskovitz,' Masha said. She had been warned for years that her cousin Rachel was 'dangerous', though nobody had explained quite what the danger was. Rachel was certainly very satirical. Masha was a vivacious young woman of twenty with a cloud of dark hair and bright hazel eyes. Her cousin was older by three years. While not so pretty, Rachel was blonde, which they both felt would be an advantage in America. They had the family name

Morgenstern, and they were first cousins, although they had grown up in different cities: Rachel in Leipzig, Masha in Berlin.

Before leaving Bremen, both girls had been subjected to stern lectures on keeping themselves pure as they embarked on new lives. Rachel, who had a facility for quoting scraps of the Torah in a nasal chant, had made Rabbi Moskovitz the subject of a number of jokes.

'Thy lewdness shall be uncovered, and mark my words, child' – Rachel wagged her finger, squinting hideously like Rabbi Moskovitz – 'thou shalt pluck off thine own breasts.' They had reached the end of the promenade and now turned around. Despite herself, Masha was laughing at Rachel's parody. It was unfortunate that just at that moment, Stravinsky had reached the deck.

Stravinsky glowered at the cousins, panting for breath after his slow climb. Masha realised with horror that the celebrated composer imagined he was the subject of their mirth. She clapped her hand over her mouth. That, however, made the situation even more uncomfortable.

Stravinsky's companion, a spinsterish woman in a lavender-tweed suit, took his arm to steady him and steered him past the cousins. As they went by, Masha noted Stravinsky's yellowed skin, faltering walk and general air of exhaustion. She felt a rush of pity.

'He looks so ill,' she exclaimed in an undertone to Rachel, 'so broken – and he thought we were laughing at him. I'm mortified.'

Katharine Wolff helped Stravinsky down the companionway. His small feet, usually so light and neat in their motions, stumbled on the stairs. His shoes, usually gleaming, were dusty. His person, usually impeccable, was crumpled. He seemed to have reached the end of his strength.

The journey from Bordeaux to Le Havre had been difficult, the roads choked with vehicles. Since the declaration of war a fortnight earlier, the whole of France had been swarming like an ants' nest disturbed by a wicked boy with a stick. The mighty German army was massing on the borders for an invasion. There had already been fighting at Saarbrucken. The British were sending an expeditionary force to bolster the French army, with its flimsy tanks and antiquated aircraft. A catastrophe loomed. All those who could were getting out.

They had arrived at the harbour with frayed nerves after many hours on a hot road, still broken-hearted after parting from Nadia Boulanger and their circle of friends. The formalities of getting on board had been prolonged and had taken their toll on Stravinsky's already depleted energies. Their baggage had not yet arrived from Bordeaux, nor their papers from the United States embassy in Paris. It was by no means certain that Stravinsky, who had just been released from quarantine, would be given the emergency visa he had applied for. Katharine, who was American, did not need one, but she had decided she would not leave France without Igor. If necessary, she would remain with him and face the consequences.

The willowy senior steward who had met them on the gangplank, and who was now leading the way, was garrulous and apologetic.

'We're going to be over capacity,' he told them. 'The *Manhattan* is fitted to take twelve hundred passengers. We're going to have more than fifteen hundred by the time we leave Cobh. It's not the way we like to do things, but under the circumstances, you understand—'

Katharine was impatient to get Igor to their cabin. 'Our baggage hasn't arrived yet and we're due to sail on Saturday.'

'Don't worry about that, Miss Wolff. I'm sure it will arrive on time.'

'What on earth makes you sure?' she snapped.

'Well, I'm expressing a hope—'

'Your hope doesn't help us in the slightest. If we have to leave without our baggage, it will be very difficult for us.' They were making their way ever downward, into the bowels of the great ocean liner. Passengers and crew members crowded the stairs. She tried to shelter her charge as best she could from the jostling. 'Is it much further, Mr Nightingale?'

'Nearly there. What I'm getting at, Miss Wolff, is that the captain has made new rules.'

'Rules?'

'Mr Stravinsky is going to be sharing his cabin.'

'Sharing? But we booked a stateroom.'

'Commodore Randall's orders, Miss Wolff. We've been instructed to turn nobody away. Sharing is the only way we can get the extra passengers on board. There will be refunds, of course. As for your good self—'

'Don't tell me I'll be sharing too!'

'I'm afraid so. You'll be in a nearby cabin with some other ladies.'

'No baggage – and sharing our cabins!' Katharine glanced at Stravinsky, but he was impassive. He seemed dazed. 'That's outrageous!'

'Very sorry for the inconvenience, but under the circumstances—'

'Who will Stravinsky be sharing with?'

The steward consulted his list. 'A Herr Thomas König is already in the cabin.'

'A German!'

'Yes. He embarked at Bremen. Here we are.'

They had stopped in front of a door. The steward drummed daintily on it with his varnished fingernails. There was no answer, so he opened it. Katharine, ever protective, bustled in ahead of Stravinsky. The cabin was occupied by a boy of around sixteen, in uniform, who was sitting on the edge of his bunk, his eyes wide. He jumped to his feet when he saw Katharine and raised his right hand in a salute. 'Heil Hitler!'

Katharine pulled the upraised hand down brusquely. 'How dare you?'

The boy seemed shocked. 'I'm sorry, Fräulein—'

She only just restrained herself from slapping the thin, hard face. 'This is France! None of that poisonous rubbish here.'

The boy's prominent ears flushed beetroot red. Stravinsky had followed Katharine into the stateroom and was now examining his fellow traveller wearily. They made an odd pair: the composer in his creased brown suit, his face a contour map of folds and pouches, and the fresh-faced boy in his pseudo-military uniform of khaki shirt and short pants, his brown socks pulled up to his knobbly knees.

Katharine took the steward's arm and pulled him back into the corridor. 'This is intolerable, Mr Nightingale. Stravinsky cannot be expected to spend the voyage with a little Nazi.'

'He's travelling on his own,' the steward murmured, leaning forward with a rush of peppermint breath. 'There are no parents with him.'

'Stravinsky is a banned composer in the Third Reich. Do you understand what that means?' The steward fluttered his hands anxiously, opening his mouth, but Katharine cut him off. 'If he were to be captured by Hitler's hordes, he would be exterminated. How can he spend the voyage in the company of this – this exemplar of Hitler Youth?'

'It will only be a week or two.'

'I insist that he be removed at once.'

Mr Nightingale licked the tip of his little finger and nervously smoothed his eyebrows into place. 'I will see what I can arrange.'

'You do that.'

Katharine went back into the cabin. Stravinsky was shaking hands solemnly with the boy. 'And may I ask, where are your parents?' he enquired, with the courtesy he showed to everyone.

'My father and mother are in Germany, sir,' the boy replied, matching Stravinsky's formality.

'You seem rather young to be travelling on your own.'

'I am eighteen, sir.' When Stravinsky looked sceptical at that, the boy squared his lean shoulders. Katharine saw that there was a little enamel swastika pinned to his lapel. 'I am going to visit the World's Fair in Flushing Meadows,' he said proudly, as though announcing that he was being sent as Ambassador Plenipotentiary to the League of Nations.

'Oh well, that's very fine,' Stravinsky replied, nodding tiredly.

Katharine looked around the cabin. It was small. There was a china washstand, an electric fan fastened on the bulkhead, a wool rug and other signs of modest comfort. Stravinsky had not been able to afford Cabin Class. She had offered to pay the difference, but he had refused. She hadn't liked to press the matter. He was very proud and felt his financial troubles keenly.

The boy gestured at the bunk he had been sitting on, which was covered with the adventure books he had been reading. 'I took this one because it's the smallest, but if you prefer it, please take it. It has the porthole, you see.'

'You're very kind,' Stravinsky said, 'but I think you should have the porthole. I will take this one next to you, if it's all the same to you.' He sat on the bed and looked up at Katharine with hollow eyes. 'I think I would like to rest a little now, chérie.'

'Yes, of course, Igor.' Katharine knelt down and began unlacing one of his shoes.

'I can do that myself,' he said, but he made no move to stop her. After a moment, the German boy knelt beside Katharine and began unlacing the other shoe. Stravinsky watched them in silence, his eyelids heavy, his lower lip drooping open.

Mr Nightingale put his knee on the bunk to draw the shades across the porthole, blocking out the bright autumn sun and casting the cabin into an ochre twilight. Katharine helped Stravinsky take off his jacket and his round-rimmed spectacles. He lay back on the pillows, closing his eyes. His features sagged, his eyes seeming to sink inward, his full lips drooping so that his teeth were exposed under his clipped moustache. His straw-coloured hair was thin. He was only fifty-seven, but Katharine had a sudden terror that he was already dying. He murmured, 'Thank you, chérie,' and waved her away.

Mr Nightingale was anxious to show her to her own cabin, so she was forced to leave him there, in the company of the German boy. She gave him a last, suspicious glare before leaving.

Mr Nightingale was gossipy as they hurried along. 'It's a great honour to have Mr Stravinsky on board, a great honour. We have quite a number of celebrities with us this trip, Miss Wolff, quite a number. Toscanini came on board yesterday. The conductor, you know.'

'Yes, I know who Toscanini is,' she said, trying to avoid the elbows of other passengers.

'He's in Cabin Class. But he's very successful, of course. Perhaps he's a pal of Mr Stravinsky's?'

'Toscanini has conducted Stravinsky's works on a number of occasions,' Katharine said stiffly. 'They have the greatest respect for one another.'

'Well, I'm sure they'll be keen to make each other's acquaintance again. A cruise is ideal for that, of course. Getting there is half the fun, isn't it? And then in Southampton we're going to be joined by the Kennedy family. Mrs Joseph P. Kennedy, the wife of the American Ambassador to Britain, and her children. They're going back to the States to get away from the bombs.'

'The bombs!'

'German air raids on London are anticipated momentarily,' the steward said with relish. He was a pretty, pink-cheeked man with carefully slicked red hair and an ingratiating manner. 'The Kennedys are quite the most glamorous family. Our American royalty. We had them on board coming out, when the Ambassador took up his post. Enchanting girls, delightful boys. I don't know what the London society papers will write about once they've left.' He took Katharine's arm to steer her through a particularly crowded area. 'Do you by any chance dance, Miss Wolff? I'm a keen dancer, myself. Red-hot on the rhumba.' He tittered. 'We shall have dancing every night, if the Captain lets us.'

Katharine was not interested in dancing. 'Are we in any danger from submarines?'

Mr Nightingale winced. 'None at all, dear lady.'

'But the *Athenia*. All those people, all those children, drowned.'

He coughed to silence her and lowered his voice. 'We don't know that it was a submarine.'

'What else could it have been but a submarine?' Katharine demanded. 'And quite clearly a passenger ship, full of civilians!'

'The Germans say Mr Churchill did it, trying to make Mr Hitler look bad.'

'Oh, what rubbish. You must be a fool if you believe Nazi propaganda.'

'Well, perhaps we'll find it was a dreadful mistake.' Mr Nightingale looked relieved to have arrived at Katharine's cabin. 'Here we are. This is yours, dear lady.' He knocked. Katharine waited to see what sort of person she had been billeted with. After a moment, the door was opened by a woman evidently halfway through her toilette, clutching a peignoir around herself. She peered at Katharine, one eye thickly rimmed with mascara, the other naked and watery.

'I hope you like gin,' she said. 'We've drunk everything else.'

Southampton

The Kennedys were sitting in the smoking room of the Royal Hotel in Southampton. Their mother sat very upright in an armchair, while the children – Jack and Rosemary, who were in their twenties, teenage Patricia and six-year-old Teddy – clustered around her on sofas. At that hour of the morning the smoking room was the quietest area in the hotel, away from the eyes and ears of the journalists who had been pursuing Jack for two days.

Now twenty-two, and still full of the importance of his mission, Jack had never seemed more grown-up and glamorous to Rosemary. She hung on her brother's words breathlessly.

'They gave me a rough ride,' Jack said, leaning back and crossing his long legs, just the way Daddy did. The newspapers piled on the coffee table between them were full of Jack's trip to Glasgow to speak to the American survivors of the *Athenia* on behalf of his father, the United States ambassador. For once it wasn't just his luminous good looks and charm that fascinated the journalists. That eighteen Americans had gone down with the *Athenia* had raised speculation the atrocity would draw America into the war. 'They're screaming for a convoy to escort them back to the States. I tried to reassure them. They've had a hell of a time. Most are still in the clothes they were wearing when they were torpedoed.'

'Did they see the submarine?' Rosemary asked.

'Oh yes,' Jack said. 'A lot of them saw the periscope and the wake of the torpedoes. And when it was dark, the sub surfaced and shelled them. That finished her off.'

'Jeez,' she said, wide-eyed.

'Rosemary,' her mother said severely, 'I wish you would watch what comes out of your mouth. Jeez stands for our Saviour's name. It's blasphemy.'

'Jack said "hell"!'

'Don't you answer me back.'

Rosemary huddled close against Jack. Mother was so irritable these days, and that made Rosemary more anxious than ever. She was constantly afraid of doing the wrong thing. Yet it always seemed like the wrong thing was just what she most wanted to do. Like laughing when she was supposed to be serious. And putting her mouth close to Jack's ear and whispering, 'Jumping Jesus on a pogo stick.'

Jack snorted. Their mother looked at them sharply, but luckily she hadn't caught what Rosemary had whispered. Rosemary was going to be twenty-one soon. Her body had turned into something she herself almost didn't recognise in the mirror. Men said she was gorgeous and a doll, and sometimes that was exactly what she felt like, a big doll that smiled and fluttered its eyelashes, while the real Rosemary was a scrap of something that had come loose inside it and rattled around, never knowing which way up she was.

'There was a little girl who died,' Jack went on. 'They showed me her body in the mortuary.'

Rosemary shuddered. 'Was there blood?'

'I only saw her face. Her eyes were open. She looked like an angel.'

Mrs Kennedy crossed herself. 'Poor child.'

Rosemary thought of that still body lying there, staring. 'But she couldn't see or hear anything?'

'Of course not, Rosie. She was dead.'

Rosemary nodded. She wished she could get the picture out of her head.

'And there was a teacher who was in the water for hours, looking after a bunch of woman students. I don't know how she survived. Some of the students are still missing. She's the one demanding a convoy.'

'Was she demanding a screw?' Rosemary whispered, her breath hot and moist in his ear. She didn't know why her doll body said these things, while the little rattling Rosemary inside quailed. He crooked his elbow around her neck and pretended to strangle her. She pinched him so hard in the ribs that despite his superior strength, he squirmed.

'No horseplay, please,' Mrs Kennedy rapped out. 'We're in public.'

They let go of each other. 'What am I going to do without you, Rose Marie?' Jack asked.

'You'll get along just fine, John Fitzgerald.' But the thought of parting from Jack was like a punch in the stomach. She slumped back into the sofa, her head hanging, her arms folded across her bosom. Seeing that Rosemary's lashes were sparkling with tears, Jack's voice softened. 'Aw, come on,' he said, 'we'll see each other in the States in a couple of months.'

'I don't want you to go into the Navy,' Rosemary said. Her lower lip quivered. 'I don't want you to be in the war.'

'America is not going to be in the war, Rosemary,' Mrs Kennedy said impatiently. 'We've been through all that.'

'Rosemary's crying,' little Teddy said, turning his Kodak Brownie her way. He snapped the shutter. He had been given the box camera on his birthday, so that he could photograph their exciting new surroundings in London, and he was inseparable from it.

'Get that thing away from me,' Rosemary said in a choked voice.

Teddy clambered over the sofa to poke the camera at Rosemary. She had been hidden away in special schools for most of his life, and she was more of a curiosity to him than a sister. 'Watch the birdie, empty-head.' He snapped the shutter again. Rosemary hit out at him clumsily, knocking the Brownie from his hands. He squealed and grabbed a fistful of Rosemary's hair. The siblings intervened swiftly: Pat lifting Teddy on to her lap and Jack stopping Rosemary from retaliating. Teddy was red-faced with fury. The Kodak had burst open. 'She's broken it,' he yelled. 'She's retarded.' He'd heard the word whispered around Rosemary and though he didn't know what it meant, he knew it hurt her worse than pulling her hair.

Pat rescued the camera and closed it. 'It's not broken,' she said.

'Everywhere you go there's trouble, Rosemary.' Mrs Kennedy was tight-lipped. 'Can you never learn to behave?'

'I don't want him sticking that thing in my face,' Rosemary said, feeling her throat all swollen and hot.

'There was no film in it,' Pat said.

'I don't care.' She was fighting down the tears. For her to be with her family – and out of school – was such a rare treat, but something always happened to spoil everything. If only Dad were here. She longed for his strong arm around her waist. 'Why does he have to call me names?'

Pat whispered in her little brother's ear. Teddy's face was sullen. 'She is retarded,' he mumbled. 'I'm not sorry.'

Rosemary flipped him the middle finger. Mrs Kennedy rose to her feet with an exasperated sigh. 'Jack, I need to talk to you.'

'Yes, Mother.'

They walked to the corner of the smoking room, where a thin glow of autumnal sunshine was filtering through the heavy drapes. Jack saw that his mother's face was strained. The sudden escalation of European politics into world war and the prospect of another long separation from her husband were taking their toll on even her resilient nature.

She put her hand on his arm. 'I'm so proud of you, Jack. You did well in Scotland.'

'I'll always do my best.'

'And you know that we have the highest hopes for you.' Her clear, cool eyes searched his. 'I don't want you to be held up by anything.'

He smiled. 'Don't worry about me, Mother.'

'It's not you I worry about.' She glanced across the room to where Pat was trying to comfort Rosemary. 'There's a man who's been pestering Rosemary.'

Jack frowned. 'Has she complained about him?'

'No. That's the problem. She encourages him.'

'Who is he?'

'He's a loose young fellow from California. A musician.'

'Well, that's three strikes against him,' Jack said.

'It's no laughing matter,' his mother said, unsmiling.

Jack shrugged. 'You'll all be on the *Manhattan* in a day or two and then your worries will be over.'

'He's got a passage on the same boat. He's even staying in this hotel. He's very persistent. And Rosemary's utterly rebellious. As soon as I showed my disapproval, she was all over him. She does it deliberately to break my heart.'

'I think she just wants to have fun.'

'You know that Rosemary cannot have fun the way other girls have fun.'

'Come on, Mother.'

'Jack, you're old enough by now to know that she's never going to be normal.'

'She just needs to grow up.'

'She's never going to grow up. It's up to us to protect her. We can't trust any man with her, let alone a man like that.'

'Does this character have a name?'

'He's called Cubby Hubbard.'

Jack smiled. '"Cubby"?'

'I've spoken to him. It didn't do any good. I want you to explain things to him properly. Tell him to stay away from Rosemary. I don't want to have to resort to the courts and the police and so forth. But I will if I have to. You understand?'

'All right. If you really want, I'll speak to him.'

'He's in the hotel now. If you ask at the desk, they'll find him. And Jack—'

He was turning to go. 'Yes?'

'Don't let him get around you.'

Jack nodded. 'Okay.'

He walked to the white marble reception desk and asked for Mr Hubbard. The clerk called his room and then passed the telephone to Jack.

'Hello, Mr Hubbard,' he said. 'My name is John Kennedy. I'm Rosemary Kennedy's brother. I wonder if we could have a talk.'

The voice that answered him was young and cheerful. 'Sure. Where and when?'

Jack checked his watch. 'I have to get back to London this afternoon, so the sooner the better.'

'No time like the present, then. I'll meet you in the bar.'

Jack waited for Hubbard at the bar, toying with a cigar. He'd started the habit at school and by now it was ingrained. But he resisted the urge to light up. He would smoke it on the way back to London, once this conversation was over. He ran it under his nose, inhaling the rich aroma.

He was thinking of what his mother had said about Rosemary – that she would never be independent, never have a life of her own. He hadn't heard it expressed with such finality before, but he knew it had to be faced. Rosemary was almost twenty-one. A lot of girls were married by that age, with children of their own. Rosemary was still a child herself.

She had been coaxed by nuns and coached by psychologists, but she couldn't add up a column of figures. She understood nothing of geography or history. The simplest academic tasks were beyond her. When doctors said she was retarded, they meant it not as an insult, but as a clinical diagnosis.

All that might be passed over – after all, none of the girls were expected to be great scholars – if she were adult in other ways. But she wasn't. There was the beauty and the warmth, to be sure, but those just made her all the more terribly vulnerable. They came with the temper tantrums and the sudden outbursts of passionate love. There was the headlong way she rushed into things, the havoc she could cause without meaning to. There was the blind way she trusted people, everybody, anybody. You could get her to do anything. Mother was right. She would need to be sheltered all her life.

'Mr Kennedy?'

Jack looked up. The arrival was a young fellow in a checked jacket, open-necked shirt and brown Bostonians, his hair slicked back in a fashionable quiff. He was stocky – Jack was six foot and lean with it – with a pleasant face. He appeared to be a little older than Jack. Not much was remarkable about him except his eyes, which were dark brown and very direct in their gaze. Jack got off his stool to shake hands. 'Mind if I ask how you came by the name Cubby?'

'My mom,' Hubbard replied. 'It stuck.'

Jack smiled. 'Figured something like that. It's noon. Have a beer?'

'Sure.'

The barman drew them each a pint of the dull, flat English beer which Jack had never come to like. Jack raised his mug. 'Mud in your eye.'

'Cheers.'

They drank, eyeing each other. 'How do you know my sister?' Jack asked.

'We met at a party in the summer.'

'So you've known Rosemary for no more than a few months.'

'I've known her long enough to be crazy about her,' Hubbard replied.

'How old are you?'

'I'm twenty-four.'

'What are you doing in Europe?'

'I saved up to go to Paris. Always wanted to hear Django Reinhardt and Stéphane Grappelli.'

'I have no idea who they are.'

'It doesn't matter. The war came along anyway and – well – Rosemary's on the *Manhattan* and where she goes, I go.'

They drank. Jack put his mug down. 'Look, I'll come to the point. We'd prefer it if you would stay away from Rosemary.'

Hubbard did not look surprised. It was almost as though he'd been expecting something like this. He replied calmly. 'If Rosemary asks me to stay away from her, of course I will.'

Jack frowned. 'Rosemary can't judge what's good for her.'

'Rosemary is the best judge of what's good for her.'

'If she was normal, that would be true.'

'She is normal.'

Jack decided to apply his charm. He gave the other man his boyish smile, leaning forward. 'You see Rosemary from the outside, as a pretty girl, and you can be forgiven for that. But we see her as she really is. She has the mental age of a six-year-old.'

Hubbard did not respond to Jack's smile. 'You ought to be ashamed to talk about your own sister that way.'

'It's the truth.'

'I plan to marry her.'

This was a lot more serious than Jack had anticipated. He tried to imagine what his father would say right now. 'What do you do for a living, Cubby?'

'I'm a bandleader.'

'What's your band called?'

'"Cubby Hubbard and The Stompers". I play guitar.'

'A big band?'

'There are seven of us.'

'Jazz?'

'Boogie-woogie.'

'You mean that Negro stuff?'

'It's getting awfully popular. We've been playing to packed houses at the Moonlight Lounge in Pasadena. We plan to have a recording contract by the end of the year. Decca are already interested. They say our stuff's perfect for the jukeboxes.'

'It sounds kind of a rackety life.'

'It's a good living. And it's what I love.'

'Would you feel safe leaving Rosemary alone with a baby while you were stomping at the Moonlight Lounge?'

'My mom and my sisters will be there for her. They can't wait to meet her. Rosemary is a wonderful girl, and with them around her, she'll do just fine.'

'Have you seen how crazy she can get?'

'Rosemary's spent her life under the skirts of a gang of old nuns. That's why she gets mad. She's frustrated. Here she is, nearly twenty-one and still at school. What kind of life is that?'

'She's still at school because she can hardly read or write.'

'I have a bunch of letters from her. Not exactly Shakespeare, but she gets her point across. She's the sweetest girl in the world.'

'Rosemary isn't always sweet. She's as strong as a lioness and she behaves like one sometimes.'

'If she doesn't marry me, what are you going to do with her? Keep her locked up the rest of her life?'

The question was a shrewd one. Jack hesitated. 'She needs more time.'

'They say you'll be president one day. On your way to the White House, Jack, wouldn't you prefer to know that your sister is happily settled with a guy who loves her and looks after her – not climbing out of the window at night?'

Jack blinked. 'What the hell does that mean?'

'It means that you and your family won't have to worry about her. She'll be in Pasadena with me and you'll be in Washington, running for president. We won't bother you none.'

'My mother wants me to tell you that she'll go to the police if she has to.'

Hubbard raised his eyebrows. 'The police?'

'You could be charged with criminal seduction.'

'You're kidding me. I've heard the stories about you, Jack, tomcatting around London. You're a fine one to talk about seduction.'

Jack grinned and finished his beer. 'Like I said, we'll do what we have to.' He glanced at his watch. 'I hope you'll think about this carefully. And I hope you'll consider my sister's happiness.'

'It's the most important thing in the world to me,' Hubbard replied as they shook hands. 'And I'm not going anywhere.'

'The strange thing,' he said to his mother, 'is that I ended up quite liking the guy.'

'Oh, Jack. I warned you he was plausible.'

'He's certainly crazy about Rosemary. But he's blind to all her problems.'

'That one has his eyes wide open, believe me.'

Jack glanced at her set face. 'According to him, he and Rosemary have known each other for months. He says she writes to him. What puzzles me is how she could have kept something like that secret. She's not capable of hiding anything.'

'Oh, you're wrong there,' Mrs Kennedy said with a bitter smile. 'She's not the innocent girl she was before we came to this country. She knows how to hide things now, all right.'

'What do you mean?'

A flush suffused his mother's lean cheeks. She was clearly struggling with what she was about to say next. 'She's been getting out of her room at night.'

'At the convent?'

'Yes.'

'How do you know?'

'The nuns told me.'

'Why don't they stop her?'

'They can't. They can do nothing with her.'

'Where does she go?'

'She goes out into the street.' His mother compressed her lips tightly for a moment. 'She goes to bars and meets men.'

'You don't mean—'

'Yes, Jack. I mean exactly that.'

Jack was stunned at the revelation. He recalled Cubby Hubbard's words about Rosemary climbing out of the window. 'Is that how she met Hubbard?'

'Well, what do you think?' she shot back.

'He struck me as more decent than that,' Jack said, rubbing his face. He was tired after his busy two days in Scotland and his mind was reeling. 'As for Rosemary—'

'As for Rosemary, I did not go through so much sacrifice to raise a slut.'

'Please don't talk like that about her.'

'A girl who goes to bars, looking for alcohol and sex? What else would you call her?'

Jack sighed. 'I have to leave for London. Dad's waiting for me. There's nothing I can do to stop Hubbard from getting on the *Manhattan* with you. We're going to have to deal with him when we get to the States.'

'I will deal with him long before that,' Mrs Kennedy said.

The Western Approaches

Out in the North Sea, a hundred miles west of the British coast, where the shipping lanes converged, Kapitän-leutnant Jürgen Todt had ordered *U-113* to heave to. The submarine was within range of British aircraft sweeping from the mainland, but it was the end of the day and the light would soon be gone. A heavy swell was rolling. The air was cold and salty, and the crew crowded at the rails, hawking and spitting up phlegm, or cupping cigarettes in the palms of their hands.

Todt's number two, Leutnant zur See Rudolf Hufnagel, stood beside him, gratefully inhaling the clean air. Less than a month out of port, *U-113* already stank. Not only were there no washing facilities for the men or their clothing, but the provisions were swiftly deteriorating. The onions, dried sausages and loaves of black bread, which were stuffed between pipes or in ducts, were sprouting white mould – rabbit's-ears, as the crew called them – and spreading a dank smell of mildew. The single usable privy (the other was stuffed full of eatables) was a malodorous swamp, outside which was always a queue of sailors waiting to empty their bowels.

The crew, most of whom were by now sporting straggling beards, were bundled into sea-jackets, except the diesel officer Ludwig, who was obsessed with vitamin D, and who had stripped to the waist. He was baring his chest to the lurid yellow sunset, apparently impervious to the icy spray, his arms upraised to catch any benefit from the fading rays.

Morale was high. There was laughter, some of it at the expense of 'Mad King' Ludwig and his sun worship. Eccentricities were prized in the early weeks of a submarine's voyage, sources of entertainment. Later, Hufnagel knew, they could become intolerable, but they had yet to experience that.

For all the good humour, Hufnagel saw that there was a perceptible barrier around the captain. None of the crew stood too close to him, or involved him in their banter. It was not that he was a martinet, or even an unpopular officer. Rather, there was an aura of coldness around him that precluded idle conversation. They knew little about him. The camaraderie, even informality, which grew around other U-boat captains, sometimes deepening into affection, had not established itself in *U-113*.

But the boat was new and the crew was new. Most of them had been selected for the service and were not volunteers. Hufnagel would have preferred more experienced men. But this crew had been hastily assembled by a submarine command which had known that war was imminent. They had all been together only a few months, most of those spent in exercises in the Baltic Sea, stalking dummy targets, practising loading torpedoes and launching attacks, testing the ship's motors, radio system and deck guns.

They had been in port in the Elbe during the last week of August. The day after the declaration of war, they had slipped out to sea again and had headed west into the Atlantic, to the hunting grounds assigned them by Admiral Dönitz. They had yet to sight an enemy vessel.

Hufnagel glanced at the skipper. The dying light which bathed Ludwig's skinny chest and gilded the death's-head painted on the conning tower also glowed in Todt's blonde fringe. Todt's pale eyes and flaxen hair had helped his progress through the ranks of the new

Kriegsmarine, which counted an Aryan appearance – and membership of the Nazi Party – as considerable advantages, advantages which Hufnagel did not share.

Todt, unlike Hufnagel, had been a member of the Nazi Party almost since its inception, and was a devoted follower of its leader, who had promised to expunge the humiliation and treachery of 1918. He had been swiftly promoted, while Hufnagel, though his senior in age and experience, was only second-in-command. Hufnagel's indifference to Nazism had counted against him, as had certain other errors.

The light was failing fast. Even Mad King Ludwig had acknowledged it and was buttoning up his shirt. An immense darkness had started to spread across the sky. But the many vigilant pairs of eyes on the conning tower had caught something in the last gleams and there were excited shouts.

Todt saw it too through the high-powered bridge binoculars, a smudge on the distant horizon, glimpsed from the top of a swell before *U-113* slid down into the trough again. He yielded the binoculars to his First Watch Officer. 'What do you see, Hufnagel?'

Hufnagel peered through the Zeiss lenses as *U-113* rose again. 'Smoke,' he said. 'Bearing fifteen degrees to our east.'

'A convoy?'

'A single vessel, in my opinion.'

'Good.' Todt turned to his crew, his pale eyes alight. 'Everyone below.'

Le Havre

Up on the bridge, the captain of the *Manhattan*, Commodore Albert Randall, was thinking about the *Athenia,* a thirteen-thousand-tonner of the White Star Line, built in Glasgow, with all the latest navigation equipment, torpedoed at night in the Western Approaches on the first day of the war.

He, who had himself been torpedoed by a German submarine in the last war, and had barely escaped with his life, could imagine the scene all too well. The screams of terror, the surge of water into the engine room, the inevitable slide into the depths. And then the chaos in the lifeboats, some sucked into the *Athenia*'s own churning propellers, others capsizing in the heavy seas. Passengers crushed against the hull, drowned in the icy water, freezing to death in their flimsy nightgowns. The brave crew sacrificing their own lives for those who'd bought hundred-dollar tickets.

It was, if nothing else, an indication of how this war was going to go. No quarter asked or given.

A large, bluff man with a determined chin, Commodore Randall had seen his share of maritime disasters and had played a gallant role in many of them. He'd saved the 274 passengers of the *Powhatan* in 1920.

Then there had been the schooner *Reine de Mers* in 1922, foundering amid mountainous seas off Newfoundland; and the Coast Guard cutter blown out to sea in a gale in 1924 off Nantucket. The crews of both those vessels owed their lives to him. And there had been a dozen rescues since.

As a result of these actions, he had been given the soubriquet 'Rescue' Randall. He was proud of the fact that his name was known to thousands and was seldom mentioned in the press without the word *heroic* attached to it. Though cultivating a reputation for modesty, he relished his fame and he knew how to capitalise on it. He liked being – like *Manhattan* herself – an emblem of American derring-do and enterprise in a world which he felt was sliding into darkness.

However, he didn't want any dramatics on this trip. Especially not since it was his last crossing, with a well-earned retirement at the end of it. And especially not with the distinguished passenger list he would be carrying. He had been applying his mind to avoiding the fate of the *Athenia*. There would be an unmistakable message to port and starboard. He stood at the window, solid as a polar bear, and looked down with satisfaction at the hoardings which had been erected on either side of the *Manhattan*'s hull.

Arturo Toscanini stood on the quayside, leaning on his cane among the bustle of stevedores and longshoremen, looking up at the great bulk of the *Manhattan*, which towered above him like a cliff face. She was the largest ship ever built in the United States, over seven hundred feet long. On each side was a hoarding painted with American flags and the legend:

MANHATTAN

UNITED STATES LINES

The idea, Toscanini presumed, was that this message, visible across miles of ocean, would deter German submarines from torpedoing the ship, as they had done with the unfortunate *Athenia*. He was not so certain that any such compunction would hinder the Nazis. Thinking back over his long and bruising battle with Mussolini, much of it fought in the sacred precincts of La Scala, he could not recall a single occasion when mercy had been shown – or conscience, or compassion, or generosity of spirit.

His dearest friends had been driven into exile, had thrown themselves out of windows, had endured arrest and torture. He himself had been beaten in the street by Mussolini's thugs. He had seen his country sink into a welter of brutality and bombast. Longing for Italy as he was, he could no longer go home without risking his life.

It would be ironic if he were to meet his fate at the hands of a U-boat crew. In May of 1915, he had been booked on the *Lusitania*, but had cut short his schedule at the Met and chugged home early on an old Italian steamer. He'd arrived in Italy to hear that the swift and glittering *Lusitania* had been sunk by a German submarine, with the loss of twelve hundred lives. Someone else had died in his cabin.

'Good morning, maestro!'

A dapper man, he tipped his fedora to the group of excited women who had recognised him. Doing so revealed that although the famous, curled-up moustaches were still dark, his hair was now white and sparse. He was used to being recognised. His portrait had been put up in every shop window. He had been hailed as the age's greatest conductor. Complete strangers greeted him, though sometimes (overexcitedly) as 'Mr Wagner' or 'Mr Beethoven.'

Toscanini pulled his fob watch out of his waistcoat pocket and consulted it. It was past noon. He hurried up the gangplank, back on to the *Manhattan*, where he made his way to the ship's radio telegraph office. It was crowded with passengers frantic for news of wives, husbands, children, lovers. The postmaster spotted Toscanini's diminutive figure behind the wall of customers at the counter. He waved the conductor over and leaned down to murmur through the gap under the glass window.

'Very sorry, Mr Toscanini. There's nothing for you today.'

'Sure?'

'Quite sure.'

'Thank you.' Toscanini tipped his hat, hiding his dismay. He felt faint as he pushed his way out through the throng. Where was she? Why had she not sent word?

Outside the telegraph office he pulled out his handkerchief and mopped his brow. He ached for Carla's steadying hand on his arm.

Communications with Lucerne were wretched now. They had stayed far too long in Kastanienbaum, lulled by the autumn beauty of the lake, shutting their ears to the rumble of mobilising and approaching conflict. War had surprised them.

He'd rushed on ahead to secure their passage on the *Manhattan*; Carla was due to have followed, but days had passed and he had heard nothing from her. He did not even know if she had left Switzerland. For all he knew, she was still in Kastanienbaum, closer to Munich than to Paris.

Ancient creatures they were now, he and Carla, married forty-two years. Like two old trees, bent by storms and beaten by suns, that leaned on one another for support. She had told him to leave without her if she did not make it to Le Havre. But he could not leave France without her. If Carla did not arrive in time, he would renounce their cabin and wait for her. And who knew when the next passenger ship would sail for America? Perhaps *Manhattan* was the last.

He stared out across the harbour. Le Havre was a gracious city, extending around the bay in pleasant sunshine. What would be left of it when the Germans had done with it, he wondered? Short-sighted as he was, he could see that the port was busy, crowded with ships of all sizes, loading and unloading, the black hulls streaked with rust. The banks of cranes swung to and fro against the pale blue sky. There was a frenetic haste to everything these days, a scramble, a stampede.

Toscanini noticed two of the ship's officers standing at either end of the deck, scanning the skies with binoculars. They were keeping watch for German warplanes, he realised, which might appear at any moment, spewing bullets and bombs. He felt sick. Grasping his cane, he stumbled down the companionway.

In their cabin that evening, Masha and Rachel Morgenstern were exchanging confidences as they prepared for dinner. There was much about one another that they did not as yet know, but they wanted very much to be friends, intimate with each other.

'Have you ever been in love?' Masha asked Rachel shyly.

'I can see from your face that *you* have, my dear cousin.'

Disconcerted, Masha turned her back quickly on Rachel. 'Can you fasten my hooks?'

Rachel smiled to herself ironically as she obliged her cousin. 'Who is it? Some nice, serious young man selected by Rabbi Moskovitz?'

'Not exactly.'

Rachel could see the skin at the back of Masha's neck flushing pink among the soft curls. 'Not exactly? What, exactly? Don't keep me in suspense.'

When Masha turned, the flush had spread all across her pretty face. 'It's not much of a story.'

'I am breathless with anticipation,' Rachel replied. 'I must know everything.'

Masha sat on the bunk, laughing awkwardly. 'You'll be very disappointed then, because it all came to nothing. I'm too ashamed to even tell you.'

'Do you want me to resort to Gestapo methods?'

Masha clasped her hands in her lap. 'Well, then. When I was seventeen, I had a beau.'

'I knew it! Proceed.'

'He was a young man called Rudi Hufnagel. He was in the Navy, in the *Ubootwaffe*. He came to see me every weekend in Berlin.'

Rachel raised her eyebrows. 'A Gentile?'

'An Aryan.'

'What did your parents say?'

'At first they were all against it. But Rudi was so polite, so charming – and so glamorous in his uniform! He had been all over the world, even to America. I think they fell in love with him quite as deeply as I did.'

'He must indeed have been a seductive fellow,' Rachel said dryly.

'Oh, no, you have the wrong idea completely. He was absolutely honourable.'

'He didn't take you to bed?'

'How can you ask me such a thing?' Masha demanded indignantly.

'Well, it has been known,' Rachel said, 'from time to time in human history.'

'That was not the case with us!'

'Not even a stolen kiss?'

Masha's stiff expression softened. 'Of course there were kisses.'

'And cuddles?'

'And cuddles,' Masha conceded.

Rachel sat next to her younger cousin. 'Now we're getting to it. How far did you go?'

'Really, Rachel, you ask the most dreadful questions!'

'Oh, come on. You can tell me. I'm not the rabbi.'

Masha's face was flushed, her eyes shining. Rachel thought she had seldom seen a prettier young woman. 'There *was* one evening . . .'

'Yes?'

'Rudi got us a box at the opera,' Masha said softly. 'Just the two of us, in the dark, hidden by the velvet curtain, and the music so lovely. And—'

'And?'

Her voice was almost inaudible. 'He put his hands—'

'Where did he put his hands?' Rachel enquired, eagerly leaning forward.

'He put his hands *everywhere*,' Masha whispered.

'Good boy,' Rachel said, half-closing her eyes as though inhaling some fine perfume. 'Did he know what he was doing?'

'Of course.'

'Those Navy men are always reliable.'

'Oh, Rachel, it was divine!' Masha exclaimed. Her reticence had gone completely. 'I've never known such feelings!'

'Better than listening to Stravinsky's *Rite of Spring*?'

'Quite, quite different,' she said firmly. 'He took me to heaven.'

'So it didn't feel like the electric chair?'

'If you laugh at me, I shan't say another word.'

'Forgive me. I know I am on sacred ground.' Rachel was smiling, but tenderly. 'However, you can't tell me that after such a divine night at the opera you never repeated the experiment?'

'Perhaps once or twice,' Masha admitted, lowering her eyes. 'You must understand that I fancied myself very much in love.'

'It sounds like more than just fancy,' Rachel said gently.

'The difficulty was in finding places,' Masha confided.

'It always is. But you managed?'

'We went out together every weekend, to the Zoo or to the Ku-Damm, sometimes to concerts or plays. If we got the chance, we would kiss and hold each other and—'

'And do what lovers do.'

'Yes. When my friends saw me on his arm I felt I would burst with pride. The Navy dress uniform is very smart, you know. Dark blue, with gold buttons—'

'Very uncomfortable at the wrong moment, I'm sure.'

'—the gold silk eagle on the breast, the braid on the cuffs—'

'Never mind the uniform. Stick with what was inside.'

'We told each other we would get married when he got his Captain's sword.'

'Despite the race laws?'

'Despite everything. The race laws weren't being strictly enforced yet. It was 1936. Rudi was sure we would get permission to marry because he was a submarine officer. We were floating on champagne. Two silly fools with stars in our eyes.'

'What happened?'

'It was silly, at first. We started to notice that there were two men always following us around the town. Not just once or twice, but everywhere we went. Rudi was amused. He called them the Two Eggs because they were so alike. He liked to mock them, pretending to make their life easier by saying in a loud voice, "Come on, Masha, let's go and have a cocktail at the Kempinski." Or, "Let's go and see the new American picture at the Universum." And then, sure enough, we would find them there when we arrived. He thought it was funny.'

Rachel watched Masha's face. 'Weren't you afraid?'

'I don't think I was, because Rudi took it as a joke. He said they were civilians and he wasn't afraid of any civilian. And I always felt so safe with him. I didn't think anything could happen to us. We just carried on as usual. We didn't try to hide anything. Rudi was very gallant. He always took my arm in public. He let everyone know that we were together, that he was proud of me.'

'That was perhaps not very prudent of him.'

'Perhaps not. But we were not in a mood to be prudent. We didn't think we were doing anything wrong.' Masha's face changed. 'And then one day the police came to our house and hammered on the door and ordered me to present myself at the station for questioning.' She was silent for a moment. 'I suppose I knew in that moment that it was all over, but I was too infatuated to accept it at first. I went down to the station with my head held high. They kept me waiting for hours, sitting on a hard chair. I could hear things happening in the cells below – beatings, men calling out for mercy. It was horrible. At last an officer came to see me. His head shaved almost to the crown, a black leather coat. You know the type.'

'I know the type,' Rachel said briefly.

'He had a thick folder full of our movements, going back weeks. The Two Eggs had written down every single detail. He demanded to know if we had been to this place together, and that place, and the other place, on and on. I said I didn't deny any of it. He asked if I were not Jewish. I said that of course I was. He asked why Rudi would associate with a Jewish girl when there were so many Aryan girls to be had. I laughed in his face and answered that if all Aryan girls were blonde and pretty, the way they were supposed to be, then I presumed Rudi would have chosen one of them.'

'For heaven's sake, Masha!'

'Yes. I think I was a little hysterical by then. I was only seventeen, remember. And in those days, one didn't really know what could happen.'

'He could have smashed your face.'

'He just stared at me, as though I were some kind of strange insect. Then he demanded to know if I was not ashamed to be destroying the career of so promising a young officer. I asked what he meant. He said that Rudi would be dishonourably discharged for going out with a Jewish girl, and would never be trusted with any kind of authority as long as he lived. As for marriage, that was out of the question. It would not be legal. If I did not leave Rudi, he would be finished. He would never serve the Reich. He would be disgraced, perhaps even imprisoned. Then this man lit a cigarette and told me to make my choice, there and then.'

Rachel didn't take her eyes off Masha. 'What did you do?'

'I walked home and I told my mother not to let Rudi in the house again. From then on, whenever he called, they said I wasn't home. I could hear my mother crying on the doorstep. Rudi wrote letters, but I didn't answer them, though I read them all before I burned them. For a long time he would stand outside the house the whole weekend, looking up at my window. I would try not to look at him through the curtains, because I didn't want him to know I was there. But I couldn't resist. He was all I wanted to see. He was—' there was a catch in her voice. 'He was everything to me.'

Rachel touched her hand gently. 'My poor Masha.'

'And then one weekend he stopped coming. His friends told me that his boat had been sent on manoeuvres in the Atlantic and that he would be gone for several months. I don't know if it was true or not. In any case, I never saw him again.'

'I'm sorry.'

Masha wiped the tears from her eyes. 'Isn't that a very silly, pointless story?'

'It's a Berlin story.'

'You know the Franz Lehar song? *In the magic glimmer of the silver light, it was nothing but a dream of happiness.*'

'Perhaps you will come across him again one day.'

'I don't think that is very likely, do you? By now, of course, he has been called up to fight. Perhaps he will die. Perhaps his submarine has already been sunk by the British. He may be at the bottom of the ocean. Or in another girl's arms. Who knows? He's not mine any more and I shouldn't care. The whole thing seems now like something I saw in the theatre, or in a dream. How much changed in Germany over the last three years, Rachel. Everything went dark as fast as night coming on a winter's evening.'

'Yes,' Rachel said quietly, 'it did.'

'You are very sympathetic,' Masha said. She put her hand almost timidly on her cousin's and looked into her rather angular face. 'I wish I'd known you better, earlier.'

Rachel looked down at the delicate hand that was laid over hers. Slowly, she covered it with her own. 'I wish that, too.'

'We should have been friends a long time ago.'

'Well . . .' Rachel didn't continue. Despite much in common – youth, music, culture – the two girls had been kept apart by their families. Or rather, Masha knew that Rachel had been kept away from her, on account of the mysterious 'danger' that had never quite been explained. And though Rachel could certainly be sarcastic, Masha was very glad of her company now. She did not think she could have faced this momentous voyage alone.

They sat in silence for a while, each lost in her own thoughts. Then the sound of the dinner gong, being beaten by a steward along the corridor outside, roused them.

'Come on,' Rachel said, withdrawing her hand and patting her cousin's shoulder, 'let's see what jokes the chefs have played on us tonight.'

Stravinsky had slept as he always did these days, fitfully and disturbed by dreams of death from which he awoke filled with a pervasive sense of dread. He stood at the washstand, fastening his bow tie with the aid of the mirror there. His fingers shook slightly. His own face stared back at him, pasty, reptilian. He was still a sick man, whatever lies the doctors told him.

The German boy was dressing, too. He had an unexpected gift for silence, the German boy. He hadn't made a sound while Stravinsky slept. Perhaps they taught them that in the Hitler Youth: knowing when to keep your mouth shut. He'd been afraid that the boy would be a nuisance, but to the contrary, he was as unobtrusive as the best sort of servant; and like the best sort of servant, apparently eager to wait on Stravinsky hand and foot. Perhaps they taught them that, too, in the

Hitler Youth. He had been brushing his own blazer carefully and now, without asking or being asked, he began to brush Stravinsky's dinner jacket.

'That's very kind,' Stravinsky said, watching the boy in the mirror, past his own haunted reflection. 'You are a thoughtful boy.'

'Do you have children of your own?' the boy asked.

Stravinsky concentrated on his bow tie. 'I had two sons and two daughters. One of my daughters is dead, now.'

'What was her name?'

'Ludmila.'

'Was it a long time ago?'

'A year ago.'

The boy considered. 'Was she sick?'

'We were all sick. My wife, my daughter and I.'

'I'm sorry.' He inspected Stravinsky's dinner jacket minutely for specks of dust. 'Did your wife die, too?'

'Yes. My wife died, too. She died a few months after my daughter. Now I am alone.'

'What did she die of?'

'Enough questions, Thomas.'

The boy looked up quickly from his task. His eyes were a sharp, pale grey, his close-cropped hair white-blonde. Freckles were scattered across the long, fox-like nose. He was an absolute example of Aryan boyhood. 'I ask too many questions,' the boy said. 'I was always told this. I apologise.'

'It doesn't matter.' Stravinsky turned from the washstand. 'You are very quiet while I sleep, for which I am grateful.' The boy helped him on with his dinner jacket, straightening the sleeves and adjusting the lapels with his thin fingers. 'How do I look?'

'*Sehr ausgezeichnet.*'

Stravinsky fitted a cigarette into the little ebony holder and lit it. The first lungful of smoke produced a racking bout of coughing. He tasted the salt in his mouth and spat dark clots of blood into the basin. The boy observed this but did not comment. 'It was tuberculosis,' he said at last, rinsing the crimson stains away. 'We all had it. But you are safe. They say I am cured.'

'I think you are dying.'

Stravinsky tried a second inhalation. 'You are as silent as the grave for hours, Thomas, but when you do talk, you are damned direct.' He coughed up more blood and spat into the basin. After a while, the coughing eased and he was able to endure the smoke in his lungs.

'Have the doctors advised you to smoke?' Thomas asked, frowning.

'They've advised me very strongly *not* to smoke. But—'

'But you don't listen to them.'

'I have a symphony to write.'

'Do you need to smoke to write a symphony?'

'It's a symphony in C. The C stands for Cigarettes.'

'Are you joking?'

'Not at all.' Stravinsky finished the cigarette and consulted his watch. 'We mustn't be late. We should go.'

'I am ready.'

As they walked to Katharine's cabin, Stravinsky had his hand on the boy's shoulder for support. He felt weak and a little confused. The crowding of the ship was abominable. Everyone was in a fervour which would not abate, he supposed, until they had left France. Katharine was ready when they arrived, wearing a formal, dark-green gown which exposed her slim shoulders, of which she was rather proud.

'How are your cabin-mates?' Stravinsky asked her.

'Ghastly,' she said with a shudder. 'They're a pair of New Jersey widows who were caught by the war while spending their late husbands' life policies on a European holiday. They intend to stay drunk until they reach New York.'

'At least they have a plan.'

Katharine turned to the boy, barely disguising her repugnance. 'I hope you are being considerate towards Monsieur Stravinsky, Thomas?'

'He smoked a cigarette in the cabin and coughed up blood, at least a tablespoon.'

'You are a little informer, Thomas,' Stravinsky said.

'Oh, Igor,' Katharine said in dismay. 'You promised you wouldn't start again.'

'Nonsense.' Stravinsky waved her concern away petulantly.

'He says he is writing a symphony in C,' Thomas said. 'He says the C stands for Cigarettes.'

'Perhaps,' Katharine said grimly, 'it stands for Coffin.'

The Cabin Class dining room was an amazing confection of glittering Americana, as though Marie Antoinette had built a palace in Wyoming and had it decorated by the Comanche. High in the lofty ceiling, crystal chandeliers illuminated colourful murals depicting redskins hunting the mighty buffalo, or greeting the white man with gifts of pumpkins and corn. Braves on mustangs galloped across a prairie framed between heavy velvet curtains. Cowboys waved their Winchesters aloft among gilded rococo swags. A sea of snowy linen and gleaming silverware covered the three dozen tables below, each one of which seated six and had a softly glowing lamp as a centrepiece.

The Commodore's table was set in the centre of the huge room, where everyone could see it and envy those invited to dine at it. Toscanini, in the place of honour beside Commodore Randall tonight, had put on his spectacles to peruse the menu. Commodore Randall, impeccable in his mess-jacket, leaned towards Toscanini like an amiable grampus. 'I recommend the live boiled lobster, Mr Toscanini, followed by the Boston *sole meunière*.'

'As a student at the conservatory in Parma,' Toscanini replied in his heavy Italian accent, 'I ate only boiled fish for three years. Since then, I eat nothing that comes from the sea.'

One of the other passengers, a plump woman from Topeka named Mrs Dabney, travelling with her largely silent husband, tugged at her immense pearls to draw attention to them. 'How romantic that you rose from poverty to pre-eminence, maestro!' she exclaimed.

'Poverty is in no sense romantic, Signora,' Toscanini retorted.

'What about Rodolfo and Mimì in *La bohème*? That's romantic, isn't it?'

'*La bohème* is an opera,' Toscanini pointed out. 'After dying of hunger, the performers get up and cash their cheques.'

Mrs Dabney laughed gaily. 'Dear maestro, do you think Mussolini will bring Italy into this war?'

'Mussolini is capable of any brutality. Only Britain can stop him.'

'We had to pull the Brits out of the fire last time,' said Dr Emmett Meese, a prominent New York surgeon. 'Why do they keep starting wars if they can't finish them? We should just let things take their course.'

'And let fascism consume Europe?'

'We have nothing to gain by getting our fingers burned.'

'It's not what you have to gain,' Toscanini commented dryly, 'it's what we have to lose.'

'It's not our fight. I say America first and to hell with the rest.'

'Mussolini offered to make me a senator,' Toscanini said. 'I told him, the emperor Caligula made his horse a senator, but I am only a donkey that you like to beat. Do you know why I hold my head like this, to one side? When I refused to play the Fascist Hymn at La Scala, Mussolini sent his men. They beat me in the street. They beat me to the ground with clubs. Ever since then, I live with the injuries. Sometimes I have to cancel engagements, because I cannot lift my arm. That is fascism.'

'Have you heard Hitler's latest?' someone said. 'He's ordered the extermination of all mental defectives in Germany.'

'The Führer gets a bad press,' said Dr Emmett Meese, 'but stopping these kinds of folks from breeding can only have a beneficial effect on the human family.'

'It would certainly have had a beneficial effect on *your* family,' Toscanini growled.

The surgeon polished his horn-rimmed glass earnestly. 'I can't say I disagree with him on the issue of the Jews, either. They've had it coming for a long time.'

'The Jews are harmless, surely?' Commodore Randall replied.

'Not in my view. And this ship is already carrying far too many of them,' Dr Meese said. 'I believe that fully half our passengers are in that category. Everywhere you look there's a hook nose or a crafty eye. Why should we be taking what Hitler doesn't want?'

'If Hitler doesn't want Albert Einstein or Yehudi Menuhin,' Randall said, 'then I reckon we can have them.'

'Our nation is bulging at the seams with riff-raff. There are hundreds of thousands of Mexican migrants roaming around the country. Not to mention the Negroes, the Italians, the Japanese and all the rest. We should pack them up and send them all home.'

'I cannot eat,' Toscanini said, pushing his chair back and getting to his feet. 'I have no appetite.'

He strode along the deck, muttering to himself. He had no intention of going back to his cabin, which he was compelled to share with five imbeciles and their assorted imbecilities. Exhausted as he was, he could neither eat nor sleep. He would rather pace the ship. The surging energies he had been born with had never permitted him to be comfortable seated or recumbent. At the Conservatory, he had even detested the instrument assigned to him, the cello, because it had to be played seated. He had never been more happy than when he'd been able to exchange the cumbersome instrument (he'd pissed in the damned thing once) for a baton.

And now, between sleeplessness and hunger, every nerve in his body crackled. Carla had not appeared. Carla was nowhere. Le Havre was dark tonight, dark as the pit, all lights extinguished in a blackout to foil German bombers. Only the stars danced dimly in the black water of the harbour.

The endless night of human stupidity! The darkness of human folly, ignorance, madness! How small a light of wisdom shone and how easily it was extinguished by the beating of leathery wings.

He took off his hat and bowed his white head on to the railing, groaning loudly to himself in the darkness.

In the Tourist Class dining room (low-ceilinged and plain) Igor Stravinsky studied the menu with a disgusted expression. The options were unappetising: vegetable soup or melon to start, fried flounder or stewed mutton to follow. There was only one sweet – rice pudding. The smells of these dishes, greasy and faintly rancid, percolated through the crowded dining room.

'We have truly left France behind us,' he remarked to Katharine ironically. The German boy sat silently beside them, his nose in a book, uninterested in food. The others at their table, who had the beaten look of refugees, discussed the menu anxiously in some foreign language.

'Would you like to go ashore and find a restaurant?' she suggested.

'I'm too tired,' he replied. 'Besides, I have to learn to be frugal.' He laid down the menu. 'I have become a character in a cartoon.'

She winced. Stravinsky's dire financial status – a perennial problem in his career – was reflected in his desperate sale of *The Rite of Spring* to Walt Disney, to be used in an animated film called *Fantasia*. 'Don't think of it like that.'

'You mistake me,' he said with a twisted smile. 'I thank God every day for Walt Disney. Without his money, I should literally be destitute.'

He coughed and wiped a little smear of blood from his lips, inspecting his handkerchief with heavy-lidded eyes. 'Everything decays. Life, art, the world. It's the natural process of dissolution. One must accept it.'

A harried steward came to take their order. They all chose the mutton, since the pervading aroma of the fish was dubious, and declined the first course. That little crimson stain on Stravinsky's handkerchief had not escaped Katharine. It frightened her that he'd started smoking again. His lungs were still ravaged. His wife Katya's tuberculosis had devastated the Stravinskys, working its way through the family like a poison. It had taken the life of their daughter Ludmila last year. Katya herself had died in March. Stravinsky had spent six months in hospital, during which time his mother had died of the disease.

It had been a terrible five years, years of personal, professional and financial loss. After his first struggles, then his explosive successes in music and ballet, moving to Paris had seemed like the culmination of Stravinsky's career. Instead, it had proved the graveyard of his hopes. Exhausted and broken-hearted, the daring young composer, once thought of as the most advanced talent in modern music, had sunk into a middle age of illness and failure. Darkness hung around him, almost visible.

Katharine knew how bitter he felt about the sale of *The Rite of Spring* to Disney. It had been the music which, more than any other piece, had made his name and had exemplified the innovative brilliance of his genius. He saw it as a public humiliation. He had been brought low and forced to sell out to the arch-purveyor of American vulgarity. Not even the enthusiasm of Walt Disney himself – who was said to have danced around the gramophone when the music was played in his office – could make up for the shame he felt.

'You haven't seen any of Disney's films,' she ventured, trying to comfort him. 'They're charming, you know. *Pinocchio* was very good. And they say that *Fantasia* will be the most original one yet. Think of it as a new medium. You've always been at the forefront of culture.'

'It's amusing, really. The role that was commissioned by Diaghilev and danced by Nijinsky will now be performed by a caricature mouse in red knickerbockers.'

'Oh, Igor.' Katharine laid her hand on his.

Thomas König looked up from his book. 'Do you mean Mickey Mouse?'

'Yes,' Stravinsky said, 'I mean Mickey Mouse.'

The boy looked impressed. 'Mickey is very famous.'

Stravinsky made a wry face. 'I am glad to hear it. What's that you're reading?'

Thomas brightened. He held up the publication. It was a colourful guidebook entitled *The New York World's Fair, The World of Tomorrow*. 'They have a huge golden robot who can walk and talk.'

'Yes?'

'He can even smoke cigarettes.'

'That is undeniably progress,' Stravinsky said, looking at the picture Thomas was showing him.

'His name is Elektro. He can count and do sums. He's full of diodes and triodes and electromagnetic cells.'

'I suppose you know all about those things,' Katharine asked, her eyes on the gleaming swastika fixed in the boy's lapel. 'Diodes and triodes and so forth.'

'A diode has only two terminals and it regulates current in one direction only, whereas a triode has three terminals – anode, cathode and grid. It's used for amplification. It's what allows Elektro to speak.'

'What else do they have at this fair of yours?' Stravinsky asked.

A little flush of pleasure touched Thomas's angular cheekbones. 'They have the Trylon and the Perisphere.'

'Indeed. And what are they?'

The boy showed them the photograph of a gigantic white sphere and an equally dazzling needle which towered above it. 'The Perisphere is eighteen storeys tall. The Trylon is sixty storeys tall. You can see them both from five miles away.'

Stravinsky gazed somewhat wistfully at the glowing geometric structures. 'And this is the world of tomorrow?'

'Oh, yes, sir.'

'They look like the deserted monuments in the paintings of de Chirico or Salvador Dali. Who lives in them?'

'The Democracity is inside the Perisphere. It's the city of the future, where everyone is perfectly happy.'

'No doubt your Führer will want a full report,' Katharine said dryly.

The arrival of the mutton stew interrupted the conversation. Katharine found the German boy hard to stomach, but at least he seemed to distract Igor a little. Perhaps Igor was reminded of his own children.

Across the dining room, Masha and Rachel Morgenstern were also observing Stravinsky. They had chosen the fried flounder, which was proving to have been a mistake.

'I'm terribly excited that Stravinsky's on board,' Masha said. 'I can't deny that. And I shall do my best to engage him in at least one conversation before we reach New York, so I can tell my grandchildren. I shall get his autograph, too. There!'

'Good luck. He looks as though he could hardly lift a pencil.'

'He's so exotic,' Masha murmured, fascinated by the composer's weary face and drooping eyelids. 'So *Russian*.'

'I should say he's just a funny little man with a funny little moustache,' Rachel replied. 'Not unlike our beloved Führer.'

'Hush!' Masha replied automatically.

'You needn't hush me. Nobody loves the Führer more than I do.'

'People could be listening.' Masha was finding it hard to shake off her terror at any disrespectful reference to Hitler. 'Be prudent, Rachel, for God's sake.'

'This fish is a more immediate threat than the Gestapo.' Rachel pushed her plate away. 'I think my piece was bad.'

'Mine was all right.'

'I'm going to be sick.'

'You're not.'

'I am. I can feel it.'

'But there's the rice pudding to come.'

'I need air. I have to go out.' Rachel rose and Masha had no choice but to follow her. Their route out of the dining room took them past Stravinsky's table. As they approached, Stravinsky raised his head slowly and Masha met his eyes. She could not stop herself from speaking.

'Oh, Monsieur Stravinsky,' she blurted out, 'I saw your *Rite of Spring* in 1934.' Everybody at the table looked up. Wanting to express the excitement she had felt, she could only stammer, 'It was – it was—'

Stravinsky stared at her dully, waiting. Rachel was pulling urgently at her arm. With everything unsaid, she allowed herself to be dragged away.

Outside, she lamented, 'Oh, I felt such a fool. I couldn't think of anything to say.' But Rachel was running up the companionway, her hand clamped over her mouth. Masha followed. When she reached the Tourist Class promenade deck, Rachel was leaning over the rail, retching. Masha went to offer what succour she could. The fish had not been nice, but Rachel had been prone to these vomiting fits ever since they'd left Bremen. She had brought up almost every meal. Masha suspected it was her way of expressing her grief and stress. She put her arm around her cousin's shoulders consolingly.

It was very dark. There were no lights to be seen either on the ship or the land, other than the searchlight which occasionally reached out from the harbourmaster's building across the vessels moored in the harbour. One of these sabre-strokes of brilliance swept across the *Manhattan* now. Masha looked up in its glare and saw, on the Lido deck above, an old man looking down on them. She gasped. The curling moustaches, the strong, passionate features, the white hair tossed by the wind: despite the wildness of the expression, there could be no doubt about it.

'It's Toscanini!' she exclaimed. 'Look, Rachel. It's Toscanini.'

Rachel looked up, but the darkness had rushed in already. She spat and wiped her mouth with her handkerchief. 'This penchant for seeing famous musicians amounts to a mania, my dear Masha. There's probably some deep psychological cause for it.'

'He was there. And he looked half-mad.'

'Tell Professor Freud all about it.'

'And now I've missed the rice pudding,' Masha mourned. She was still hungry, but as usual after vomiting, Rachel was restless and wanting distraction.

'Let's go to the bar and have a beer. Perhaps you'll see Mozart there.'

Southampton

Rosemary waited until Luella Hennessey's breathing grew regular and deep. The devoted family nurse had been given the bed next to hers, an unlikely watchdog between Rosemary and the door. But Luella was tired after a day dealing with the younger children, and Rosemary knew how to wait. She was adept at the whole thing, easing the bedclothes off, sliding her legs out, slipping on her dress without a sound. She knew how to open and close the door without so much as a click. She'd had a lot of practice.

Outside, she slipped on her shoes. She was giggling to herself as she flitted down the corridors of the hotel. Because of the war – she already hated the war – the lights were turned down almost to nothing at all.

She met nobody on the stairs. The place was as dead as a graveyard at two in the morning. But Cubby had left his door unlocked, as he had promised. She glided in without a sound, her heart starting to race. Cubby was her darling. There was nobody like Cubby. He never did anything that frightened her or hurt her. He wasn't like everyone else, even her brothers, who got impatient with her and pushed her away when they'd had enough of her. His love for her was something new in her life: a love that didn't ask her to be any different from what she was, never yelled at her or mocked.

Cubby was awake, reading a paperback in bed. She jumped on to him joyfully.

'Oh God, I've missed you,' she moaned, hugging him tightly. 'Oh God, oh God.'

He squirmed under her substantial weight. She was all knees and elbows, digging into uncomfortable places on his body. Her mouth, wet and hot, locked on his and flooded it with saliva. He managed to roll her off, though she was strong and determined. 'Rosie. You came!'

''Course I came. Didn't you want me?'

'I want you more than anything in the world.'

'Good.'

'Are you sure nobody saw you leave?'

'I'm not *stoopid.*' She jumped up and in one fluid movement, hauled off her dress. She was naked beneath it, her full breasts rebounding. She came back to him, bringing an intoxicating wave of her body scent. 'Kiss me properly.'

He was always shocked at her daring, she who could be so timid in public. 'Honey, put your clothes back on.'

'Why?'

'We agreed—'

'Are you afraid Mother will burst in?' She put on her mother's stern face and voice. '*Mister* Hubbard. *Phwhat* are you doing with my daughter? *Don't* you know that *Jesus H. Christ* and all his angels will punish you with *eternal hellfire*?'

'Please, honey,' Hubbard begged, 'put your dress back on.'

She blinked at him, her face flushed. 'Don't you want me?'

'More than anything in all the world.'

She reached between his legs. 'I want you, you, you.'

'We said we would wait.'

'I'm no good at waiting.'

He tried to prise her fingers off. 'It's one of the things we all have to learn, honey.'

Her skin prickled all over with disappointment. 'We did it before. Why can't we do it now?'

'There'll be plenty of time for all that.'

'When we're married?'

'Yes, when we're married.'

'You promise?'

'I promise.'

'My hubby, Cubby!' She snuggled up beside him, sliding a strong leg across him. 'You've promised. You can't break a promise.'

'I never break my promises.'

'I get scared when I think you don't want me any more.'

'I'll never stop wanting you. You're the most wonderful girl in the world.'

'Say it again!'

'You're wonderful.'

'Again, again!'

'I'll get your name tattooed over my heart.' Cubby stroked her hair. 'I have to tell you something. Your brother Jack came to see me today.'

She cringed. 'What did he say?'

'He said your mother wants me to go away.'

Her fingernails dug into him. '*Don't*,' she said fiercely.

'I'm not going anywhere. I told him that, too.'

'Did you tell him we're going to get married?'

'Yes. He wasn't very impressed.'

'I don't care. I'm going to be Mrs Hubbard,' she said passionately.

'Yes, baby, you are.'

'And we'll have our own home. Our very own.'

'Yes, my Rosemary Rose.' She was rubbing her thigh over his loins. With Rosemary warm and naked in his arms, he was finding it terribly hard to control himself. She was supremely confident in this, if in little else in her life. Sex came to her with the naturalness of a healthy, lusty, wild animal. A lioness, as the Kennedy boy had called her this morning. She felt no guilt about her body, no inhibitions about her desires. He knew she had been with other men, that they'd abused her naiveté, got her to do things. He hated to think of those others to whom she had given herself so artlessly. But he knew that none of it had touched her. She was still innocent, pure in a way he'd never seen in anyone else.

'Our very, very own home. With fine things everywhere. And Jack and everyone will come to visit us there. And they'll see all my fine things all around, won't they?'

'As fine as I can afford,' he said, smiling.

'And they'll see me there with my beautiful baby. Being a wonderful mother. And the baby calling me Mamma. And they'll treat me just like one of them. I won't be "empty head" any more.'

He kissed her tenderly. 'No, my darling.'

'I won't be "retarded" any more, will I?'

'I hate that word,' he said. 'Please don't use it.'

'And we'll go for rides on your motorcycle.'

'You bet.'

'I'll hold on tight, tight.'

'You'll never let me go.'

'Do you really love me?' she said, looking into his face eagerly. 'Really and truly?' Her lips were parted, her green eyes luminous. She had a slight squint. It sometimes gave the impression that she was looking not at him, but past him, to something beyond. It was the only flaw in her beauty and it melted his heart. He cupped her soft, rounded cheeks in his palms. He could scarcely believe that this lovely woman could be his.

'You are my life, Rosemary.'

'I'm so happy when you say that.' She straddled him, rubbing herself against him. 'Cubby, my Cubby, my own Cubby!'

'Rosemary, wait,' he gasped.

She was panting with excitement, her hips thrusting rhythmically. The softness of her body was enfolding him. He knew that now she was in her stride, there was no stopping her. It was cruel to even try. He took hold of her mobile hips and in seconds he was inside her. She gave a broken cry as he pushed deep into her. Her eyes had become unfocused. She smiled down at him blindly. As she began to rock, she dug her nails hard and rhythmically into the muscles of his chest. *A lioness*, he thought, she was a lioness conquering her prey, devouring him; and it was heaven to be devoured. Her fingers bit into his shoulders, his stomach, his arms. There would be cuts and marks in the morning to remind him of this.

She loved it fast. He grew swiftly bigger and harder, she hotter and wetter. She angled her sturdy hips to give them both the maximum pleasure. She was no longer calling his name, just uttering gasps. It never took either of them very long to climax. They wanted each other far too urgently for niceties. He felt her insides tighten and ripple around him, dragging him into her world. She bent down and bit his neck, her command to join her in bliss. He obeyed, pouring himself into her. For a long moment she held him like that, a prisoner of her teeth and claws and loins. Then, with a shuddering sigh, she nestled languidly beside him again. 'Oh, I feel good, I feel *sooo* good. Do you feel good?'

'You didn't give me time to get any protection on, honey.' He got his breath back. 'You're going to get pregnant, Rosie.'

'I want our baby.' Her voice was thick and dreamy. 'I can't wait to have our baby. How many babies will we have?'

He laughed breathlessly. 'Let's start with just the one and see how it goes.'

'I want five. Six! Tell me about our house.'

'Well,' he said, gathering her in his arms, 'it will be in Pasadena. The sun always shines there. And it will be cosy and neat and bright and full of happiness.'

'With a garden?'

'Oh, sure. Not like the big gardens you're used to, but it will be pretty, with lots of flowers.'

'And I'll sit there with our baby.'

'Yes, you will.'

'I can't wait.' She gave a great sigh. 'When will we be married?'

'I've been thinking about that. I think it should be as soon as possible.'

She propped herself up on one elbow, excited. '*Tomorrow*?'

Cubby smiled. 'It can't be tomorrow, honey.'

'When, then?'

'Perhaps soon after we arrive in New York.'

'In St Pat's?'

'Not in St Pat's,' he said regretfully. 'It'll have to be a registry office. Your family aren't going to be happy. But they wouldn't have come even if it was in the cathedral.'

Rosemary thought about that for a moment. Then she lay back down again. 'It doesn't matter,' she said. 'I can still wear white, can't I?'

'Of course you can.'

'And have a bouquet?'

'White roses.'

'White roses and cream lilies.'

'You'll be so lovely.'

'You're my Cubby hubby. My hubby Cubby.'

'I'm yours.'

'You're mine.'

They were her last words. She fell into one of her swift, deep slumbers, her body becoming heavy and inert against him. He held her close to his heart, aching with love, knowing that in half an hour he would have to wake her and send her back to her own room again.

The Western Approaches

The blazing wreck lit up the night, a spectacle which almost the entire crew of *U-113* had come on to the deck to see. It was their first kill of the war. Initially, there had been cheering and congratulations, but these had died down as they watched the stricken ship consumed in the fire which had been started by the two torpedoes they'd launched just after midnight.

She was the *Robert Recorde*, a 3,000-ton merchantman, built in Newcastle upon Tyne, registered in Cardiff, carrying a cargo of timber from Canada to the Clyde. This information had been provided by one of the survivors, whom they'd fished out of the sea, a sixteen-year-old boy rating named Howell Lewis. He was badly burned, and they'd dropped him near one of the lifeboats to be picked up. There were only three of these. The rest had been shattered when Todt had ordered the bridge and radio room to be machine-gunned. The British sailors huddled in the lifeboats shouted at the submarine as *U-113* rumbled between them, playing its searchlight around the floating wreckage. The U-boat crew stared back silently, some taking turns to use the night-glasses.

'What are they saying?' Todt asked Hufnagel, who was beside him in the conning tower.

'They say their lifeboats are taking on water,' replied Hufnagel, who spoke some English. 'And they say they have wounded. They are asking for medical assistance.'

Krupp, the medical officer, was on the bridge. 'We could give them some first-aid supplies, Captain. We have enough.'

One of the lifeboats, which seemed to have an officer in it, began to row raggedly towards the U-boat, the men on board calling out hoarsely. Todt drew the Luger from his holster and fired three shots towards them. There was a scream and the sailors huddled for cover in the boat, dropping their oars. 'Tell them I'll use the flak gun on them,' Todt commanded Hufnagel, who relayed the warning in English. To drive the point home, Todt ordered the machine gun to be trained on the lifeboats. The men in them fell silent, with sullen faces.

The *Robert Recorde* was settling in the water, but the torpedoes had evidently not done enough to send her to the bottom quickly. One of them, in fact, though it had made contact, had failed to explode. Flames were pouring up into the night sky in long, rolling surges of orange, shedding enough heat to make some of the observers shield their faces. Hufnagel watched through his binoculars. A lukewarm attitude towards National Socialism had slowed his progress through the ranks. Then he had fallen in love with Masha Morgenstern, practically on the morning of the Nuremberg Laws. As a result, he had waited in vain for his own command; while Todt had benefited from accelerated promotion. Hufnagel, not a jealous man, regarded it as part of his duty to encourage and advise his younger commander. 'She's full of wood. She'll burn all night. Like a beacon.'

They were only a hundred miles east of Rockall. Hufnagel was right to be concerned. Fascinated as he was by the blaze, Todt gave the order to the deck gun crew. 'Five rounds, rapid fire. Amidships. Waterline.'

The blasts from the deck gun lit up the sea and the boats in it. There were cries of rage or despair from the survivors in the lifeboats. For the first few moments it seemed the target was unaffected, despite the gaping holes that the explosive shells had torn in her hull. Then *Robert Recorde* began to sink fast. She went down by the bows, her rusty stern rising out of the water, ignominiously revealing her rudder gear and her single screw. For a few minutes, the stern of the merchantman towered over the scene, unearthly in the U-boat's spotlight. Then, with a long groan, she sank into the depths. With the flames extinguished, the night rushed in and the stars began to be visible. The air became icy.

'*Waidmannsheil*,' Hufnagel said quietly to the captain.

Leaving a bridge watch strapped to the deck rail to endure the cold and the rough sea, the crew went below. It was their first kill and some of the excited younger men clamoured for a tot of schnapps, or at least a bottle of beer from the store that clinked in the galley. But Todt did not give the order. Instead, he retired to his quarters and drew the thin curtain which separated him from the crew.

The boat's gramophone was in the captain's quarters, connected to a series of speakers attached to the bulkheads throughout *U-113*. Also in the captain's quarters was the boat's collection of gramophone records, personally selected by Todt. These included the *Unser Führer* set of Adolf Hitler's speeches as well as recordings of Beethoven, Wagner and Bruckner. A hiss from the speakers announced that Todt had put the needle on to a record and shortly, the opening chords of Bruckner's mighty Eighth Symphony rolled through every compartment of the boat.

This choice was not popular with everyone. Most of the crew were very young and almost all were novices.

Some settled down with eyes closed and folded hands to listen dutifully or doze. Others were restless after being in action. The men had their own gramophone in the forward torpedo room, which also served as the crew's quarters, with their own collection of records, not all of which were officially sanctioned; but there was no competing with Bruckner. They turned instead, as *U-113* surged through the night, to their usual pastimes: looking at photographs of their families and girlfriends, playing chess on little portable boards, or leafing through dog-eared magazines they had already read a dozen times.

Le Havre

Aboard the *Manhattan*, moored in Le Havre, Stravinsky had been dreaming of the Trylon and the Perisphere. They towered, white as bone, in a de Chirico landscape of empty palaces, twilight skies and marmoreal clouds. He dreamed he was walking slowly towards them, his hands outstretched, knowing he would never reach them. He was not sure what had awoken him until he heard it again – a stifled sob. He wondered if he had been crying in his sleep, something that happened to him from time to time. But the sound was made by someone else.

He raised himself in bed and switched on the lamp. Groping for his spectacles, he put them on his nose and peered at Thomas in the bunk next to his. The boy had buried his face in his pillow, but his thin shoulders were convulsing.

Stravinsky spoke quietly. 'Child.'

The boy stopped moving. He slowly raised his head from the pillow. His face was a tragic mask, his eyelids swollen. 'I didn't mean to wake you.'

'I'm a light sleeper.' Stravinsky inspected his little travelling clock, a parting gift from Nadia Boulanger. It was long after midnight. 'Why are you crying?'

'I miss my family so much.'

'You'll see them again soon.'

The boy dug the heels of his hands into his eyes. 'I will never see them.'

'Why do you say that?'

'They took them away.' His lips were trembling. 'They came in the night with the truck, and took them all, my mother and father, my uncle and my aunt.'

'Who took them? Where were they taken?' The boy didn't answer, and the questions hung in the air. Stravinsky knew that modern Germany was a state in which people were arrested at night and never returned, and nobody asked why or where. 'But why didn't they take you, Thomas?'

'They didn't find me, because my mother made me sleep with the neighbour, Frau König.'

'I see.' Stravinsky tried to unravel what the boy was saying. 'Your neighbour's name is König?'

'Yes.'

'She was a relation?'

'No.'

'But your name is König, too.'

'No. My name is—' The boy stopped, his face panicky.

Stravinsky raised his hand tiredly. 'You need not tell me your name. Your mother sent you to sleep with this Frau König to keep you safe?'

'It was an arrangement.'

'What sort of arrangement?'

'My mother gave Frau König her things. Her gold sovereigns.'

'To take care of you?'

'Frau König's son died. Last year. So she had a spare bed.'

'And a passport?' Stravinsky guessed.

The boy looked up quickly, his tear-stained face scared and guilty. 'I should not have said anything.'

'No, you should not,' Stravinsky said. 'And you must not say it again. Not to anybody.'

Thomas twisted his hands together. 'I won't.'

'Especially not when you enter the United States. Whatever your name was before, you are Thomas König now. When you show your passport to the immigration officer, you must not flinch. You understand?'

'Yes,' the boy whispered.

'And you must not breathe a word of this to anyone on board. Not to anyone.' Stravinsky raised his finger sternly. 'Not a soul. Or you will be sent back to Germany.'

'I think I would rather go back and die than live alone,' the boy said in a low voice.

'That is nonsense,' Stravinsky said sharply, then looked at him more compassionately. 'It may seem preferable to you to give up now, but you have a life to live, Thomas. You have a duty to live it for the ones you have left behind. Do some good in the world to repay the evil that was done to you and to them. Otherwise where would the world end up?' He paused. 'What were they arrested for?'

'My father and my uncle said things about the Nazis. They confessed against Hitler in the church.'

'Confessed? What do you mean? What confession? What church?'

'They are pastors. Lutherans. They call it the Confessing Church, because they believe they must speak the truth openly, before God, no matter what. They said that the treatment of the Jewish people was wicked. They were warned many times, and my mother begged them to be silent, but they wouldn't be silent.'

'And for that they were arrested?'

'They have been sent to a concentration camp.'

'So you are not a Nazi, after all?'

'No. They expelled me from school because I would not give the Hitler salute or join the Hitler Youth.'

'You were going the same way as your father and uncle? Your mother must have been distraught. How old are you, really?'

'Sixteen.'

'That is more believable. You don't look eighteen.'

'I watched everything from Frau König's window,' Thomas went on. 'But my mother didn't even look up at me as they took her away!' The boy started sobbing in earnest, burying his face in his hands.

'The reason for that,' Stravinsky said, 'was that she did not want to betray your hiding place.' Thomas quietened, making only those little gasps that had disturbed Stravinsky's nightmare. Stravinsky took a cigarette from the pack in his bedside cabinet, then thought better of lighting it. He put it away again. 'Come, Thomas,' he said at last. 'Sit with me.'

Thomas groped his way to Stravinsky's side. Stravinsky put his arm around the boy's shoulders. 'Honour your mother's sacrifice. Do what she asked you to do. You must be the best Hitler Youth in the world now, at least until you are settled in America, and safe from harm. You understand?'

Thomas nodded.

'Play your part. Be eighteen, not sixteen. Be a good Nazi. I will help you. Thomas König is not such a bad name. Eh? It was a good thing that Frau König kept her part of the bargain. But then, you brought her dead son back to life, and that is no mean feat.' He offered Thomas his handkerchief. 'Have you slept at all?'

The boy shook his head. 'I can't stop thinking about them. I think they are all dead by now.'

Stravinsky could make no comment on that. 'You should try to sleep. Would you like me to tell you a story?'

'Yes, please.'

'Then put your head on the pillow.' The boy obeyed, lying back and gazing up at Stravinsky with bleary eyes. 'I will tell you about my first great success. Yes?'

'Yes, please.'

'It was a long time ago, in the spring of 1913. I was a young man, I suppose about nine or ten years older than you are now. Nobody had heard of me. I had composed a ballet called *The Rite of Spring*. It was the story of a young woman who is so full of life that she cannot stop dancing, and in the end dances herself to death. It was to be performed in Paris, at the Théâtre des Champs-Élysées, by the Ballets Russes. On the opening night, everybody came in their smartest clothes. They were expecting a pleasant, dull evening – you know?' Stravinsky folded his arms and bowed his head in imitation of the Dying Swan. The boy nodded. 'But my music was considered very revolutionary. Nobody had heard anything like it before. It was harsh, what we call dissonant. Do you know what dissonance is?'

'No,' Thomas replied.

'You understand diodes and triodes, but not dissonance? Well, let us say that dissonance is when the composer squeezes lemon-juice in your eyes. You understand?'

The boy nodded. 'I think so.'

'So there was the dissonant music, to begin with. The audience started to shout and whistle. They weren't happy. Other people were interested in the dissonance, and told them to shut up. And then, among all this tumult, the dancers appeared on the stage, young girls and boys. But they danced in a new way. Like this.' Stravinsky made exaggerated, angular jerks with his arms and head. This brought a slight smile to the boy's lips. 'This was also something nobody had seen before. So the audience began to howl and stamp even more, and the ones who were enjoying it began to shout back even louder. But all this was as nothing to what happened when the star of the show appeared. Do you know who Nijinsky is?'

'Well, Nijinsky was the greatest dancer in the world, but between you and me—' Stravinsky twirled his forefinger around his ear. 'He was a little crazy. In fact, more than a little crazy. And his dancing was crazy, too.' His dark eyes opened very wide to express insanity. 'Completely crazy – or so it seemed to those bourgeois people who had come to see frilly tutus and nice legs. So instead of watching and listening, they began to fight each other, right there in the theatre. They made so much noise that the performance could hardly continue. I was very angry. I got up from my seat and I told them, "Excuse me, but go to the devil, all of you." And I walked out. I left them to fight and stamp and scratch each other's faces and insult my art. I walked around the Champs-Élysées in a temper. But I could hear the rioting from streets away. It was a disaster.'

'You said it was your greatest success,' the boy said sleepily.

'And that is true. The next day, the newspapers were full of the story. Everyone was talking about *The Rite of Spring*. And the next night, all of Paris came to see what these crazy Russians were doing. By the end of the week, everybody had heard of Igor Stravinsky. I was the most celebrated madman in France. So you see, my greatest success was a disaster.'

The boy smiled, but his eyelids were heavy now. 'I would like to have seen that.'

'The sight of a stockbroker punching a hole in another stockbroker's opera hat is a touching spectacle. But close your eyes now, Thomas.' He watched the boy's face slacken as he drifted into an exhausted sleep. He reached out and touched the short blonde hair lightly. This motherless lamb had slipped away from the wolves. The son of Christians who dared criticise the regime, a crime which had carried a death-warrant, he had assumed the name of a dead boy. And his mother had taken his true identity with her to her grave. Her parting gift to him, a theft that had saved his life.

When he was certain Thomas would not wake again, Stravinsky sighed heavily, and lay down beside him, wondering whether sleep would come again.

'I have good news,' Katharine told Stravinsky the next morning at breakfast. 'Our baggage has arrived during the night. And so have our papers. Just in time – we sail tomorrow.' Stravinsky nodded without much interest as he stirred his coffee. He had slept badly, she thought. The dining room was even more crowded today, the waiters rushing to and fro with laden trays. The ship was being joined by passengers all the time, and the atmosphere of urgency was growing. 'Where's your little Nazi?' she asked.

'Still asleep. He passed a bad night.'

'You seem to enjoy his company.'

'He tells me about things.'

'The World's Fair?'

'He's particularly interested in the scientific displays.'

She pulled a face. 'These Fascists and their worship of machinery.'

Igor seemed unable to even hold his head up. He spoke to his coffee. 'One day, I suppose, we will see an orchestra of robots play a symphony written by a calculating machine.'

'I hope I'm not around to see that day.'

'One never knows what one will see in one's lifetime,' he said.

She laid her hand over his. 'We are leaving Europe tomorrow, Igor.'

'And perhaps for the last time,' he replied.

'You're depressed. But remember, you're going to a new life. Leaving behind the past, with its sorrows.'

'I'm leaving my dead behind. My wife, my child, my parents. A man should not be separated from his dead.'

'That's morbid,' she said.

He raised his eyes heavily to hers. 'I feel that I am leaving half of myself behind me. I don't think I will ever compose again.'

'Oh, Igor, no.' Shocked, Katharine pressed his hand, trying to shake him out of this mood. 'Don't say that. What about your Symphony in Cigarette?'

'I will never complete it. My life's work has been a failure.'

'It hasn't. You are still at the forefront of music.'

'I'm a little old to be a daring young composer any more,' he replied sardonically, 'don't you think, my dear?'

Katharine poured him more coffee without replying. Since the 1920s, Igor had been in a liaison with Vera de Bosset, a love affair to which poor Katya, a chronic invalid, had acquiesced, sometimes nobly, sometimes with feeble rages. And now Igor had lost Vera, with her huge eyes and long limbs, who could express herself in dance or in brilliant, witty paintings; she was the half of himself that was being left behind. Wife, daughter, mother and lover – Igor had lost all four female archetypes in the last year. What would Jung have said?

Across the room, Rachel and Masha Morgenstern were also in elegiac mood. In Rachel's case, it was mock-elegy.

'Ah, my dear Masha,' she said, spreading marmalade on her toast, 'we are the last two rosebuds on the bush. The last breath of perfume before the bottle is stoppered forever. Cultured, pretty, gay, in us you see the last two *kneidels* on the plate, before it is taken back to the kitchen and scraped into the bin.' She bit a corner off her toast, and continued with her mouth full. 'The last two *bublitchki* the fat man just couldn't eat.'

'I get the picture,' Masha cut in. 'You need not continue.'

'What are you staring at?' Rachel asked, noticing that her cousin's attention was elsewhere. She looked over her shoulder and rolled her eyes facetiously. 'Oh, of course. The great Stravinsky-Korsakoff. Honestly, I don't know what you see in that man. He's as yellow as a lemon this morning, and looks twice as sour.'

'It breaks my heart to see him so sad.'

'Indeed, he is sadder than the last *latke* that has been left on the saucer, and is starting to curl at the edges.'

'You cannot be serious for one moment, can you?'

'I could try, if there was anything to be serious about.'

'But there is not?'

'There is not.'

'Well, I am glad your life is so free of trouble, dear cousin Rachel. Have you finished your breakfast?'

'I think so.'

'Then let us go to the promenade deck, and watch you vomit it up for the seagulls.'

Rachel clasped her hands prettily. 'Oh, can we? What an appealing idea. Let's not delay.'

But as Masha rose from her chair and turned to go, there was a ripping sound. The coat which she always wore had caught on the edge of the table. She clutched at the fabric in dismay, turning pale. 'Rachel! My coat!'

'Quick, take a hold of it.'

'Help me.'

Rachel snatched up the torn hem of Masha's leather coat, rolling it in her fingers. 'Quickly. Back to our cabin.'

In this somewhat ungainly fashion, with Rachel holding Masha's coat absurdly like a page lifting the train of a queen, they made their way out of the dining room. Stravinsky did not look up as they passed, but Katharine stared at them curiously.

Luckily, the cabin which they shared with a young Hungarian woman who spoke neither German nor English was temporarily empty, the bunks unmade and feminine clothing scattered all over the floor. They locked the door, and Masha carefully took off the coat.

The tear was a bad one, and the contents of the hem were sliding out, a thin chamois leather pipe. Masha unfolded the soft leather to reveal a string of dark-red rubies. 'They nearly fell out in the restaurant. The stitching has all ripped away.'

'Can you fix it?'

Masha shook her head. 'I can't sew like our grandmother.'

'Let me try.' Rachel got the little sewing kit out of her suitcase and sat down to inspect the coat. 'The mend will be conspicuous,' she said seriously, for once not making a joke of the situation. 'What if the American customs officers notice it?'

'Do you think they would confiscate the stones?'

'They will make us pay duty.'

'With what? We haven't got a penny.' The German authorities, indeed, had allowed each of them to take only the farcical sum of ten Reichsmarks, less than five American dollars, out of the country. And one suitcase of clothing apiece.

Masha, who had inherited a house in Berlin, had been forced to relinquish her title in the property to the State before she could get a 'Jewish Passport', entitling her to leave. Then, too, there had been the crippling emigration taxes which had been imposed on the family for the privilege of letting the two girls escape. The necessary documents required filled a thick dossier.

Nor was there any great welcome waiting across the Atlantic. To have had even a remote chance of entering the United States, the Morgensterns had been compelled to find several sponsors willing to give affidavits. They were required to prove that they could support themselves which, considering that they had been robbed blind by the Nazi state, was almost unfeasible. They had then been given numbers in a waiting list within the small quota established for Germany. The girls had been forced to undergo a humiliating physical examination at the United States consulate. It had all seemed impossibly hard until, at the very last moment, their numbers had come up. They had left Bremen with the iron gates almost literally crashing shut on their heels.

This little string of red stones represented the final gasp of a once-wealthy family, now reduced to pauperdom.

The girls stared at one another, the last two *latkes* on the saucer. 'I could wear them round my neck from now on,' Masha suggested.

'Everybody would see. They would be stolen long before we reached New York.'

'On board this ship? Surely not.'

'My dear cousin, what planet do you think you inhabit? We are Jews.'

'But not everybody hates Jews.'

'When you find someone who loves us, would you kindly let me know? I'll just have to make as good a job of it as I can,' Rachel said.

Masha nodded. She watched Rachel sewing the maroon lining, her fair head bent over the work, and reflected – but did not comment – upon the interesting fact that this was the first time since leaving Germany that Rachel had neglected to vomit up a meal. 'You've never told me whether you were ever in love, Rachel.'

'Haven't I?'

'Not a word. You never talk about yourself.'

'Perhaps there's nothing to talk about.'

'I don't believe that for one moment. Why are you so enigmatic?'

Rachel examined her stitches closely. 'I've learned to keep myself hidden away, like these rubies.'

'So there *was* someone!'

Rachel lifted her shoulders. 'Perhaps there was a certain someone.'

'Tell me about him!'

Rachel's smile had a certain secretive quality. It lifted the corners of her eyes, turning her high cheekbones into little apples. 'You're too young.'

'Nonsense,' Masha scoffed. 'I told you about Rudi, didn't I?'

'Yes, you told me about Rudi.'

'Well, then. What was his name?'

'I can't tell you.'

'At least tell me his first name!'

'I can't even tell you that.'

Masha was fidgeting with excitement. 'Somebody famous, then!'

'No. Not famous.'

'What, then?' Masha's eyes opened very wide. 'Married!' she gasped.

Rachel drew up the crimson thread carefully. 'No, not married.'

'Thank goodness for that.' She laid her hand on her mouth. 'Oh. I've guessed.'

'Have you?'

'A Gentile. And your family objected.'

'You're very clever,' Rachel said, 'but that was not the difficulty.'

'What was the difficulty, then? Tell me!'

'Stop asking questions. You're distracting me.'

'And you're exasperating me!'

'If I don't make these stitches neat, the customs men will confiscate our precious rubies.'

'It's not fair,' Masha exclaimed. 'I told you all about Rudi.'

'Of course you did. You are incapable of keeping a secret.'

'There shouldn't be secrets between us.' When Rachel didn't reply, but just kept smiling and sewing, Masha went on plaintively, 'I think you're very unkind to keep things hidden from me. I know hardly anything about you, and we're first cousins. We used to have fun when we were children, didn't we?'

'Yes.'

'We used to play duettinos by Clementi together on the piano, do you remember?'

'Of course I remember.'

'And then they started keeping us apart. When I asked to see you, they said you were a bad influence.'

Rachel seemed wryly amused. 'Did they indeed? Well, you should be warned.'

'But we only have each other, now. And I like your influence.'

Rachel lifted her cool blue eyes to Masha's. 'Do you?'

'Yes. You're rather cynical, you know. You don't have a good word to say about anybody. But I've grown to like that. It makes me feel grown-up.'

'Really?'

'I'm too romantic. I know it. I always have stars in my eyes. You help me to question things.'

'Well, the question before us now is whether this repair will pass muster,' Rachel replied, lifting the hem of the coat to show her cousin. 'What do you think?'

Masha examined it critically. 'A man on a galloping horse might not notice.'

'We shall have to be content with that. Be careful not to catch it on anything again, or you'll be scattering precious stones like the girl in the fairy tale. Let's go and get some sun.'

They went up to the deck together, with Masha none the wiser about this mysterious love-affair of Rachel's.

'At least,' she begged, 'tell me his initials.'

'No.'

'How can you be such a tease? You'll make me hate you!'

'I hope not,' Rachel said gravely; but no matter how Masha pleaded and bullied, Rachel refused to be drawn further on the subject.

Southampton

The discussion between Rosemary and her mother about Cubby Hubbard was not going well.

'You never used to be a liar, Rosemary,' Mrs Kennedy said, her voice rising sharply. 'The Devil has got into you.'

'I'm not lying,' Rosemary said sullenly.

'If you're not lying, then Nurse Hennessey is. And I know which of the two of you I believe. Look at me, Rosemary. She says she woke up at two in the morning to find you coming back into the room. Where had you been?'

Rosemary refused to meet her mother's eyes. 'I didn't go anywhere.'

'You went to Mr Hubbard's room, didn't you?'

For a moment, it seemed as though Rosemary was going to deny it again. Then her face, which had been set in a scowl, crumpled. 'I love him.'

Mrs Kennedy groaned, turning away from her daughter with a mixture of pity and disgust. 'You poor fool. Don't you understand what you've done?'

'I haven't done anything bad.' Rosemary's cheeks were red, her eyes shining with tears.

'Of course you've done something bad. I don't expect you to understand difficult things, but this isn't difficult. Going to that man's bed is a mortal sin.'

'It's not a sin if we get married.'

'Is that what he tells you? That's nothing but a wicked lie. He only wants one thing.'

'We're going to get married and have a house. And a baby.'

'A baby! You can't even look after yourself. How could you look after a baby, you poor fool?'

'I'm not a fool.' Rosemary had been sitting on the bed, still huddled in her dressing gown. She rose to her feet now. She was considerably taller and bigger than her mother, and with her swollen face and wild hair, she was intimidating. Mrs Kennedy took a step back despite herself. 'Don't call me a fool!'

'You're worse than a fool. You're in deadly sin.'

'Why am I different from everyone else? Why do you treat me differently? It's not fair!'

'I treat you as you deserve to be treated.'

'You don't love me.'

'Of course I don't love you when the Devil is in you.'

'He's not. He's in *you.*'

'How dare you challenge me, Rosemary? Say the Act of Contrition right now.'

'You spoil everything. *Everything.*'

'Get on your knees and say it.'

'I *can* have a baby. I *can* get married. I *will.* I'm *not* retarded. I'm *not* bad.'

'Look at yourself,' her mother retorted. 'How could you possibly be trusted with a helpless infant? If you had a baby, you'd kill it in a week.'

Rosemary could feel herself slipping into chaos. '*I would not kill my baby.*'

'That man is degrading you for his own filthy lust, twisting you round his finger. You will never see him again. Say the Act of Contrition right now. *O my God, I am heartily sorry for having offended Thee, and I detest—*'

'I won't say it. I will see him!'

'I forbid it. The thing is finished, Rosemary.'

Rosemary ran to the bathroom and slammed the door.

Mrs Kennedy found she was trembling. Her stomach ached. She'd always been able to reduce Rosemary to obedience, or at least wretchedness, but it was getting harder and harder. The child had her father's strength, her father's will.

She went to the window and looked out on Lime Street. The cars were moving slowly in a steady drizzle. Most had already been fitted with the odd little hoods on their headlamps that were supposed to make them invisible to German bombers during the blackout. Every day brought the war closer. And the *Manhattan*, inexplicably, was stuck in France.

What was she going to do about Rosemary? It had happened without her being aware of it. The child had been shut away for so long in convents and special schools, while she got on with the other eight children. She'd done her best, nobody could have done more, but she'd had to give her time to the ones who were—

The ones who were right in the head.

She was her father's daughter. She had that in her which also drove her husband, that lust. That refusal to understand that carnal desires were shameful and sinful. She saw Joe in Rosemary's face, that sexually confident grin. She heard Joe in Rosemary's laugh, in the way her voice coarsened when she was thwarted. She smelled Joe in Rosemary's shameless appetite for life.

Hadn't Joe flaunted his mistresses in front of them all for years? He'd had the pick of them, film stars, starlets, chorus girls, the famous and the infamous, he'd had them all. He was with the latest one, a buxom secretary, right now. What example was that for a child? And if she reproached him – for his brazenness, because God knew she never reproached him for his sin – he laughed in her face.

From such a father came such a daughter.

She'd subordinated her life to Joe's ambition, his pursuit of power and wealth. He'd given her much in return, but the pain he had inflicted over the years was incalculable, though she could never speak of it to anyone. The thought of coping with Rosemary's lust from now on was horrible. How would she manage her? Nobody could manage her.

By the time the nuns had told her what the girl had been up to, it was too late. Rosemary's virginity was gone. Her innocence was gone. She had become corrupted. So beautiful to look at, but rotten inside, rotten before she was ripe. Sneaking out to rut with strangers. Drinking and smoking. And with her limited mental capacities, she couldn't even understand what she had done wrong. Any more than a bitch in heat could understand that it was wrong to run after—

And now here there was this cheap nobody filling her head with absurd ideas of wedlock and motherhood. As though Rosemary could even say her Hail Marys or recite her ABCs. She was no more ready for marriage than she was to fly to the moon. Ten to one he was in it for the money. That kind of man always was. He was looking to be paid off.

Jack had gotten nowhere with him. As for Joe, it was beneath his dignity to deal with a boy who played the guitar in a nightclub. Hadn't it always been Mother who'd administered punishments, with a hanger out of the closet? While Dad just grinned? She would have to speak to Cubby Hubbard herself.

Mrs Kennedy went to the bathroom door and banged on it with her fist. 'Rosemary, come out.'

'I won't!' came the tearful reply.

Mrs Kennedy tried the handle. The child was too simple to even lock the door. It opened, revealing Rosemary huddled on the floor next to the sink, crying bitterly. Mrs Kennedy felt that visceral wrench of mingled revulsion and pity again. 'Get up,' she said quietly. Slowly, Rosemary pulled herself to her feet. Her face was blotchy, her eyes swollen almost shut with crying. 'Wash your face,' Mrs Kennedy commanded. 'You're coming to church with me. You'll make a full confession to the priest. You'll take Communion with me. And then I am going to speak to Mr Hubbard. I'm going to put a stop to this.'

'No, Mother!'

'Wash your face and get dressed.'

'Please don't do this.' Rosemary clutched at her mother. 'Please, Mother. Please don't. *Please don't.*'

'You leave me no choice,' Mrs Kennedy said coldly. 'Let me go, Rosemary.'

But Rosemary was sliding towards her, her face turned blindly up to her mother. 'I'm begging you, begging you, begging you. Please don't. Please, Mother.'

'Get up off your knees.' She tried to prise her daughter's fingers from her clothes, but Rosemary was strong, and the flimsy material ripped. 'Look what you've done!'

Rosemary's fists pounded into Mrs Kennedy's thigh, sending her staggering back. The girl was no longer articulate. A scream of rage was swelling from her throat, piercing and inhuman. Her eyes had rolled back in her head. Her limbs flailed, legs kicking out, fists pounding at anything near her. Mrs Kennedy backed away. These frenzies had been common during Rosemary's childhood, when she'd been frustrated in a cherished desire, but she'd hoped they were over. In a child they had been bad enough. In an adult woman they were frightening. 'You can scream your head off,' she said breathlessly, 'it's not going to make any difference.'

She went to call Luella Hennessey, leaving Rosemary to thrash on the floor.

Cubby Hubbard's thoughts were with Rosemary. He was remembering the first time he had seen her, at her sister's party in London. He'd glimpsed her across the room, so pretty and yet looking overwhelmed by it all. Her eyes were beautiful, but somehow blind. And when he'd asked her to dance, she'd seemed astonished. Later, she'd told him that men never asked her to dance, at least not a second time. They seemed frightened of her. Sometimes they laughed and said cruel things behind her back.

He'd been astounded by her, once he'd got close to her; by her beauty, her innocence, her vulnerability. He'd been filled with a powerful need to protect her. He could think of little else from then on.

She didn't just need protecting from the world, from the predatory men he'd soon learned about; but from her family, too – those arrogant Kennedys, to whom she was an embarrassment, to be hidden away. With all the boys heading for Washington, a crazy sister was not an advantage. So they kept her locked up like something shameful. What did they think was going to happen to her? Did they think she'd be happy to rot in an ivory tower the rest of her life?

He sat at his breakfast table now, staring at the starched white linen in front of him. Getting Rosemary away from the Kennedys would not be an easy task. She was like some princess in a fairy tale, protected by dragons. But once they were married, she would be his, his alone. There would be nothing anyone could do to come between them or take her away from him.

'Mr Hubbard?'

He looked up. Mrs Joseph P. Kennedy was standing at his table, wearing a severe grey wool suit. Her face was stony. He rose to his feet. 'Good morning, Mrs Kennedy.'

'Come with me, please.'

He had just ordered his breakfast, but he didn't think fit to mention that. 'Sure.' He followed her out into the street. It was a wet morning, and the doorman gave them a large umbrella. He opened this and held it over Mrs Kennedy's head as they walked along. She was a thin, brusque woman, and she walked fast. He had no idea where they were going.

'I understand my daughter visited you in the night,' she said.

Hubbard felt his face flush. 'I'm not going to lie about that.'

She could see the bite on his neck, inflicted by her daughter's teeth in the throes of copulation. She felt nauseated. 'You realise that I could go to the nearest policeman and have you arrested?'

There was, in fact, a large policeman standing on the street corner, majestic in a shiny cape. 'Look, I'm glad of the chance to talk to you about Rosemary. I care about her very deeply.'

'My daughter is at present suffering a violent seizure on the bathroom floor. That is what your "caring very deeply" has done for her.'

'You mean that you've driven her half crazy,' he retorted angrily. 'Have you called a doctor?'

'Don't presume to instruct me in what I should or should not do with my own daughter.' Her face tightened. 'What will it take to get you to leave Rosemary alone?'

'What are you talking about?'

She didn't look at him, but kept her face averted, even though he was hurrying close beside her with the umbrella. 'How much?'

'How much what?'

'How much money, if you force me to be crude.'

He was astonished. 'I don't want your money.'

'Everybody wants money. You're an itinerant musician – which would never allow you to give Rosemary the kind of life she's accustomed to, let alone the nursing care she will require all her life.'

'I do okay. But I believe that Rosemary only wants one thing in life, and that is love.'

'A very pretty speech. If you're not in this for the money, then you're a fool as well as a knave.'

'You can insult me as much as you please,' Cubby replied. 'It won't make any difference to my feelings for Rosemary. I've already told you that I love her. I told your son the same thing. I would rather have your blessing.'

'You will never have that.'

'Then I'll do without it.'

He was a little out of breath. Mrs Kennedy was a good walker. They had been making brisk progress up the hill, and had now reached a church, which was (to Hubbard's eyes) a hideous Victorian structure of blackened brick. Workmen were boarding up the stained-glass windows against German bombs, and laying sandbags around the foundations. She turned to him, her eyes the same colour as the autumn sky. 'And that is your last word?'

'It is.'

'Then we part as enemies, Mr Hubbard.' She reached out her gloved hand. He thought she wanted to shake hands for a moment, but she only wanted the umbrella. He gave it to her. She turned without another word and went quickly into the church. He made his way back to the hotel, turning up the collar of his leather jacket against the rain. Her last, ominous words rang in his ears.

Le Havre

His head full of tumult, a roaring in his ears, Arturo Toscanini strode the deck, muttering to himself. His fellow passengers had by now learned to keep out of his way. There had been some collisions and furious altercations at first. But even though the ship grew more crowded daily, promenaders had learned caution.

Toscanini himself was oblivious to everyone around him. He paced all day and he paced all night. He had neither visited his cabin nor slept. As for food, he had kept himself alive by bursting into the kitchen at odd hours (he had not revisited the Comanche dining hall) and tearing at whatever he could find – stale bread, slices of beef. It was the way he had always eaten, on his feet.

Carla had not appeared. Carla was lost somewhere in the swarming ants' nest that was Europe, while Hitler's armies battered down the gates. But the tension was terrible. *La forza del destino, inexorable fate that drives me on to a foreign shore! Orphan and wanderer, tortured by fearful dreams! Weeping, I leave thee, beloved homeland! Farewell!* Only Verdi could capture the pathos, the horror.

A sudden gust of wind swept the hat from his head. Toscanini snatched at it unsuccessfully. It bowled along the deck, scurrying between the passengers, some of whom made efforts to catch it. But it was too cunning, and evaded all grasping hands, rolling along on its brim until it came up against an immaculate pair of spats. A long-fingered white hand picked it up. It belonged to none other than Igor Stravinsky, who was walking the deck with a teenage boy who appeared to be wearing the uniform of the Hitler Youth.

Stravinsky restored the errant hat to its owner. 'Good morning, maestro. We had heard you were on board.'

Toscanini clutched the fedora. 'When do we sail, Igor? Have you some idea?'

'Not today, at any rate,' Stravinsky replied. He indicated *Manhattan*'s red, white and blue funnels, which towered silently over them. 'The engines have not yet been started, and the stewards tell us that the bunkers have not yet been filled with fuel, either.'

'Incredible,' Toscanini burst out, 'that they cannot say when we sail.'

The two men made an odd contrast: the Italian conductor dishevelled by the wind and his emotion, the Russian composer impeccably turned out in homburg hat, plus-fours, argyle socks and spats, as though for a promenade through the Bois de Boulogne. 'I understand you are waiting for your wife?'

Toscanini groaned by way of an answer. He raised his arms to the autumn sky, his gnarled fingers crooked, his lined face anguished.

'Calm yourself, maestro,' Stravinsky said. 'She will come. There is time. Passengers are still boarding.' Indeed, a group of new passengers was even now hurrying up the gangplank, lugging suitcases and trailing coats. The ark would sink under their weight soon. 'They tell us that you don't go to your cabin or the dining room.'

'I cannot stand the company of idiots.'

'You should not have become a conductor, then,' Stravinsky replied.

Toscanini was unamused. 'You laugh, but I cry,' he said angrily.

'I am not laughing. I have left my wife behind – in her grave.' Stravinsky was in a mood of weary irony. 'My young friend Thomas here has been telling me about a talking robot they have in America. It can do sums and smoke cigarettes. Perhaps your occupation and mine will be usurped by such inventions in time.'

Toscanini groaned again. He yearned for Lake Maggiore, for Isolino, for the *palazzo* on the island where he had made his home, in a coppice of cypresses and pines, in a thicket of peace. He yearned for Italy and Italians. For how many years would he be condemned to spend his life on an alien shore, among crazy foreigners?

'I was invited,' Stravinsky went on, 'by the manufacturer Pleyel to transcribe my compositions for the Auto-Pleyela, their mechanical piano. The music is conveyed on to perforated paper rolls, which are put into the device. Through a system of membranes and pneumatic valves, the machine then plays the music exactly as the composer transcribed it. No need for a conductor or a performer. What do you think of that?'

'That is a diabolical invention,' Toscanini retorted.

Stravinsky shrugged. 'I hope to leave a series of model performances to guide future interpreters. A composer hears every sort of distortion of his work, which of course prevents the public from getting any true idea of his intentions.'

Toscanini drew himself up stiffly. 'Are you saying you were dissatisfied with my conducting of your *Petrushka* in Venice?'

'Of course not.'

'I take no liberties,' Toscanini went on, deeply offended. 'I have never tried to enforce my own ideas from the podium. I have always had the utmost contempt for that kind of conductor, in love with showy effects and self-aggrandisement.'

'Of course, maestro.'

'I rely on my iron discipline, my mastery of the score, my excellent memory. My only desire is to enter the spirit and intention of the composer.'

'Indeed, maestro,' Stravinsky said blandly. 'Yet is it not a pity that your Promethean energy and marvellous talents should almost always be wasted on such eternally repeated works as fragments of Verdi and Wagner that have long since grown stale?'

'Stale!'

'I mean in the sense that food exposed for too long on a buffet will inevitably lose its freshness and become mouldy.'

'Mouldy!'

'Concert programmes,' Stravinsky went on, 'contain too much that is wearisomely familiar, don't you agree?'

'Luckily,' Toscanini snapped, provoked beyond endurance, 'we have composers who do not scruple to mangle the rules of music beyond all comprehension in the pursuit of something new!'

Stravinsky tipped his hat, as though he had received some exquisite compliment, and walked on, accompanied by the pale German youth.

No sooner had this irritation passed, however, when Toscanini was confronted with a second, in the shape of two young women, who had been standing behind Stravinsky, forming a kind of queue.

'Oh, maestro,' one said breathlessly, 'please could you autograph this?'

Toscanini was about to snarl a rebuff when he noticed that the young woman in question was extremely pretty, her expression appealing. 'Hmmm?'

'This is all I have,' she went on, 'but if you were to sign it, it would be a great honour!'

The thing she was holding out, he now saw, was a Tourist Class dining room menu. He caught the words *mutton stew* on the list of fare. He took it and the proffered pen. 'To whom should I inscribe it?'

'My name is Masha Morgenstern. And this is my cousin, Rachel Morgenstern.'

She was of the type that he liked best – petite but curvaceous, with a heart-shaped face and a full mouth. He glanced over her shoulder.

The other girl, though of a more austere type, with angular cheekbones and the cold blue eyes of a Siamese cat, was also attractive in her way.

'You young ladies are travelling to New York?'

'Yes, maestro.'

'Emigrating?'

'We are Jews.' She looked up at him shyly. Her lips were parted, the gloss of youth upon them, fresher than any paint. Toscanini stroked his moustache with the tip of the young woman's pen. His recent annoyance with Stravinsky was fading swiftly. Even thoughts of Carla had receded. Under his scrutiny, she dropped her gaze modestly. Her eyelashes were thick and soft as owl's feathers. The sun caught the golden glow of down on her cheeks. He felt a stirring. One could imagine such a face smiling up at one shyly from the pillow. 'I wish you luck in your new home, my dears.'

He uncapped the pen and wrote, in his elegantly sprawling hand,

'Me, pellegrina ed orfana,

Lungi dal patrio nido.

Un fato inesorabile

Sospinge a stranio lido . . .'

He signed it with his name.

Masha took it from him and gasped. 'Why, it's Verdi! From *La forza del destino*! Oh, maestro, I will treasure this all my life!'

He beamed at her. 'I hope we will see one another many times more on this voyage.'

Rendered speechless by this gracious condescension, Masha nodded. Flushing, she allowed herself to be led away by Rachel.

'Old goat,' Rachel said shortly.

'Hush!' Masha exclaimed in shock. She looked over her shoulder. Toscanini, who appeared not to have heard Rachel's observation, raised his hat after them. 'Whatever do you mean?'

'He was practically undressing you with his eyes.'

'That good, kind old man? Nonsense!'

'He's still leering at your backside.'

Masha pulled her arm out of Rachel's. 'You're awful sometimes, Rachel.'

'I thought you admired my awfulness.'

'But you see the worst in everyone.'

'Toscanini is no saint, believe me.'

'Look what he has written,' Masha said, holding up the menu. 'So apt. Such sensitivity. What a wonderful soul, Rachel.'

'Make sure he doesn't get you alone in a dark corner,' was all that Rachel would comment.

The Western Approaches

Jürgen Todt was in a state of nervous elation. He had sunk two more vessels within forty-eight hours. It was true that they had been small fry – a 1,500-ton collier limping along the Irish coast, and a 2,000-ton freighter carrying pig iron to the Clyde – but his total was already approaching seven thousand tons sunk. At this rate, the Knight's Cross would be his in a matter of weeks.

In the lens of his periscope now was a fishing smack of around 250 tons. She was so close that he could read the name on her bows, *Kitty of Coleraine*, and underneath that, the name of her owner, a Northern Irish fisheries company.

She was fair game. And he lusted for her. But *U-113*'s complement of sixteen torpedoes was already reduced to nine. To use a torpedo on such a small prize would be wasteful. He weighed up his options, then closed the handles of the periscope and pushed it down with a pneumatic hiss.

'We'll take her with the deck gun,' he said.

'That will be hard,' Rudi Hufnagel noted. 'It's rough up there.'

Todt ignored his watch officer. 'Action stations. Prepare to surface.'

U-113 surfaced in moderately heavy seas, about fifty yards off the fishing boat's starboard quarter. Todt broached the U-boat so that it was parallel to *Kitty of Coleraine*. It was early in the evening, and very cold.

The crew went into action fast, clambering out of the conning tower and on to the rolling deck. Their captain had brought them within range of the RAF's Sunderland flying-boats, so what had to be done had to be done quickly.

The gun crew of four lugged the heavy 20mm flak gun along the deck and mounted it on the firing-platform behind the conning tower. The swell made the work difficult; waves dashed over the mounting, the men slid and fell, saved from being swept away only by their safety-lines.

'Take out the bridge, quick,' Todt commanded, the binoculars to his face. 'Rapid fire.'

The Oerlikon opened fire, its twin barrels pumping shells into *Kitty of Coleraine*'s wheelhouse. The flimsy little structure collapsed almost immediately, the radio mast sagging down into the water. It was a miracle of gunnery, given the conditions. They could see crew members running in panic for the single lifeboat, which was slung on a davit over the stern. The gun crew ceased firing as the ammunition canisters emptied.

'Reload!' Todt screamed at them. 'Keep firing.'

'We're giving them a chance to abandon ship, Captain,' the chief gunner called up to the conning tower.

'The bridge, the bridge, God damn you. They may be sending a radio message right now.'

The gun crew locked the fresh canisters in place and opened fire again. The wheelhouse disintegrated in the storm of shells, its wooden wreckage now ablaze. Some of the Irish crew, scrambling to ship the lifeboat, were caught in the barrage of shells, their bodies spinning like rag dolls.

'Again! Again!' Todt commanded. 'Don't stop until I give the order.'

The rest of the U-boat crew watched from the bridge while Todt ordered the gunners to keep firing until the smack's deck was a blazing ruin. The single smokestack was gone, all the tackle and rigging had been shot away. Though they'd tried to spare the lifeboat, the heavy seas had made accurate aiming impossible, and a shell had hit it, blowing off most of one side. It dangled uselessly over the transom.

Todt studied the fishing boat tensely through his binoculars, wiping them impatiently as condensation formed in the lenses. Satisfied that there was no further movement, he leaned over the rail to the heavier cannon. 'Now, the waterline,' he shouted.

The cannon crew obeyed, raking *Kitty of Coleraine*'s hull with half a dozen 88mm shells. The little boat listed heavily and began to founder.

Todt circled *U-113* around the sinking fishing boat. The crew stared in silence at the morning's work. As the deck submerged, *Kitty of Coleraine*'s cargo of fish started to float out of the hold, like the disgorged last meal of some stricken animal. Silvery, the fish drifted among the oil that slicked the sea.

Other things were drifting, too: the men's cots, their few possessions, unused life jackets. Some of the flotsam was human, no longer intact, blackened lumps of men barely breaking surface as they wallowed in the swell. And there were two living men, too dazed to call for help, clinging to the same lifebelt.

'I count sixteen bodies,' Hufnagel said without inflection. 'Including the survivors.' The sea-spray had frozen in his and Todt's eyebrows and beards, white forests riming their faces. There was no hope for the men in the sea. 'We could have warned them before we opened fire.'

'So they could radio for a plane to come and sink us?'

'We could have told them to keep radio silence and ship their lifeboat. That is the procedure we are asked to follow.'

'This is not a gentleman's game,' Todt retorted. 'It's war.'

'Yes, Kapitän.'

'We can hardly stop every ship for a friendly chat. What would you say, three hundred tons?'

'I would say less. Perhaps two hundred and sixty.'

'Good enough. Put that in the log,' Todt commanded.

The silence among the crew continued as the U-boat slipped away from the kill. Many of them were the sons of Baltic fishermen. Seeing those bodies broken by the anti-aircraft gun had left a bad taste. 'Boys and old men,' as Ludwig the diesel officer muttered, opening a can of peaches he'd saved for such an occasion, when he would want something sweet. 'No warning given. Just goodbye, nice to meet you.'

The men crowded around the electric heaters, but they did little to mitigate the piercing cold. Condensation glistened on the bulkheads and on the menacing hulks of the torpedoes in their tubes.

Todt had chosen a Hitler speech to play on *U-113*'s gramophone. It was one they had heard many times before, and most tried to shut their ears to the ranting voice that echoed out of the speakers.

In the officer's mess, Rudi Hufnagel tried to analyse the Führer's words as he stared into his coffee. They were full of sound and fury, but the more he heard them the less sense they made to him.

He had been present at the lunch party given on the *Tirpitz* at the naval base in Gotenhafen when Hitler had come to inspect the new generation of U-boats, a few years earlier. As one of the most promising young officers in the *Ubootwaffe* at that time, he'd been given a seat diagonally opposite Hitler. He'd had an opportunity to observe the Führer at close hand. With the lock of hair plastered across his forehead and the absurd toothbrush moustache, he had seemed to Hufnagel like the new boy who arrives at school in mid-term, trying to appear manly among men, monopolising the conversation, never asking a single question, trying to show that he knew every detail about everything before he was even informed. Hufnagel had not been impressed.

Hufnagel's father, a veteran naval officer of the last war and a man of few words, had summed up the Nazi phenomenon contemptuously: 'When small people get big ideas, watch out.'

That Hitler had surrounded himself with thugs and murderers had cast a darker shadow on the years that followed. But by then it was too late for anyone to do anything. The thing was unstoppable. And Hufnagel's own career in the U-boat service had already foundered on the rocks, lured by the Jewish siren, Masha Morgenstern.

Le Havre

Manhattan's engines had started in the early hours of the morning. The vibration woke Toscanini, who had finally fallen asleep in one of the wooden loungers on the promenade deck, wrapped in his cloak. He jumped to his feet, cursing the force of destiny and tearing his hair in despair. He had been pacing ever since.

The atmosphere of the ship had changed. The crew were bustling in every quarter, busy with preparations for casting off. The passengers were in states of varying emotions, exultation, relief or wretchedness. And down on the quayside, a large crowd had already gathered, either for the spectacle of a great ship's departure, or to bid farewell, perhaps forever, to loved ones. Those who were about to depart crowded at the rails, leaning over perilously to shout messages to those who were remaining on shore. Their voices were inaudible above the hubbub, but perhaps the expressions on their faces and the tears on their cheeks were enough to convey their feelings.

The beat of the engines was transmitted through the deck, up the legs and into the chest, where it rattled the heart. The two red, white and blue funnels were pouring steam into the sky. It surged up in volcanic clouds, rolling across the sky and casting diaphanous veils of shadow over the multitudes below.

Toscanini stood grasping a stanchion, surrounded by his baggage. He'd had it brought up from the hold and placed on the deck near the gangplank. If there was no word from Carla, at the last minute, just before the ship cast off, he would have everything carried ashore. He and Carla would have to wait for the next sailing – if there was one.

The war news was terrifying. The Germans' superiority was becoming established without doubt. Not only were their weapons more modern and more deadly, but their tactics had evolved since the last great conflict. It was becoming clear that they had no intentions of attacking the vast concrete fortifications of the much-vaunted Maginot Line, dug deep into the French earth to resist the Hun hordes. They were simply going to circumvent it. Their mechanised armies were already streaming around it, their warplanes were thundering over it. The concept of war as armies locked in trenches was as outdated as Homer. The new war was a lightning war. It would all be over in the blink of an eye. Hitler would be in Paris in three months, in a month, in a week, tomorrow.

The multifarious crowd below blurred in Toscanini's vision. His head was spinning; his limbs were numb. They could no longer support him. He, who never sat down if he could help it, now sank on to his leather-bound trunk like an old man.

Mr Nightingale had arranged the tour. He had been reluctant at first, because as he pointed out, the engineers would not welcome a visit at this busy juncture, and there would be plenty of opportunity later on during the voyage; but the dollar bills Stravinsky had slipped into his hand had eased matters considerably.

As for Thomas König, he was trembling with excitement. It was all he could do to remember his manners, and offer to let Stravinsky go first. Gravely, Stravinsky declined the honour. They entered *Manhattan*'s forward engine room, the boy leading the way, the composer behind him.

The narrow corridor opened into a space as vast as a concert hall. The orchestra that was playing in it was deafening, overwhelming. Every range was filled, from the shrill hissing of cymbals to the thunder of basses and tubas, the deep concussions of kettledrums, the blare of brass and roar of cellos, the piping of flutes and piccolos.

They gazed up at the columns and pipes of steel that were producing this colossal symphony, the banks of glass gauges, the immense wheels which vibrated the very teeth in one's head. Billowing steam, escaping from gleaming valves, made the air hot and damp. The painted metal surfaces dripped with it, the faces of the men shone with it as they gazed up at the hundreds of dials, writing down the readings of each.

'The temperature in the furnace is currently three thousand, five hundred degrees,' the engineer shouted, his voice barely audible over the symphony. 'It will go even higher when we're under way. At full power, the boilers can consume forty tons of fuel every hour, and produce a hundred and sixty thousand horsepower.'

Stravinsky was dazed. He could hear the hoof beats of those one hundred and sixty thousand horses, pounding out a rhythm of power and purpose. He had not expected this greatness, this might. He had wanted only to arrange a distraction for the boy, who had been crying again at the prospect of leaving everything he knew behind. They followed the engineer along the walkway between the towering banks of machinery. He was shouting out figures – seven hundred of this, fifty thousand of that – but his voice was mostly drowned out in the cacophony.

Thomas, however, was transfixed, his pale eyes shining, his mouth half-open with wonder as he worshiped in this cathedral of steel, this temple of energy. His thin hands clutched at railings, as though his knees were weak. So many glass dials, red-painted wheels, so many brass and iron and aluminium and bronze shapes that gleamed, so many thick springs that compressed and opened under pressure of unimaginable forces. He was overwhelmed. He did not need to hear the figures to understand that this was a dwelling place of gods and monsters. As they approached the turbines, he gripped Stravinsky's hand tightly.

'Saturated steam is produced in these tubes,' the engineer bawled at them, mopping his brow with an oily rag, 'and is then superheated in the furnace before being fed into the engines at four hundred pounds per square inch and seven hundred degrees Fahrenheit. The hot fumes from the furnace are vented through the funnels. That accounts for the smoke you can see being made.'

'I feel like Jonah in the bowels of the whale,' Stravinsky said to Thomas, but the boy either didn't hear or didn't understand.

'The *Manhattan* has four propellers,' the engineer continued. 'The technical name is screws. They are made of manganese bronze, and each one is over thirty feet high – taller than a suburban house. The outer propellers are driven—' He was interrupted by a subordinate who had hurried over to him with a clipboard. He fell silent, studying the figures.

The German boy was still clutching Stravinsky's hand. They stood staring around them, feeling the thrumming of the giant turbine in their bodies. Stravinsky was suddenly aware that all this giant energy was devoted to one end – departure. This mighty engine had been set in motion for the single purpose of taking him – and some hundreds of other souls – from Europe to America.

The imminence of the voyage, which had somehow not seemed real to him until this moment, struck him like a physical blow. He felt dizzy, breathless. He was leaving France, leaving behind decades of his life, huge pieces of himself. He was leaving behind Vera and the dead. He was leaving everything that was his: and going to a world which was not his.

His mouth fell open stupidly as he grasped the immensity of it all. One life had ended. Another had yet to begin. He was as helpless as though his physical body had been caught in these giant machines, and was being flung God knew where. He felt heavy. He took off his steel-rimmed spectacles, and tremblingly put them in his breast pocket. The engine room became a blur, but he no longer wanted to see its gleaming precision, anyway. Thomas König's hand was gripping his tightly. 'We are two wayfarers,' he said, turning to the boy. 'We are about to be set adrift on the currents of the world.'

Thomas didn't answer. The engineer checked his watch and turned to them, fist on hip. He stared at them with undisguised resentment.

'I think he wants us to leave now,' Stravinsky said to Thomas. The boy nodded obediently. He led Stravinsky out of the thundering chamber, carefully guiding the composer's uncertain steps.

Standing in the shadow of the Cabin Class lifeboats, Masha and Rachel Morgenstern were receiving an unexpected visitor who had come to see them off: a distant relation, Moshe Perelman, who had once played second violin in the *Berliner Philharmoniker*, before he'd lost his job to a non-Jew. He was in his seventies, looking pinched in a coat that was too thin for the weather, and shoes that were down at heel. He seemed to have fallen on hard times. Neither of the girls had seen him for many years, and might not (as they later agreed) have recognised him, had they passed him on the street, though he had once been very distinguished-looking. But for his part, he seemed grateful to be received by them.

'I'm hoping for a sailing in the next month or two,' he told them, rubbing his ungloved hands together with a papery sound. 'Only, my documents are not through yet. I have applied to America, to Great Britain and to Argentina. One waits, one waits, one waits.'

'We know all about that, don't we, Masha?' Rachel said.

'You'll never guess who is on the boat with us, Uncle Perelman,' Masha said, wanting to cheer the old fellow up. 'Igor Stravinsky. *And* Arturo Toscanini.'

Uncle Perelman gave a laugh that was half-embarrassed, half-deprecatory. 'Oh, I scarcely know who such people are any longer. That is no longer my world.'

'Are you not playing in an orchestra here in Paris?' Masha asked politely.

'No, no, my dear. I have not performed in many years. They took, in any case, the fiddle away from me.'

Masha recalled that Uncle Perelman had been the owner of a valuable instrument, a Stradivarius. 'I'm very sorry to hear that.'

'Yes, yes. It was confiscated by the *Reichskulturkammer*. They said it was in danger of being damaged, played by such bungling hands as mine.' He laughed again. 'And I am sure they were right, quite right. I left Germany soon after that and came here to Paris.'

'So what do you do now?'

'I have a facility for figures.' He tittered. 'I do a little bookkeeping. On a small scale, you understand. It's convenient for my customers. I go to their shops after hours and' – Uncle Perelman fluttered his fingers – 'I make the numbers come out straight.'

'How clever of you,' Rachel said, trying to sound bright. 'And Aunt Perelman?'

'No longer with us.' He laid a finger on his lips as both girls began to utter condolences. 'Thank you, but please, not a word. Her suffering is over. I carry her precious memory here.' He touched his heart.

'Uncle Perelman, you look so cold. We found this scarf on the floor, being trampled on. It's a little dirty, but it's very good quality, and I am sure it can be cleaned.' Rachel held out the scarf she and Masha had found lying on the deck.

Uncle Perelman inspected it wistfully. 'It's certainly very beautiful. But the rightful owner—'

'I am sure the rightful owner won't want it now that it's dirty,' Rachel said firmly. 'Besides, he can certainly afford to buy another one. There are very rich people on board.'

Uncle Perelman looked as though he were going to refuse, but his bony hands acted independently of his will, taking the wool scarf eagerly, and tucking it in his threadbare coat. 'So kind, my dears. So very kind.' He looked around him. 'This is certainly a beautiful ship you have got here.'

'Trust me, we're not in Cabin Class,' Rachel said. 'We couldn't afford this. We just sneaked here from the cattle sheds to look smart for you.'

'It was very kind of you to come and see us off,' Masha added. 'Please send our love to everyone at home.'

Uncle Perelman winced. He began rubbing his papery hands together again. He seemed very uncomfortable. 'My dears, my dears. I have been asked to come to you to pass on some news. I wish there were more time for me to prepare you for it, but your beautiful ship is about to leave.'

'News?'

'Bad news.'

Masha had gone very pale. 'From Berlin?'

'It is from Berlin.'

'About our relations?'

'It is about your relations.' The old man, too, had become pale. He seemed to want to lead them to guess what his news was, rather than tell them directly. Masha saw his dry lips trembling, and she burst into violent tears.

'They are all dead,' she sobbed. 'They've been killed.'

'No, no.' Uncle Perelman laid his hand on her arm compassionately. 'Not killed, not killed. Only resettled.'

'*Resettled*?' Rachel repeated. Unlike Masha, who was now unable to speak, and Uncle Perelman himself, who was weeping openly, she was dry-eyed. 'How comfortable that sounds. Who has been resettled, exactly?'

'All of them.'

'Our parents?'

'All four of your parents.' Uncle Perelman wiped his sunken cheeks. 'Your uncles, aunts, your grandparents, your cousins, everyone by the name of Morgenstern. They have all gone. Strangers are already living in their apartments.'

Masha had buried her face against Rachel's breast, feeling as though her heart was breaking. Rachel put her arms around her cousin. 'And where have they been resettled?'

'That is not known. In the East. That was all that was said. A full report will be given by the authorities when the resettlement is complete. They were allowed to take some clothing and personal possessions.'

'How kind of the authorities. And in the East, where one hears that the climate is so healthy at this time of the year. We must be grateful to them.' Uncle Perelman was unable to reply. 'Is there no one left, then?'

'No one,' he replied.

'When did this resettlement happen?'

'The day after you left Bremen.'

'You hear this, Masha?' Rachel said to her sobbing cousin. 'We have missed a wonderful adventure by a bare twenty-four hours. What atrocious luck.'

Uncle Perelman stared at Rachel with bleary eyes. He seemed not to know how to respond to Rachel's ironies. 'I am sorry,' he said. 'I would not wish to be the one to tell you this, but there was no one else. I have been very clumsy, and I apologise.'

'You were very kind, Uncle Perelman,' Rachel said. 'You weren't clumsy at all. We expected this to happen. We are the lucky ones, if you can call it luck.' Her voice broke for the first time. 'Though what we have done to deserve—' She could not go on.

'I urge you to be strong,' Uncle Perelman said, mopping his eyes. 'To love God, and to remember who you are, and where you came from.'

'How can we love a God,' Masha cried out, raising her head from Rachel's shoulder, 'who does this to us?'

Uncle Perelman spread his hands helplessly and repeated, 'Love God and remember who you are.'

'I am going back to Germany,' Masha said.

The *Manhattan*'s horn, fixed to the forward stack, issued a great blare of sound, loud enough to vibrate the decks underfoot and send the last visitors scurrying for the gangplank. It sounded to Toscanini like the opening chord of some terrible Prelude. A steward laid a compassionate hand on his shoulder.

'We cast off in ten minutes, maestro.'

He nodded. The porter he had paid to carry his luggage ashore hurried up to the conductor, pushing a trolley.

'Going ashore, maestro?'

'Yes,' Toscanini said, almost inaudibly. He shuddered all over, and rose slowly to his feet. The porter began loading the trunks on to his trolley. People streamed around them, shouting, laughing and crying. Toscanini pulled his fedora firmly on to his head, and squared his shoulders.

'Okay. We go.'

They made their way on to the gangplank. It was thronged with visitors streaming off the *Manhattan*. The quayside was now densely packed with many thousands of people. Paper streamers and serpentines were already cascading down the side of the ship, celebratory tokens on an occasion that had little of celebration in it.

Toscanini's eyes were full of tears, but he kept his chin held high. He did not look back at the liner he was leaving, its giant stacks pouring smoke. What would become of them now? Would they be trapped here by Hitler's armies, after all? Were they doomed to end their days in a concentration camp, or against the pockmarked wall of a firing squad? Would they never see their children again? There were no answers to these questions. *La forza del destino*. It could not be resisted. He blinked away the tears.

At the very bottom of the ramp, he was confronted by a rotund little woman bundled into a green coat with fur trimmings at the neck and sleeves, about to get on the gangplank. Her Loden hat was decked with enamel good-luck charms: a cloverleaf, a white rabbit, an edelweiss. She frowned at Toscanini.

'Where are you going, Arturo?'

He was brought up short. 'Ah,' he said. 'You've arrived.'

'You see me, don't you?'

'Of course I see you.'

'You can't imagine the journey I've had,' Carla said crossly. 'The whole of Europe has gone mad. Including you, I think.' She rapped the trolley sharply with her umbrella. 'Get these things back on board. Don't you know the ship is about to leave?'

'Of course I know that,' he snapped.

She took his arm as the porter heaved the laden trolley around, and began to trundle back up the ramp. 'Why aren't you wearing the scarf I gave you, that cashmere one?'

He clutched his throat. 'I put it on this morning. I think I may have dropped it somewhere.'

'You're becoming impossibly forgetful,' Carla said severely. 'It was expensive. Really, you are hopeless without me.'

'Without you,' he growled, 'life was a lot quieter.'

After his visit to the engine room, Thomas had been unable to stop talking about the sights he had seen. They had made an immense impression on him. Words poured out of him: so many degrees Fahrenheit, so many pounds per square inch, so much boiler horsepower, he remembered all the figures precisely.

He, Thomas and Katharine had gone up to the games deck, the highest part of the ship. It was crowded with passengers, but they found a place at the railing. Two tugs had arrived alongside the *Manhattan*. As they nosed her away from the wharf, pouring black smoke, the great liner seemed to give a shudder all along her steel body.

Down on the quayside, a band was playing 'The Star-Spangled Banner', but the thumping of the anthem was barely audible over the cheering of the multitude. At least, it was presumably cheering; at times, it sounded like wailing. Streamers and confetti poured from the ship, snaking down on to the crowds below, a final, tenuous link with Europe that was soon broken.

The tugs nudged *Manhattan* into the channel, leaving behind her empty berth, where mats of coloured streamers floated in the oily, grey water. The liner moved steadily away from shore. The sound of the band grew distant. Already, there was a new perspective. The buildings of Le Havre appeared smaller, a toy town for children. The security of the harbour gave way to a prospect of the open sea, dark blue and mottled with the sunlight that streamed through the patchy cloud cover.

The tugs fell away on either side. Again, *Manhattan* shuddered, more deeply this time. Her gears had engaged. She uttered another long blast on her hooter to indicate that she was making way under her own steam. The tugs responded, and so did every other vessel nearby. Thomas clapped his hands over his ears to shut out the huge sound. Stravinsky patted him on the shoulder, and then stared at the receding shapes of France. The ship felt different now, purposeful. She steamed steadily out of the harbour towards the open sea.

The crowds that lined the *digue nord* at the mouth of the harbour were densely packed, but largely silent. As the ship passed them, Stravinsky noticed a few waving hands and fluttering handkerchiefs, but by and large, the last Frenchmen he saw simply stood passively, watching the ship sail away.

The English Channel

The radio transcript was delivered to Commodore Randall as he dined in Tourist Class, which it was his habit to do two or three times on each voyage. Unlike some captains, he was not above joining the hundred-dollar passengers now and then, and conferring upon them the reflection of his glory.

They were having a rough crossing of the Channel. Plates slid across the tables as *Manhattan* rolled. Half the tables in the dining room were empty. Commodore Randall's dinner companions included the Russian composer Stravinsky and his companion, Miss Wolff, who had both been staring at their plates during his anecdotes, showing little of the sympathy or excitement one might have expected from highly sensitive persons.

Randall paused in his narrative as the steward put the slip of paper into his hand, and studied the message. The first line was enough to make Randall swiftly fold it again and put it into his jacket pocket. He glared at the fool who didn't know better than to bring such messages into dining rooms, but the man was already hurrying away. He would make sure someone had a word with him later.

'And so it was,' he continued, steadying his wayward plate, 'that the story, which began so badly, had a happy ending.'

The German boy with the swastika on his lapel, who had been the only listener hanging eagerly on the captain's words, spoke anxiously in his guttural English. 'But you have not said what happened next. Was nobody drowned?'

'We didn't lose a single soul,' Commodore Randall replied. 'It was all in a day's work for me and my crew, but for some reason the newspapers got a hold of the story, and imagine my surprise, on returning to New York, to be given a ticker-tape parade.'

'What is this, please?'

Randall smiled indulgently at the pale youth. 'I and my crew were driven in an open car down Broadway, from the Battery to City Hall. We were showered with confetti and streamers all the way.' Randall was already pushing back his chair preparatory to leaving the table. 'But I must excuse myself. We'll be in Southampton by morning. I bid you good night, ladies and gentlemen.'

With a snappy salute, he left the dining room, nothing loth to forego the rest of his dinner, a hash of beef which, between the fat and the gristle, required careful navigation. He would fill the empty place inside him later. For now, he was more concerned to examine the transcript he had been handed.

He read it on the bridge, watched by a group of officers who already knew the contents. It consisted of a series of Marconigrams. The first read:

> SOS FROM BRITISH CARGO SHIP ROBERT RECORDE POSN 54 22 N 1705. TORPEDOED BY GERMAN SUBMARINE. 23 CREW SOME STILL ABOARD. SINKING. URGENT.

The position given was in the Western Approaches, along the route which *Manhattan* herself would shortly be traversing. The second Marconigram, sent an hour later, read:

> M.V. PEARL PRINCESS. DISTANCE FROM YOU 30. STEERING FULL STEAM AHEAD TO YOUR ASSISTANCE.

The third was also from the *Pearl Princess*, and had been sent to the British Admiralty some six hours later:

> REACHED LAST POSITION OF ROBERT RECORDE. OIL SLICK AND WRECKAGE FOUND. NO SIGN VESSEL OR LIFEBOATS. CONTINUING SEARCH.

Randall folded the paper and looked up at his officers. 'Anything since?'

'Nothing, Commodore.'

'Well, gentlemen. We know what we're up against. We'll be setting special watches. I'll order a lifeboat drill as soon as we leave the British Isles.'

'Will we be plotting an evasive course, sir?'

'No.'

The first officer cleared his throat. 'The British Admiralty advised—'

'I'm fully aware of the advice of the British Admiralty,' Commodore Randall growled, turning a cold eye on the man. 'It applies to British shipping. We are a United States vessel.'

'Yes, Commodore.'

There was a silence. The Admiralty announcement had been sent from London on the first day of the war, advising all shipping to travel at speed in a zigzag pattern to avoid submarine attacks. Randall's officers watched him, waiting.

'Well?' he demanded, glaring back at them. 'Spit it out.'

'Sir,' the navigator began, 'we're going to be carrying fifteen hundred passengers on this trip. The *Athenia*—'

'The *Athenia* was making full steam, showing no lights, and plotting a zigzag course. Am I wrong in what I say?'

'No, Commodore.'

'And she was still torpedoed?'

The men all took an automatic step to maintain their balance as *Manhattan* rolled in a trough. 'Yes, Commodore.'

'There you have it. A fatal decision by the British skipper. A darkened ship, jinking constantly, making full speed. What would arouse greater suspicion in a U-boat captain? The German assumed *Athenia* was a troopship or an armed merchant cruiser. He acted accordingly.'

The officers shuffled, but nobody made a reply.

'Running and hiding is not the answer. Creeping along is not the answer. Remember Farragut at Mobile Bay, gentlemen. Damn the torpedoes. Safety lies in boldness. I may go so far as to say that glory lies in boldness. I will plot the same passage that I have sailed all my life. We will show lights at night. We are Americans, and I'll be damned if we will skulk like curs. The world knows that it tangles with the United States at its cost.'

The reference to Farragut at the Battle of Mobile Bay had not had a reassuring effect on the ship's officers, and when Commodore Randall had left the bridge to complete his dinner in his cabin, there was a muttered confabulation among them. While not quite old enough to have served in that glorious engagement, Commodore Randall was now in his sixties, and as one of them remarked, 'The old man has survived so many adventures that now he believes he is immortal.'

The Morgenstern cousins had not attended the evening meal. They had stayed in their cabin for most of the day. Masha had cried so much that she could hardly see to pack.

Rachel took her arm. 'Enough nonsense with the suitcase, please.'

'Why don't you cry?'

'They couldn't make me cry at kindergarten. They couldn't make me cry at school. They couldn't make me cry at the conservatory. I will not let them make me cry now.'

'But our parents,' Masha said. 'Oh my God, poor Mama and Papa. To think of them cold and alone in some terrible place. We should never have left them.' She returned blindly to folding things into the valise.

'There is nothing you can do, Masha,' Rachel said flatly. 'We knew this would happen. That is why they made such a great effort to get us out. It's hateful to think of squandering that sacrifice.'

'I'm going back to join them.'

'To be sent to a camp?'

'They're old and weak. I can at least take care of them, wherever they are.'

'Do you imagine they will be happy to see you come back?'

Masha swept the things off her side table into the valise. 'I don't want to be the last.'

'Think of it as being the first,' Rachel replied.

'Do you realise that our family name will die out?' Masha asked, taking clothes off the hangers in the closet.

Rachel reached in her bedside drawer for the little bottle of smelling salts. 'My dear, our family name died out a hundred and fifty years ago. Nobody even remembers what it was. They chose to call us after the morning star in the hopes that it would stop the Gentiles from persecuting us, but it only made us easier for them to find.' She waved the vial under Masha's nose. Masha's head jerked involuntarily as the fumes of *sal volatile* struck her sinuses. She reeled back from the suitcase she had been packing. 'It was a long struggle,' Rachel went on, 'and now it is over. There will be no Jews left in Germany.'

'Don't say that,' Masha begged in a broken voice. 'That stuff stinks. Put it away.'

Rachel closed the lid of the suitcase. She put an arm around her cousin's soft shoulders. 'When we reach New York we'll get information about them. And if the information is not good, we'll have a kaddish sung for them. But you will not get off the boat at Southampton.'

'You cannot stop me.'

'I will have you locked in the hold, if necessary.'

Masha peered at her blearily. 'Don't you have feelings?'

'I have feelings,' Rachel said quietly. 'I have feelings inside, without displays or fuss.'

Masha wept in silence for a while, her head on Rachel's shoulder. At last she said, 'You're different from me. You're brave. It takes a special kind of person to want to live when everyone you love has vanished. I am not such a person. I will get off the boat at Southampton. The British authorities must send me back to Germany. You take the rubies, go to America on your own. I don't want to live with this burden any more.'

'The burden of life, you mean.'

'Yes, I mean the burden of life. This life. We grew up like those fish in glass bowls. We knew that terrible things were happening just beyond the glass, but we looked inward.'

'And now the bowl has broken.'

'Yes. But the bowl *was* our life. I can't survive outside it.' She sat up. 'Let me pack my suitcase, Rachel. Don't stop me.'

'Very well,' Rachel said after a pause. 'If that is what you really want. I'm going to dinner.'

Stravinsky looked up from his plate as the young woman took the empty seat at their table. She was a German Jewess of the blonde type, it seemed, very pale, and with a set expression on her face.

'I may as well say from the start that I'm not an admirer of your music, Monsieur Stravinsky.' She spoke good French with little accent. 'But my cousin is. She's the one who attempted to speak to you the other night, here, at dinner. You remember?'

Stravinsky glanced at Katharine, who was frowning, then back at the Jewess. 'I am at a loss, Fräulein.'

'She is very pretty, with brown hair. She wore a red leather coat.'

'Perhaps I recall such a person,' Stravinsky said dubiously. 'What of her?'

'Her name is Masha. She is in our cabin now, packing her suitcase. She intends to disembark at Southampton.'

'Indeed.'

'But we are on our way to New York. Our families sacrificed everything so that we could leave Germany. We have heard that all those who remain of our families – both hers and mine – have been sent to Silesia.' Stravinsky saw her eyes land on the swastika that gleamed in Thomas's buttonhole. 'Now Masha says she is going back to Germany to perish with them. She won't listen to me.'

'What is it particularly about my music that you do not like?'

The young woman's eyes flashed. 'I am not here to talk about your music. I am here to talk about my cousin. Don't you hear me? She intends to disembark tomorrow and go back to her death in Germany.'

Katharine leaned forward. 'What is it you expect Monsieur Stravinsky to do?'

'Talk to her. Persuade her out of this suicidal course of action.'

Stravinsky rested his cheek wearily on his fist. 'And what makes you think I might have the slightest influence on your cousin?'

'She is a passionate admirer of your music. So much so that when she listened to your *Rite of Spring*, she felt her heart leap out of her chest. She became speechless in your presence. She'll listen to you if to nobody else on this ship.'

'Young woman, if I have no desire to continue my own life, I can hardly persuade a stranger to cling to hers.'

'You're old, and it's fit you should feel that way. She's a child. There is not much time. We will be in Southampton in a few hours.' The young woman rose abruptly. 'Her name is Masha Morgenstern, and she is in Cabin 321.'

She hurried away from the table without looking back.

'The melodramas of youth,' Katharine remarked dryly. 'Extraordinary.'

Stravinsky pushed away the congealing bowl of stew, which he had barely touched. 'You don't believe this tale?'

'I find it, as I say, theatrical.'

'You don't think I should follow it up?'

'I think you should go to bed. You look exhausted. Don't get involved in these histrionics.'

Stravinsky turned to Thomas. 'And what do you think, Thomas?'

Thomas was staring after Rachel. 'It's true that her friend came to our table, but couldn't speak. The two of them usually sit over there.' He turned and pointed to an empty table across the room.

'Ah. You've noticed them. Why? Because they are pretty?'

'I notice everyone,' Thomas said, the sharp ridges of his cheekbones colouring.

'You hear this?' Stravinsky said to Katharine. 'Two sparrows are sold for a farthing, but one does not fall without Thomas noticing.'

'You're not thinking of going to these young women? It is certain to be a trap of some kind.'

'I'm not so much afraid of that,' he replied, dabbing his pendulous lips with his napkin and pushing away from the table, 'but I don't think I can be of any use in their present predicament. You are right, chérie. Let's go to our beds.'

Rachel heard the tap at the door, and hurried to open it. She was bitterly disappointed to find that the caller was not Stravinsky, but the German boy who had been sitting beside him.

'What do you want?' she demanded curtly.

He was blushing hotly. 'I have – I have—'

'Did Stravinsky send you?'

He shook his head dumbly, staggering a little as the ship rolled.

'Then why have you come sniffing around here?'

'I have something to show the other Fräulein.'

'You can have nothing to say that she would be interested in,' Rachel retorted. She indicated the swastika on his jacket. 'Take that hideous thing off.'

'I made a promise to always wear it.'

'To the Führer?'

'To my mother.'

'Your mother is a good Nazi, it seems.'

Masha came to peer over Rachel's shoulder with swollen eyes. 'Who is it? Oh, it's Monsieur Stravinsky's little friend. Why are you here?'

The boy, acutely shy, swallowed, the knot of his Adam's apple jumping in his lean throat. 'I would like – like to show you something.'

Masha glanced interrogatively at Rachel, who shook her head. 'Well, I suppose you should come in, then.'

Rachel glared at Masha. 'The boy is a Hitler spy. I don't want him in our cabin.'

'He is a child,' Masha said wearily. 'What harm can he do?'

'You know what harm these people can do,' Rachel retorted. But against her wishes, Masha admitted the boy.

'What is it you want to show me?' Masha asked.

'Here.' He took something from under his arm.

Masha looked at it blearily. 'A book is always a good thing. First, what's your name?'

'Thomas König.'

Masha patted the space beside her on the bunk, where her suitcase lay open. 'Then come and sit with me, Thomas König, and show me your book.'

The boy opened the book eagerly on his lap. 'It's about the World's Fair in New York. I'm— I'm going there.'

'You must be very excited, Thomas König.'

'Oh, yes!' He showed her the photographs, some of which were in colour. 'This is the Trylon, and this is the Perisphere. The Perisphere is eighteen storeys tall and 628 feet in circumference. The Trylon is sixty storeys tall. You can see them from five miles distant.'

Rachel was on the point of pushing the youth out, with his cropped head and his proudly displayed swastika. But Masha, for some reason, was willing to indulge him. 'That is very tall.'

'And look, this is the Court of Power. It's joined on to the Plaza of Light. These are the fountains which play music and are lit in colours at night. And here is the Singing Tower of Light.' He bent his narrow head over the photograph. 'It says "Westinghouse". That's an American electrical company. They have a display of all the ways electricity can be used.'

'Including to extract confessions?' Rachel asked.

Masha laid a finger on her lips to silence her cousin. 'What else?'

He turned to a page he had marked. 'This is the General Electric Pavilion. Do you see this apparatus? It creates a lightning bolt of ten million volts. The onlookers are blinded and deafened.'

'Isn't that frightening for them?' Masha asked gently.

'Yes, but I will go there nevertheless. I'm not afraid.'

'You are very brave.'

'There are a lot of statues of naked people. Both men and women. But you don't have to look at them if you don't want to. And all the film stars are there. Johnny Weissmuller comes every day. He is Tarzan, you know. His name is German, but he is Hungarian.'

'So much the worse for him,' Rachel said dryly.

'And Gertrude Ederle. She was the first woman to swim the English Channel. Her parents were Germans.'

'Have you done?' Rachel demanded.

The boy began to stammer again. 'There are inventions of all kinds – and – and – there are robots and machines—'

Masha laid her hand on the book. 'Tell me, Thomas, why do you want to show me these things?'

'I invite you to come and see them with me, Fräulein.'

Masha uttered a little sound like a laugh. 'How kind of you.'

'I have two tickets.' Carefully, he took the bright coupons out of the inside cover of the book. 'This one is for a child and the other is for an adult. The adult one is for you. Look, they have the Trylon and the Perisphere printed on them. You see? And underneath it says "The World of Tomorrow, Admit One". Take it.'

'I will not be going to America, but thank you.'

'Please,' he said.

'Thomas, this ticket surely belongs to a relative. An uncle, perhaps.'

'No, it's yours. I am giving it to you.'

'What has got into your head?' she asked wonderingly.

His ears were glowing red again, but he met her eyes. 'If you get off the boat in Southampton, you will not be able to see the World's Fair with me,' he said. 'And if you go back to Germany, they will kill you.' There was a silence. The boy got up, all elbows and knees. Even his thighs were flushing now. 'You may keep the book as long as you like. I've read it all.' He presented it to her, and bowed formally. 'You mustn't lose the ticket, Fräulein, or you will have to buy another.'

He hurried to the door, and waited there with his face averted until Rachel, without a word, let him out.

When he reached his cabin, Thomas found Stravinsky lying on his bunk, half-undressed, with one arm flung over his eyes.

'You have to do something,' he said sharply.

Stravinsky peered at him with bleary eyes. 'About what?'

'About Fräulein Morgenstern.'

'Is that where you have been? To her cabin?'

'I gave her my ticket to the World's Fair. But I don't think she will use it.'

'Thomas,' Stravinsky said wearily, 'didn't you promise me that you would stay in character? That you wouldn't betray yourself to anyone on board this ship?'

'Yes,' Thomas replied tersely.

'Well, then? What good Nazi would bother himself with the fate of a Jewess?'

'They will kill her there!' the boy burst out. 'Don't you understand? You cannot be so cold!'

'You remind me of my own children,' Stravinsky replied ironically. 'I feel quite paternal when you insult me. Are you in love with this female?'

Thomas's face twisted. 'I am only a boy in her eyes.'

'That is certainly true, and remember that you are even younger than you claim. I hope you understand that there is no chance of her returning your feelings.'

'My feelings have nothing to do with it.'

'It seems to me they have a great deal to do with it. What is she to you?'

'She is beautiful,' Thomas shot back. 'The most beautiful girl I ever saw.'

'I assure you she is quite an ordinary young person,' Stravinsky said gently.

'She is not *ordinary*. She is sensitive, and kind, and gentle, and special. How can you think her *ordinary*?'

'And you love her.'

'If that's what you want to call it.'

'You are certainly a very strange boy,' Stravinsky commented. He stared at the pale, passionate face. 'What do you expect me to do, Thomas?'

'You must think of something. You are the only one she respects. It's your duty!'

'I warn you, Thomas, if you give yourself away because of this infatuation, they will turn you back in New York, and you will be sent home to Germany.'

'I don't care about that.'

'But I do.'

'You must help!'

'If I agree to think about it, will you leave me in peace? I have a migraine.'

'Yes, I promise.'

Stravinsky covered his aching eyes again. 'Then not a sound more out of you until morning.'

Thomas sat hunched on the edge of his bunk as Stravinsky drifted into an uneasy sleep. His mind was in turmoil. He had blurted out his feelings without thought. But from the instant he had seen Masha Morgenstern, something magical had entered his life, something that made him feel strong enough and brave enough to endure the loss of his family and face the terrors of an unknown future.

It was as though, in the arid desert that his young life had become, he had stumbled across an oasis, a pool full of sweet water that rippled and shimmered and that might sustain him.

In her presence he felt a quiet joy, in her absence an empty yearning. He had fastened on her, and though he could not have said why, he knew that what he felt was as intangible as the air he breathed, and as real.

Was this love, as Stravinsky had called it? He hadn't thought of it as that. Love, he had been taught, was what you felt for God. But God hadn't given Thomas much cause to love Him. His father, always so remote and severe, had climbed proudly into the Gestapo truck, and had embraced martyrdom in the name of love. He had led with him his brother and their wives, leaving Thomas an orphan.

He had always seemed more real in his church than in their home, where he was so often silent. When the Brownshirts had picketed Saint-Johannes, turning away parishioners and breaking the stained-glass windows, his face had been alight with joy. He had marched past the glowering faces and threatening rifle butts with his head held high.

That was admirable, to be sure. It was in the tradition of Martin Luther, the founder of their church. But what Thomas felt was something different. It was not a desire to die, but a desire to live. God could do without him. God was already claiming truckloads of lives. If he was to serve, Thomas would serve Masha. If he was to love, he would love Masha. He knew that there was a gulf between them, and it was unlikely that he could ever bridge it, but the thrilling, breathtaking fact of her existence was enough to give his life meaning.

Stravinsky cried out quietly in his sleep, an inarticulate sound of grief. Thomas covered him gently with the blanket, soothing him. Here was another strange, dry man, who had imperceptibly taken the place of his father. He trusted Stravinsky, and trusted that he would find a way to keep Masha Morgenstern from marching, as his father had done, to her doom.

A bitter wind swept off the Channel, scouring the superstructure of the *Manhattan*. On the promenade deck, sheltered by the canvas awnings that the crew had stretched to keep out the wet, Toscanini and Carla huddled under rugs. Both had been wretchedly sick. The mountainous grey waves rolled past, queasily glimpsed by the light that was flaked off *Manhattan* by the gale.

'Yet again you have betrayed me,' Carla said. 'Yet again. After so many betrayals and humiliations.'

'Is now the time to discuss this?' he growled into his blanket.

'I found her letters when I was packing in Kastanienbaum.'

Toscanini grunted. 'I hope you were entertained.' But he glanced at her out of the corners of his eyes.

'I was disgusted. An old man like you. Shameful.'

He drew his bushy eyebrows down, huddling deeper into the rug, wishing he could shut out her voice, which shook with anger and pain. 'I do not expect you to understand.'

'Understand!' Carla retched futilely over the bowl she held. Her stomach had long since emptied. 'No, I do not understand. I found the menstrual bandages she sent you. The posies of her pubic hair. *Flowers from my little garden*. What kind of woman sends such things to a man?'

'A woman such as you could never understand.'

'A sexual maniac. Pathological. And younger than your own daughters.'

'She is not younger,' he muttered.

'She is barely older than them. She was their friend. What would they say if they knew? Did you think of that, Arturo? As for the correspondence, I have never read such obscenities. They appalled me.'

'Why did you persist in reading, then?'

'The folly of it, Arturo. What if her husband comes across these things? She will end up like poor Gretel Neppach.'

'Don't be melodramatic.'

'Melodramatic! If this thing is discovered, you will be ruined. We will all be ruined. What possessed you to take such a risk?'

'Her marriage is unhappy.'

'You were jealous of her husband, you mean. He is young and virile. While you can barely empty your bladder.'

'In any case, it is all over now.'

She retched again, groaning. 'Did it take another war to end it?'

'What did you do with the correspondence?' he asked, his voice barely audible above the wind that battered the canvas awnings.

'I burned the flowers from her little garden.'

'And the letters?'

'I have brought them to you. So that you can see your folly.'

He made no reply, but he thought, *thank God, they are all that's left me.*

'She must be a madwoman. And you are the same. A mad old man. *Psychopathia sexualis senilis.* That is what Dr Eisenberger called it.'

He opened one eye. 'You showed the correspondence to Eisenberger?'

'I asked for his opinion on your sanity. He said it was a form of sexual dementia of the elderly. He attributed it to syphilis.'

'I do not have syphilis,' he snarled, glaring at her. 'You had no right to show my private letters to that prating Swiss fool. Is that what you were occupied with all this time, while I waited for you in an agony?'

'I nearly didn't come.' She lay back in the deckchair, exhausted. 'I wish I were dead. You have broken my heart for the last time.'

'You have never understood my passionate nature, Carla.'

'Haven't I supported you for forty years? Looked after your business affairs? Nursed you when you were ill and put up with all your madness? And you say I do not understand you.'

'There is a dimension of me that you never shared. That you always refused to share.'

'The old story again. Your justification for licentiousness. It's finished, Artú. I am leaving you.'

'I will never give you a divorce,' he said quickly.

'A divorce?' She laughed bitterly. 'I will not dignify your treachery with a *divorce*. Besides, unlike you, I believe in the sanctity of marriage.'

'What are you talking about, then?'

'A legal separation. I will go my way and you will go yours. I want nothing more to do with you.'

'What about the children?'

'You old fool, do you think they don't know by now what you are? Worry about your public, rather. When they find out that the great Toscanini is a fraud, a lying, deceitful wretch who cannot keep his hands off women half his age, then you will have something to worry about.'

'Carla, I cannot live without you.'

'You should have thought of that before.' She heaved herself to her feet with difficulty. She had once been a ballerina, her body alive with grace. In the past forty years her body, like her face, had grown heavy. What had once been a grave beauty had become lumpishness. 'I'm going to my cabin. You may stay here and freeze to death, for all I care.'

Toscanini watched her make her way down the deck, tottering as the ship surged. She had been allocated a stateroom to herself, a great honour on such a crowded voyage, but the door was clearly locked to him.

When she had vanished, he lowered his chin on to his chest. How was he going to face an existence without Carla? His art had been his life, and she had taken care of all the rest for four decades. She had been the roof under which he had sheltered.

Of course he had been unfaithful to her. But the daemon that possessed him demanded the regular sacrifice of a young woman's body. Sometimes two or three at a time. The daemon insisted that he obey its commands to sin, to lose himself in passion without considering the consequences. To be as wild as those ancients who rutted with every woman they met, with goats and birds and trees and stones. Without that wildness, the daemon would withdraw its gift, and he would be nothing.

His gift was everything to him – this ability to bring out the best in a performer, an orchestra, a lover.

He allowed the thought of Ada Mainardi to come into his mind. The gulf of separation was sickening. He missed her with a pain that was like death. And mingled with the pain, that rush of desire to the heart.

Those last weeks in Kastanienbaum had been dreadful. The agonising difficulties of seeing Ada for more than a fleeting moment had driven him half-mad. And then, out of a clear sky, the thunderclap of Gretel Neppach's death. The daughter of his dear friend, Bruno Walter; that lovely girl, who for years had been begging her husband for a divorce. Instead, he had shot her as she slept, and then turned the revolver upon himself.

The tragedy had burst on them all like the judgment of a wrathful God. The days after it had been a slow nightmare: the wretched funeral, at which the only other mourners had been the Walters and Ezio, Gretel's lover. The pitiful spectacle of Bruno, shattered by grief, begging him to take his place at the Lucerne Festival. Of course, he'd had to agree. But how had he managed to conduct Mozart in Bruno's place? Mozart 40! The G minor symphony! With the tears streaming down his face on the podium!

And of course, Carla was right, in her blunt way. It could have ended like that with him and Ada. If Mainardi had lost his reason as Neppach did, who knew how it could have ended?

As much as the eruption of war into their lives, it had been those two revolver shots that had sobered them. That *what if.*

There had been moments over the course of the affair when he would have welcomed a bullet in the heart, either to end the wretchedness, or because Ada had given him a joy he would not experience again in his life.

Yes, he had been mad. A madness that Carla would never understand. He clutched the blanket in his hands as he remembered Ada, in that hotel room, crouched between his thighs, his manhood quivering in her mouth. Those terrible kisses that had sucked his soul from his body.

And then he, in turn, returning that cannibal kiss, intoxicated by her, addicted to her, while she cried out *Artú, Artú, you are my god.*

Yes, he had begged Ada for those flowers from her garden, for the handkerchiefs stained with her blood, the downy curls from her sex. He had been unable to think of a life without her. And now it was here, that life without her. She in Fascist Italy, he on his way to America. It was not likely they would ever meet again, in this world or the next.

How would he survive, without Ada, without Carla?

Southampton

The SS *Manhattan* steamed up the silver Solent with black clouds trailing from her stacks and spreading into the leaden morning sky. The overnight crossing had been rough, but not unbearably so, and scores of passengers had turned out of their bunks early to be on deck for the arrival at Southampton. They were visible from shore, crowding the rails in groups, muffled against the cold.

The sky over the docks was filled with hundreds of elephantine barrage balloons. The docks themselves bristled with anti-aircraft batteries. Anxious Tommies with Lewis guns peered from little molehills of sandbags. Along the wharf, dozens of troop transports were moored, steady tides of khaki cannon fodder trudging on to each one. A quarter of a million men were bound for France.

In her hotel smoking room, poised against a view of the harbour, Fanny Ward, the Eternal Beauty, was entertaining the Press.

'Miss Ward, are you afraid of bombing?'

Miss Ward bridled. 'I'm not running away, if that's what you mean. I'm returning to New York to fill several stage and radio engagements.'

Nobody was so ungentlemanly as to ask what those engagements might be, or to point out that she was leaving behind her beautiful

Berkeley Square apartment, with its antiques gathered over a long career in silent films and vaudeville.

'As a friend of England, what do you think of America's Neutrality Act?'

'Oh, I can't say anything about that.' At her age, Fanny Ward had to be careful with lighting. She had put herself with her back to the window. A lace veil bobbed over her eyes, where time had wreaked most havoc. Once a sexually alluring beauty with a bee-stung mouth, she knew that the best that could be said about her now was that she was a pretty old woman. As for her once-voluptuous figure, although she still affected flapperish clothes, it was a flapper in winter that she presented now, wrapped to the throat, trimmed in furs, with kid gloves on her hands and a cloche hat pulled down over her dancing curls.

'Do you think this war will last as long as the Great War?'

'My goodness, I'm far too young to remember *that*,' she replied indignantly. This drew laughter. They all knew that Miss Ward's agelessness had by now become an act in itself, carried out with the conspiratorial wink of a pleated eyelid.

'Are you worried about your salon in Paris, Miss Ward?'

She had opened a beauty shop in Paris in the 1920s, called The Fountain of Youth, which had added considerably to her mystique. 'Not at all,' she cried gaily. She forbore to mention that she had already sold it.

'Are you going to miss your friends in London, Fanny?'

The question was a pointed one. Miss Ward counted among her friendships a warm attachment to Elizabeth, the former Duchess of York, catapulted on to the throne of England by the abdication of the King, her brother-in-law, three years earlier. To be the confidante of the Queen of England was no small thing.

'Oh, I'm not going for more than a month or two,' she said gaily. 'My friends will survive without me for that long, I am sure.' She wagged a gloved finger at the cameras. 'Didn't I say no flashbulbs?'

'So you're optimistic about the war?'

'Oh, very. But gentlemen, you must have mercy on a girl. I have to prepare for the voyage.'

'Miss Ward, can we have just a few more poses?'

'Naughty, naughty boys.'

She obligingly threw some kittenish poses, redolent of the Edwardian era, lifting one foot prettily behind her, pulling out her spectacular pearls (frankly envied by her friend Queen Elizabeth) and tilting her head back. The flashbulbs sizzled, despite her admonishment. Her movements dislodged a cloud of face powder, momentarily bright against her silhouette, as though she were literally crumbling into dust before their eyes.

'Miss Ward. Miss Ward!'

But Fanny was making her bow and heading for the exit.

Mrs Kennedy was waiting to be connected to her husband. The telephone lines were maddeningly congested as a result of the war. And quite possibly, she thought, he would be occupied with his bouncy new secretary (whose smirking presence she'd had to put up with for the past few weeks) and too busy to talk to his wife. Rosemary was sobbing on the bed.

'I can't stand this much longer,' she said through clenched teeth. 'Can't you shut her up, Patricia?'

'I'm scared of her.' At fifteen, Pat was no match for Rosemary when she was like this. Her sister was capable of lashing out at anyone who approached. Rosemary was the eldest sister, bigger and more robust than Pat in every way. Only Eunice among the girls, and Jack and Joe among the boys, could deal with her tantrums. Even Mother didn't seem able to do anything any more.

'Don't be a goose,' Mrs Kennedy said tersely. 'Try and distract her.'

Pat twisted her hands together, shaking her head. 'Mother, please don't make me.'

Joe was finally on the line, his voice impatient. 'Hello? Hello?'

'It's me. I can't cope with this any longer, Joe.'

'Cope with what?' he asked cautiously.

'Rosemary is becoming impossible. She's throwing one of her tantrums as we speak. Luella's not here. I just have Pat to help me, and the poor child is terrified. Rosemary is like a wild beast.'

'What set her off?' Joseph Kennedy asked wearily.

'This man, of course. I've prevented her from seeing him and she's raging. All she thinks of is—' She glanced at Pat, who was listening, pale-faced. 'You know what,' she concluded, tight-lipped.

'She's in love with him?'

'That's dignifying it. It's unbridled lust.'

He sighed. 'Jack said he spoke to the fellow.'

'It's Rosemary who is intractable. She's obstinate beyond belief.' Mrs Kennedy covered the mouthpiece and hissed at Pat. 'This is not for your ears. Do as I say. Go to your sister. Don't you *dare* disobey me!'

Reluctantly, partly because she wanted to hear what Rosemary had been doing with 'that boy' and partly because she was afraid, Pat obeyed. She picked up the latest copy of *Hollywood Magazine,* which she had been reading, and went to sit beside Rosemary on the bed.

'They're remaking *The Hunchback of Notre Dame*, Rosie,' she said, 'with Charles Laughton and Maureen O'Hara. Do you want me to read you the article?' She showed Rosemary the page, but she might not have been there at all. Rosemary was lying on her side with her face half-buried in the pillow, her body convulsing with strange, choking sobs.

Pat persevered. 'A bear escaped on to the set while they were filming. They thought it was foaming at the mouth, and everyone ran away screaming, but it was just eating a bowl of ice cream. Isn't that funny?'

Rosemary was only dimly aware of her sister's presence. She was in a wilderness, battered by every sound, clawed by the light. Everything hurt. Nothing made any sense. Except pain. She couldn't bear her own feelings. She couldn't bear the skin that was wrapped around her flesh or the hair that clung to her sweaty face. She couldn't bear the organs inside her; she could feel every one of them in rebellion. She couldn't bear her own bones. But there wasn't anywhere to go. Because she was the wilderness, and everything was howling around inside her and nothing was bearable. She wanted Cubby, but she couldn't let him see her like this. She couldn't even think of him like this. He didn't belong in here.

'It takes three hours to put on Charles Laughton's make-up,' Pat went on, 'and an hour to take it off, so they can only film for a short while every day. He has such a chubby, cute face. I guess it takes a lot of work to turn him into a monster.'

The word *monster* lanced through Rosemary's wilderness like a lightning bolt, cracking open the sky, becoming a snarling shape with fangs and claws. She tried to bury herself, like a terrified animal, but her world was rock, unyielding.

Pat looked up at Rosemary, and saw that there were now watery, red stains on the pillow. Her heart sank. Rosemary's tantrums were really awful lately. She dreaded the thought of the voyage to come, and wondered how they were going to cope with Rosemary in the States, without Dad. She turned to another of her magazines, *Film Weekly*.

'Hitch is coming to the US. That's Alfred Hitchcock. He says he wants to direct American stars for a change. He says British actresses bottle up their feelings. He says you can throw them into an ice-bath and they come up still trying to look aloof and dignified.' She giggled.

Rosemary covered her face clumsily with her hands, sobbing. The light from the window was savage, stabbing into her eyes, prying between her fingers to get into her brain. She hadn't understood anything of what Pat had said except the word *ice-bath*. She could feel the piercing cold of the ice, feel the slippery blocks sliding across her skin, pushing inside her. Everything was too cold, too hot, too hard, too loud, too raw. Everything tortured her. The only sense anything made was pain.

'Please stop crying, Rosie,' Pat begged in a quavering voice. But the stains on Rosemary's pillow were bright red now. Pat put the magazines down and stroked Rosemary's convulsing shoulders. 'Mother,' she called out, 'she's biting her tongue real bad.'

Exasperated, Mrs Kennedy came away from the telephone to look at Rosemary. She groaned. 'You stupid, wilful girl. What is the point of this?' She pushed Pat out of the way and shook Rosemary hard. 'These dramatics impress nobody.' The shaking had the effect of silencing the jerky sobs for a moment. Mrs Kennedy hauled Rosemary upright and pulled her mouth open. She had champed her tongue until it bled. Her face was swollen and blank, all her beauty gone. She glared at her mother for a moment, then her eyes rolled away. She spat bloodily.

'Don't you spit at me,' Mrs Kennedy said furiously. 'Go and wash your mouth out. Get up, get up.'

With the aid of Pat, she got Rosemary to her feet and pushed her towards the bathroom. Rosemary stumbled inside. Mrs Kennedy went back to the phone, leaving Pat hovering nervously outside the bathroom door. The sounds from within were scary, as though there were a wild thing in there. She cracked the door open and peered in. Rosemary was groping at the blank wall, leaving streaks of bloodstained saliva on the white tiles.

'There's nothing there, Rosie,' Pat whispered.

But Rosemary could see the door in front of her. Except there was no handle. And push as hard as she may, it wouldn't open. There was no way out.

'There's nothing there, Rosie. Please come and rinse your mouth.' She tried to steer her sister to the sink, but Rosemary abruptly turned on her, flailing in panic. 'You're hurting me,' Pat gasped, trying to protect her face. 'Stop it!'

Those awful sobs were coming faster now, sounding more like choking than crying. She didn't even look like herself any more.

She grabbed at Rosemary's wrists, but Rosemary was far too strong for her to subdue. She clawed and panted and thrashed. Pat was forced to back away, gasping, 'Okay, okay, *okay*. I'm not touching you.'

Something raced through the wilderness of Rosemary's mind. A yellow animal, with its ears back.

She recognised it. The yellow cat that her brothers had trapped in a fishing net in the rambling garden at Hyannis Port. It had rolled its eyes and hissed and bared its teeth and fought for its life, while the boys had laughed and tormented it. She could see it now, as vividly as though it were happening in front of her.

Why did the boys do that? Why did they hurt and torture weak things? They said it was a game, but it wasn't. She knew, because they did the same thing to her when the mood took them. They said they loved something and then they hurt it for fun. Why? She'd begged them to free the yellow cat, and eventually they had done so. It had streaked away across the sand, not stopping till it was out of sight. But she didn't know how to free herself from the invisible net that had closed around her.

Her bladder was bursting. She couldn't bear it any longer. She fumbled her skirt up and squatted on the floor, her underpants around her knees.

Pat ran back out. 'Mother, she's going to pee on the floor.'

'Well, stop her.'

'I can't. She's hitting me in the face every time I come near her. She doesn't know what she's doing.'

'She knows very well what she's doing.'

'Mother, please come.' Pat dissolved into tears, too upset to continue.

'I'll call you back,' Mrs Kennedy said to her husband, and replaced the receiver. She went to the bathroom, where Rosemary was crouching in a spreading puddle. 'Oh, for the love of God. Don't you see the lavatory right next to you?'

All around Rosemary was flashing light, roaring sound. Her own pee running over her thighs was like boiling water. She tried to squirm away from it.

'We have to call someone,' Pat said, appalled.

'There's no one to call. We can't let anyone see her like this. Nobody can know. Do you understand?'

'Yes, Mother.'

'Come out of here. Leave her.'

'But Mother—'

Mrs Kennedy pushed Pat out and closed the bathroom door on Rosemary. 'She'll come to her senses in there. Until then, there's nothing to be done.'

Mrs Kennedy went to the window and shed some tears of her own, crying silently into a handkerchief. Rosemary had been in secure schools from puberty onward. With all the other children to deal with, there had been little option but to shut her behind high walls, leave her in the hands of devoted nuns who had dieted her, schooled her, drilled her, supported her, loved her, and attempted vainly to discipline her. She had been safe.

But it had become increasingly difficult to keep Rosemary shut away. She had turned into a beautiful young woman, and the press were hungry for news, eager to photograph her. So far, those who knew the truth had remained obligingly silent. But their discretion could not be relied upon forever. And the terrible reality was that Rosemary was getting worse, not better.

Mrs Kennedy was conscious that an era was coming to an end. Over these past two, glittering years, the most glamorous years of a life that had not been short of glamour, she had dined with the King and Queen of England (beef on a Friday once). She had been in every newspaper, met every celebrity, sparkled like a diamond. She had played golf with diplomats and film stars, had seen the great art, music and ballet of Europe, holidayed in the south of France. Teddy, at seven, had received his First Communion from the Pope himself in Rome.

All that was over. Joe's diplomatic career was now in jeopardy, despite the folderol that continued. His support for Hitler would never be forgiven or forgotten by the Brits now that war had broken out. The only hope for his remaining as ambassador – and continuing his political career in the United States thereafter – was an early peace settlement. Or, of course, a German victory.

For her and the children, there was little option but to return to the safety of America. And there, a solution to the problem of Rosemary would need to be found.

The Western Approaches

An absurd confrontation had arisen aboard *U-113* in the lull produced by several days without action of any kind. Captain Todt had subjected the boat to a prolonged programme of Hitler speeches.

The crew bore this for several hours, and then countered the musical tyranny by setting off their own gramophone at full volume. They chose a selection of songs from popular German films of the past ten years. For a while, *Mein Gorilla hat 'ne Villa im Zoo* competed cacophonously with Brünnhilde, rendering the forward section of *U-113* almost uninhabitable.

On a destroyer, such a minor mutiny would have resulted in disciplinary action, even courts-martial; but the submarine service was different, as Leutnant Hufnagel pointed out to the captain. The nervous pressure of long voyages in U-boats could be explosive, and some high spirits had to be tolerated among the crew, so as to keep morale high.

Todt responded by cutting off the men's supply of tinned cream, condensed milk and butter. These delicacies, kept in a cupboard to which only he had the key, were crucial to the men's happiness (especially the condensed milk, which they loved to put in their coffee).

Hufnagel approached the captain, determined to end the growing feud between the commander and the crew.

'Kapitän, surely the crew deserve a rest?'

'You have taken it upon yourself to defend them, I see.' Hufnagel was dismayed to see that the commander's hands were trembling and his jaw clenched tight under the straggling blonde beard. This ridiculous contretemps was telling on his nerves, where another man would have laughed it away. 'Have you come to tell me to turn off the words of our Führer in favour of some frivolous Semitic rubbish?'

'Not at all, Captain. It's simply that long speeches are—'

'Long speeches are what?'

'As a general rule,' Hufnagel tried again, 'it is wise for us all, during a long voyage, to leave politics in port.'

'*Politics?*' Todt was genuinely astounded. 'The speeches of the Führer are not *political.* They are above *politics.*'

'Hitler is a politician,' Hufnagel replied cautiously, 'if nothing else.'

'What does that mean?' Todt demanded, growing pale. '*If nothing else*?'

'I mean that he is the chief politician of our country.'

'You are determined to insult Adolf Hitler in my presence?'

'It's not meant as an insult,' Hufnagel replied, growing even quieter. 'He's the leader of the ruling party.'

'He is our Führer. The politicians are the ones who bear the guilt of the catastrophe of 1918, the hour of our deepest degradation and dishonour. It was the Führer who, with his superhuman willpower and energy, saved our nation.'

'I do not deny that, of course. I am concerned only with the morale of the crew.'

'The morale of the crew is the very reason that I am playing the Führer's speeches.' Todt held up the sleeve of the record, which showed a painting of a giant Adolf Hitler emerging from a mass of tiny, ordinary people, rather like a *Fleischkäse* being formed from crumbs of meat.

'Hitler is the apotheosis of the German *volk*, Hufnagel. It is the values embodied in Hitler which are sadly lacking in this crew. It has been my misfortune to inherit the problems of other captains.'

'They are a well-motivated and hard-working crew,' Hufnagel replied. 'In their time off, they benefit from laughter and relaxation.'

'A mind which is not capable of responding to the speeches of Adolf Hitler must be dull and swinish indeed.'

'I didn't say they weren't capable of responding. Only that they are energetic young men who need to loosen up from time to time.' He tried a smile. 'These young crews don't fight for the Führer, or even for Germany. They fight for each other, because they know that if one dies, they all die.'

'They do not fight for the Führer? I will make a note of this conversation in the captain's log,' Todt said, with an unmistakable threat in his voice. He was trembling all the more, and now no longer meeting Hufnagel's eye.

Hufnagel decided to give up. He saluted Todt and turned to leave the captain's quarters. As he opened the curtain, however, something occurred to him, and he turned back.

'What did you mean by saying that you have inherited the problems of other captains?'

Todt did not look up from his log, in which he was energetically writing. 'It's no secret that this crew is made up of misfits and rejects.'

Hufnagel paused. 'That's the first I've heard of it.'

'I was warned when I was given this command that the crew contained a high proportion of borderline cases.'

'Really? Does that include me?'

Todt finally met Hufnagel's eyes. 'Your adherence to National Socialist principles has been in question from the start, Hufnagel. That is no secret, either. It is well-known that you conducted a liaison with a Jewish woman in Berlin.'

'I see.'

'I shudder to think of it. Mad folly! How could you defile your racial lineage in that way? I would sooner embrace a serpent or a crocodile.' Todt capped his fountain pen. He used ink, not pencil, which could be rubbed out. 'Close the curtain when you have left.'

Hufnagel made his way slowly forward to the torpedo room, thinking of Masha Morgenstern. *A liaison with a Jewish woman in Berlin.* Yes, it had been mad folly. He had crippled his career during those few months. But was not first love always mad folly? And had those mad, foolish months not been the happiest of his life? It had been a dream of another life, with the most beautiful woman in the world on his arm, laughing at the Two Eggs who followed them everywhere, floating on champagne.

And hardly before it had begun, it was over; and he was standing in the snow, looking up at her window, knowing he would never see her again.

He had certainly never loved any woman other than seventeen-year-old Masha Morgenstern. He was probably going to finish this war on the bottom of the ocean. He could at least say he had loved with all his heart, even if he had subsequently lost. That was something to take to the bottom of the ocean.

Southampton

'I call this a damned disgrace,' Dr Meese told Commodore Randall. They were on the upper deck, seventy feet above the waterline, looking down at the stream of new passengers coming aboard. 'These people aren't Americans by any stretch of the imagination. Look at them, Commodore. Yet more aliens. Hebrews, Levantines, Semites – whatever you want to call them.'

'They are refugees, Dr Meese. Do you want me to order my crew to beat them back with oars?'

'Where are you going to put all this garbage?'

'I've instructed the stewards to prepare emergency sleeping quarters in the grand salons, the palm courts, the gymnasiums and the ship's post office.'

Meese snorted. 'So we'll be picking our way over recumbent bodies? Why it'll be like a Bowery flophouse on a Saturday night.'

'There was a time,' Commodore Randall said, 'when as a young swab I was glad to find the shelter of a Bowery flophouse.'

'You cannot tell me that you are proud to be bringing this unsavoury collection of oddities into the United States? You might as well inject a healthy man with the cholera bacillus.'

'I have saved a few lives in my time, Dr Meese,' the Commodore said easily, laying a large flipper on Meese's shoulder, 'and if God spares me, I will save a few more. It's not a question of pride, but of common humanity.'

Annoyed by the Commodore's imperturbable calm, Dr Meese tipped his hat and walked off whistling, with his hands in his pockets. The Commodore turned to his first officer, who was standing beside him, and who had made no contribution to the conversation thus far. 'These Britishers are preparing for a scrap, by the looks of things, George.'

George Symonds, who had made many a voyage with Randall, nodded his head, gazing at the gun emplacements all around the harbour, and then up at the fleets of barrage balloons overhead. They had seen much the same sort of preparations in Bremen and Le Havre. 'My money's on the German dog.'

'You think it's the better animal?'

'I think it's bigger than all the others put together, and has the sharpest bite. And I don't see how the old bulldog can beat it without our help.'

'Let's hope it doesn't come to that. One is liable to get bitten in a dog fight.'

'You never can tell with a dog fight, Commodore.'

'Masha, I'm begging you not to do this.'

Rachel's usual ironic composure was breaking down as she followed her cousin, who was hauling the suitcase up the companionway. She had remained stoical through so much in the past decade. What should have been her youth had been consumed in the rising conflagration of Jew-hatred which the Nazis had lit and fanned. Her education had been curtailed, her property, her home and finally her family had been taken from her. She had been forced into exile. All that she had borne with stoicism. But this last blow was too much to bear.

'Masha, please.'

Masha merely shook her head. Her face was ghastly. She hadn't slept or eaten. They emerged on the deck, finding it thronged with people jostling and milling in a fine drizzle which had begun to fall. Masha blundered through the crowd towards the gangplank.

'Now then, now then, what's all this?' At the top of the gangplank they were brought up short by the figure of Mr Nightingale, the senior steward, looking very seamanlike in a slick oilskin coat. He looked Rachel up and down. 'You're going to catch your death of cold, young lady. Where are you off to?'

'She's disembarking,' Rachel said, now crying helplessly.

'Your geography's not very good,' Mr Nightingale said archly. 'I'm certain your ticket says New York. This is Southampton.'

'Her parents have been sent to a concentration camp by the Gestapo. She wants to go and join them.'

'My goodness. And what do you think disembarking here is going to accomplish?'

'If they are going to die,' Masha said in a choked voice, 'then I will die with them.'

'Do you know what you are?' Mr Nightingale asked.

Masha looked at him with eyes that were almost swollen shut by the salt tears, uncomprehending.

'You're an enemy alien, that's what you are.' Mr Nightingale jerked his thumb at the rain-blurred outline of Southampton behind him. 'That country's at war with your country. Which means that as soon as you set foot off this gangplank, you'll be detained. If you look, you can see the policeman who'll arrest you, standing there in his size-twelve boots. You won't ever get back to Germany. You'll be sent to some internment camp in some dreary place like the Isle of Man, and you'll sit there for years and years and years.'

Igor Stravinsky and the young German boy had now arrived, sheltering under the same umbrella. Mr Nightingale turned to the composer.

'Am I right, Monsieur Stravinsky? Am I right in what I say?'

'I believe you are.' He turned to Masha Morgenstern, and took her hand. 'My dear child, I beg you to listen to me. You must consider—'

Whatever Stravinsky was about to say was cut short. A thunderous volley of gunfire suddenly rolled over the harbour. Deafened and panicking, passengers scattered, pushing each other out of the way, some diving for the shelter of the lifeboats, others crouching where they stood with their hands over their heads. Everyone was looking up at the skies. Some of the women were instantly in hysterics. Their screaming could hardly be heard over the guns and the sirens, which were now wailing.

'It's an air raid,' a man shouted as he ran past. 'Get under cover!'

Thomas had thrown his arms around Masha, and was trying to shelter her as she cowered on the deck in shock.

'Everybody stay calm.' The ship's quartermaster had appeared, megaphone in hand, making his way among the terrified crowd. 'Stay calm. There is no danger. The anti-aircraft batteries are having air-raid practice, that is all. Remain calm.'

The thunder of the firing spread around the docks. The smoke from the guns was filling the air, grey and sulphurous, luridly lit by the muzzle flashes. The macabre warble of sirens had now been taken up all around the harbour. Despite the quartermaster's assurances, every report sent a shockwave through the crowd. People hurried off the deck, shaken, dragging screaming children who had been terrified out of their wits.

Mr Nightingale turned back to Masha, who was trembling. 'Now, Miss Morgenstern. I'm going to have a hot cup of beef tea sent to your cabin. You drink that, and have a good cry, and think about things.'

Thomas released Masha and helped her to get back on her feet. The shock and noise seemed to have dazed her. 'I will take your suitcase back to your cabin, Fräulein.'

Masha allowed Thomas to take it from her nerveless fingers. It weighed little. She had given most of her clothes to Rachel.

Stravinsky put his arm through Masha's to support her, since she seemed unsteady on her legs.

'I understand that young Thomas has given you a ticket to the world of tomorrow,' he said, as he and Rachel steered her gently away between them. 'I think you should take it.'

It was four o'clock in the afternoon by the time Cubby Hubbard got to his cabin. There had been an extraordinarily long line of passengers ahead of him, and much confusion and ill-temper at times through the day. The repeated air-raid practices by the shore batteries had told on everyone's nerves. People were complaining of headaches, their nerves rattled. The shocking anger of those guns had brought home the reality of the war more than any broadcast speech or strident newspaper article.

The ship was already well over capacity. It was said that there were not enough in the kitchens to cater for all the extra passengers who would need to be fed, and that some three dozen Irish cooks would be taken aboard in Queenstown.

He'd had no sight of the Kennedy family. They had been secluded in their suite in the hotel since his interview with the matriarch. He presumed they would be in First Class, while he of course was in Tourist.

His cabin was meant for two, but now contained four. The three others were young Canadians of his own age, all (somewhat to his disgust, since he liked a good time) training to be Methodist ministers. Like Cubby himself, they had been on a tour of Europe. They were in a state of considerable excitement.

'We were stranded in France,' the freshest and pinkest of them told Cubby in his weird Canuck accent. 'Our passage home was on the *Britannic.* She's owned by the White Star Line, the same people that own the *Athenia.* When *Athenia* was torpedoed – guess what? They cancelled our ship.'

'We managed to obtain a passage on the *Manhattan* through the grace of God,' another said.

'We were in the hands of Providence,' the pink one assured Cubby earnestly.

'It was a singular deliverance for us all,' the third said, his Bible in hand. 'The Lord conducted us safely through manifold dangers.'

While Cubby unpacked, they began an earnest discussion of St Paul, whom they clearly regarded as the prototype of their own peregrinations. It looked like being a dull trip home if he couldn't – as he anticipated he wouldn't – see much of Rosemary during the voyage.

When the dinner bell sounded, the Canadians took each other's hands to pray before going to the dining room. They invited Cubby to join them, but he declined politely, and set off on his own.

Strolling along the corridor, he came upon Mr Nightingale, the malleable senior steward, knocking on a passenger's door with a tray in one hand, on which was poised a brightly coloured drink. The occupant, a plump man wearing a flowery dressing gown, threw open the door.

'Is that my cocktail?' the passenger asked gaily.

'Your cock, my tail,' Mr Nightingale carolled, slipping into the cabin and slamming the door behind him.

Puzzled by this exchange, Cubby made his way to supper.

London

Joseph P. Kennedy, the United States ambassador to the court of St James, was up late in his private study.

It had been a long day. Since the outbreak of war there had been lines of people right around the imposing Mayfair mansion every day, screaming for passports, visas and other documents. His staff were exhausted. And today there had been a formal embassy dinner with a host of grandees: the Duke and Duchess of Beaufort, the Duke and Duchess of Devonshire, the Earl of Such-and-Such, the Viscountess of So-and-So, the Honourable This, the Grand Panjandrum That – the usual crowd, bursting with the bitter comments and the poison barbs which the British upper classes were so adept at launching. God rot them all.

All of them hated him and knew that he hated them in return. They had all read the bulletin – 'Ambassador recalled to Washington for consultations' – and were praying that he had been fired.

But Roosevelt wouldn't dare fire him yet. Not with the war just begun, and the full might of the Nazis yet to be unleashed. Roosevelt was many things, but he wasn't a fool.

Kennedy loosened his silk tie, unfastened his collar, and ran his fingers through his thinning red hair. He needed a real drink. He sat behind his broad, leather-topped desk and poured himself a large Dewar's. The amber stuff glowed in the Waterford crystal tumbler as he held it to the lamp. It had been his favourite whisky ever since the 1930s, when shiploads of it had built his fortune. He drained the glass and then poured another, beginning to relax.

Not that he was looking forward to the interview with Roosevelt. He didn't hate the man. In fact they called one another friends. But there was in him much that could turn to hate – a long tally of humiliations and slights, going back twenty years. Roosevelt enjoyed taking his money, letting him believe he was part of the inner circle, then showing him clearly that he was not. The assaults on his dignity were no less vicious for being disguised as pranks.

Roosevelt had made him drop his trousers in the Oval Office to get this job. He'd stood there in his undershorts, his pale brow burning with shame as Roosevelt chuckled at his bare legs and told him he was too bandy-legged to be ambassador to Britain.

'You'll have to wear knee-britches and silk stockings to court,' Roosevelt had chortled, 'and you're about the most bow-legged Irishman I've ever seen. You'd make America a laughing-stock.'

This, from a man in a wheelchair.

That was why Roosevelt did it, of course; because he was stuck in that chair while men like Joe strode and kicked and screwed their way through life. It was the envy of a cripple, refined into sadism.

So he'd had to drop his pants to get the job. Well, he'd done worse. Bow-legged Irishman he might be, he'd got the job (in long pants) and faced the Brits on his own terms. He would endure anything to get where he was headed.

As for Roosevelt, a reckoning was coming. Kennedy believed fervently that the poisonous old gimp would be defeated in 1940. His day was done, as was that of the Jew financiers who supported and funded him. Roosevelt would be relegated to the wilderness, the Jews would all be shipped off to Africa, and the way would be paved for a red-headed, bow-legged Irishman to reign in the Oval Office.

And by then – he also firmly believed – the Luftwaffe would have reduced London to smoking ruins, and England to subservience. Churchill would be hanged; Hitler would be master of all Europe.

He'd told them so tonight, over the port and cigars. He never scrupled to tell the truth. 'You can't stop the Germans,' he'd told them, 'so you'd better learn to live with them.'

How he enjoyed the disgust that curdled their faces. He knew they called him 'Jittery Joe' and hummed *Run Rabbit Run* behind his back. God rot them all. Their day was done, too. They thought he didn't know that they were spying on him, their much-vaunted MI5, opening his diplomatic bag, intercepting his cables. Well, he knew right enough, and he didn't care.

At least he would be home for Christmas.

The official line was that none of the Kennedys would leave England until every American had been repatriated, but that of course wasn't true. Joe Junior had sailed already on the RMS *Mauretania*. Jack would be on the New York flight in a few days. His wife, Teddy and the girls were waiting for the arrival of the SS *Manhattan* from Le Havre.

He would get them all home as soon as he could. The German ambassador had privately told him what was coming: a rain of fire such as the world had never seen, devastation on an awesome scale. 'Get your family out,' von Ribbentrop had whispered. 'When this is done, we will need men like you, men who understand our Jewish policy so perfectly, men with whom we can build the future.'

And by God, he looked forward to that day.

The telephone on his desk buzzed. He picked it up. 'Yes?'

'She's here, sir.'

He checked his watch. It was two a.m. 'What condition is she in?'

'Quiet.'

'Have them bring her up.' He drained the second glass of whisky and poured himself a third. He'd drunk nothing more than water during the interminable banquet tonight, damned if he would give them the satisfaction of adding 'sodden Paddy' to the book of insults they compiled on him. But he was the son of a man who'd started life as a saloon-keeper, and he knew hard drink was medicine for anger. It didn't kill it; it kept it alive and burning, so you didn't forget it.

There was a knock at the door. He pulled his suspenders up and squared his shoulders, fixing a bright grin on his face. 'Come in,' he called.

His eldest daughter had grown into a tall, curvaceous beauty in the last couple of years. But the woman who was led in to his study now was dishevelled and dazed, her head bowed. She bore little resemblance to the vivacious Rosemary he'd last seen a few days earlier.

His smile faded. He got up and hurried over to her. 'Hello, Rosie.'

She didn't seem to know where she was, and looked around dazedly, her face blotched, her lids swollen. Then her dull gaze landed on his face. 'Oh, Daddy!' she whispered.

She collapsed into his arms. He enfolded her, pressing her face into his broad chest. 'Rosie, my Rosie. You're safe, now.'

The nurse who had brought her into the room stood back, her hands clasped dutifully around the handle of her Gladstone bag. 'She's had a strong sedative, sir. She might be a little confused.'

'When's her next dose due?'

'As soon as she seems to be getting agitated again.'

'Have you got the stuff?'

'Yes, sir.'

'Put it on my desk. I'll give it to her.'

The nurse took the packets out of her bag and laid them on the desk in a row. 'A single dose stirred in a glass of water,' she murmured. 'Whenever necessary. She goes out like a light.'

He nodded, still holding Rosemary, who had buckled against him, her body getting heavier in his arms. 'I'll call you if I need you. You can go.'

When they were alone, Kennedy lifted his daughter's head and looked into her face. Her features were blurred, coarsened, as though someone had beaten her with fists, though there were no injuries to be seen. Her beauty had gone. She looked, he thought, hideous.

'God damn it,' he said angrily, 'how could you let yourself get into this state?'

His displeasure, always terrible to her, made her break out in fresh tears. 'I'm so – sorry – Daddy.' The medicine they had given her made it hard for her to talk properly. Her tongue lolled in her mouth, her words slurred into each other.

He gave her a handkerchief. 'Clean yourself up.'

She swayed as she tried clumsily to wipe her eyes and nose. She had been barely conscious during the drive from Southampton, lying on the back seat of the car, her misery suppressed by the medicine, all her functions slowed to a standstill so she could hardly even breathe, her heart a slow thud. Now she felt as though she had been broken all in pieces, and put together wrong. Her head ached dreadfully. She could barely see. Her father's softly lit study swam around her. All she knew was that Cubby was far away, and that her mother had promised she would never see him again. The grief of that was like a vast chasm, at the edge of which she teetered, only prevented from falling in by the thinnest of threads.

'Tell me about this boy.' Daddy always knew what she was thinking. Daddy knew her better than anyone. 'Have you slept with him?'

'Yes, Daddy,' she whispered.

He didn't scream at her, the way Mother did, but his expression made her want to curl up and die. 'Did you go all the way?'

'Yes, Daddy.'

'How many times?'

'I – I don't know.'

'Ten times? Twenty?'

'I – I don't know, Daddy.'

'Are you pregnant?'

'I don't – don't think so. But I want a baby!' He had put on his glasses and was looking at her intently, one fist on his hip. 'Please don't be angry with me,' she begged. 'I love him!'

His face grew more hawk-like for a moment, his eyebrows coming down. He turned and filled the whisky glass on his desk. 'Drink,' he said, pushing it into her hand.

Rosemary tried to obey, but the stuff burned her throat, which was swollen and raw from all the crying she'd done. She choked. 'Can I have ginger ale with it?'

'I don't have any here. Throw it down, Rosie. You'll feel better.'

She closed her eyes and drank the whisky obediently. She got it down in two gulps, but her head instantly began to spin even more wildly. She staggered.

'Stand up straight.'

'Daddy, I have to go back. The ship – the ship is leaving.'

'Yes. But you'll be staying here.'

'No,' she moaned, shaking her head from side to side desperately, 'no, no, no.'

He took the empty glass from her. 'You have to forget him, Rosie.'

'No, Daddy!'

He spoke slowly, reasonably. 'Even if I would accept a son-in-law like that – a musician, and a Protestant into the bargain – you're not ready for marriage.'

Rosemary struggled to articulate her anguish through the fog of the whisky and the sedative. 'I am, I am. I love him!'

He gripped her arms in strong hands, shaking her. The green glitter in his eyes was cold. 'You don't love any man more than you love your Daddy, do you?'

She hung her head. 'Daddy . . .'

He shook her harder. 'Do you?'

'No, Daddy,' she whispered.

'Good,' he said. 'And you know that no man will ever love you better than I do, don't you?'

'Yes, Daddy.'

'You know that I've taken care of you all your life. You know that no man could have taken better care of you. Don't you?'

'Yes,' she said.

'All your life. From when you were a little, tiny girl. I dried your first tears.' He rubbed his thumb under her brimming eyes. 'Just as I'm drying your tears now. Isn't that right?'

A heavy calm was settling over her, following the slow, rhythmical cadence of his voice, an acceptance that was like despair. But it was better than the anguish. It stopped her from falling into the chasm. 'Yes, Daddy,' she said dully.

'You see, Rosie, the difference between me and all other men is that I understand you. Nobody else can. Nobody else ever will. I'm sure this Cubby is a nice enough boy, but he can never know you the way I know you. Sooner or later, he'll find out what you really are, and then he'll hurt you. He'll go away. I will never hurt you. And I will never go away. I will always be here.'

'Daddy . . .' She swayed against him. He took her in his arms again, stroking her tangled hair with one hand.

'It's all over now,' he said quietly. 'You'll forget everything and then you'll be better again. Calm again. It's going to be great. The best. You and me. Nobody else. You'd like that, wouldn't you? Just you and me?'

She nodded her head, no longer able to speak.

'Good.' He studied her face. 'You're so tired. This has been bad for you, Rosie. Very bad. We can't let this happen again, can we?'

She shook her head.

'You need to sleep, now. Go to your room and get into bed.'

She walked away from him slowly, like a woman in a dream, her eyes almost closed. He made sure she got out of the door without bumping herself, and watched her drift down the dimly lit corridor and vanish into the shadows.

Then he went back to the telephone on his desk and called his wife.

'She's arrived safely,' he told her. 'She's calm now. I'm putting her to bed. Everything's under control.'

The Western Approaches

Servicing the torpedoes was a regular task which nobody enjoyed, least of all the crew who had to live in the company of the greasy monsters. It didn't help that the sea continued to be very rough. *U-113* pitched and rolled violently, causing even the nimblest sailors to lose their footing and slide into metal projections which seemed designed to imprint the human body with a rich diversity of bruises.

In the forward torpedo room, the torpedo mechanics were hauling the long, heavy 'fish' out of their racks, using the hoists installed for that purpose. The things were twenty-five feet long, weighing three thousand pounds, eight hundred pounds of which was high explosive. They were complex beasts, with tails and fins and brains and teeth, and they could swim at a speed of forty knots.

The few ratings who had chosen to remain watched the torpedomen unbolt the access hatches of the torpedoes and work in their tangled entrails. The rest were squatting along the passageways, some with miniature chess-boards between them: Rudi Hufnagel, in an effort to combat the tensions bred by boredom and fear on board, had organised a chess tournament.

He had drawn up a league table with considerable care. Out of forty-eight crew members, twenty-three were chess players. All of them had signed up eagerly. Somewhat to Hufnagel's surprise, Todt put his name on the list, and as luck would have it, the commander drew Hufnagel for his first match. They played in the captain's quarters, wedged around his fold-down table. Todt wore his white captain's cap, perhaps to remind Hufnagel who was boss.

'Chess,' Todt said, inserting his pieces into the little holes on the board, 'is an intrinsically Aryan game.'

'I thought it was Persian.'

'Exactly so. The Persians are descended from ancient Aryan races. It is from the very word "Aryan" that they draw the name of their country, Iran. The meaning of the word "Aryan" is free, noble and strong.' Todt made his first move and scratched at an ugly red rash that had spread around his groin. Despite the cold, he was wearing shorts so as to air the inflammation.

'That's very interesting,' Hufnagel said, making his countermove. He was wondering whether to try to win his match or whether it would be more diplomatic to allow the captain to beat him.

'Do you know that I found recordings by Vladimir Horowitz in the crew's music collection?' Todt said.

'That is very serious,' Hufnagel replied gravely.

Todt did not pick up the irony in his tone. 'The difference between music made by Aryans and music made by Jews is the difference between healthy air and poison gas. Any contact with Jews spreads an infection, insidious but deadly, which eventually overpowers the strongest organism. The danger of Jewish infection is something you ignored when you took one of their females to your bed.'

Hufnagel had a memory of a night at the opera, of a soft body in his arms, of soft lips on his. He moved a pawn, saying nothing.

'And this is not to mention the case of negro music, which although different, is equally dangerous. Negro music attempts to excite the worst passions in man, to drag man down to the level of a jungle ape. It drives the listener to sexual excess of the worst kind. And in the United States, of course, the Negroes have been given a dominant place.'

'If you say so,' Hufnagel replied dryly.

'They are allowed to dominate in music and sport, to name but two areas.'

Hufnagel hid a sour smile. No sooner had the Nazis banned Aryans from frolicking to the rhythms of Louis Armstrong and Duke Ellington when along had come Jesse Owens and his Negro teammates to sweep past pure-blooded Germans at the Berlin Olympics – and that under the nose of the Führer. 'Shocking,' he murmured.

'Shocking indeed. This worship of the savage is the surest sign that the American culture is doomed.'

Half-listening to Todt's high-flown analysis of what he called 'nigger-music', Hufnagel tried to disguise his boredom. Unlike Todt, he had visited America, albeit briefly. Their training ship had docked at Baltimore, Maryland, and a group of them had caught the train to New York to do some sightseeing.

They'd been careful not to show swastikas or other emblems, knowing that Nazism was already held in opprobrium by many people. He remembered the first Negroes he had seen, their lively grace, their seeming good-fellowship, mingled with a certain humorous cynicism.

They had strolled around Harlem, looking at the dark folk and listening to their music spilling out of shabby doorways, along with the smell of spicy cooking. He'd been struck by the difference between them and the hard-faced, thrusting, white New Yorkers who bustled like ants from one skyscraper to another.

He studied the board. Perhaps in his enthusiasm for the topic, Todt had made an unwise move. Hufnagel capitalised on this quietly, bringing up a knight which had been previously held back, strengthening his command of the middle of the board. As they played, they could hear noises from the bows of the U-boat, where the torpedomen were working, the rattle of chain winches and the clank of tools on metal casings.

Todt continued. 'This war, Hufnagel, is not being waged for profit or land. We are Teutonic knights, going to war against an enemy who spreads his tentacles right around the globe. If we allow infection to spread here, under our very armour, then, Hufnagel, we are beaten before we begin.' He scratched his crotch, looking more closely at the board. 'I see I have made bad moves.'

'One or two, Captain. All is not yet lost,' Hufnagel said, contemplating making a bad move of his own so that Todt could recover the initiative.

'You still have not answered my earlier question.'

'What question was that, Captain?'

'How you could have brought yourself to have intercourse with a Jewess.' Todt raised his hollow eyes to Hufnagel's. 'It's the most disgusting thing I ever heard. It makes my gorge rise.'

'Yes, you said as much before.'

'Was she very hirsute?' Todt's lean cheeks flushed as he asked the question. 'I have heard that Jewish women have an abnormal quantity of bodily hair, particularly in the reproductive regions. It reaches to the knees in some cases. It's said that this can be used to identify a Jewess, even if she attempts to conceal her race.'

'I am unable to comment on that,' Hufnagel said icily.

'But surely your experience—'

Hufnagel cut in. 'My experience is not one which I choose to share. It is a private matter.'

Todt's eyes flicked from the board to Hufnagel's face. 'You still entertain feelings for this Jewess, then?'

'I refuse to discuss it.'

'Then you are not to be trusted, Hufnagel. You have been corrupted, as all are corrupted by contact with Jews.'

'That is nonsense,' Hufnagel replied tersely.

'In the moment of crisis, you will fail the Fatherland. That is inevitable.'

Todt moved his queen, another bad move. Hufnagel now had his opponent in his sights, and victory was more or less inevitable. Todt, if he was any sort of a player, could see that. And Hufnagel now had no intention of losing the match.

Southampton

Fanny Ward, now aboard the *Manhattan*, had not gone to dinner. She had provided her own nourishment in the form of a little hamper from Fortnum & Mason. Since Dotty's death last year, she did not care for public appearances. The press conference she had given in the hotel had to be endured because one endured such things as part of one's profession. But the death of a child changed one. One no longer wanted to see so much of the world. Or be seen by it.

The lovely Commodore Randall, whom she knew well, had made sure she'd got a cabin to herself, even if it was a tiny one. Such a gentleman, for all his saltiness. She appreciated such courtesies all the more now that fewer and fewer people knew who she was, The Eternal Beauty, The Perennial Flapper. The Girl Who Wouldn't Grow Old.

But she had grown old.

She sat at her dressing table, pulling her rings off. There was something about fabulous diamonds on gnarled fingers that made one shudder. But that was what one was reduced to. The bare bones.

Some of those reporters had been laughing at her, she was sure of it. Not the laughter of delight, but mocking laughter. Did they know what she had been? That men had lost their reason over her, that she had been the most fashionable woman in London for a time, that she had been directed by Cecil B. DeMille? A few, perhaps.

As one aged, one entered a funnel. One's circle of acquaintance shrunk, there were fewer people each year who had shared one's life, who knew who one was. But the loss of a child was the most terrible thing of all.

Fanny removed her wig of chestnut curls and stored it carefully in its box. Her own hair, secured by a net, was now too sparse to bother dyeing, and lay lank and white across her skull.

At least Dotty had died a glamorous death. She had raised Dotty to understand the importance of glamour. And no death could be more glamorous than perishing beside one's husband, the sixth Baron Plunkett, in a plane owned by William Randolph Hearst, on one's way to stay as a guest at San Simeon. It would be talked of for years.

Of course, one didn't like to dwell on the details. Dotty and Terence, trapped in the plane's cabin, engulfed in flames. It didn't do to look at the details of anything, really.

Fanny pulled off her false eyelashes carefully, her lids stretching into watery pouches as she did so. Of course the children would be well taken care of, raised by Lord Plunkett's sister and brother-in-law. It simply hurt, that was all, to be left with the last years to fill, and no Dotty. Her love-child. The child of her great love.

Fanny wiped off her lipstick. The cupid's bow vanished, leaving a thin, bitter gash. Running back to America was humiliating, but one was terrified of the bombing. Simply terrified. The last war had been bad enough. She'd come to London at the turn of the century, when things had got rather too hot for her in New York, and the last three decades had been marvellous, simply marvellous. But now they were over.

She didn't expect that she would ever be back. Or that London would survive Hitler's bombs. But one couldn't say that, of course.

She wiped away the powder and rouge, watching in the mirror as her own face emerged, washed-out, haggard, unhappy.

For years they'd been asking her, what's your secret, Miss Ward? Is it surgery? Do you eat monkey gland? Usually she told them it was a secret facial treatment passed on to her by Gaby Deslys, and available (for a substantial outlay) at her salon in Paris, in six weekly sessions.

The truth, of course, was that it was all simply an illusion, carefully maintained, and possible only because those charming gentlemen of the press participated in the conspiracy, printing photographs of her that were twenty years old, retouching negatives, lavishing lies on her. She hoped they would continue the conspiracy. It would be too tedious to have to grow old in public, as well as in private.

She rubbed cream into her face and hands. In the cruel light of the vanity mirror, this made her face gleam like a skull, her hands appear even bonier. Putting away her potions, she rose and removed her dress. With it came the strategically-sewn padding that had given her body its youthful curves. She hung the garment in the closet, and wrapped a dressing gown around herself.

Gaunt, frail and almost hairless, she opened the Fortnum's hamper and investigated the contents. A game pie, a bottle of port, a cold chicken. She picked at the food with skinny fingers. She would take her teeth out after supper.

Alone in her own cabin, Carla Toscanini had also been thinking about the death of a child. But her Giorgio had died at the age of six, not in adulthood. Diphtheria had choked the innocent life out of him before he could even open his wings.

She had been four years married when she'd had Giorgio. Not yet twenty-three. And Arturo was already unfaithful to her.

She had discovered it through his carelessness, his arrogance. He had been receiving the woman's love letters under a clownish assumed name at the local post office. It hadn't taken Carla long to identify the woman: Rosina Storchio, the handsome young soprano whose vivid personality was propelling her to operatic stardom at that time.

But Arturo had not been interested in Rosina Storchio's larynx. His interests had been in another organ altogether. The letters made that clear. Carla had confronted him with his treachery, screaming. It was a scene to be repeated many times over the course of their marriage, but this had been the first time, and she'd had a lot to learn. She'd still thought she could stop him.

Raging, she'd scoured every post office for miles around, hunting down his illicit correspondence. He'd simply used other anagrams of his name, even more clownish (Icinio Artú-Rostan and the like). She'd stood like an idiot, burning with humiliation, at the *post restante* counters, rifling through other peoples' mail, looking for Storchio's huge, extravagant calligraphy on the envelopes, while the postmasters watched her in mingled pity and scorn. It had been impossible to track down all Arturo's aliases. She had followed his footsteps, dogged him for weeks. He had given her the slip every time.

It was a fire she couldn't extinguish. He promised to renounce Storchio, swore on his mother's soul she meant nothing to him. But he always found a way to go back to her.

He had been with Storchio when Giorgio had died, six years later. She'd had to face her child's death alone.

Carla had never forgiven him for that. She should have left him then. But her heart was broken in so many pieces that she was half-dead with grief; and besides, she was expecting Wanda. Where would she go, with her belly out to here, and two children under ten years old?

Well, Rosina Storchio had had her punishments. The son she'd had with Arturo had been born crippled and paralysed, and had died at sixteen. Her voice, small to begin with, had disintegrated through over-use. She'd retired young, and it had been twenty years since anyone had heard of her. It was said that she too was now paralysed, living alone in obscurity. She'd never married.

Contemplating this litany of tragedy gave Carla no satisfaction. Her own pain was still too great to take pleasure in anyone else's. But she felt that justice had been served.

She undressed now, hoping she would find sleep tonight. She had almost not come to Le Havre. Finding those filthy letters of Ada Mainardi's had knocked her down, after so many times of being knocked down. She'd started to feel sure that her husband was now too old for these adventures. She'd been wrong.

She'd sat staring at the lake for days, stunned. The telegram boy had come climbing up to the house every day, with ever-more-frantic messages from Artú. She'd ignored them.

At length she had been forced out of her inertia by sheer self-preservation. Their landlord had implored her to pack up and go. If she did not leave Switzerland, he'd warned, she would spend the war here, possibly interned, separated from her children. There was no point in that.

She'd made a bonfire in the garden, and had burned much of the correspondence. Not only the handkerchiefs stained with Ada's blood, and the little nosegays of hair tied artistically with silk thread, but other letters as well, from other women – because there had been those, too. Artú's sexual energies, like all his other energies, were inexhaustible.

Even then, she had almost set off not west, to France, but south, to Milan. Yes; she'd contemplated taking her maiden name and slipping back into Italy, to sit out the war alone. Only the thought of the children had stopped her.

At sixty-three, her expression had grown severe, her features jowly. Her body was thickened, her temperament curdled. She no longer cared what she looked like, and habitually wore black. Heavy, heavy, she was heavy, her heart was heavy, her face and her life were heavy upon her.

She should have left Artú after Storchio, but there had been too many things stopping her.

Not any more. Enough was enough.

The next day, the air-raid drills were repeated. The guns began firing at nine in the morning. The children on board the *Manhattan* were wrought to a pitch of excitement by the commotion, running around howling, arms outstretched in imitation of fighter planes, or plummeting to the deck, trailing imaginary flames. For the adults, the exercise was more trying. Each blast made one's body jerk involuntarily, or as Katharine Wolff put it more colloquially, jump out of one's skin.

She and Stravinsky were breakfasting with Thomas König and the German girls who had caused such a scene yesterday. They were all jaded today, particularly the younger of the girls, who was clearly distressed by the guns.

'I can't bear to hear them any more,' Masha said, covering her ears and shutting her eyes. 'When will they stop?'

'They are very disagreeable,' Thomas said in his awkwardly formal way. He reached out to touch her hand in an oddly adult gesture of comfort.

'I would have thought you would find them very agreeable indeed,' Rachel snapped at him. She never missed a chance to attack the boy. 'Isn't this the very sound your Führer loves most?'

Stravinsky, wearing a black crew-necked sweater, seemed to find that amusing. 'Ah yes, Thomas is a fervent little Nazi. You should hear him quoting passages from *Mein Kampf*. Explain, Thomas, what the Führer tells us about modern music.'

Thomas withdrew his hand from Masha's. 'The Führer tells us that modern music contains germs which are infecting our society, and by which we are bound to rot and perish,' the boy said in a monotone, his face flushing scarlet, his eyes on his plate. He had been made to memorise these wisdoms at school, until his expulsion, and his youthful memory retained them; but having to trot them out in front of Masha and Rachel was excruciating.

'You see?' Stravinsky said to Rachel. 'You and the Führer are agreed in your opinion of my music.'

'I have never said any such thing,' Rachel retorted. 'I merely said I didn't care for it.'

'And tell us, Thomas,' Stravinsky said with a malicious glint, 'where does Hitler say we modern composers belong?'

Thomas gritted his teeth. 'In a sanatorium.'

'Once again we cannot fault the Führer's prescience, for that is exactly where I have spent the last year. My late wife and daughter, indeed, spent most of their lives in a sanatorium.' He turned to Masha. 'Do you know Haute-Savoie, young lady?'

'I have seen Mont Blanc,' Masha said dully.

'Ah yes. Very large. Very white. Our sanatorium lay at the foot. One opened the curtains and there it was. Very large. Very white.' None of them was eating much, but Stravinsky was carefully peeling an apple with a little pearl-handled fruit knife. 'It was a celebrated sanatorium. No less a person than Marie Curie came there. We used to see her, my wife and I, creeping into the sun to get warm. They were treating her for tuberculosis – Madame Curie, I mean – but the diagnosis was mistaken. She had given herself pernicious anaemia by the unwise habit of carrying radium around in her pockets. She died. Large doses of radiation, as with my music, are less healthy than small ones.'

'You have a strange sense of humour,' Rachel commented shortly.

'I have no sense of humour at all. Thomas can attest to that. He relates to me all the Führer's excellent jokes, but I am never amused. It must be a deficiency of intellect on my part.'

Rachel merely shook her head at Stravinsky's whims. She watched Masha constantly, anxiously. She laid her hand on her cousin's brow now. 'You are hot. Are you getting a fever?' Masha seemed not to hear, her face remaining desolate.

'I understand that you two young people have studied music?' Stravinsky said.

'I studied at the violin faculty at the Conservatory in Leipzig for two years,' Rachel replied. 'But I was suspended on hygienic grounds.'

'Your Jewishness was infectious?'

'That is what they told me. Which was amusing, since the Conservatory was founded a hundred years ago by Felix Mendelssohn.'

'A Jew. And now a banned composer, like myself. What does Hitler teach us about Jews and taste, Thomas?'

Thomas writhed. 'There is no Jewish art,' he replied automatically, the colour rising into his face again, 'but the – the Jews have succeeded in poisoning public taste.'

'There you have it. So much for Mendelssohn.'

'I've often wondered why Hitler bothers himself about such subjects as music,' Katharine said.

'Because he is himself an artist,' Stravinsky replied.

'If he were really an artist,' she said, 'the world would be a safer place.'

Stravinsky shook his finger emphatically. 'Oh no. Artists are the most dangerous people on earth. Your army general may kill a few thousand, but your artist thinks nothing of exterminating millions.' He turned back to Rachel. 'What about your young cousin, Fräulein Morgenstern? Is she musical, too?'

'Masha is an amateur pianist of some talent. But she was not permitted to enter any conservatory. Also on the grounds of being infectious.'

'Her lack of professional formation no doubt explains her dubious enthusiasm for my music.' Having peeled the apple smoothly, he sliced it into four quarters, and gave one to each of the others. 'If you find the time lying heavy on your hands, I have a little work for you.'

'Work?'

'I have with me the partial score of my symphony, but the manuscript is in rough, with all my corrections and scratchings-out. Perhaps I could prevail upon the two of you to copy the work out in fair?'

'What will you pay?' Rachel asked swiftly.

'Rachel!' Masha exclaimed in dismay, lifting her head. 'It will be an honour to do the work – without pay, of course.'

'You want payment in dollars, I presume?' the composer asked Rachel, ignoring Masha.

'Of course.'

'Very well, I will pay fifty cents per manuscript page. There are some eighty pages. And I will subtract twenty-five cents for every error. Two errors, no pay. Three errors, you pay me.'

'There will be no errors.'

'That remains to be seen.'

'And you will supply pens, ink and manuscript paper at no cost to us,' Rachel pressed.

Masha, embarrassed by Rachel's businesslike dealings, dug her fingers into her cousin's arm. 'We can find our own materials,' she hissed.

'I will supply materials,' Stravinsky conceded. 'But for any page that you spoil, you will pay me ten cents. Delivery to be before we dock in New York.'

Rachel held out her hand. 'It's a deal.'

They shook hands solemnly. 'Thomas will bring the manuscript to your cabin this evening.'

'I cannot believe, Igor,' Katharine said quietly to him, 'that you are entrusting your precious manuscripts to these perfect strangers. For all you know, they will sell them, and you will never see them again.'

'Fräulein Morgenstern is completely honest,' Thomas said sharply, glaring at Katharine. His face was now flushed with anger, rather than discomfort. 'You have no right to doubt her.'

'This is the first time I have heard a Nazi vouching for the honesty of a Jew,' Katharine said in a dry voice.

Stravinsky smoothed his greasy, blonde hair wearily. 'I am going back to bed. These guns tire my mind and make my head ache.'

As they all left the dining room, Rachel fell into step beside Stravinsky. 'Was it your idea to send the Hitler Youth to our cabin the other night?'

'Not at all. It was Thomas's own idea. He's not a bad fellow for a National Socialist.'

'He's infatuated with my cousin.'

'I wouldn't go as far as that.'

'Haven't you seen the way he moons over her?' Rachel glanced over her shoulder. Thomas was walking close beside Masha behind them, listening intently to what she was saying. His face was rapt. 'I find it repellent. Disgusting. He's like a dog that licks one's hand, but wants to bite.'

'We all know that Nazis have sharp teeth,' Stravinsky said, 'but this one is just a puppy. You should be able to kick him away easily enough.'

'I shall do my best,' Rachel said grimly.

Thomas König arrived at the girls' door, carrying a portmanteau holding Stravinsky's manuscripts. The boy was awkward, as he always was in the girls' presence. Rachel greeted him coldly, but Masha invited him eagerly into the little cabin.

'Imagine, Rachel. Original manuscripts from the hand of Igor Stravinsky!'

'Just imagine,' Rachel said ironically. 'Let's hope the great man is neat in his writing.'

'He's always so neat in his personal appearance. Quite fastidious, isn't he, Thomas?' She patted the place next to her on the bunk. 'Sit here beside me.'

The boy obeyed, pressing his hands between his knees. Rachel opened the portmanteau reverently. The sheaves of pages inside were densely written, with plentiful crossings-out and scribbled lines in French and Russian. Odd bits of paper, scraps of envelopes and even margins torn from magazines, were glued here and there with lines of music scribbled on them.

'Oh, what a lot of dots,' Rachel commented sardonically.

Thomas cleared his throat. 'Herr Stravinsky says you need not copy out his annotations. Only the staves.'

'My heart is beating fast,' Masha said, handling the pages as though they were holy writ. 'This is such a privilege!'

Thomas glanced at her face, and then away again. He found being in this cabin, with its scents, its articles of feminine clothing strewn around, and above all, the proximity of Masha Morgenstern, overwhelming. His heart, like Masha's, was beating fast.

'You have removed your swastika badge,' Rachel said, looking down at him.

'Yes, Fräulein.'

'Are you disobeying your mother's wishes out of sensitivity for our feelings?'

He swallowed. 'I know that the Fräuleins find it distasteful.'

'You needn't bother on our account. We are Germans, like yourself, and quite used to seeing the thing everywhere one looks. Put it back on.'

'It's quite all right.'

'It is not all right,' Rachel snapped. 'In Germany, we are obliged to wear a yellow star so that the world can see we are Jews. I don't see why you shouldn't wear a swastika to tell the world you are a Nazi. Put it back on.'

'Leave him alone,' Masha said.

'Why should I leave him alone? Put it on, I say.' She watched while Thomas, his fingers shaking somewhat, fished the pin from his pocket and reattached it to his lapel. 'We are also obliged to change our names to "Sara" or "Israel". I think we should call you "Adolf" from now on.'

'He's just a boy,' Masha said, leafing through the manuscript, her soft brown hair falling around her face. 'He doesn't understand these things.'

'He understands, all right. Don't you, Adolf?'

'I understand,' Thomas said, almost inaudibly.

'Look at the facility with which Stravinsky writes,' Masha exclaimed. 'It simply pours out of him, wherever he is. He scribbles on whatever comes to hand. Can you imagine having such a quantity of beauty in your head?'

'I can't imagine transcribing such a quantity of rubbish at fifty cents a page,' Rachel retorted. 'I hope you're going to do the lion's share. I have better things to do.'

'But what if I make mistakes?'

'Then you will pay for them. You heard the great Stravinsky-Korsakoff.'

'If the Fräulein wishes,' Thomas said in a small voice, 'I can check the pages for any errors.'

'You're very sweet, Thomas,' Masha said, laying her hand on the boy's knee. He started as though he had been burned with a red-hot iron.

'You're not going to disembark – are you?' he said in a whisper, his pale grey eyes fixed on hers.

Masha sighed. 'I've been told that I can't.' She smiled sadly at Thomas. 'I still have your ticket to the World's Fair. I can't really keep it, you know. I'll give it back to you.'

Thomas felt a flutter of dismay. The ticket was his only, tenuous link to Masha once they arrived in America. 'Oh no. It's yours. I beg you to keep it. You don't have to go with me. You can go any day you choose.'

Rachel was observing the boy narrowly. 'Young Adolf is in love with you, Masha.'

At once, the blood rushed into Thomas's face, reaching the roots of his hair. Rachel laughed mockingly. Masha shot her a reproving glance, and then patted Thomas on the knee again. 'Pay no attention to her. She's a dreadful tease.'

But Rachel's malice – or perhaps that gentle hand on his knee – was too much for Thomas. He jumped to his feet, made them a bow, and hurried out of the cabin.

'You're cruel, Rachel,' Masha said. 'Why do you torment him?'

'I hate the sight of him. Besides, it gives me a little pleasure.'

'He's a sensitive boy.'

'Oh, very. He has the hots for *you*.'

'Really, Rachel. It's nothing so adult as "having the hots". And it's a reason to show him some consideration.'

'There was a dwarf in our apartment building in Leipzig. She was tiny, like a child, even though she was thirty years old, with little stunted arms and legs. But do you know, Masha, she could play the violin with surpassing sweetness. I don't think I ever heard a sweeter tone. She asked me to give her lessons from time to time. Her arms were too short to hold the violin under her chin, so she played it like a cello. They came for her, the SS men, and took her away.'

'I don't want to hear any more horrible stories,' Masha said, with tears in her eyes.

'They didn't show *her* much consideration. I saw two of them swinging her like a sack between them, laughing on the way to the van. I said nothing, because I knew I would be next. By now she has been exterminated. Don't waste your pity on that boy. He'll be back in Germany baiting Jews while you and I are begging for our bread on the streets of New York.'

'If we do this work of Stravinsky's, we'll have at least forty dollars more,' Masha said, wanting to get Rachel off such bitter subjects. 'Shall we make a start?'

'And by the way,' Katharine pointed out sharply, 'you can ill afford forty dollars for a task you don't need doing.'

'It will be useful to have fair copies of those two movements.'

'I happen to know that fair copies of those two movements have already been sent to your publisher.'

'Exactly. That is why I require further fair copies for myself.'

She snorted at this prevarication. 'Those forty dollars would have bought you a Cabin Class ticket.'

'I am happy with my cabin.' He was playing patience in the Tourist Class smoking room, his legs wrapped in a rug, a cigarette in a holder clamped between his teeth. From time to time, when he was frustrated by the way the cards turned out, he muttered filthy expletives in Russian, imagining that she couldn't understand. 'There is nothing wrong with the cabin at all.'

'And what about the food?'

'I have never been very interested in food.'

'Nonsense, Igor,' she said roundly. 'You know you are a gourmet.'

'Shit on your mother,' he muttered to the cards in Russian.

'I understand what you are saying. I have enough Russian for that. And I see you cheating.'

Irritably, he gathered up the cards and shuffled the deck. 'How can I play, with you sitting there like a crow, pecking at me?'

'If you wanted to give those women charity, you could have just handed them the cash. You didn't have to risk your precious autograph manuscripts.'

'It is not a question of charity,' he replied, starting to lay out a new game. 'It's a business transaction.'

She lit a cigarette and began to buff her nails. 'You are absurdly trusting.'

Thomas König arrived at their table, his pale face set. 'I gave them the portmanteau.'

'Good boy.'

'Why do you always repeat that I am a Nazi to them?' he asked tensely.

Stravinsky looked up, adjusting his spectacles. 'But you are. Aren't you?'

'You make them hate me. Especially the older one.'

'Is that not in the natural order of things?'

'It's hard for me.'

'And yet you must bear it,' Stravinsky replied with a warning note in his voice. 'You have no choice.'

'You could at least not make a point of it every chance you get.'

'I don't think they need reminding of what you are. And my advice to you is not to annoy the elder Fräulein Morgenstern. She has a very sharp tongue.'

Thomas grimaced and walked off without replying.

'What was that all about?' Katharine asked.

Stravinsky returned to his cards. 'I suspect he has formed a sentimental attachment to one of the Jewesses.'

'How ironic. The softer one, I should guess.'

'Indeed, the other is something of a virago.'

'I hope he doesn't have any expectation of it being reciprocated.'

'I shouldn't imagine he is so foolish. He worships from afar. He is considerably younger, in any case.'

'I don't like him.'

'Is he not a man and a brother?'

'He is merely your cabin-mate.'

'Indeed. On life's journey, like us all. He will learn from us and we will learn from him. Aha.' Chewing on his cigarette holder with satisfaction, he began to move the cards around successfully. 'You note I am not cheating. Please do not tell me when I win that I have used underhand means.'

Masha had worked for much of the night on the Stravinsky score. Rachel had been wise enough to leave her to it. Despite being rudely awoken by the anti-aircraft batteries, after having got to sleep only a couple of hours earlier, Masha was ready for breakfast, and full of the music she had been transcribing.

'You can have no idea how wonderful it is,' she exclaimed to her cousin as they made their way to the dining room.

'Is it the roaring of lions or the trumpeting of elephants?'

'Neither. It's the most elegant, refined music you ever heard – well, since Beethoven, anyway.'

'Since Beethoven!'

'It's full of enchanting rhythmic variations. And Rachel, it's so clever.'

'Oh, I am sure it is *clever*.'

'And witty.'

'I will tighten my stays before reading it, so as not to break a rib laughing.'

As they made their way to the dining room, they encountered Arturo Toscanini, walking at great speed, as always. He almost collided with them, and began to utter curses in Italian, before his dark eyes, flashing beneath his tangled eyebrows, registered who they were.

'Ah!' he exclaimed, pulling himself up. 'The beautiful *signorine*.' He lifted his hat and showed his brownish teeth in a smile. '*Buongiorno, buongiorno!*'

'Good morning, maestro,' Masha replied.

Toscanini took Masha's hand in both of his and raised it to his lips. 'I was told of your unhappy news. I offer my condolences.'

'How kind of you, maestro,' Masha said, moved by this attention from the great man. Rachel, however, remained tight-lipped.

Toscanini pressed another kiss on Masha's knuckles, his eyes fixed hypnotically on hers. 'That mean little man in his ridiculous chauffeur's uniform! How I loathe him.'

'Do you mean Hitler?' Masha asked timidly.

'They asked me to return to Bayreuth in 1933, to conduct *The Ring*. With Hitler sitting in the front row? The bloated Goering beside him? And that hideous gnome Goebbels on the other side? Never!' He kissed Masha's hand again. 'They sent me ten thousand Deutschmarks. I sent them back. Hitler himself wrote to me, pleading. Do you know what I told him?'

'What?' Masha asked breathlessly.

'I told him, Toscanini says Tosca-no-no!' He burst out laughing. 'What has Wagner to do with Hitler?'

'Quite a lot, it seems,' Rachel put in dryly. 'The effect of the former on the latter is noxious. I sometimes ask myself whether the war would have started if Hitler hadn't been such a regular visitor at Bayreuth.'

Toscanini, who had still been pressing kisses on Masha's hand, threw it down furiously. His face flushed dangerously. 'Wagner expresses all that is sublime in the human condition,' Toscanini thundered, 'Hitler all that is most execrable.'

'Oh, yes,' Masha exclaimed, thrilling to the conductor's fiercely curling moustaches and flashing eyes.

Toscanini shook his finger in Rachel's face. 'Do not blame the composer of *Parsifal* for Hitler!' He pushed past the girls and hurried away on his peregrinations.

'The maestro is so fiery, isn't he?' Masha said in awe.

'Half-mad, you mean,' Rachel commented.

They arrived at their table to find Stravinsky, Katharine Wolff and Thomas König already seated. The boy got up with perfect manners, his eyes flicking apprehensively from Rachel to Masha.

'I've been copying out your manuscript, Monsieur Stravinsky,' Masha said eagerly.

'I hope you are not making expensive mistakes,' Stravinsky said, looking at her from under hooded eyelids.

'Oh no, I'm being very careful. But the music is so classical in form. It's nothing like *The Rite of Spring*.'

'My dear, it's at least fifteen years since I began composing in the neo-classical style, and at least twenty-five since I wrote *The Rite of Spring*. Are you disappointed?'

'Not at all. The music is wonderful. I'm surprised, that's all.'

'My life has been a long vista of surprised faces,' he replied. 'Unpleasantly surprised, I might add. They complained when I wrote new music, and said they wanted to hear classical forms. Now that I write classical forms, they complain and say they want to hear new music again. But one thing I cannot do is go backwards. I cannot be false to my aspirations.'

'Of course not,' Masha said, shocked at the idea. They ordered breakfast, and Masha and Stravinsky entered into a discussion of the accented off-beats in the music she was copying.

'Have you seen what your great army is doing to Poland, Adolf?' Rachel asked Thomas. 'You must be very proud.'

'It's pitiful,' Katharine said. 'I was in tears in the night, listening to Polish Radio on my short-wave. They put on a Chopin nocturne. I had to switch it off. I couldn't bear it. Even the women in my cabin were crying, and God knows they're not sensitive souls. That poor, tragic country! Between Stalin and Hitler, God help them.'

Thomas stared at his plate, pale-faced as the two women discussed the invasion. The dining room was completely full, and passengers were crowding at the doors, demanding tables. The overtaxed stewards were pleading in vain for them to form orderly lines. Those who had tables were shouting impatiently for food, which was emerging all too slowly from the kitchen. The crash of dropped crockery was becoming more frequent, the atmosphere more charged.

The SS *Manhattan* had been in Southampton harbour for a week already, and passengers were still coming aboard along the steep, narrow gangway, a steady flow of humanity, or as Dr Emmett Meese indignantly put it, human garbage.

Those already on board were showing signs of strain. Some, like Rachel and Masha Morgenstern, who had embarked in Bremen, had already been on the ship for a fortnight, and felt themselves to be choked by the ship's surroundings. These prolonged stays in port were hard to bear.

The sound of a bell cut through the hubbub. The public address system crackled.

'Attention all passengers. This is the chief purser. The Manhattan *will be sailing tomorrow morning at oh-six-hundred hours.'*

There was a moment of silence. Then the entire dining room erupted into cheers. The purser could barely be heard announcing that all passengers had to be on board by eleven p.m., and all visitors had to have left the ship by the same time, and repeating the announcement in French and German.

Masha looked at Thomas and saw the tears running down his cheeks. She rose quickly from her chair and put her arms around him. She had made up her mind to be especially kind to him, even if Rachel enjoyed sharpening her claws on him. He was just a boy, and his solicitude had touched her.

'Don't cry, Thomas. You'll be at the World's Fair very soon.'

Enveloped in her warmth and fragrant softness, Thomas had no words. She kissed his cheek and gave him her handkerchief, which he pressed to his face with both his hands.

Hertfordshire

The car pulled up in front of the big white mansion. Rosemary didn't want to get out, but Daddy said, 'I'm not in the mood to argue with you, Rosemary,' and she knew that tone of voice, which always made her shrink inside. She got out of the car and looked around her.

She didn't really like the countryside. She didn't understand it, with its silence and its emptiness and the way people fussed about things like the view and the trees and cows. And she'd been crying all the way from London and she couldn't see very much because her eyes were all swollen. But when Daddy said, 'Isn't this grand?' Rosemary nodded and said it was grand.

Daddy held her hand as they went into the house. It smelled like all the schools she had been to, of floor polish and cooking and the rubber boots lined up in the hallway. The smiling nun took them to see the Mother Superior in her office.

'This is Rosemary,' Daddy said.

Mother Isabel took one look at Rosemary and asked, 'Have you been crying, Rosemary?'

Rosemary didn't say anything but Daddy said, 'She's having a very emotional time lately. I'm afraid we've been asking far too much of her.

Engagements, appearances, dances. The embassy is a very public place. The press never leave her alone. There's a lot of pressure.'

Mother Isabel nodded sympathetically. She was old but you could tell right away she wasn't one to be messed around with. 'Oh yes. Of course, Rosemary's face is already familiar to us from the newspapers. It's natural that they would take an interest in such a lovely young woman, but the attention must be difficult.'

'Very difficult.'

'Your life will be much quieter here, Rosemary,' Mother Isabel said, touching Rosemary on the shoulder. 'You'll find it very much more peaceful than London. But I promise you won't be lonely or bored here.'

'I don't want to be here,' Rosemary sobbed. 'I want to be with Daddy.'

Mother Isabel had a box of Pond's tissues on her desk, perhaps because a lot of people cried in this room. She pulled one out with a little pop and gave it to Rosemary to staunch the tears that were pouring down her cheeks. 'Daddy will be only an hour's drive away.'

'I'll see you every weekend, Rosie.'

'And you'll be much safer here than in London,' Mother Isabel went on, 'now that the war has started.'

'I don't want to be in school any more,' Rosemary said in a loud wail.

Mother Isabel opened her eyes very wide. 'Oh, but my dear, you're not *in school* any more. Belmont House is a teacher training college. Didn't you know that?'

'You're going to be a teacher, Rosie,' Daddy said. 'It's what you've always wanted, isn't it?'

Rosemary stared at her shoes but she stopped crying.

'It's the start of a new life for you,' Daddy said. 'No more stress. No more strain.'

'We'll expect you to work hard,' Mother Isabel said. 'But we find that working with children is one of God's gifts. There is no more rewarding occupation. Your father tells me that you love children?'

Rosemary sniffled. 'Yes.'

'All those who love children are loved by them in return,' Mother Isabel said. 'But there are some individuals who are blessed with a special gift, because they are especially close to childhood. Something tells me that you are one of these, Rosemary.'

She looked up at last, blotting her nose. 'I do love children.'

Mother Isabel smiled in a way that reminded Rosemary of the statues of Mary. 'It's a sacred love. It's not like any other kind of love. It's pure. Divine. Other kinds of love can bring us pain. They can bring us to sin, terrible sin, mortal sin. But God's divine love can wash away that sin. And God's love is so often channelled through His little ones. Do you understand, Rosemary?'

Rosemary knew that Mother Isabel was talking about Cubby. She felt her mouth twist into a sullen shape. She missed Cubby terribly. And he hadn't even written. She groped in her pocket for her cigarettes and put one in her mouth.

'We don't allow smoking at Belmont House,' Mother Isabel said, her voice changing slightly, just enough to show that she was displeased. 'We'll have to ask you to get rid of that particular habit.'

'Perhaps you might make an exception for Rosie,' Daddy said quickly. 'She finds the habit very relaxing. Maybe she could be allowed to smoke in the garden? I know she'd appreciate that dispensation. And I'd be personally very grateful.'

Mother Isabel thought about that for a moment. 'Very well,' she said, folding her hands. 'We don't want to impose unnecessary hardships on Rosemary. But not in the building, if you please.' She took the cigarette from Rosemary's lips deftly and dropped it in the wastepaper basket. 'Your father tells me you will soon have your twenty-first birthday.'

Rosemary nodded, looking longingly at the cigarette which lay in the trash.

'We'll arrange something special for that. It won't pass unmarked.' She pressed a bell on her desk. 'I'm going to ask Sister Clare to show you around while your father and I have a little talk.'

But while they waited for Sister Clare, Mother Isabel and Daddy started their little talk anyway, with their voices lowered, as though she couldn't hear what they were saying.

'Now, Mother Isabel,' Daddy said, 'you just let me know how I can help you here at Belmont House. I'd like to show my gratitude in any way I can.'

'We always need help, Mr Kennedy. I could give you a list as long as your arm.'

Daddy stuck his hand out, grinning. 'As you can see, I have long arms, Mother Isabel.'

Mother Isabel laughed. Daddy was tall. 'Well, let's see whether Rosemary is going to be happy here.'

'I have a feeling that Rosemary is going to be very happy here.'

'Belmont House is a happy place, Mr Kennedy. Our Benedictine brothers say *Ora et Labora*.'

'"Pray and work".'

'Exactly. We believe that work is the best kind of prayer. We also believe that keeping young people fully occupied is the best way to keep them on the straight and narrow and avoid divagations into sin.'

'I couldn't agree more.'

'For a young woman with Rosemary's difficulties – and perhaps weaknesses as well – filling every hour of every day is of the utmost importance. It keeps the mind occupied. And the influence of children cannot be overestimated. They guide us surely and effortlessly to God. Their innocence is often the best medicine for a guilty heart, and their laughter the best medicine for a heavy one.'

'Amen to that. I have nine, myself.'

'Needless to say, you may rest easy that here at Belmont House, Rosemary will be well protected from the outside world. She will not be receiving any' – Mother Isabel glanced at Rosemary – 'callers such as you would not wish her to receive.'

'That's very important to us.'

'May I ask how serious the – ah – problem was?'

'It seems they were seeing each other as often as they could.'

'By *seeing each other* you mean—'

'All the way, yes.'

'And emotionally?'

'Well,' Daddy said, also glancing at Rosemary, 'she doesn't have the emotional capacity for very deep feelings. I think it was more physical than anything else. She's not a child any more, if you get my point.'

'I do, indeed. You may feel that the damage has been done, in that regard. But our experience is that there is no damage which cannot be healed. We'll get her mind off' – she waved her hand – 'certain topics. And we'll direct her thoughts to higher ones. Whatever can be keeping Sister Clare?' She pressed the bell again.

'Her mother and I are also concerned about her weight,' Daddy said, looking at Rosemary critically. 'She's much too fond of sweet things. She's gotten herself much too fat. It attracts unwanted attention. We're hoping you can do something about that.'

'We certainly can. We'll make sure—'

But Rosemary never got to hear the rest of that, because the smiling nun finally appeared and took her off to tour the school. As soon as she was out of Mother Isabel's office, she lit a cigarette and inhaled deeply. The nun's smile faded.

'What are *you* looking at?' Rosemary demanded.

The Solent

The *Manhattan* sailed promptly at six. Every ship in Southampton, including the troop transports that were themselves preparing to leave for France, sounded horns, steam whistles or sirens. The unearthly chorus sounded to those on board like wails of woe and despair, despite the customary carnival of streamers and confetti that trailed from the high decks of the liner, fragile links with shore that were soon torn apart, joining the debris in the water.

Masha Morgenstern felt as though her heart were being torn out of her. Unable to watch the docks receding behind *Manhattan*, she left Rachel waving at the rail, and clung to the huge trumpet of a ventilator intake, pressing her face against the cold metal. She would never see her parents again.

She felt a hand on her arm, and looked up blearily. It was Thomas, his face twisted in sympathy.

'Oh, Thomas,' she blurted out, 'this world is a travesty, a travesty.' She drew his head on to her breast and held him tightly.

As the great liner steamed down the Solent, Cubby Hubbard hunted for a sight of Rosemary Kennedy. He pushed his way through the emotional throngs of people on every deck, craning to see over the hats (he was not a very tall young man). He knew that the Kennedys were keeping to their stateroom. One of the stewards had told him that. He'd heard nothing from Rosemary for days. He was concerned. He knew that her mother would have made her life difficult, and Rosemary didn't respond well to having her life made difficult. He wanted badly to see her.

At last, leaning back over the rail on the lower deck, he got a glimpse of Luella Hennessey, the family nanny. She was on the deck above him, waving a handkerchief. Beside her was Patricia, Rosemary's younger sister. Cubby made for the companionway which connected the two decks, but the going was difficult. The stairs were jammed with people who blocked his ascent. He was breathless and dishevelled by the time he got to the First Class deck.

He glimpsed Pat Kennedy's blue woollen beret at the rail, and fought his way over to her. He managed to elbow himself a place beside her. *Manhattan* uttered a deep, bone-jarring blast on her horn. The docks were already a mile away up Southampton water.

'Where's Rosemary?' he asked in a low voice.

Pat turned to Cubby in surprise. She stared at him, her mouth half-open, but didn't answer.

'Is she okay?' Cubby demanded.

Pat shook her head slightly. Her freckled face was pinched with the cold. She looked frightened. 'No. She's—'

Luella Hennessey, now aware of Cubby's presence, took Pat's arm and pulled her away before she could say anything more. Cubby called after her, but apart from a last glance over her shoulder, Pat was helpless. Cubby leaned on the rail, biting his lip in frustration as he watched them disappear into the crowd.

As *Manhattan* turned west, Commodore Randall was on the bridge, his binoculars to his eyes, watching the horizon.

'Heard the news from France, George?' he asked his first officer.

'Yes, Sir.'

'If France falls, the Germans will control the Atlantic coast from Brest to Bordeaux. They'll be hundreds of miles closer to Allied shipping lanes. They'll build airfields and U-boat bases all the way along the Channel.'

'It'll be the end of Southampton, Plymouth and Portsmouth. The south coast ports will be far too dangerous to use. Shipping will have to use Liverpool or even Glasgow instead.'

'And what's more, the Germans will be perfectly poised for an invasion of Britain.'

George Symonds nodded. 'It's a bad lookout, Commodore.'

Randall grunted like a walrus, lowering his binoculars. 'I'm retiring at the end of this trip. I don't mind telling you, I'm damn glad to be getting out, too.'

Arturo Toscanini was at *Manhattan*'s stern, looking down at the ship's wake.

He reached into the pocket of his overcoat and took out the sheaf of letters that Carla had brought him from Kastanienbaum. Ada's letters, bound together by a length of purple ribbon, the ribbon from her slip which he'd begged her to give him after they'd made love for the first time.

He had read them all over the past two days, often with his heart pounding. So much passion! So much feeling!

Toscanini relaxed his fingers slowly. There had been others before Ada. But she—

She had been the love of his life. Ah, that cliché on the lips of every cheap Romeo. *The love of my life*. But when you considered it, when you really understood it, it was a sentence pronounced by the most terrible of judges, echoing down the barren years that remained.

He raised the letters to his nose, trying to catch the scent of Ada's perfume over the salty wind that buffeted him. There! The faintest, sweetest trace of *violette di Parma*. He inhaled it deeply into his lungs, and then with a groan threw the sheaf of letters away from him. The purple knot unravelled; the letters tumbled in the wind like dying doves, spiralling down into the churning maelstrom of the liner's wake. For a moment there was a flash of purple silk in the foam, a scattering of dainty envelopes; and then the correspondence was sucked into the deep and gone forever.

Carla Toscanini was in her little cabin, breakfasting off toast and coffee. She had never adopted the Anglo-Saxon custom of a cooked breakfast; and in any case, there was her figure to think of. If she put on any more weight, she would have nothing to wear. And she couldn't be bothered to go back into corsets.

She hadn't seen her husband for two days, though the stewards told her he tramped the decks ceaselessly. That frenetic engine inside Artú beat with greater energy than ever; but the housing was growing frailer, and one day the engine was going to shake it all to pieces, and that would be the end of Arturo Toscanini.

Why had she not suspected Ada, thirty years younger than Artú, and with all the right qualifications? Perhaps because Ada's husband had been young and handsome, and Italy's foremost cellist. She should have remembered that Artú could conquer any woman, and feared no rival, no matter how young and handsome. Mainardi must have known. Perhaps he had been compliant, even complicit? The tyrant Toscanini subjugated men as easily as women. He was demoniac.

The word *genius*, so often thrown carelessly at Artú, had a dark shadow that few people considered. To the ancients it meant the god that ruled each person's life and passions and appetites. The greater the genius, the greater the appetites. And the more implacable the rule. Artú's genius was a monster. If one were to see it as it really was, it would not be a little man with white hair. It would be a towering, horned thing, rampant, destructive, mad.

That was perhaps what his adoring public really worshipped, if the truth were known. Not the music, but the madness.

The children, of course, knew more than she did. They saw what she preferred to close her eyes to. As one of them said, 'Papà casts his net wide.'

Did Artú have no scruples? There had been a line in one of Ada's letters that had stuck in Carla's mind:

You write that your conscience is always fighting with your will, that you hate yourself, are disgusted with yourself! But my darling—

Perhaps he felt remorse, from time to time, when the horned thing was exhausted. But not enough to bring him back to sanity. And one could not live with a madman.

She was sixty-two now. At sixty-two, her own mother had been an old woman, already dying. But times had changed. A woman of sixty-two these days was not yet old. There was still enjoyment left in life, for all the tragedies that had beset her – the death of her own child and those of her sister, the ravages among the family of drug addiction and cancer.

Out from under Artú's shadow, she could live a little before the end came. Enjoy what was left of her life. Take refuge from the storm. And find some peace.

Fanny Ward, the Perennial Flapper, had eaten nothing as yet, though her hamper still contained most of the cold chicken and half the game pie. She had remained in her bunk, with the silk sheets (she had brought her own on board) pulled over her head during the noisy departure from Southampton. She hadn't wanted to see or hear any of it. It was far too painful.

She got up now and went to her window, opening the curtain cautiously. She peered out, anxious that she might still catch a glimpse of the country she was leaving with so much sorrow. To her dismay, there was still land to be seen: chalky white cliffs gleaming in the watery sunshine, with a sparse green topping; chalky white rocks sticking out of the sea like a few last teeth; a chalky white lighthouse, painted with fading red stripes.

She stared blankly at these things, feeling the dull ache in her heart. At least there were no towns, no signs of humanity to be seen. She was leaving behind half her life, and she had a deep foreboding that she would never return to it again. All her lovely things, some of them priceless, now stored in a sandbagged basement. Her friends, her life, her peace, all gone.

Sighing, she drew the curtains closed and set about the long task of preparing herself to face the day.

Young Teddy Kennedy was fascinated by the little people. They were called Hoffman's Midget Marvels. There were eight of them, and they were holding court in the Observation Lounge, seated in a group on a banquette so they could be photographed. They were all dressed fashionably, four miniature ladies and four miniature gentlemen, and their miniature suitcases had been arranged around them for extra effect. None of them were any bigger than Teddy himself, and he was only seven. The smallest was so tiny that their manager, Mr Harry Hoffman (in a jacket with very wide shoulders and smiling very widely) was bouncing him on his knee. Although he was tiny, you could see that he was really quite old, older than the manager, with a face like a wizened apple, and he looked cross at being bounced, which made everyone laugh even more.

Teddy took a photo with his Brownie while the midget men all lifted their hats and the midget ladies all crossed their legs. Some of the ladies were very pretty. Their manager explained that they were en route to the World's Fair in New York, where they would live in Little Miracle City, a whole midget town, with midget houses fitted with midget furniture and kitchens.

'Come visit them there, ladies and gentlemen, boys and girls. You can walk around their tiny town, and see them living their lives, just like real people. Tell all your friends.'

Teddy wanted to get closer and take a photo of the prettiest of the midget ladies, but his mother stopped him and said she didn't think the whole thing was very nice at all. He was reluctant to be pulled away. He asked his mother if they could go to the World's Fair and see the midgets there, and she said that they could certainly go to the World's Fair, but there were much more interesting things to be seen than human beings put on show like performing monkeys. She said it was on a par with tattooed ladies and sword swallowers. Teddy wanted to see a tattooed lady, and looked around carefully, but there weren't any to be seen.

Igor Stravinsky sat with his head in his hands on the edge of his bunk. Katharine sat beside him, with her arm around his shoulders. Despite his long struggle, he had finally given in to the desolation inside him. He felt that his irony and worldliness had sloughed off him like the dry skin of some reptile, leaving him emotionally naked, unable to continue the masquerade.

'Everything is finished,' he whispered. 'You are right, Katharine. It's the end. The end of art, the end of music, the end of everything that matters. The end of me. I cannot express the anguish I feel.'

'You'll recover, Igor.' She rocked him, feeling how frail his body had become. He was all bones. He smelled sick. 'Everything will get better, you'll see. You'll start composing again. As for the war, they can't possibly win. The world won't let them win.'

'The world has let them win before, these people. Over and over again.'

'America won't let it happen this time. There's a new life waiting for you there.'

'I'm too old to begin again.'

'You feel like that now, but you're exhausted, grieving. You'll get strong again. There's so much life in you, Igor. Don't give up.'

Commodore Randall had warned the passengers that they might be heading into some bad weather once they had called in at Cobh. The more experienced travellers prepared by lining up in the deckchairs along the sunny side of the ship to soak up all the warmth they could, their chins lifted to catch what solar rays there were, their legs wrapped in rugs.

There was strong competition for the deckchairs on the over-crowded *Manhattan*. Miss Fanny Ward, who had taken the wise precaution of slipping Mr Nightingale a five-dollar note beforehand, was one of the fortunate ones. He conducted her to a prime spot, sheltered from the wind, yet catching the full benefit of the hazy sun.

Miss Ward stretched out carefully on the deckchair, trying to ease her knees into position without too much clicking and creaking. An unwise movement would have her hobbling for a week. Mr Nightingale got the cushions behind her head just the way she liked them, adjusting the rug gently around her feet. She half-expected him to kiss her tenderly on the forehead before leaving. They had sailed together many times.

She had slept badly the night before. She closed her eyes behind the dark sunglasses, composing her mind for a morning nap. Irritatingly, however, the child on the deckchair beside her was singing 'Some Day My Prince Will Come', a song which Miss Ward particularly detested. She tried to shut out the piping voice in vain. It continued, thin and true, to the end of the song, and then began again.

Miss Ward sat up to look severely at the child. She found herself staring at a little girl of considerable beauty, around seven years old, with a cloud of dark hair and large, lilac-blue eyes. She stopped singing, and looked back at Miss Ward from under impossibly thick eyelashes.

'Am I annoying you?' the child asked with adult composure.

'It's not my favourite song,' Miss Ward said.

'It's *my* favourite song,' the child replied. 'It's from *Snow White and the Seven Dwarfs*.'

'Yes, I know that.'

'Have you seen it?'

'No.'

'*I've* seen it three times. And they've got it in the ship's cinema. So I'm going to see it again.'

'Each to his own,' Miss Ward replied.

'I'm going to be a film star,' the child volunteered.

Miss Ward settled back down again and closed her eyes. 'Good luck to you.'

'I'm going to America to do a screen test for Paramount.'

Miss Ward sighed. 'What's your name, child?'

'Elizabeth Taylor.'

'Well, Elizabeth Taylor, what makes you think you're going to get a screen test with Paramount?'

'It's all arranged,' the child said calmly. 'It might be MGM. Louis B. Meyer wants me especially. It could be Universal. But I'd rather it was Paramount.'

This made Miss Ward sit up again. The child was strangely convincing in the matter-of-fact way she spoke of the great Hollywood studios. Miss Ward studied her more carefully. She was a ravishing little thing with an upturned nose and a look of the young Vivien Leigh about her. 'You'd rather it were Paramount, eh?'

'Yes.'

'Is your father arranging all this?'

'My mother *and* my father. That's them, over there.' She pointed to an attractive young couple who were leaning on the rail, the man taking photographs of the woman, who was posing with her straw hat dangling from her hand. 'My brother's coming, too. I can sing and dance. I've been to Madame Vacani's school of ballet.'

'Have you indeed.'

'She said I had star quality.'

'I can see that.'

'I'm not sure whether to be a film star or an actress.'

'I'm an actress myself, you know,' Miss Ward offered.

Elizabeth Taylor looked at her with incredulous violet eyes, but was too polite to express open disbelief. 'Oh really?'

'Yes. My name is Fanny Ward. I've been in thirty films.'

'What films?'

'You wouldn't have seen them.' As it happened, her most famous films had been made in the silent era, and were now as dead as the dodo.

'*I'm* going to be in lots of films,' Elizabeth replied, unimpressed.

'I imagine you will,' Miss Ward said dryly. The child had beauty, self-confidence and presence. In a film industry which fawned on child stars, and promoted them relentlessly, young Elizabeth had a decent chance of success. But Miss Ward wondered whether her handsome, confident parents knew what a hard road lay ahead of the child. How much sorrow and disappointment would she endure in her life? How many times would the studios chew her up and spit her out before every vestige of happiness had been sucked out of her? And then, when she was no longer a child, would she join the long list of forgotten infant prodigies in alcoholic homes?

Approaching the end of her own career, Miss Ward felt she should have some words of wisdom for this hopeful, starting out on the rocky road to the heights. But there was nothing she could say that would be believed, or wouldn't be instantly forgotten. She felt worn and sad. Without another word, she put her sunglasses back on and lay back down. Beside her, Elizabeth Taylor continued singing 'Some Day My Prince Will Come'.

In their cabin, Rachel was trying to console Masha. They were together on one of the bunks, Masha lying back against Rachel, with her aching head pillowed on Rachel's shoulder. Rachel held her tight, kissing her temple.

'Don't cry any more, Masha. You're exhausted.'

'I can't stop thinking about Mama and Papa. Don't you think about yours?'

'Yes, of course, my dear.'

'Then why don't you cry too?'

'I suppose,' Rachel replied slowly, 'because I had already parted from them.'

'I said goodbye to Mama and Papa in Bremen. But I always thought I would see them again.'

'My parting with my parents was some years ago,' Rachel said quietly, 'and of a more definitive nature. We've seen very little of each other since then.'

'Was it because of this love affair of yours?'

'Yes, it was.'

'I'm sorry, darling. I didn't know.' Masha pressed the palms of her hands against her swollen eyelids. 'I shouldn't have tried to pry into something so painful.'

'It's all right.' Rachel gently took Masha's hands away from her eyes to stop her rubbing them. 'Her name was Dorothea.'

'Whose name was Dorothea?' Masha asked tiredly.

'The person you have been so curious to know about.'

Masha was puzzled for a moment. Then she sat up and peered at her cousin closely. 'A *woman*?'

'Yes, a woman.'

Masha gasped. 'Rachel!'

'She was older than I, an assistant teacher at the conservatory, which of course made it all far worse.'

'Are you telling me that you are a—' Masha stopped herself before uttering the word.

Rachel nodded. 'Ever since I can remember, I've known I was what you cannot bring yourself to name. Now you understand why your family thought I was a danger to you. Are you appalled?'

'How can I be appalled when I love you so?' Masha asked. 'But – don't you like men?'

'As a class, you mean? I don't dislike them. But I cannot desire them.'

'Perhaps you just haven't met the right one, yet,' Masha said innocently.

'I think it goes a little deeper than that,' Rachel replied, her tone light.

'Did something happen to you to make you this way?'

'What should have happened to me, Masha?'

'I don't know – a bad experience with a man, perhaps.'

Rachel smiled a little wearily. 'Do you think that's what makes us one thing or another? A bad experience?'

'Sometimes it does, I'm sure.'

'Not in my case. I never had any confusion about myself or what I wanted. Do you think I don't feel the same tenderness you do? The same yearning, the same desire – the same love? I longed for my Dorothea long before I knew she existed. And when she entered my life, I thanked God for her.'

'I don't know what to say.'

'Trust me,' Rachel replied wryly, 'everything that could be said on the matter has already been said a thousand times. My ears are still ringing with it. My father even took me to the celebrated Professor Freud in Vienna, which by the way was very expensive, in the hopes that I could be cured by psychoanalysis.'

'What did Professor Freud say?'

'He said that I was incurable. In the sense that I did not need to be cured. He said that my condition was neither an illness nor a neurotic conflict, and that eliminating my feelings was not possible or desirable. I liked him very much, as a matter of fact. To be spoken to like a human being was worth whatever it cost my father.' She made a bitter face. 'Naturally, that didn't please *him*. It did nothing to soothe his outrage to be told by the great Sigmund Freud that my disgusting perversion, as my father called it, was innate biology.'

'Oh, Rachel. How awful.'

'Freud told him, in my presence, that in most cases, any "cure" achieved is just a superficial compliance to avoid conflict. I added that I wasn't the bravest woman on earth, but that I had enough courage not to pretend to be something I was not. So we went back to Leipzig no happier than we left it.'

'And your friend – Dorothea?'

'They tried to forbid me from seeing her of course. And then the Nazis expelled me from the conservatory anyway, because I was a Jew, so it seemed that was that. But I found I couldn't live without Dorothea.

I left my father's house, and got work, and we set up in a small apartment together.'

'That sounds so cosy,' Masha said wistfully.

'We were very happy for a while, even though our families disowned us both. But as you once put it, the darkness came swiftly. It started to become obvious that I couldn't continue to live in Germany. Like you, I had a brush with the Gestapo which left me bruised in body and soul. I always had difficulty in keeping my mouth shut. My parents decided that, wicked as I was, they would help me to emigrate. Of course, I refused their help at first – but it was Dorothea herself who persuaded me to go in the end.'

'And she stayed behind?'

'It broke my heart to leave her,' Rachel said calmly. 'It breaks my heart every morning to awaken without her beside me. She had planned to join me in America, once she got her visa, but now that the war has begun, I don't know whether we'll ever see one another again. We parted four months ago in Leipzig, and I've heard almost nothing from her since then.'

Masha touched her cousin's hand timidly. 'I'm so sorry. How much you've kept inside, Rachel. I wish you'd confided in me before.'

'One never knows how people will react.'

'Did you think I would be disgusted?'

'I thought you might be alarmed.' The corners of Rachel's eyes lifted for a moment in that secret smile. 'When other women find out, I often see a look of trepidation on their faces. Perhaps they think I might pounce on them like a hungry lioness. But I assure you, you're safe from me.'

Masha kissed her. 'Of course I am. How could I think otherwise? You don't want anybody except your Dorothea.'

'You're right, I should have spoken earlier. But I've learned to live inside myself, Masha. I live a concealed life. I've had to hide what I was, not only from society at large, and especially from the Nazis, to whom

I am an abomination, but from my own family. I've grown some sharp corners as a result. I'm like one of those suits of armour one sees in museums, all spikes and uncomfortable protrusions. I know that. I'm very glad you've learned to put up with me.'

'I'll do much better from now on,' Masha said. 'And I know you will find Dorothea again, when all this is over.'

Rachel shrugged. 'If the Nazis neglect to send her to a camp. And the British neglect to drop a bomb on her. I don't entertain hopes. I've learned not to.'

'Don't talk like that.' Masha, who had found some distraction from her grief in these intriguing revelations, settled herself among the pillows. 'Tell me about her. Don't hold anything back!'

'What is it you want to know?'

'I'm sure she's beautiful. Tell me what she looks like.'

'I don't know whether you'd think her beautiful,' Rachel said reflectively. 'She is to me, but most others think her plain. She's tall and slender. She wears round-rimmed glasses which she hates to take off because her eyesight is poor. Her hair is the same colour as yours, and very long. She usually wears it braided and coiled around her head in the old-fashioned German style, but when she lets it loose, it hangs all the way down her back.'

'She sounds very interesting.'

'She's a brilliant musicologist. She was assigned to me as my music theory tutor in my first year. I hadn't paid her too much attention at first – I was a sulky girl in those days, and stared at my shoes most of the time. But the first time we were alone together in her room, I saw her properly at last. She seemed to me like—'

'Like what?' Masha demanded as Rachel hesitated.

'Like a perfect, unopened seashell that one finds on a beach. I couldn't take my eyes off her while she talked about pitch, duration, rhythm and tempo. She noticed me staring at her. I saw her face suddenly flush to a deep pink, like a musk-rose. It was the most extraordinary transformation. Her eyes became liquid. I saw her lips swell and grow moist. She had become beautiful in a moment. And I, for my part, felt I had come alive for the first time in years.'

'I've had that feeling,' Masha whispered. 'So you knew at once?'

'I knew,' Rachel agreed. 'But we continued in the same way for a few weeks, I sitting there staring at her, she enduring my stare with her colour coming and going every few minutes. The tension was unbearable. And yet I was deliriously happy inside. And it was I who made the first move.'

'What did you do?'

'I waited until the end of the tutorial one day, and then I said to her, "I've been longing to kiss you since the moment I saw you."'

Masha leaned forward breathlessly. 'You were so bold! Did she allow you to kiss her?'

'Not then. After all, she was older and wiser – and far more cautious – than I. She had a great deal more to lose. Her position, her reputation. I was eighteen, and ready to burst out of my skin. She simply gathered her books and hurried out of the room.'

'How disappointing!'

'Not altogether. I'd seen the look on her face. And I wasn't about to give up. Once I set my heart on something, I usually get it.' Rachel smiled. 'I am a lioness, after all.'

'You pursued her?'

'I pursued and stalked and laid in wait. I left flowers on her desk. I told her what I wanted with my eyes. I sat close to her in the concert hall. I followed her everywhere, up the marble staircases, in the cloisters, in the refectory. I pushed my bicycle behind her in the street. It was autumn, and she wore a long, English houndstooth coat that drove me wild with desire. The smell of burning leaves is forever associated in my mind with that period. She fled from me, but she looked over her shoulder. And at last—'

'At last—?'

'At last she was mine.'

'What was it like, the first time?' Masha demanded.

'As to that, my dear, you will have to use your imagination.'

'You can't stop there!'

'I can and I will. And you are exhausted. You need to sleep.'

'How do you expect me to sleep now?' Masha complained.

'I think you'll find it easier than you think.' She held out her arms.

Masha, still protesting, sank against her cousin's breast and was enfolded. And despite her reluctance, as Rachel had predicted, sleep came on swift wings.

Cubby Hubbard had thought it over and thought he had a pretty good idea of what 'your cock, my tail' had meant, and it wasn't very nice; but whatever it meant, it meant that Mr Nightingale was an easy-going sort of guy who could be approached with a proposition. He grabbed the steward's arm as he flitted past.

'Say, Mr Nightingale—'

'Yes, Mr Hubbard?'

'If I needed to get a message to a passenger, could you deliver it?'

The steward put a manicured finger archly to his cheek. 'That depends on the passenger.'

'It's Miss Rosemary Kennedy. She's in First Class.'

'And why would you be sending messages to Miss Kennedy?' Mr Nightingale asked suspiciously.

'We're engaged to be married. We're crazy about each other. But her family don't approve of me. They don't think I'm good enough for her. They're trying to keep us apart. I know she's on board, but I haven't seen her once since we left Southampton. I'm pretty sure they're keeping her locked up in her cabin. She'll be desperate to hear from me. If I could just get a note to her, telling her I love her, and that we'll see each other in New York—'

Mr Nightingale's guarded expression had softened during the recital of this fairy-tale account. 'Well, Mr Hubbard, I have to say that's very romantic and all, but . . .' He paused as Cubby discreetly slipped the note he'd written, plus a five-dollar bill into his top pocket. 'But now that you come to mention it, I'm going to be in First Class this afternoon. I'll see what I can do. Leave it with me.'

Carrying hundreds of extra passengers as she was, *Manhattan* was slow to feed her charges. Dinner began early and finished late. In the First Class dining room (which was panelled in American oak, and studded for some reason with the huge heads of buffalo, elk, moose, grizzly bear and caribou) the tables were still crowded, though it was close to midnight.

Families with children and the elderly had eaten early and gone their ways. As the evening progressed, the dining room filled with more glamorous diners. Men in evening jackets and women in long gowns came in from the bar, laughing, trailing the scents of expensive perfume and cigars, sparkling with diamonds. These were passengers of the upper crust, people who moved in the same circles, knew each other, and knew what was what.

At the Commodore's table, in the centre of the dining room, the crème de la crème had gathered. The party included Fanny Ward, the Eternal Beauty, Mrs Joseph Kennedy, the wife of the American ambassador; and Madame Quo Tai-Chi, the plump and pretty young wife of the Chinese ambassador.

The two ambassadresses, of course, were well acquainted with one another, though there was not a great deal of warmth between them. Mrs Kennedy privately considered Madame Quo Tai-Chi rather a coarse little woman, though she had supposedly written a book on Chinese art. In London she had presented a fulsomely inscribed copy to Mrs Kennedy, which Mrs Kennedy thought showed far too many airs and graces.

Nor had she forgiven Madame Quo for the public humiliation of a gala dinner given at the mansion in Portland Place, at which Chinese dishes had been served – with *chopsticks*. After watching Mrs Kennedy struggling with these primitive implements, Madame Quo had scuttled round the table and – with everybody laughing and applauding, including the malicious Russian Ambassador, Maisky – assisted her to eat, positively ladling noodles into her mouth like a mother with a messy child.

For her part, Madame Quo regarded the entire American administration, and most particularly its representative, Joseph P. Kennedy, as a gang of loathsome hypocrites. Savaged for a decade by Japanese aggression, which had wrested away the vast resources of Manchuria, China had been begging America and Britain in vain for help. Even now, her husband was pleading with His Majesty's government to stop selling guns and planes to the Japanese, guns and planes which had already killed hundreds of thousands of Chinese.

'What an enchanting outfit, Madame Quo,' Mrs Kennedy said.

Madame Quo's cheongsam was pale pink, piped in crimson and embroidered all over with silver thread. 'It required six months to make,' Madame Quo said, accepting the tribute with a gracious nod. But she did not return the compliment. That was one up to Madame Quo. Mrs Kennedy was aware that she'd made a mistake with the black dress tonight, which showed her shoulders; once she'd taken off her stole, she felt dowdy, cold and skinny. 'You're travelling with your children, Mrs Kennedy?'

'With three of them.'

'You have so many, of course. Thirteen, isn't it?'

Mrs Kennedy smiled thinly. 'Nine.' Madame Quo had two boys, *Merlin*, if you please, and Edward.

'How is your daughter Rosemary?' Madame Quo asked, toying with one of her spectacular jade earrings, which were a vivid green and no doubt ancient and priceless, unless they came from Hong Kong. 'Such an original young lady.' She accompanied this with a pitying smile on her smooth face, indicating that 'original' was intended in this context to signify 'crazy as a coot'.

'She's doing extremely well,' Mrs Kennedy said robustly. 'She has just qualified as a nursery school teacher. She loves the little ones.'

'Ah,' Madame Quo said sympathetically, turning her head to toy with the earring on the other side. 'My sons and I are heading to Tucson. We always spend the winter in Arizona. Such a perfect winter climate.'

This gave Mrs Kennedy a much-needed opening. 'Oh it is, it is. By a coincidence, we met the lady from whom you rented a house last year, Mrs Robert G. Nelson. A charming person.'

Madame Quo nodded blandly at this sally, though it must have stung. The Mrs Robert G. Nelson in question had won damages of several hundred dollars against Madame Quo for stolen silverware, broken china, and the house left in a disgusting state. So much for Chinese culture.

Mrs Kennedy turned her back on Madame Quo and addressed herself to Fanny Ward, who was painted like a doll, and wearing an extraordinary garment of luridly flowered silk, gathered in a jewelled knot right over her you-know-what, as though anyone were still interested in *that*.

'I was so sad to say goodbye to their Majesties. They told me that they intend to remain in London, whatever happens.'

Miss Ward was looking glazed. She had already spent a couple of hours in the bar, hoisting back gin and tonics. She nodded a little too vigorously now, making the feathers in her extraordinary headdress dance. It contained what must surely be real diamonds, and was perched on top of what must surely be a wig, a very unconvincing one. 'Not lacking in courage,' she said, enunciating very distinctly. 'And the dear girls. Wanting to do their part, they told me. A beacon of inspiration.'

'I presume there are air-raid shelters in Buckingham Palace?'

'Basements. Lots of them,' Miss Ward agreed, her feathers nodding. Her famous eyes, heavily ringed with mascara, were bloodshot oysters tonight. Perhaps she'd been crying, or trying too hard not to. 'So brave. Not running away, like us.'

'*I* am not running away,' Madame Quo said sharply. 'I always spend the winter in Arizona. I shall be back to London in the spring.'

'Nonsense,' Miss Ward said. 'Why should you? Not your war.'

'It is very much our war. For us it began in 1931. Manchuria, Shanghai, Nanking. Ten million Chinese are dead. Your turn, now. The Japanese are already preparing to attack America and Britain.'

'Now, now, no warmongering,' Mrs Kennedy said.

'You would be a fool not to know that's true,' Madame Quo retorted, 'and I don't believe you are a fool, Mrs Kennedy.'

A four-piece jazz orchestra had been setting up in a corner of the room, and the waiters had been clearing tables away in front of the bandstand. The musicians now struck up 'Begin the Beguine', a clarinet taking the lead.

'They're playing for their passage,' Commodore Randall said. 'Refugees, all four of them. Apparently Herr Hitler doesn't approve of their kind of music.'

Diners abandoned their food to dance. The syrupy melody lines stopped conversation for a while. Couples glided to and fro under the glowering gaze of the great land-animals whose heads were mounted above them.

'I wonder,' Miss Ward said brightly, 'if their bodies are on the other side.'

'Whose bodies?' Mrs Kennedy asked.

'Those bison and moose and things. We should go and have a look.'

'Your husband,' Madame Quo went on, 'has been singing the same song for years, Mrs Kennedy. Peace in our time, and all that. But it's the wrong song now. The gospel of isolationism is dead. It died in 1917.'

Mrs Kennedy looked at Madame Quo with dislike. 'You know I can't comment on American policy,' she said stiffly.

'He's not only out of step with the British government, but with your own State Department. Fawning on Hitler, egging on Neville Chamberlain and all those smart Nazi sympathisers at Cliveden.'

Mrs Kennedy's lean cheeks were flushed. 'I don't intend to sit here and be scolded by you.'

'You must scold your husband. He can't go around loudly insisting that Hitler is going to win this war. Nothing could be more distasteful in an American ambassador. And he's setting himself in direct opposition to your President.'

'I suppose you know just what our President thinks,' she snapped.

'Everyone knows what your President thinks.'

'Wanting to commit another whole generation of young men to the fire? To save a rotten old house that ought to be pulled down?'

'I understand that history impels you Irish to consider Great Britain a hated enemy, Mrs Kennedy. But I assure you, you would find the Nazis a great deal worse. They're rotten too, but in quite a different way.'

'I've had enough.'

'Your husband is committing political suicide,' Madame Quo said as Mrs Kennedy rose. 'He's going to be sent back to Washington in disgrace if he doesn't change his tune.'

Stony-faced, Mrs Kennedy swept up her stole and stalked out of the dining room, ignoring the others at the table. Being lectured by that little woman was too much to bear.

She walked along the promenade deck, trying to cool the heat out of her face. There were too many things to bear. Unhappiness and worry weighed on her intolerably.

What to do with Rosemary. Joe's diplomatic career heading for the rocks, along with the whole damned country. The looming war. The dreadful prospect of the boys enlisting.

Was Madame Quo right? There were others who said the same things. After everything Joe had done for Roosevelt! They had courted Roosevelt for two decades, raising millions for his campaigns, preaching the Roosevelt doctrine, even sending planeloads of live crabs and lobsters to the White House. But as was the way with politicians, Roosevelt would drop Joe in a heartbeat if it was expedient. And Madame Quo had been right in one thing, at least: it was becoming expedient to drop Joe.

She hurried back to her cabin to call her husband.

Cobh

Manhattan sailed into Cobh harbour with a long blast of her horn. The call echoed around the foggy little town, rebounding from the towering bulk of the cathedral, the rows of houses painted yellow and pink and blue, and the terminal buildings that clustered at the water's edge.

The ship's passengers crowded at the rails to gawp at the place, remote, pretty and somehow melancholy, perched at the edge of the Atlantic, the last landfall for over three thousand miles.

Unfortunately, the sturdy little tug which was nudging them into their berth was on the windward side of the *Manhattan*, and as its motors roared, its funnel expelled a cloud of dense black smoke which surged up the high sides of the ship and billowed across the deck, choking the passengers and covering them with soot.

Up on the bridge, Commodore Randall looked at the quaint vista of Cobh, arranged like a nebulous picture postcard around the bay. How many Irish men and women had passed through here on their way to New York, and a new life in a new world? And how many shipwrecked passengers had been brought back here, with nothing more than the drenched clothes on their backs, thanking God for a deliverance from the deep?

Titanic had sailed from here on her maiden voyage, never to be seen again. *Lusitania*'s handful of survivors had been brought here after the submarine sent her to the bottom in '15. The *Celtic*, the *Vanguard*, so many others, a catalogue of departures and catastrophes.

Cobh had seen all that, lives launched, voyages started and ended; but now the harbour lay quiet. Where usually a dozen great ocean liners were berthed here, this morning the *Manhattan* was the only one. The war had stopped the British, German and French lines from calling in. They would not return until the war was over. And as for American ones, there were damned few, and all of those were heading for home.

As they approached the dock, the sound of a band could be heard, playing 'The Star-Spangled Banner'. The mist drifted clear, revealing the musicians, their uniforms starched, their brass instruments gleaming, pink cheeks distended with musical wind. Behind them, held back by a row of black-uniformed police, was a crowd of some two or three thousand people, waving flags and cheering. And beyond the trumpeting of the band, the forty-nine bells of St Colman's cathedral could be heard pealing energetically.

'They must have missed us,' George Symonds remarked. 'We've berthed here more times than I can remember, but they never rang the bells for us before.'

Randall merely grunted. He was not in a jocular mood. He had received a radio message the day before from the American vice-consul in Cork, Robert Patterson. He knew the diplomat would be waiting to board as soon as they were berthed. He was not looking forward to that particular interview.

And news had reached them of the last American ship to sail from Cobh, the SS *Iroquois*, captained by his old friend Edgar Chelton, with whom he had served in the last war. It had been a disastrous voyage. Heavily overcrowded, and having endured a three-day storm, the *Iroquois* had delivered her passengers in poor shape – many with sprains and black eyes from having been rolled out of their cots, and worse, complaining bitterly about the way they had been treated by the captain. There had been insufficient food, they had been jammed in like cattle, the conditions had been insanitary, the crew rude and aggressive.

Ominously, halfway through this unpleasant voyage, Grand Admiral Erich Raeder, the head of the German navy, had warned the United States naval attaché in Berlin that the *Iroquois* would be 'torpedoed and sunk, just like the *Athenia*'.

When this news had been radioed to Captain Chelton, he'd taken immediate precautions. All radio sets on board had been disabled, every nook and cranny of the cabins had been searched, and the passengers had been made to line up one by one in the trunk room to have their baggage searched. That had added panic to an already chaotic situation. Randall was determined not to end his own career on such a low note.

The fog clung to Cobh as Cobh clung to Ireland, tenacious and grey. It skulked in the streets, never lifting, just changing its contours. The passengers on the observation deck were admiring the quaintness of the place and taking photographs. Dr Meese was telling Mrs Dabney and anyone else who would listen that Cobh was pronounced 'cove'. The British, he said, had tried to rename the place 'Queenstown', after Queen Victoria, but the obstinate Irish had patiently outworn that, and reverted to the old name. At least two and a half million Hibernians, he said, had emigrated to America through this little place. He added, in all modesty, that his own family had come over on the *Mayflower*, and had settled in Virginia in 1682. No Johnny-come-lately, he.

As they crowded to the shore rails of the ship, *Manhattan* listed perceptibly to that side. The purser had to use his megaphone to order passengers back from the rail. Their weight was too great for the balance of the ship.

Manhattan docked gingerly in the fog. The gangplank was set up, and the shore crowd surged forward, all but overwhelming the line of nervous young Irish policemen, who had valiantly linked arms to restrain the rush. They managed to push the mob back, but with difficulty. The passengers on the decks fell silent at the sight of this struggle.

The first person on board, as Commodore Randall had anticipated, was Robert Patterson, the American vice-consul, a harassed-looking young man from Ann Arbor, Michigan. Randall met him on the bridge.

'Boy, am I glad to see *you*,' he greeted Randall, wringing the Commodore's hand fervently. 'I've got six hundred Americans for you.'

'And I've got a hundred places for you,' Randall replied briefly.

The vice-consul looked aghast. 'A hundred? What about the rest?'

'They're going to have to wait, Mr Patterson.'

'Wait for what?'

'Ships are being requisitioned. It's just a question of time.'

'My God, they'll lynch me. Can't you take more?'

'I have over seven hundred extra already. And aside from passengers, I'm due to take on twenty extra kitchen staff here.'

The vice-consul reeled. He steadied himself against the compass table. 'But – but I've promised them all a place on *Manhattan*.'

'Well, you shouldn't have done that. I can take a hundred and that's it. I can't risk overloading my ship. You'll have to choose a hundred of the most deserving cases. Women and children first is the law of the sea. Able-bodied young men will have to go to the end of the line.'

Patterson rubbed his face as though trying to wake himself from a dream. 'Where will they go? Most of them are running out of money already.'

A steward had made a large pot of strong coffee for Commodore Randall. He poured the vice-consul a cup and handed it to him. 'I suggest you make a general appeal to all the hotels and private houses to offer whatever lodgings they can to American refugees, until such time as they can be offered a passage home. You can tell them Uncle Sam will refund them in due course.'

Patterson gulped his coffee, scalding his mouth. 'It's not the Irish I'm worried about. It's the Americans. They're busting their britches to get home.'

Commodore Randall looked at the tranquil surroundings of Cobh town, with its charming old houses. 'I don't think the Nazis are arriving here any time soon,' he pointed out dryly.

'You tell them that. They've been camped in my office for weeks, screaming about submarines.'

'They don't have to worry their heads about submarines.'

'If the United States gets into this war, they do.' He gestured at the huge American flags painted on *Manhattan*'s sides. 'Those will make a nice, fat target. They want to get home before we find ourselves caught up in it.'

'How the hell have six hundred Americans ended up here, anyway?'

'There's been a rumour going around that US ships aren't going to travel to Europe any longer – that Cobh is going to be where they turn around from now on.'

'That's not true.'

'It's what everyone believes. So they all came here to be sure of getting a ship.'

Randall sighed. 'Whatever the case, I can't take more than a hundred. And we've been delayed enough already. I want to sail in two days. You need to go out to that crowd and explain things.'

Though Commodore Randall had not encouraged any of his passengers to go ashore in Cobh, Mrs Dabney and a party of others could not resist the lure of the charming old town. With their cameras at the ready, they climbed the steep streets up to the gigantic edifice of St Colman's cathedral, which dominated the harbour, encrusted with every neo-Gothic embellishment that its Victorian architect could think of. From here (the fog having started to clear) they were able to admire the azure bay spread out below them, dotted with green islands, and watch the inquisitive sailboats which were nosing in from all quarters of County Cork to inspect the proud bulk of their own *Manhattan*.

Nor did their progress through the town go unremarked. Shopkeepers emerged from little corner shops to lavish charm upon them, along with unbeatable offers of woollens, tweeds, whiskies and original, guaranteed authentic souvenirs from the *Titanic*. Their dollars were readily exchanged for these good things. The only disagreeable incident arose when an American couple with a little boy in tow accosted them, demanding not very politely that they intercede with the hard-hearted Commodore Randall to allow them a passage home.

Escaping from this importunate family, they made their way back down to the docks, there to admire the painted fishing boats in the harbour, and the elaborate wrought-iron bandstand in the Boggy Road. A local hostelry, advertising a pie and Guinness lunch for five shillings, caught their attention, and they went in, with appetites sharpened by their shore excursion.

Back on the *Manhattan*, Commodore Randall was not having such a relaxing morning. Far from pacifying the large group of Americans hoping for a passage home, the vice-consul had returned with a vociferous delegation of some twenty men and women, determined to do battle with the skipper. The group was too large to entertain on the bridge, so they adjourned to the First Class smoking room.

'We're not taking no for an answer, sir.' The spokesman of the group was a loud, fat man named Reverend Ezekiel Perkins, the spiritual director of something called The Nordic Tabernacle, who had been leading a party to Rome to confront the Antichrist in the Vatican, when war had broken out. Randall took an immediate dislike to the man, but heard him out. 'We have heard that this ship is carrying many hundreds of aliens. Non-Americans, sir, not to put too fine a point on it. Our question to you is, why are we to be excluded from travelling on a United States ship, when foreign nationals are welcomed aboard?'

'The answer is simply that they have tickets, and you don't.' At the back of the group he saw Dr Meese, and thought he knew who had given the delegation their information, and encouraged this mission.

The Reverend Perkins' face darkened. 'We have tried in vain to buy tickets, sir. We have queued with our dollars in our hands at the ticket office here in Cobh, and have been told that we cannot get places on the *Manhattan* for love nor money.'

'We're already well over capacity.'

'We are Americans. We are Christians, sir. We demand to be treated as such.'

'As I told Mr Patterson here, I'm able to take a hundred extra passengers—'

Far from pleasing the deputation, this caused an uproar which prevented the Commodore from finishing.

'A hundred places are of no use to us,' the Reverend Perkins said stridently, his voice rising with practised ease over the others. 'There are over six hundred of us! How do you suggest we choose who should leave and who should remain?'

'As I said to Mr Patterson, women and children should have priority—'

'That is inhuman, sir. Are you proposing to tear Christian American families apart in this time of crisis?'

'I have offered you a solution, and you must take it, or wait for the next United States vessel to call in at Cobh.'

'And when will that be?' a woman called.

'Within the week, assuredly.'

'If anyone is to wait in Cobh, it should be the foreigners you have on board,' Perkins declared. There was noisy agreement from the others. 'You should put them off the ship immediately, and give their places to us. Let the aliens wait for the next ship – if it comes.'

'I have never done such a thing in all my career,' Randall said shortly. 'And I don't intend to start now.'

'They do not have the rights of American citizens, sir. Their welfare should not come before ours.'

'Don't browbeat me, Mr Perkins,' the Commodore growled. 'I have room for a hundred, and no more. And I will be sailing tomorrow, so make up your minds quickly.' He rose from his chair, adjusting the sleeves of his jacket, on which were the unbroken gold bars of his rank. 'I bid you good day.'

The *Manhattan*'s post office had taken delivery of a mailbag from the postmaster in Cobh. The letters, from all over Europe, were distributed to the passengers by the bellboy. There was one for Rachel Morgenstern, a pale mauve oblong covered in stamps and stickers. It had been forwarded from Le Havre to Southampton, and from there to Ireland.

'It's from Dorothea,' Rachel said. She tore it open swiftly, and the colour drained from her face as she read.

'What does she say?' Masha asked anxiously.

'She was arrested by the Gestapo.'

Masha's hand flew to her mouth. 'Oh no.'

'She was caught when they raided a club we used to go to. It was a harmless place, just somewhere we could meet without being pestered by Romeos.' Rachel's voice was dead. 'She was interrogated for three days. They released her when her health broke down, but she's still under suspicion, and waiting to hear what they will do next.'

'I'm so sorry.'

Rachel read on. 'She's been sacked from the academy. She has no money. She doesn't know how she will survive. She can't pay the rent. Rationing is in force now, there's little food in the shops, and the winter is coming.'

'What will she do?'

'The only relations she has are her sister's family in the country, but they haven't spoken to her for years because of what she is.' Rachel lowered the letter, her face bleak. 'She says she will get married.'

'Married! To whom?'

'Heinrich Vogelfänger. He's a professor at the academy. He's pursued her for years, but of course she was never interested.' Rachel folded the letter mechanically. 'The Gestapo have told her that if she marries and becomes pregnant within a year, they will leave her alone. Otherwise she will be sent to the women's concentration camp in Ravensbrück.'

Masha laid her hand timidly on her cousin's arm. 'Darling, I'm so sorry,' she repeated helplessly.

'What choice does she have? It's what women like us have done for centuries,' Rachel replied, her expression hard. 'And the Fatherland needs children. The authorities prefer to save a healthy Aryan woman for reproduction. A few blonde children, and she will be spared. Else she is of no use to the state.'

Masha tried to comfort Rachel, but Rachel shook her off. Her face remained stony, as though the letter and its contents had meant little to her. 'A lot happens in three months,' was the only further comment she would make.

Later in the day, however, Masha found her crying bitterly in their cabin. The young Hungarian woman with whom they were sharing was attempting futilely to console her, talking loudly in her own language. Masha shooed her out and gathered Rachel in her arms.

'Don't cry, don't cry my darling,' she whispered.

'I will never see her again.' Rachel wept like a woman who wept seldom, saving up her grief until it broke all walls. Her severe façade was gone, her prettiness, such as it had been, destroyed. Her tears poured out unchecked. 'Up to now I had some hope. But it's all gone, Masha. All gone.'

The third deputation to the Commodore was much smaller, but promised to be more effective. It came in the shape of Mrs Joseph P. Kennedy, holding her youngest son, Teddy, by the hand. They arrived on the bridge shortly after lunch. She was wearing a pale-green twin-set and pearls, both of which set off her eyes, which seemed to have taken on a softer hue in the Irish sea. The boy, in an obvious compliment to Randall, was wearing a sailor top in navy blue and white, complete with a square collar knotted under his chin.

'Might I have a word, Commodore?' she asked.

Groaning inwardly, Randall forced himself to smile. 'Of course, Mrs Kennedy.'

'It's about our unfortunate fellow Americans who are stranded here in Cobh. I hope you don't think me too forward, but their plight touched me deeply, and I took the liberty of calling my husband in London.'

'I see.'

'He replied, of course, that this is a matter entirely for you to decide.'

'Quite so.'

She gave him a charming smile. 'But he has asked me to beg you, dear Commodore, to do everything you possibly can to help these poor folk. They are truly in a sad plight.'

Randall spread his large paws. 'But Mrs Kennedy, you know how overcrowded the *Manhattan* already is. And I'm sure you know what happened on the *Iroquois*.'

'The *Iroquois* was an old tub. The *Manhattan* is an awfully big ship.'

'The size of the ship has no bearing on the number of passengers it can conveniently carry. *Manhattan* was designed to offer a luxurious experience. She is not equipped as a troopship might be. Almost every possible space has been used. Extra cots have been put in all the cabins and staterooms. People are sleeping in the public areas. It's already taking many hours each day to feed them all. How can I take more? We're crossing the Atlantic. Three thousand nautical miles!'

'I do remember a little geography,' she smiled.

'We're risking serious problems of food, water, ventilation, hygiene, comfort, movement around the ship, fresh air, risk of infection—'

'But isn't the distress they face on shore even greater than any discomfort they may face on board?'

Commodore Randall, baffled by Mrs Kennedy, noticed that her young son was staring around the bridge. 'Would you like to drive the ship, sonny?' he suggested amiably, indicating the control room, where the gleaming brass telegraph signals stood like golden sentries.

'The ship isn't going anywhere,' Teddy pointed out with cold logic. 'It's stopped.'

'Well, you could pretend.'

Teddy frowned. 'What for?' he asked.

'Wouldn't you be able to stretch the limits just a little,' Mrs Kennedy wheedled. 'Just to, let's say *two* hundred? My husband would take it as personal favour.' She laid her fingers on the heavy gold bar on his sleeve, looking up at him. The beauty of her youth had faded somewhat, but she could still be very appealing. And she was the wife of the influential Joseph P. Kennedy. 'As for myself, I could ask you no greater favour – *Rescue* Randall.'

Commodore Randall produced a groan somewhat like a harpooned walrus. 'Oh, very well, Mrs Kennedy. To please you – nobody else, mind – I will take two hundred.'

She beamed and blew him a kiss. 'I'll see you get a medal for this.'

'Indeed.'

'We're all in your hands, you know, Commodore. You are our guardian angel.'

'Yes, ma'am,' he sighed, 'I know that.'

Leaving the bridge victorious, Mrs Kennedy suggested to young Teddy that he get some exercise and warm his cold legs by seeing how fast he could run three times around the great forward derrick. Although this did not seem a very appealing prospect, he knew better than to defy his mother, and he set off at a reluctant jog.

In his absence, Mrs Kennedy unfolded the letter which Mr Nightingale had given her. She read it through again. It was from Cubby Hubbard to Rosemary, and it was a thoroughly contemptible document, with its protestations of love couched in the most clichéd forms (the boy was steeped in the language of popular music) and its bold invitations to his 'honey' to 'give everybody the slip' and rendezvous in New York. In the hands of an attorney, this would be enough evidence to ensure a conviction on the grounds of criminal seduction, particularly as there was clear evidence, from certain passages in the letter, that sexual intercourse had already taken place. And that further sexual intercourse was envisaged. She uttered an exclamation of disgust.

Going to law, however, was no longer needed. Joe, in his clever way, had solved the problem. Joe always solved the problem. He could be relied on for that.

She tore the letter carefully into small pieces, walked to the rail, and scattered them into the sea.

Two hundred extra voyagers had somehow been squeezed aboard the *Manhattan*. That brought her passenger compliment up to almost nineteen hundred. Together with the crew and the extra help they'd taken on, the ship was carrying well over twenty-three hundred souls. She was overloaded and she felt overloaded.

Commodore Randall had not involved himself in the decisions as to who would sail and who would stay, but he understood that there had been acrimonious arguments on the subject. Nor was he surprised that the Reverend Ezekiel Perkins had made sure that he was one of the saved, rather than staying to shepherd his remaining flock in Cobh – and was, in fact, one of the first on board, where he soon struck up a close alliance with Dr Emmett Meese of New York.

The ship had been re-provisioned, and the overworked kitchens had welcomed a score of new cooks, which promised to speed up mealtimes as they crossed the wide Atlantic.

Following the example of his old friend Captain Chelton, Randall had the baggage of the new arrivals examined thoroughly, and conducted a careful search of the entire ship, including the trunk hold, for anything suspicious. He was feeling uncharacteristically nervous about his last crossing. But when the searches were complete, and *Manhattan* found innocent of explosive devices, there was no reason to postpone sailing any longer.

To guard against any unpleasant last-minute incidents, he cancelled permission for any of the passengers or crew to go ashore, and had the pursers make sure that all visitors were ushered off the ship by noon.

The next morning, *Manhattan* left Cork Harbour, accompanied by all the good wishes of the ships around her. By evening, the wild cliffs of Ireland were fading dim and violet behind her, and she turned her bows to the cold Atlantic.

The Western Approaches

It was *U-113*'s youngest crewmember, a hydrophone operator, who first picked up the sound of a four-screw ship. He sent for the First Watch Officer.

'A destroyer?' Hufnagel asked, holding the earphone to his ear.

The operator shook his head. 'She's still too far away to tell. Around twenty miles. We need to submerge and stop engines to be sure.'

'Very well.'

Hufnagel went to Todt's cabin with the request. Todt got out of his bunk and gave the order. *U-113* submerged to twenty meters and turned off all her engines. Hanging motionless in the dark sea, the U-boat's crew were silent while the hydrophone and radio operators listened to the swishing in their headphones and made careful calculations.

After fifteen minutes, they had an answer. 'It's not a warship. We think it's either a tanker or a liner.'

Furthermore, they had triangulated the position and bearing of the other vessel as lying almost directly on the U-boat's track. Four screws meant a large vessel, at least fifteen thousand tons. The atmosphere on board changed. Emerging from his sulk, Kapitän-leutnant Todt ordered the torpedomen out of the engine room and into their natural habitat, to check over the monsters and ensure that this time there were to be no errors.

Hufnagel, too, felt the thrill of excitement. To return with at least one major prize might redeem his career.

He and Todt went up on to the bridge. *U-113* was now making full speed to intersect with the target vessel. She surged through the swells as though eager for the appointment. The night was foggy and very dark, with no moon. They were heading closer to the enemy coast with every minute that passed.

'We'll reach her at about 05:00 hours,' Todt said. 'My intention is to get this done in darkness and be gone before the British can respond.'

'I agree.'

Todt hugged himself against the intense cold. 'Make no mistake, Hufnagel. This is our chance.'

Hufnagel nodded but said nothing.

SS Manhattan

Manhattan's kitchens, stimulated by the fresh cooks who had joined at Cobh, provided a gala dinner for everyone aboard, complete with Irish crabs and lobsters and crates of Irish stout. After dinner, fortified by the alcohol, the passengers arranged an impromptu entertainment in the Smoking Room.

Hoffman's Midget Marvels started the proceedings with a scene from *Snow White and the Seven Dwarfs.* The prettiest one, whom Teddy Kennedy admired, played a sleepy Snow White in a very short slip and a paper crown. The other seven played the Dwarfs. They sang 'Whistle While You Work' in husky voices, wearing beards made of cotton wool, and took turns to kiss Snow White, lifting her slip to peer under it and share what they found with the onlookers. Their antics and bawdy remarks caused much hilarity among an audience wanting to blow off some steam.

Thomas König, viewing this performance with acute discomfort, found himself wondering whether the World's Fair was going to be the sober, scientific symposium that he had imagined. This mockery of things he held sacred was giving him an intimation of America as a land of brash vulgarity and crude sexuality, very different from the chaste German romanticism he had been brought up with.

He watched, bemused, as Miss Elizabeth Taylor clambered on to the stage and sang 'Some Day my Prince Will Come', with her violet eyes raised heavenward, to loud applause. Her proud mother announced to everyone that she had performed in front of the King and Queen of England, information which seemed to surprise young Elizabeth herself.

Mrs Dabney then launched into a recitation of *When Lilacs Last in the Dooryard Bloom'd*, Walt Whitman's elegy for Abraham Lincoln, which people around Thomas murmured was very apt for the time and place, though it went on somewhat long, and was perhaps imperfectly remembered here and there.

Thomas leaned over to Masha and whispered, 'Won't you play something, Fräulein Morgenstern?'

'It's been months since I touched a piano,' she replied. 'I'm so out of practice.'

'You cannot be worse than this,' Thomas pointed out, as Mrs Dabney groped for her next lines.

She giggled. 'That's true.'

'Won't you play?' He blushed. Rachel had scorned to attend the entertainment, and he felt bold in her absence. 'For me. I have never heard you play.'

She smiled. 'Very well, if it will please you. For you, Thomas.'

Masha went to the piano and sat to a scattering of applause. After a moment's reflection, she began to play *Träumerei* by Schumann. An absolute silence fell as the wistful, touching melody drifted through the room. Masha played without flaw, and with a delicacy of touch that made several people in the audience begin crying.

Among those who wept was Thomas, who felt with every note – as perhaps others did – that his tarnished dreams were being brightened again, that his hurts were being healed, that his dying hopes were being rekindled. He had kept the handkerchief she had given him like a precious relic. He pressed it to his mouth now, inhaling the faint scent that still clung to it. It was Masha's particular scent: vanilla and apricots, it seemed to him at times; at other times, something darker, aloes and musk.

Masha finished to rapturous clapping, and took her seat next to Thomas again.

'Thank you,' he whispered.

She saw his wet cheeks. 'I didn't mean to make you sad,' she said.

'I'm not sad. It was very beautiful.'

Katharine Wolff, perhaps not wanting to be outdone, followed Masha at the piano, and played a medley of national anthems, the French, the British, the American and a fourth which caused some puzzlement until it was revealed to be the Irish national anthem, otherwise known as 'A Soldier's Song'.

There was more applause as Miss Fanny Ward looked in on the proceedings, glassy-eyed in a magnificent gold lamé gown with a cascading, beaded headdress in the style of ancient Heliopolis. But she declined to perform, other than to smile lopsidedly at everyone around her. And the two great musicians on board, Stravinsky and Toscanini, both kept out of the way.

The highlight of the evening was provided by a mysterious, svelte and exquisite woman, hitherto unnoticed by anybody on board, who appeared in a grass skirt and a coconut brassiere, accompanying herself on the ukulele while she sang 'My Little Grass Shack in Kealakekua' in a sultry contralto, getting all the Hawaiian words right and shaking her hips in the most provocative way.

It was whispered excitedly that this must surely be the Mexican actress Dolores del Río, who it was assumed must have been keeping to her stateroom to avoid the press of admirers. But astonishingly, at the end of her song the sultry lady pulled off her wig and revealed herself to be none other than Mr Nightingale, the senior steward, who in addition to all his other talents, was seen to have very good legs. He used them to make a sensational exit, hula-ing around the room, swishing his skirt and leaving a section of the audience open-mouthed and another section stamping and wolf-whistling.

It took some time to restore order after this. Members of the ship's crew, watching from the wings, were especially vociferous in their appreciation. One was heard to say it was 'Naughty Nightie's best ever'.

The Reverend Ezekiel Perkins of the Nordic Tabernacle now got on to the stage and announced that he felt it incumbent upon him to offer a little lecture on 'Improving the Health of the Next Generation'. This apparently involved the sterilising of Negroes, Jews, Mexicans and abnormal individuals such as Mr Nightingale and Hoffman's Midget Marvels, to prevent them from contaminating the nascent American race.

Masha became agitated at this flood of urbanely expressed hatred, and rose to leave. Thomas walked her to the exit. Several of the audience followed suit, either because they were also offended by the Reverend Perkins' address, or because it was not as short as he had promised.

At the door, Thomas touched Masha's hand. 'Thank you again for tonight.' He gazed into her face, feeling that he was more deeply in love than ever. 'I will never forget it.'

Masha laughed, disengaging her hand from his. 'In Yiddish we call that sort of music *schmaltz.* Dripping with sentiment, you know? But it's a sweet piece. I'm glad you enjoyed it. Goodnight, Thomas.'

She slipped away. Thomas leaned against the wall dreamily as the Smoking Room emptied and the stewards cleared up and turned off the lights.

U-113

The ship was a dim silhouette in the pre-dawn darkness, but she was showing lights that revealed her outline. Todt, trembling all over, had the silhouette recognition chart open, his forefinger skimming along the list.

'I have her,' he whispered, as though the British crew could somehow hear him across two miles of sea. 'She is the *Duchess of Atholl*.'

'Are you sure?'

'As sure as my life. Over twenty-four thousand tons gross. My God. Look at the size of her.'

Hufnagel knew that he was whispering partly because the prize was so great. It was the roll of the dice that recoups all the gambler's losses. The stag that steps out of the woods just as the hunter shoulders his rifle to return home empty-handed. To go back with a bag like this was the dream of every U-boat captain. It would lead to commendations, medals, promotions, parades, the covers of magazines.

But there was no record of the *Duchess of Atholl* having been converted as a troop carrier. Hufnagel studied the silhouette chart with his pocket flashlight.

'She's a passenger vessel,' he said quietly. 'We can't sink her without warning. There will be terrible loss of life.'

'Causing loss of life to the enemy is the purpose of war,' Todt retorted.

'She isn't armed. There will be women and children on board. The rules of war—'

'Don't lecture me about the rules of war,' Todt said.

'We must signal her to launch her lifeboats.'

'You are mad.'

'*You* are mad if you think sending hundreds of civilians to the bottom will do you or the Reich any good. For God's sake, man. Think! Remember the *Lusitania*.'

'Go below at once, Hufnagel. Or I will shoot you.'

Hufnagel waited, staring at the shadowy figure of his captain. He had the conviction that the man confronting him was a coward, whose will was weaker than Hufnagel's own. When Todt's hand made no move towards the pistol at his side, he turned to the rating who was standing nervously by the signal lamp. 'Signal her to stop.' He spelled out the English words for the signalman: STOP SHIP.

The frightened rating glanced at Todt. There was no response from him. The rating switched on the lamp. The dazzling beam speared through the darkness towards the ship. After waiting a few seconds for the ship to notice the light, the rating began to rattle the signal slats open and shut.

SS Manhattan

Commodore Randall had spent most of the night on the bridge. He had looked in on the talent show, but had not found anything very amusing to keep him. The feeling of anxiety would not leave him. He went back to the wheelhouse and made himself a nuisance there, keeping everyone on the qui vive. George Symonds persuaded him to turn in during the darkest hour before dawn, and he went along to his cabin, yawning.

He had just fallen asleep when he was awoken by the sensation of his ship's engines powering down. He was already pulling his uniform over his pyjamas when a rating began pounding on his cabin door.

He reached the bridge a few minutes later to find George Symonds and his other officers staring at the flickering light of a communication lamp out in the darkness.

'It's a German submarine,' Symonds said tersely. 'She's signalling us to stop the ship. I gave the "All Stop" order.'

'You did the right thing. Signal back "American ship". Keep signalling that at one-minute intervals. In the meantime, I want the radio completely silent. No transmissions at any cost. All watertight doors closed and all crew at action stations. Sound the general alarm and get all the passengers into the lifeboats.'

Symonds did not question his captain's orders. The cadet in charge of the signal blinker relayed the message rapidly to the unknown submarine. *Manhattan*'s alarm bells began to ring throughout the ship, in the crew's quarters, in the public areas where the cots were set out in rows, and in every passenger cabin.

Fanny Ward awoke in terror with a vision of the flames that had engulfed Dotty and Terence, hearing their dreadful screams in her ears. But the screams were the strident calls of an alarm that wouldn't stop. She heaved off the heavy eiderdown and went to peer out of her door. The corridor was full of people in their nightclothes, and stewards shouting instructions about lifeboats.

'Is it a drill?' she asked of a man in uniform pushing past, her voice quavering.

'No, Miss, it's not a drill. Get your life jacket on and get to the lifeboats as quick as you can, and don't take anything with you.'

She groped her way to the chest of drawers and took out her jewellery box. It was massive and heavy, far too massive and heavy for her to carry very far. She unlocked it with unsteady fingers and opened the lid. Inside, tucked into the satin-lined shelves and compartments, was the best of her jewellery. She stared at the glittering array with watery eyes. The rings, the brooches. The heavy bracelets, the necklaces and collarets, the tiaras. Such a mass of gold and platinum, of diamonds, rubies, emeralds. Which should she take? The most valuable? The ones with most sentimental value?

The shrilling of the alarm invaded her head. It wouldn't let her think clearly. Blindly, she clutched at the glittering mass and pulled out two handfuls at random. She began thrusting bangles on to her wrists, rings on to her fingers.

Thomas König had awoken instantly, knowing exactly what he must do. He rolled out of bed and grabbed his clothes and his life jacket, pulling them on over his pyjamas. Ignoring the confused Stravinsky, who was querulously asking what was going on, he went out of the door and ran towards the Morgenstern girls' cabin. People were starting to spill out of their doors, choking the passageways, but he lowered his hard head and butted his way through, giving no quarter and asking none.

Reaching their cabin, he hammered on the door, and then burst in. Less than three minutes had passed since the alarm had begun to sound, and the girls were still in their nightgowns, in a state of panic, pulling possessions out of their closets.

'Leave all that,' Thomas said sharply. 'Get dressed quickly.' They stared at him dazedly. '*Get dressed*,' he commanded. 'Leave everything. There may not be much time.'

His voice, suddenly that of a young man, rather than a boy, seemed to penetrate their confusion. They began to pull on their clothes.

'What's happening?' Rachel demanded.

'We have to get to the lifeboats. Get dressed. Warm things. Put on warm things. Quickly.' Masha snatched up her precious red leather coat while Thomas reached under their bunks and hauled out the life jackets that were stowed there.

Toscanini had been dozing in a deckchair, wrapped up in three blankets against the biting Atlantic cold. He leaped to his feet, cursing, and hurried to the rail. Out in the blackness, a dazzling pinpoint of light was flickering. An enemy submarine! The ship was about to be torpedoed.

'Carla!' he exclaimed. He snatched up his cane and hurried off to find her. But he had no sooner reached the top of the companionway when a torrent of passengers emerged, driving him back. He tried to fight his way down through the throng, but he was far too frail to make any headway. He was pushed aside like a dry leaf, and found himself sitting on the deck, without his hat, his stick, or breath in his lungs.

U-113

U-113's torpedoes had all been loaded into the launching tubes. The U-boat was now within two miles of the target. Since the ship had obligingly stopped, there could be no doubt about the bearing, speed or range. The vessel was the biggest and easiest target they had ever had.

Todt had manoeuvred the U-boat into position off the other vessel's port amidships, where her torpedoes would go straight into the engine room.

Todt himself was at the master sight on the bridge. He had taken all the readings, and passed them to the target-bearing transmitter, an anonymous grey box which contained an advanced, high-powered calculator that had already fed the information into the brains of the three weapons. They would run true, homing to their target with deadly intent.

Even a single strike at the water line would inflict a mortal wound: great loss of life, the sea pouring into the engine compartment, the ship starting to founder. Three strikes would be hard to survive.

'Flood torpedo tubes one, three and four,' Todt commanded.

The answer came through the intercom. 'Flooding tubes one, three and four.'

The sound of water rushing into the tubes came to their ears.

'I'm going to signal them to abandon ship,' Hufnagel said.

Todt did not take his face away from the aiming column. He had the cross hairs fixed on the centre of the ship. 'I will give them ten minutes,' he said.

Hufnagel turned to the signalman who was waiting beside the blinker. 'Send: "Will sink you. Ten minutes to abandon ship".'

'I don't know how to send it in English,' the rating said sheepishly.

'I'll write it out for you.' Hufnagel took his notebook from his pocket and wrote the English words for the signalman. 'Don't make any mistakes.'

SS Manhattan

Commodore Randall was on the bridge when the new signal came in. He watched the blinking light impassively.

'They're giving us ten minutes to abandon ship,' the rating stammered nervously but unnecessarily, for they had all understood the Morse Code.

'Heave to,' he commanded the helmsman. The great liner swung slowly to starboard, presenting the U-boat with its broad side.

'You're giving them a perfect target,' Symonds said in dismay.

'I'm giving them a good look at our funnel. Get as many lights on it as you can. And keep signalling, "American ship".'

He had deemed it best not to order a lifeboat drill before now. The *Manhattan* was so heavily overcrowded that it would inevitably cause chaos. And the truth was that the ship's sixteen passenger lifeboats, together with two for the crew, were inadequate for the number of souls that would have to be saved. The realising of this would have caused unnecessary dismay among those on board. Like the *Titanic*, there were going to be hundreds who would have to either jump or go down with the ship. He himself knew he would choose the latter option.

'How is manning the lifeboats progressing?' he asked.

'Surprisingly little panic,' Symonds replied. 'It's going to take longer than ten minutes, though. And there will be a lot of passengers left standing.'

'We'll put the excess passengers in the crew lifeboats. You agree?'

'Aye-aye, Captain.'

Randall grunted and trained his night-glasses on the location of the U-boat, around a mile and a quarter away. After that last, ominous signal, she had remained silent. He could just make out a light, presumably on her jackstaff.

'Strange,' he said in a conversational tone. 'Here's a group of boys eager to do the right thing by their country. Probably kind to animals and good to their mothers. If you met them at a baseball game they'd be fine fellows whose hands you would shake. Yet here they are, itching to kill us all, even though they know that doing that is going to break thousands of hearts just like their mothers' hearts, and wreck thousands of innocent lives, just like their own lives. Can you figure that out, George?'

'No, sir, I cannot.'

'Me neither.'

'They're signalling again,' the cadet called.

They watched in silence. This time the message was even shorter:

'Ten minutes.'

Randall turned to the signalman. 'Change the message. Send: "Manhattan, American liner". Keep sending that. Don't stop.'

'Sending,' the cadet said, operating the blinker with arms that were by now starting to ache.

'What if they don't understand English?' Symonds asked.

'Then let's keep them busy consulting their dictionaries, rather than calculating torpedo trajectories, George.'

Nobody recognised Fanny Ward as the sailor pushed her on to her lifeboat. Her knobbly hands so loaded with rings and bangles that she could hardly lift them, her scrawny neck so weighted with necklaces that her head drooped, she stumbled over the thwarts and almost fell on to Mrs Kennedy.

'Help the old lady,' Mrs Kennedy snapped at Patricia. Pat grabbed Miss Ward's arm and guided her to her seat. She collapsed into it with a gasp. Wigless, unpainted, she crumpled into her life jacket like an old tortoise drawing its head and limbs into its shell. Mrs Kennedy suddenly perceived that the old woman was the Eternal Beauty, wearing a fortune in heavy jewellery.

If that old crone falls overboard, she thought to herself, *she'll go straight to the bottom with all her bullion.*

Madame Quo Tai-Chi was hampered, as she clambered into the lifeboat, by the Ming Dynasty vase she was clutching to her chest. The thing was huge, nearly half as big as she was, ornately (and auspiciously) painted with horses galloping over waves. It was four hundred years old, as priceless as it was fragile. But it caused resentment among the other occupants of the lifeboats, as did the second Ming vase, only slightly less huge, carried by her young son Edward, who followed close behind her.

'You can't bring those damned things on to the lifeboat,' someone exclaimed. 'Throw them overboard!'

Mrs Quo, who had already had an argument with the rating who'd tried to wrest the thing out of her arms, ignored the complaint. 'Make room,' she commanded imperiously. She pushed herself into her rightful place, using her surprisingly sharp elbows to make room. As she settled down, it was revealed that, in addition to the Ming vase, she was also carrying, tucked into her life jacket, a large, signed and framed photograph of Madame Chiang Kai-Shek. Her son followed suit, inserting himself next to her. Holding tightly on to the vase, she and Madame Chiang stared grimly ahead.

Thomas König helped Masha to pull the life preserver over her head. The thing was very bulky, made of rubberised fabric, a bilious yellow in colour, and festooned with a confusing tangle of toggles and straps. Thomas, however, seemed to understand how the thing was intended to work. He tied the tapes securely at her back, pulling them tight. Then he performed the same task for Rachel. Both young women were in a state of confused alarm, like everyone else; but Thomas appeared to know just what he was doing. He shepherded them out of their cabin and into the passageway, which was jammed with passengers. 'That way,' he commanded. The going was difficult. But halfway to the exit, Masha suddenly swung round.

'Stravinsky's manuscript. It's still in the cabin!'

'Forget it,' Thomas said, pulling her arm, 'we have to get to the lifeboats. The ship may go down at any moment.'

But Masha burst into tears. 'He trusted me with it. I can't lose it!'

'Stay here.' Pushing the girls into an alcove, Thomas fought his way back along the corridor to the girls' cabin. Bruised and breathless, he found the portfolio on the little writing desk, and snatched it up. He stuffed it into his own life jacket and went back to find Masha and Rachel.

'I've got it,' he said tersely as he reached them. 'No more delays, come.'

The lifeboat deck was chaotic, seething with hordes of passengers in livid-yellow life jackets trying to find salvation. Those who had been put in cabins had been allocated numbered seats on the boats. But all those who had been billeted in the public areas – many hundreds of people – had none. The crew were bawling orders through loudhailers, telling those who had no numbers to make for the crew lifeboats in the stern of the ship. But some were clambering into lifeboats not meant for them, and others were being pushed aside in the crush; and some, still under the impression that this was a drill, were asking whether they could go back to their cabins, now. But it was not a drill.

Bleary-eyed children clutching dogs and cats trotted in the wake of fathers clutching babies. Mothers with little ones hanging on their skirts hunted frantically for their boats. They passed an elderly man being hauled out of his wheelchair and dumped unceremoniously into a boat.

Alternately pulling and pushing the girls along, Thomas forged a path through the mob. 'Thomas, where are you taking us?' Rachel shouted.

'Your boat is number sixteen. It's the very last one at the rear of the ship, on this side.'

'How do you know that?' she demanded.

He didn't waste his breath replying. Reaching their lifeboat, he gave their names to the rating stationed there, and then helped them climb aboard.

'Aren't you coming?' Masha called from her seat.

He shook his head. 'I'm going to get Monsieur Stravinsky.'

'Thomas, no. Come back!'

But he was already gone.

Cubby Hubbard, bundled into his life preserver, was running from lifeboat to lifeboat, hunting for Rosemary. She was nowhere to be seen. But at last he caught sight of Mrs Kennedy, sitting in one of the boats with Teddy and Patricia. He hauled himself into the boat and clambered over the cursing passengers.

'Where's Rosemary?' he demanded.

Mrs Kennedy, who seemed dazed by events, turned to face him. 'Rosemary?' she repeated, as though hearing the name for the first time.

'Yes, Rosemary. Where is she? I don't see her anywhere!'

Her eyes focused on Cubby, recognising him. Her expression hardened. 'Rosemary's not on the ship, you poor fool.'

'What?'

'I sent her back to her father. Do you really think I would leave her to your tender mercies?'

He stared at her blankly, thunderstruck. A rating laid a heavy hand on his shoulder. 'This isn't your lifeboat, son. You have to get out of the way.'

Stunned, Cubby allowed himself to be led away. Mrs Kennedy's eyes followed him. She put her arms around her children and held them tight. For all her care, for all her ceaseless struggle to strengthen and protect them, they were about to be set adrift on the wide, rough sea of the world, there to sink or swim as God and the fates decided.

U-113

'They're manning the lifeboats,' Hufnagel reported, watching through his night-glasses.

'Ten minutes are almost up,' Todt replied, hunched over the bridge aiming column beside him.

'They need more time.'

'Are any lifeboats in the water?'

'Not yet.'

'A torpedo in their guts will hurry them up. I am ready to launch.' His hand was on the torpedo launch lever.

'Wait.' Hufnagel moved forward, focusing his glasses and cursing the condensation in them. 'I can see her funnels.' His voice changed. 'They're red, white and blue.'

'The British colours,' Todt said impatiently.

'Also the American ones. *Duchess of Atholl's* funnels are yellow and black.'

'For God's sake, man. We can establish her identity from the survivors.'

'She keeps signalling that she's an American ship.'

'Of course – to save herself.'

'There's also something painted on her sides. You'd better take a look.'

Todt tore himself away from the aiming column with a curse. 'You are wasting precious minutes, Hufnagel.' He snatched the binoculars from his first officer and held them to his eyes.

'You see?' Hufnagel prompted.

After a moment, Todt thrust the binoculars back at Hufnagel. 'She is the *Duchess of Atholl*,' he said curtly. 'Prepare to fire.'

SS Manhattan

Thomas König had fought his way back to the cabin and had found Stravinsky sitting on his bunk in a clouded state, staring at his unlaced shoes. As he'd done on the very first morning, he now knelt at the composer's feet and fastened the laces tightly.

'What is happening, Thomas?' Stravinsky dully asked the top of Thomas's head.

'They say it's a German submarine. It's going to torpedo us.'

'But this is an American vessel.'

Thomas grimaced. 'That will make little difference to them.' He spoke from hard experience of Nazi measures. 'They already see America as an enemy.' Having laced Stravinsky's shoes, he helped the older man to stand, and tried to fit the life jacket over his head.

Stravinsky pushed him away. 'I don't want that thing.'

'You have to wear it,' Thomas said briskly. 'It will keep you afloat if you end up in the water.'

'I don't care to remain afloat,' Stravinsky said petulantly. 'I prefer to go down with the ship.'

'We have to get to our lifeboat quickly. There isn't any time.'

'Let someone else have my place on the lifeboat. I'm staying here.'

Thomas stared at him for a moment. 'Don't be a stupid old fool.'

Had it been shouted as an insult, it might have angered Stravinsky, and determined him to remain in his cabin; but the matter-of-fact way it was spoken was somehow calming. Silently, he allowed the boy to pull the bulky yellow thing over his head and tie the straps in a secure knot.

Thomas took Stravinsky's hand. 'Hold tight. We have to hurry.'

He pulled Stravinsky out of the cabin and along the passageway. Almost all the passengers were on the open decks or in the boats now. Stravinsky was tired, and the ascent from the ship's underworld was steep. His feet occasionally stumbled on the metal stairs. But the boy pulled him upright each time, and at last they reached the top deck.

The scene was to Stravinsky's eyes like the Last Judgment. He stared, open-mouthed. Two thousand passengers had come up from below. In the harsh deck lights, the life preservers they wore gleamed like folded golden wings about to open and take flight. The figures had already all but filled the boats, and yet hundreds more queued at each one. Overhead, the sky arched pitch black.

Thomas did not allow him to pause. He dragged Stravinsky towards the senior steward, Mr Nightingale, who was directing passengers to their boat stations with a list in his hands.

'It's Monsieur Stravinsky,' Thomas shouted. 'He's in boat twelve, but there are too many passengers trying to get on.'

'We can't leave Monsieur Stravinsky behind,' Mr Nightingale said cheerfully. 'The ballet-lovers of the world would be very annoyed with us.'

Deftly, he got the milling queue of passengers to make way, and ushered Stravinsky on to the lifeboat.

U-113

Todt had the cross hairs of the master sight set amidships on the target. The red lights on the calculator were glowing, indicating that the machine was making its final calculations. There was a breathless silence in the control room, broken only by the voices of the captain and the torpedo aimer.

'Calculating.'

All eyes flicked to the calculator's lights, which had turned white.

'Calculations complete. Ready to fire.

Rudi Hufnagel came clattering down from the bridge. 'I see the American flag painted on the side,' he said tautly. 'And the name of the ship. The captain was not lying. She's the SS *Manhattan*. Do you hear me, Captain? She's the *Manhattan*.' He offered Todt the glasses. 'Go up and take a look.'

'It makes no difference,' Todt replied, ignoring the proffered binoculars.

'No difference? Are you mad? She is a neutral ship!'

'She is filled with enemies of the Reich. That makes her a legitimate target.'

'We know nothing about her passengers. And if we sink her, it will bring America into the war!'

'That is inevitable, in any case. Hitler has spoken many times of Roosevelt's weakness. America is a mongrel nation, weakened by the blood of the Jews and the Negroes. They will never have the fighting capacity of an Aryan race. They are not even armed, Hufnagel. It will take them years to rearm. We have nothing to fear from them.'

'Are we really discussing these ridiculous issues here and now?' Hufnagel asked incredulously.

'You are right.' Todt swung back to the aiming column. He put his eyes to the viewfinder and grasped the launch lever. 'Prepare to launch torpedo one.' On the panel before him, the red lights went out obediently and the white 'ready' light came on.

'No.' Hufnagel grasped the shoulder of Todt's jacket and pulled the commander away from the column. 'You can't do this, Todt.'

Todt's pale grey eyes were alight. 'I expected this, Hufnagel. You are not going to cheat me of this prize.' He pulled the Luger from his holster and cocked it. He pointed the pistol at Hufnagel's face. 'Stand back or I will shoot you in the head.'

'You had better shoot, then,' Hufnagel muttered, moving forward to grapple with his captain.

'I knew that you would fail in the moment of crisis. Jew-lover.' Todt pulled the trigger.

SS Manhattan

Stravinsky had found himself, whether through coincidence or plan, seated beside Arturo Toscanini, who had been helped aboard the lifeboat in a state of shattered nerves by his plump little wife. The two men said nothing to each other. There seemed to be nothing to say. But as they stared at each other, each man recognised in the other's face the same state of exhaustion and despair, the same bitterness. Beside them sat Carla Toscanini and Katharine Wolff.

'Getting there is half the fun!' Mr Nightingale said gaily. He pulled the lever, and the lifeboat swung out over the sea. Jolted and finding themselves swaying seventy feet in the air, with nothing but a sheer drop between them and the icy water below, the passengers screamed and grabbed on to each other or the gunwales. The boats were now so full that almost half the passengers in each were having to stand.

Stravinsky and Toscanini both turned to look over the side of their lifeboat. Far below them, the sea was black, laced with chains of foam. Their boat dangled unsteadily, lurching as the *Manhattan* rolled in the swell. They stared into the abyss, each one recognising it for what it was, death staring back at them.

It came to each man quite suddenly that, for all the disillusionment of life that had passed, there was still life to be lived. Still music to be played, women to be loved. Still a little sunlight left on the mountainside.

They turned away, shuddering, from the darkness that yawned beneath them.

Naughty Nightie, who had behaved with exemplary calm and good humour from the start of the crisis, moved down the line, dispensing jokes to each group of passengers and yanking the release levers like a cheerful hangman. One by one, the lifeboats swung out on their davits, ready to be lowered on the Commodore's command. Shrieking adults and wailing children clutched at each other.

The Commodore himself was showing little emotion as he stood at the window of his bridge, staring into the darkness. 'Why don't they say anything?' he asked rhetorically. 'They must see our funnels by now. They must see the Stars and Stripes.'

'The ten minutes were up a long time ago,' Symonds said, looking at his chronometer. He was very tense. 'The lifeboats have all been swung out. Shall I give the order to lower them?'

'No.'

'But, Commodore—'

'If we lower the lifeboats, he'll torpedo us right away. It's like admitting we're a legitimate target.'

Randall saw the officers on the bridge glance at one another. Stress was written clear on every face. 'So what do we do?' Symonds demanded.

'We keep signalling who we are, and wait for them to understand,' Rescue Randall replied calmly. It was essential for him to maintain imperturbable control and not be swayed by his officers' panic. 'Is there any fresh coffee, gentlemen?'

U-113

The pistol fired in his face had half-blinded and deafened Hufnagel, but he was surprised to find himself alive. The bullet had struck him in the left shoulder. He did not know how badly he had been injured, only that he could no longer use that arm. He didn't flinch, however, as he grasped Todt's pistol and wrenched it aside. For a moment the two men wrestled, their faces an inch apart. There was another shot. Hufnagel felt something sear his arm.

Then new hands were intervening, dragging them apart. Dimly, he saw the faces of the crewmen, among them Krupp, the medical officer.

'You've been shot,' Krupp said urgently. 'Let me examine the wound.'

'The captain is in an unfit mental state,' Hufnagel gasped. He saw Krupp flinch and back away from him, and realised that he had somehow got possession of Todt's Luger, and was waving it dangerously. Hufnagel lowered his arm. Blood immediately streamed down his hand and spattered on the floor plates. He had been shot a second time, the bullet tearing the flesh of his right forearm open. He could feel no pain. 'That is an American liner,' he said urgently. 'The *Manhattan*. Attacking her would be a serious breach of our orders. I am relieving the captain of his command.'

'Do you know what you're doing, Rudi?' Krupp asked quietly.

'Come and see.' Hufnagel dragged himself up to the conning tower again, followed by the others.

The sun was about to rise, and the sky was flushed with the first reddish light of dawn. Looking across the two miles that separated them from the other vessel, those with good eyesight could now see, even without the aid of binoculars, the huge American flag that was painted on her side. A man uttered a curse of dismay or surprise. Otherwise they were all silent. Todt seemed to be dazed by what he had done. He put his head in his hands and crouched down, making no attempt to resume his command.

Hufnagel noticed that the signalman was huddled in the corner of the conning tower next to his overturned lamp, terrified at the sight of the bloodstained second officer brandishing a Luger.

'Get up,' he commanded. 'Prepare to send.' The man scrambled to his feet, pulling on his cap, which had come off, and pushing the lamp back into place.

SS Manhattan

'They're signalling again,' George Symonds said urgently.

They all watched the flickering light, brilliant against the glowing dawn sky, and read out the letters as they were transmitted, slower than before: 'A-P-O-L-O-G-Y. M-I-S-T-A-K-E. P-L-E-A-S-E C-O-N-T-I-N-U-E.'

Randall showed little emotion. 'Ask him to confirm his message.'

The cadet relayed the query. A few moments later, the reply came: 'M-I-S-T-A-K-E. G-O A-H-E-A-D P-L-E-A-S-E. G-O-O-D-B-Y-E.'

'Signal "Received". Start engines.' The deep rumble of *Manhattan*'s engines began to throb under their feet. 'Ahead slow.'

The tension hadn't left the bridge. If anything, it had increased. 'Should we get the passengers out of the lifeboats?' Symonds asked.

'No hurry,' Randall replied calmly. 'Let's get some distance between Mister Mistake and us first.'

'Aye-aye, Sir.'

Commodore Randall had his binoculars trained on the U-boat. 'I'd give a lot to overhear the conversation that's taking place on her bridge at this moment,' he muttered.

As the *Manhattan* moved forward slowly in the water, they all watched the U-boat intently. The rim of the sun emerged from the horizon, sending a shaft along the surface of the sea. The tips of the millions of waves turned translucent green. It had become a sea of jade.

A bellboy ran on to the bridge, a boy of fourteen, the brass buttons on his uniform still awry from the haste with which he had dressed that morning.

'Sir! There's another submarine on the port beam.'

The officers moved in a body to the port deck to look. Without doubt, several miles away, another submarine had surfaced, her shape gilded in the flat light of the rising sun. They could see her hull and the lump of her conning tower.

'Has she seen us?' Symonds asked.

'I don't care to find out,' the Commodore retorted. 'And I don't want any more conversations with undersea boats. Swing us into the sun, helmsman. Full ahead all engines.'

The manoeuvre brought the second visitor to their stern. *Manhattan*'s one hundred and sixty-five thousand horses began to gallop, pushing her to her full speed of twenty knots and heading straight into the brilliance of the rising sun. The great liner settled her stern in the water and drove ahead. Either blinded or uninterested, the second submarine soon fell astern and vanished.

'I believe I've aged ten years in the last hour,' Commodore Randall remarked. 'Shall we secure lifeboat stations, George?'

'Aye-aye, Sir.' Symonds went on rather shaky legs to let the passengers out of the boats.

U-113

None of the crew were quite sure what to do with Kapitän-leutnant Jürgen Todt. Since being relieved of his command, he had not spoken a word. He went straight to his quarters and remained there, which many of them thought was ominous; they imagined he would be writing furiously in his notorious log, preparing a report which would have them all shot on their return to Germany.

Rudi Hufnagel, however, was in need of immediate medical attention. He had been wounded twice and he was losing a lot of blood. The first of Todt's bullets had glanced across his left shoulder, damaging bone and muscle. The other, ostensibly more superficial wound, was the one that Krupp found most hard to deal with. The bullet had torn open the veins of Hufnagel's right forearm, and blood was pouring out as the First Watch Officer lay slumped on the floor, starting to lose consciousness.

Krupp bandaged the arm as tightly as he could, but the scarlet blossomed through the gauze instantly and spilled on to the metal deck-plates, making them slippery underfoot.

'Tie a tourniquet above the elbow,' someone advised. 'That will stop it.'

'I can't cut off the circulation altogether,' Krupp said helplessly. 'By the time we get back to Kiel he'll have lost the arm.' With a seriously wounded man to care for now, and very little real experience, the twenty-three-year-old Krupp was overwhelmed, and on the edge of tears. There was a hubbub of conflicting advice from the men standing around him: to raise the wounded arm above Hufnagel's head, to make Hufnagel lie down, to cauterise the wound with the electrician's soldering-irons.

The sharp voice of the hydrophone operator cut through this babble.

'Torpedo launched.'

They all turned to stare at the man, who was hunched over, with his hands clamped on to his headphones. 'We haven't launched a torpedo,' Krupp said stupidly.

'Enemy torpedo,' the hydrophone operator said. 'Starboard stern. One thousand metres. Closing at thirty knots.'

There was a moment of silence. In the confusion of the last few minutes, and with their two senior officers out of action, the inexperienced crew had neglected the primary rule of submarine warfare – to keep a watch at all times. They now had less than a minute to respond to the torpedo which had been launched at them.

'Secure hatches!' Krupp screamed. 'Prepare to dive.'

Leaving Hufnagel bleeding on the floor, the men rushed to their posts, closing the watertight doors, gulping water into the ballast tanks, revving the motors. The seconds ticked by. The remainder of the crew rushed to the forward compartment to weigh *U-113*'s nose down. At his station, the hydrophone operator murmured, almost admiringly, 'It's a British submarine. They crept up behind us while we weren't looking.'

U-113 was just starting her dive when the torpedo struck her stern. The explosion ripped through the compartments, bursting the watertight doors open, hurling men and machinery in all directions, plunging the U-boat into darkness and opening her like a sardine can to the plundering sea.

SS Manhattan

Rachel Morgenstern was reluctantly forced to admit that Thomas König had been helpful during the crisis. Without his assistance, the girls would have found the experience very difficult; and it was doubtful whether Stravinsky would have made it to the lifeboat at all.

'Of course, you did it for Masha,' Rachel said to Thomas. 'You prefer Masha to me, don't you, Adolf?'

'I like you both the same,' Thomas replied awkwardly. Rachel made him very nervous.

'Liar. You think I am an ugly, spiteful Jewess.'

'You are not ugly,' he replied, flushing, 'and your religion is not important to me.'

'Liar again. Nor have you denied that I am spiteful.'

'You are not spiteful.'

'Liar a third time.' She considered him with her sharp blue eyes. 'How did you know which was our lifeboat?'

'I found it out.'

'When?'

'The first day I saw you.'

'So you could impress my cousin?'

'So that I could be useful.'

'How lucky we Jews are to have a little Nazi looking out for us. You were useful, I suppose.' Grudgingly, she leaned forward and touched her lips to his cheek. 'There. You had better go and wash that off now, before the Führer finds out about it.'

Thomas would far rather the kiss had come from Masha, but he accepted it with good grace. Masha did not kiss him, but she took Thomas's hand in her own and walked along the deck with him. 'You have never told me about your mother,' she said. When he made no reply, but just looked away, she went on, 'I would like her to know what a good, brave young man she raised.'

Well-intentioned as this remark was, it had the effect of emptying the cup of Thomas's happiness in an instant, leaving him bereft, taking him back to the moment he had last seen his mother. 'It was nothing,' he mumbled.

'It was not nothing,' Masha replied. 'You looked after us.'

'The submarine didn't even fire a torpedo.' Thomas felt almost disappointed, as if that eventuality would have enabled him to show true heroism, rescuing Masha from the waves.

Masha smiled, perhaps reading his thoughts. 'That's not the point. You behaved like a grown-up. Like a man.'

Thomas squirmed, both at the praise and at the reminder of his youth. 'It was only my duty.'

'I think it was more than duty,' Masha replied gently. 'From the start, you've been very kind to us. It's meant a great deal to me. To both of us. If my cousin is harsh with you, I want you to remember that her life has been hard. She's suffered at the hands of the Nazis. The way she treats you isn't personal.'

Thomas felt that it was very personal indeed, though he didn't say so. He was still aching for a kiss from Masha's soft lips, which he was watching yearningly; but it didn't come. Masha simply pressed his hand, looking warmly into his eyes. 'Thank you, Thomas. I won't forget it.'

And he had to be content with that.

Miss Fanny Ward was in a highly agitated state. She had called Mr Nightingale into her stateroom and was clutching at him with tears in her eyes.

'I know someone has stolen them. And they're precious, so precious. It's not just the value of the stones, Mr Nightingale. They were given to me by Dotty's father. They're diamonds of the first water from South Africa. I would lose anything sooner than those. We must search the ship. Every cabin, every suitcase.'

'Now then, Miss Ward,' he said soothingly. 'Now *then*. I couldn't help noticing, in the lifeboats last night, that you were wearing rather a lot of jewellery. Is it possible that in all the excitement, you dropped the rings overboard?'

'Look,' she said piteously, holding out her hands for him to see. 'They hardly fit over my knuckles any more. They simply can't fall off!'

'Let's retrace your steps. Where were you when the alarm went off?'

She pointed to the bed. 'Asleep.'

'So you got up.'

'I got up and I opened the door to ask what was going on. They told me there was a submarine. So I ran to my jewellery box and I took as many of my things as I could carry.'

'Did you put the two diamond rings on?'

'Oh, I can't remember. I can't remember if I did or not.'

'And you've searched your jewellery box thoroughly?'

'I've had every single thing out,' she wailed. 'I believe someone came into my cabin while I was in the lifeboat, and simply helped themselves!'

'Let's see, now.' Mr Nightingale inspected the heavy, inlaid box. Then he took the walnut chest of drawers on which the box stood, and showing a surprising turn of strength, pulled it away from the bulkhead. He insinuated his slender body in the gap behind it, and bent down. When he straightened again, he was holding something in his hand.

'One,' he said, presenting Miss Ward with a sparkling diamond ring, 'and two.' He gave her the other.

Her face turned pink with delight, and for a moment it was as though she were indeed eternally young, eternally pretty.

'Oh, Mr Nightingale. You are wonderful. They must have fallen down there while I was digging through the box.'

'All's well,' Mr Nightingale said, pushing the chest of drawers back into its alcove, 'that ends well.'

'You must think me an awful old fool,' she said, looking up at him through sparse, wet lashes. 'But you know, at my age – well, this is all I have left.'

'You still have your beauty,' Mr Nightingale replied gallantly.

'You're a brave man,' Miss Ward said gently. 'In more ways than one. We all saw that the crew lifeboat was given up to the passengers.'

'Just doing our job,' he replied airily. 'I've been doing this for a lot of years, as you well know, Miss Ward. And the passengers behaved awfully well.'

'It's one thing to endure dangling in a lifeboat; but it's quite another to face going down with your ship and keeping a smile on your lips.' Miss Ward selected a handsome ruby ring from her hoard and slipped it on to Mr Nightingale's finger. 'I don't know if I'll ever make this voyage again. This is something for you to remember me by.'

Flushed with pleasure, Mr Nightingale took her knobbly little claws in his own well-manicured hands and kissed them. 'Bless you, Miss Ward.'

'Bless you,' she murmured, 'Naughty Nightie.'

HMS Tisiphone

HMS *Tisiphone*, a spanking new Tclass submarine, recently completed by the VickersArmstrong's engineering works in BarrowinFurness, sliced through the sparkling waves to investigate the results of the morning's stalk. The mood on board was one of elation. Her crew, led by one of the Royal Navy's youngest submarine skippers, Lieutenant-Commander George Henry Cottrell, crowded the deck, scanning the water around them. The 4-inch gun was manned, but there was no need for it; the single torpedo they had launched had sent the enemy submarine straight to the bottom. The Germans, as they all agreed, hadn't even seen them coming.

Tisiphone eased through the floating debris and oil. They were looking for any survivors, but the crew were also eager for souvenirs of their first kill of the war. An enterprising AB was using a boathook to fish objects out of the drink. He was rewarded with a few German sailor's caps, which were stuffed with kapok, and had floated to the surface. The men squabbled over these trophies eagerly.

'Is there a boat's name on any of them?' Cottrell called out from the conning tower.

'No, sir.'

They passed by the trash of onions, fragments of rubber and waterlogged debris of all sorts which floated languidly in the swell. A group of life jackets was revealed in a distant trough. The men shouted down to the control room, and *Tisiphone* nosed towards it.

Cottrell leaned on the rail over the eager ratings. 'Keep an eye out for submerged wreckage.'

'Aye-aye, sir.'

'This one's alive!'

The shout brought the crew of HMS *Tisiphone* scrambling to the starboard side to get a look. They had seen several bodies so far, mostly floating face down. But the boathook had pulled in a figure that moved feebly in the water, his pale face stark under a straggling beard, locks of hair plastered across the high forehead.

'Come on, Fritz.' Hands hauled the German on to the deck, where he lay dazed and staring. He was uninjured but in a state of shock, shivering violently with the cold and seemingly unable to understand or answer the questions he was asked. There were no insignia to be seen on his overalls. They began to wrap him in a blanket against hypothermia.

German voices could now be heard shouting hoarsely from the sea.

'There are a few more of the buggers.'

Another four oily and exhausted German sailors were pulled on to the deck.

'This one's in a bad way,' the AB reported. They took off the life jacket and examined the man's wounds. 'Looks like he's been shot.'

'Shot?' Cottrell repeated. He clambered down from the conning tower to see the injured survivor at closer hand. Pushing his cap back on his head, he squatted in front of the German, who had been propped up against the turret. The German's eyes were closed, but he was breathing shallowly. This man was too badly hurt to even tremble with the cold. Tentatively, Cottrell touched his uninjured arm. The man opened his eyes slowly and focused on Cottrell.

'Hallo, Tommy,' he murmured.

'It's George, actually,' Cottrell said. 'Do you speak English?'

'Little bit.'

'That makes things easier. What's your name?'

'Leutnant zur See Rudolf Hufnagel.'

This was rather too much of a mouthful for Cottrell to attempt. 'Right. Are you the captain?'

The German shook his head slowly. 'First Watch Officer.'

'And the name of your boat?'

'*U-113*.'

'Thank you.' Cottrell indicated Hufnagel's wounds. 'Just to be clear, we didn't shoot you. We only torpedoed your sub.'

Hufnagel nodded wearily. 'I know this.'

'Would you like to tell me who did shoot you?'

The German moved his bedraggled head in the direction of the other survivor, closing his eyes again. 'That man.'

'A member of your crew shot you?'

'He is the captain.'

'What's his name?'

'You must ask him that.'

'What did he shoot you for?'

'Mutiny.'

'Mutiny?' Cottrell repeated in some surprise.

The medical officer interrupted. 'I need to tie off that arm, sir. He's losing a lot of blood.'

'Yes, I can see that.' Cottrell stood up to let the medic get at the German. 'There's one of our destroyers in the vicinity. She's heading towards us now. We're going to get you on her as soon as she arrives. All right?' He saw Hufnagel nod slightly. 'In the meantime, we're going to scout round for any more members of your crew. We've got five of you so far.'

Unexpectedly, the first survivor, who had been silent up to now, began to shout in German, his voice hoarse, his expression wild. He was pointing at Hufnagel furiously.

Cottrell looked around at his petty officers. 'What's wrong with him?' Cottrell asked.

'No idea, sir.'

'What's he saying about you?' Cottrell asked Hufnagel.

'He says I am a traitor, and that I will be shot when the war is won.'

Cottrell grunted. 'Can someone shut him up, please.'

The sailor shook the German's arm brusquely. 'Stow it, Fritz. The war is all over for you.'

SS Manhattan

Having missed Thomas at breakfast, Masha went to look for him in one of his favourite refuges, the little triangular breakwater deck at the very front of the boat. Few passengers lingered there; it was filled with derricks and loading machinery, and always very windy, with a good chance of being drenched by spray. No hat or scarf was safe there. But she knew that Thomas liked to hang over the rail and stare at the empty horizon ahead, thinking his thoughts, whatever they were.

She found him sheltering from the wind in the lee of a winch motor, his chin resting on his knees, his arms clasping his shins. She sat down beside him. The cold had sharpened his features, making him look like one of those stray dogs one saw in Berlin parks, too aloof to beg for scraps, yet eyeing every morsel hungrily.

'I didn't mean to upset you yesterday,' she said.

'It's all right.'

'I shouldn't have mentioned your mother. I know you must miss your parents. I miss mine. I miss Berlin. I miss all the people there.'

'I'm sorry, Fräulein Morgenstern.'

'Oh, you must call me Masha now. Haven't we got beyond "Fräulein"? I hope we have. When you call me that, you make me feel like a schoolteacher.' She laid her hand gently on his shoulder. 'You remind me very much of someone.'

'Who?'

'Someone I was once very fond of.'

He turned to look at her, his cheek on his knee. 'Do I look like him?'

'I don't mean in that way. But he cared for me, as you do. And he was always considerate and kind, as you are. He thought of ways to help me before I even knew that I needed help. You are the same. You will make some lucky woman a wonderful husband someday.'

He had nothing to say to that.

Masha went on, her voice even softer. 'I am very grateful for everything you've done for me, Thomas. You've been very gallant. I know that—' Masha hesitated. 'I think that you have perhaps developed feelings for me. Feelings that are more like those of a man than a boy.' She saw that his cheeks were crimson now. She took her hand away from his shoulder. 'I don't mean to embarrass you. I know how painful such feelings can be. Especially when there is no possibility of their being reciprocated. I mean only,' she hastened to add, 'that there is a gap of several years between you and me—'

'I know all that,' Thomas said in a tight voice. 'I understand. You need not explain, Fräulein.'

'Masha.'

'Masha,' he repeated, almost inaudibly.

'I just don't want you to be wounded. These feelings can help us to grow, or they can hurt us very much. I would rather it was the former than the latter. I would not wish to repay your regard by injuring you. But if you should feel pain, I want you to know that the pain passes. With time. It fades, and makes a place for new feelings to grow, feelings for someone else, someone who can share them with you.' Masha looked at Thomas but he made no reply, his head hunched between his shoulders. 'And by then,' she went on, 'I promise that you will have forgotten all about me.'

'Please don't say anything else,' Thomas whispered.

'I've been very clumsy. Forgive me.' Masha picked herself up and held out her hand to him. 'I didn't see you at breakfast. You must be starving. Let's go and have lunch.'

Since learning that Rosemary was not on the ship, Cubby Hubbard had been desolate.

He paced along the deck now, hunched around his wretchedness, passing the rows of deckchairs where happier passengers were lounging at their ease. The chances of his seeing Rosemary again anytime soon were vanishingly small. He could never get back to London until the war was over. Nor could she easily come to the States except under heavy escort. Guarded in a tower somewhere in England, she was more than ever a lost princess in a fairy tale.

He paused in his walk and leaned on the railing to stare at the rolling Atlantic which now separated him from Rosemary.

'I presume,' said a quiet voice behind him, 'that you are wishing for wings to fly.'

Cubby turned. The words had come from a woman reclining on the lounger closest to him. She was in her seventies he guessed, wrapped in a diaphanous, embroidered shawl that looked as though it had come from India or somewhere, a large panama hat and a pair of dark glasses shading her face. 'I beg your pardon?' he said.

She removed her sunglasses, revealing that her eyes, though lined with age, were a bright blue. She was lipsticked and powdered with great care to present an appearance of youth. 'You don't know the song? *The water is wide and I can't get o'er, neither have I wings to fly.* My name is Fanny Ward. I don't mean to intrude on your thoughts. I couldn't help overhearing your exchange with Mrs Kennedy in the lifeboat the other night.'

'Oh. Yes.'

'It was her daughter you were speaking of? Rosemary, the eldest.'

Cubby nodded. 'Yes.'

'A very pretty girl.'

Cubby winced. 'She's the loveliest woman in the world.'

Miss Ward considered him appraisingly. 'First love is a beautiful thing. There's nothing like it.'

'The whole business is hopeless,' Cubby replied heavily.

'Oh, it always is. In my young day, girls were never allowed to marry their first love. It simply wasn't done. One's parents swiftly intervened. The man was told never to darken the threshold again and one was packed off to reflect on one's folly in some dull and remote location until the season was over. One was supposed to be grateful in later life. For having been rescued from a terrible mistake, I mean.'

'Is that what happened to you?' Cubby asked.

Miss Ward examined the brilliant rings on her fingers. 'Well, I was rather a naughty girl, and I ran away to be with my first love.'

'Did you? What happened?'

'It's too long a story to tell you now. But it was considered terribly wrong. One was meant to accept the intervention. And one's feelings were to be folded in tissue paper in a secret drawer and never referred to again.' She cocked her head. 'You don't mind my speaking to you of this? I'm old enough to be your grandmother, after all.'

'I don't mind at all.' Cubby was glad, rather than otherwise, to have this interest taken in his unhappiness. 'Your face is familiar. Are you in the movies?'

Miss Ward merely smiled. 'First love is never forgotten,' she went on. 'It's the only love that remains fresh and potent for a lifetime. It's the truest and most innocent of loves, exactly because it can never come to fruition. Do you understand what I mean?'

'Not exactly.'

'It never grows old; you see? It's as fleeting as the morning dew, yet it clings to us all our lives. It becomes part of our existence. It's probably the last thing we remember on our deathbeds.'

Cubby had been listening to the old creature with a growing feeling of discomfort. In her queer, gossamer wrap, with her pale-blue eyes, she was like an elderly fairy of some sort, laying a spell upon him. 'We don't want to give it all up,' he said sullenly. 'We want to get married.'

'Oh, you mustn't think of it,' Miss Ward exclaimed. 'First love is far too precious. It's not of this world. It asks nothing and gives all. It has nothing to do with the trade and barter of marriage – the dreary practicalities of rent and children and dirty dishes and all that.'

'But that's exactly what we want.'

'Would you lead a goddess to the kitchen sink? First love is divine. It belongs in the realm of the soul. Keep it there, young man.'

She replaced her dark glasses, and the advice (if that was what it had been) appeared to be at an end. It had hardly consoled Cubby.

He braced himself to speak to Mrs Kennedy.

He tipped his hat to Miss Ward and found his way to the Kennedy stateroom and tapped at the door. Mrs Kennedy herself opened it. Although he saw her in his mind as a dragon, complete with scales and fiery breath, she looked pale and tired today.

'You don't give up, do you?' she greeted him.

'I just want to know that she's okay,' he replied quietly.

'If you're asking whether she's weeping and wailing without you – the answer is no. She's with her father, and she's very happy.'

'I'm glad to hear that.'

'And don't bother writing her any more love letters. She won't get them.'

He swallowed that without comment. 'What happens if they bomb London?'

'She's somewhere safe, Mr Hubbard. It has never been my policy to expose my children to harm.'

'I don't mean Rosemary any harm.' When she made no comment, he went on, 'I do care for her very much.'

'You think you do.'

'I know I do.'

'Perhaps you can even kid yourself that you didn't do her any harm. But you did. Just like all the others who took advantage of her.'

'I didn't take advantage of her.'

'You are no better than a man who has sexual relations with a child.'

He flushed. 'She's not a child.'

'Not in body, perhaps. But everywhere it matters – in her heart, in her mind, in her soul – Rosemary is a child. She will always be a child. Your idea of marrying her is not just absurd, it's obscene.'

'So is locking her up,' he retorted. 'How long do you think you can keep her shut in a convent?'

'The rest of her life, if that's what it takes to protect her.' She looked at him with hostile green eyes. 'Rosemary is as happy as Larry without you. She's forgotten you already.'

'I don't believe that for one moment.'

She laughed shortly. 'How dare you contradict me to my face? You've got some nerve, coming to me like this.'

'Like I said, I do love her. I don't want to live without her.'

'In that case, I suggest you go to the rail and throw yourself over.'

'You're a cruel woman,' he exclaimed, stung by her coldness.

'Then you wouldn't like me as a mother-in-law,' she retorted. 'If you use extravagant language, you can expect to be mocked. You're a young man who sees what he wants to see and hears what he wants to hear.' She reached into her pocket. 'You have no right to read this, but I want you to understand, once and for all.' She handed him the telegram.

He unfolded it. It had been sent to the ship from London the day before. The pasted lines of printed capitals covered the whole page:

HAD RING-A-DING AFTERNOON TEA AT BELMONT HOUSE WITH ROSEMARY. LOOKED CHARMING AND WAS PRAISED BY EVERYBODY. LOVES THE PLACE. SAYS 'MOST WONDERFULEST' SCHOOL SHE HAS BEEN TO.

ALL SERENE AND HAPPY. NO SIGN OF PINING FOR YOU OR CHILDREN. MUCH LESS DEMANDED OF HER NOW. SHELTERED FROM STRESS AND KEPT OCCUPIED. VERY RELAXED. IDEAL LIFE FOR HER.

SISTERS CONSTANTLY REMARKING ON 'MARKED IMPROVEMENT' IN HER ATTITUDE AND STUDIES. AM VERY OPTIMISTIC.

HAVE INSTALLED TELEPHONE LINE AND FIREFIGHTING EQUIPMENT FOR THEM. SEE ROSEMARY EVERY WEEKEND. DON'T WORRY ANY MORE. JACK AND JOE JR HEADING HOME SOON. MUCH LOVE TO YOU AND KIDS. JOE.

Cubby handed the telegram back to Mrs Kennedy. 'Sounds like he is talking about a six-year-old,' he mumbled. But his eyes felt hot and there was a hard knot in his throat.

Mrs Kennedy put the telegram back in her pocket. 'You think me unkind, Mr Hubbard. But I'm going to give you some advice that is the kindest thing anyone will say to you: get on with your life and forget Rosemary.'

She closed the door in his face.

Igor Stravinsky was coughing heavily into his handkerchief that night. Masha laid her hand on his arm.

'You should not be smoking. This is killing you.'

'It's not – the smoking – which is killing me.'

He spat into the handkerchief. It was a dark night, but by the dim light on the promenade deck, where they reclined side by side, she could see the red stain on the linen.

'You are not well.'

He let his head sag back against the cushion, gasping for breath. 'How far – have you got – with my symphony?'

'I've copied forty pages. It's a great privilege. But—'

'But?'

'The music is not in any sense Russian, Monsieur Stravinsky.'

He was silent for a long while. 'I do not feel myself to be a Russian in any sense,' he said at last. 'I consider myself a French citizen.'

'Why have you stopped working on it?'

He made a weary gesture with the bloodstained handkerchief. 'I have stopped everything, Masha.'

'Even living?' she asked. 'Forgive me, but you told my cousin that you wanted to die.'

'I am old. I have lived. And I have lost a wife, a child. You are still young. You haven't had a child yet. You can't stop living until you've reproduced, that's the law of nature.'

'And what if I were to lose my child, the way you've lost yours?'

'You have to hazard everything,' he replied. 'That is the law of nature too. Risk everything, your whole being, on that throw of the dice.'

'And how do you survive the death of a child, Monsieur Stravinsky?'

'Maybe you don't.'

'Then how are we supposed to make sense of life?' she asked. 'Are you telling me you can't leave until you've had your heart broken?'

'Perhaps, yes.'

'And to whom does it matter, whether you suffer or not?'

'To God, perhaps.'

'I don't believe in God any more.'

'I do.' Stravinsky sat up and coughed up blood again. 'But not in a God who keeps us from harm.'

'What sort of God, then?'

He rose with an effort to his feet. 'I think of God as a stern country schoolmaster. He calls us one by one, to write something on the blackboard before he will let us go home. Some of us write beautiful things, some of us write nonsense, some make glaring errors. For some of us, the chalk snaps in our fingers before we can finish.'

Masha watched him walk slowly away, then she rose and went to the rail alone. The moon had not yet risen, there were no stars. The lights of the ship glimmered on the nearest waves, but beyond, all was blackness.

Masha leaned on the rail, thinking about the letter Rachel had received in Cobh, before the submarine. Did she feel any differently towards Rachel, since Rachel had revealed her inner self? She felt that she didn't. She was too fond of her cousin to be disturbed in any way. She felt, more than anything else, compassion for the difficulties Rachel had faced in her life, pity for her isolation and her sorrows. But there was much that was strange about Rachel that had now been explained, and which she had begun to understand.

'You are sad tonight.'

Masha turned. Arturo Toscanini had joined her at the rail, wrapped in a heavy coat and scarf against the cold. 'It's a sad world, maestro,' she replied.

'I feel it also.' He struck his breast. 'This is broken.'

'I'm so sorry.'

He stood beside her, his face in shadow, the deck lights making a silvery halo of his sparse hair. 'But you are too young to feel such things.'

'I don't think it matters how old one is.'

'Perhaps that's true. When I was young, I suffered from profound bouts of melancholy.'

'I'm not normally a melancholy person,' Masha replied with a catch in her voice. 'But I've heard so much terrible news of late. Sometimes it overwhelms me.'

'Poor little bird.' He put his arm around her shoulders. Grateful for the fatherly reassurance, Masha laid her head on Toscanini's shoulder.

'You are so kind, maestro.'

'It pains me to see you all alone in the world,' he replied in a husky voice. 'So young and so beautiful. I should like to help you.'

It was almost like having Papa back. She nestled into him. 'Oh, maestro—'

But before she could finish her sentence, he was kissing her. She was astonished to feel his bristly moustache prickling against her nose, his lips sucking at hers. 'So young,' he repeated, munching greedily, enveloping her in a miasma of bad teeth, 'so beautiful—'

'Maestro!' Masha exclaimed in horror.

'Let me console you. I understand, I understand everything!'

'Please, maestro!' She struggled to get away from him.

His wiry arms were surprisingly strong, and he was very determined. 'Don't fight me. I can make you happy, *piccolina*.'

'Let me go!'

'Patatina, dai.' He had lapsed into Italian, and was murmuring endearments to her as his whiskery kisses, like the attentions of an elderly terrier, planted themselves on her mouth, cheeks and eyes.

'Maestro, stop!'

'Carissima!' The conductor's nimble fingers were prying under her coat, searching for the curves of her breasts.

'Say, what's going on here?' The interruption had come in the form of a burly young passenger in a checked jacket, his hair slicked back in the defiant quiff which was popular with young Americans these days. 'Is everything okay?'

Toscanini appeared momentarily baffled, his tongue still protruding, his eyes rolling. However, his arms relaxed, and Masha extricated herself swiftly from his amorous grasp. 'Thank you,' she said breathlessly to the young American.

'I'll walk you to your cabin.' The American offered his arm. She took it gratefully.

'*Carissima*!' Toscanini bleated in dismay as Masha and her rescuer made their escape down the deck.

'Who's that old billy goat?' the American asked.

Masha took out her handkerchief and wiped the spittle off her face in disgust. 'It's Arturo Toscanini.'

'The conductor?'

'Yes.'

'Gee. I hope I did the right thing. You looked kind of reluctant, so I thought I better say something.'

'I think he got carried away.'

'He's old enough to be your grandfather.'

'Yes. I don't know whether to laugh or cry.'

'He ought to be ashamed of himself. My name's Cubby Hubbard, by the way.'

'I'm Masha Morgenstern.' She glanced over her shoulder, anxious that Toscanini would follow her; but he had vanished. 'I'm so glad you were there.'

'No problem. I've seen you and your friend around the ship. I guess you're getting away from Hitler?'

'Yes. And you're going home?'

The American's pleasantly chubby face looked unhappy. 'I'm going to enlist as soon as I get back.'

'But America's not in the war.'

'Not yet. But I reckon we soon will be. I thought I'd get an early start. So when it happens, I already have some rank, you know what I mean?'

'I suppose that's one way of looking at it,' Masha said uncertainly. 'Do you come from a family of soldiers?'

'No. Matter of fact, I'm a musician. But—'

'But?'

'Well, I've had a disappointment. I don't feel the same way about things any more.'

'A disappointment in love?' Masha asked.

'You could say that.'

'Did she choose someone else?'

He sighed. 'Other people chose for her.'

'Oh. I'm sorry. I know how that feels,' Masha said quietly.

'You do? Well, I guess we're in the same boat. The whole thing was just a dream.'

'You mustn't say that.'

'I shouldn't have tried to kid myself it could ever work. A couple of days ago an old lady – I think she was a witch – told me you should never mix dreams with reality.'

'But you can't live without your dreams,' Masha said wistfully.

'Well, that's all I have now. I don't see my future the way I did before. A few weeks ago, I was in Paris, listening to Django Reinhardt. I was kidding myself that one day I could be as good as that. But I just realised I'll never be as good as that. No point in even trying. So it's the Navy for me.'

Masha glanced at his face. Under the youthful plumpness there was a square, dogged strength. 'I hope you go back to your music one day.'

'You never know.'

'No, you never know.'

He escorted her to her cabin, where she thanked him and disengaged her arm. She went through the door, half-giggling, half-tearful. 'Oh, Rachel!'

'What's the matter?' Rachel demanded.

'Toscanini. He's been trying to make love to me on the promenade deck.'

Rachel rose angrily. 'What did he do, the wretch?'

'Oh, it's too absurd. He put his arm around me, and I thought he was just trying to be nice, but then he started kissing me and calling me *piccolina* and *patatina*—'

'How disgusting.'

'But such a nice young American came to my rescue. He told me he's going to enlist. I feel so sad for him.'

'Never mind him. Didn't I warn you not to let Toscanini get you in some dark corner?' Rachel said.

'But he's so old! I never imagined he could behave like that—'

'We must complain to the Commodore.'

'Oh, don't be silly. Everybody will laugh at us.'

'He's a revolting creature. His wife is on board!'

Masha sat down and began to laugh breathlessly. 'Well, at least I can tell my grandchildren I was kissed by Toscanini.'

'You,' Rachel said dryly, 'and a few hundred others.'

HMS Tisiphone

Altogether, HMS *Tisiphone* picked up five survivors of *U-113*, including Todt, Hufnagel and Krupp. The five of them had all been in the control room, and had managed to make their escape through the conning tower hatch in the first few minutes as the U-boat went down. It was Krupp who had ensured Hufnagel's survival, taking precious moments to fit him with a life jacket at the risk of his own life.

The rest of the crew, including the men in the stern of the boat, where the torpedo had struck, those who had rushed into the forward compartment, those in the engine room and those in the sickbay, had all perished with the submarine. Forty-three men were dead. Hufnagel tried to absorb this as his injuries were treated by a well-meaning but clumsy British petty officer.

Almost everyone he had known aboard *U-113*, a small world, but a world nevertheless, was gone. He would never see any of them again. It was a thing almost impossible to comprehend. Most of them had been barely over twenty. He himself was only a few years older than that, and nothing in his life had prepared him for these past weeks. He felt altered in vital ways, a man apart, as though he had in reality gone down with the iron coffin, and a stranger had been put in his place.

The well-meaning officer gave him a swig of scotch from a bottle, to fortify him against the pain of the crude stitches with which he was trying to hold together Hufnagel's torn and bleeding arm. It was a mistake. The raw alcohol made Hufnagel confused and then violently ill. The bed which he had borrowed from a British sailor had to be changed.

The British crew, fresh out of port, were clean and groomed. He and the other four survivors had been dirty and unkempt even before *U-113* had been sunk. They were far worse now, covered in oil and filth. The only emotion he was able to feel at first was a vague shame at his own appearance and that of his fellow Germans.

The British skipper, Cottrell, was inquisitive. He was eager to talk, and looked in on Hufnagel now and then as they waited to rendezvous with the destroyer which would take charge of the captured Germans. He was a pink-cheeked, gingery man who affected a pipe, and seemed to Hufnagel like the cartoon of a typical Englishman.

'May I ask,' he enquired during one of his visits, 'what you were up to with the *Manhattan*?'

'Our captain got it into his head that he was going to torpedo her.'

'Didn't you see the American flags painted on her sides?'

'Yes. We had a disagreement about that.'

'And that's when this so-called mutiny took place?'

'It had started some time earlier, I think.'

'But this is when he shot you?'

'Yes.'

Cottrell puffed on his unlit pipe, producing a whistling sound which apparently give him as much satisfaction as real tobacco smoke. 'I don't mean to interrogate you. They'll do that when you get to England. But it seems you saved a lot of innocent lives. You're not a Nazi, I take it?'

Hufnagel couldn't think of an answer which would explain his feelings without seeming disloyal to his country. 'I am a German.'

'Yes, of course you are. The reason I ask is because your skipper's still Heil-Hitlering and raving about you.'

'Yes, I hear him.' Todt was perfectly audible a few bunks away, accusing Hufnagel of treason.

'He seems awfully cut up. I suppose the fact that you were all so busy arguing about the *Manhattan* explains how we were able to surprise you.'

'I suppose so.'

'Did you serve in the last war, old chap?' Cottrell asked innocently.

Hufnagel realised he must look very decrepit indeed. 'I wasn't born yet when it started.'

'Oh, I see. So you're about the same age as me. Well, the closest I'd been to battle was breaking a tooth on some buckshot in a roast pheasant. Your boat was our first kill.'

'I congratulate you,' Hufnagel said dryly.

'Thank you.' Cottrell champed on his innocuous pipe. 'I'm glad you survived. Sorry about your crew.'

'You didn't start the war.'

'Neither of us started the war. There's not much point in worrying about it, is there?'

'No. If you worry about it, you won't last very long. Like Hamlet.'

'Oh, you've heard of Hamlet?'

'We read Shakespeare at school.'

'Odd, that.'

Hufnagel, weak with pain and loss of blood, found himself wishing Cottrell would go away and leave him alone. 'What is odd?'

'Our two countries being at war again.'

'You always start it.'

'Not exactly.' Cottrell opened his mouth to launch on a defence, but seeing Hufnagel's drained face, thought better of it, and drew the curtain again.

SS Manhattan

'They say we will be in New York in four days,' Stravinsky announced at breakfast the next morning.

'You sound happy about it,' Katharine observed.

'Why should I not be happy about it?' He dabbed egg yolk off his lips. 'It is our journey's end, after all. The start of a new life.'

In Le Havre, a matter of three weeks earlier, he had been bemoaning the end of an old life, Katharine reflected; but she did not utter the thought. She was glad to see him starting to look buoyant again, shedding his weariness and despair. Even the tone of his skin was improved, as though the blood beneath were circulating more vigorously. 'I think you quite enjoyed our encounter with the German submarine.'

'There was a certain exhilaration in evading death,' he acknowledged. 'And now to be speeding away is also very pleasant. We are making an average of twenty-two knots. And the weather ahead of us is fine. I found this out from the steward, Mr Nightingale. The information cost me five dollars.'

'Why did you have to pay five dollars?' Thomas asked.

'A sprat to catch a mackerel. There is a sweepstake of a hundred dollars. Armed with this information I was careful to buy a low number. A hundred and fifty-three.'

'I don't understand what you are talking about,' Masha said.

'They are betting on how many hours it will take us to reach New York,' Katharine said. 'Though if you think Mr Nightingale isn't selling the same information to every passenger who asks him, you are more naïve than I imagined, Igor.'

He smiled sardonically. 'Perhaps I am. An innocent lamb arriving to be shorn by the cunning Americans.'

'In my experience,' she retorted, 'it's usually Americans who are taken in by Old World guile and deceit.'

'I'm glad to hear that,' Rachel put in. 'I look forward to spinning my Jewish web again. The Führer made it rather difficult for us to practise our wiles.' She glanced at Katharine. 'You are Jewish, aren't you?'

'I am an atheist,' Katharine replied, irritated as always by the question.

'Ah. This means what, exactly?'

'It means I do not care to categorise myself as adhering to one outmoded system of beliefs or another.'

'One can see you have not lived in the Third Reich,' Rachel said dryly.

'Rachel,' Masha whispered, 'you are being impertinent.'

'In the Third Reich,' Rachel went on, 'it does not matter how you characterise yourself. One does not enjoy the luxury of categorising oneself. It matters only how the authorities categorise you.'

'I am aware of how things stand in the Third Reich,' Katharine said stiffly.

'That is very clever of you, having had no practical experience of life there, as well as not adhering to any outmoded system of beliefs.'

Stravinsky was amused. 'It seems it's your turn to suffer the elder Miss Morgenstern's ironical barbs, Katharine. Have you tired of tormenting young Thomas, Miss Morgenstern?'

'I will get to Thomas by and by,' Rachel said with a glint in her ice-blue eyes.

Thomas looked up from his plate with a wan smile. 'For my part, you can skip over me, Fräulein. I will donate my turn to someone else.'

Rachel stared for a moment, then gave a sharp laugh. 'So there is a little wit in that head of yours.'

As they left the breakfast table, Masha took Rachel's arm. 'Don't you think there is some mystery surrounding Thomas?' she whispered.

'What mystery might that be?'

'He seems so young.'

'He is eighteen.'

'I don't think he's telling the truth about *that*. And where are his parents, for another thing?'

'They are probably high Nazis, and too busy to leave Germany. He is going to stay with his uncle, isn't he?'

'It's strange that they let their son travel so many thousands of miles all alone, during wartime.'

'If I had a son like *that*, I would drown him in a bucket.'

'Rachel!' Masha exclaimed. 'Sometimes you go too far.'

'That,' Rachel said grimly, 'is my speciality.'

'Wasn't he very helpful when the submarine came?'

'That was only because he's in love with you.'

'Constantly reiterating that he's in love with me doesn't explain him, Rachel. There is more to him than that. He has a sense of duty, of responsibility, of human kindness that someone must have taught him. And you were very rude to Miss Wolff at breakfast.'

'She gets on my nerves, declaring she can choose whether to be a Jew or not.'

'You know that there have been times when you and I have both wanted to pass as Gentiles,' Masha said.

'That was quite different. That was a question of saving ourselves from a beating, or worse. She is in no danger. She does it because she is ashamed of her Jewishness.'

'How do you know that?'

'I know that sort of woman.'

'You're very unreasonable. I don't think you have the right to judge Miss Wolff.'

'Besides,' Rachel added, 'I am sure she is ashamed of something else about herself.'

'What do you mean?'

'I mean that she has the same preferences as I do, but denies them.'

'You think she's a lesbian?'

'She doesn't have the courage to be a lesbian, so she despises women who do.'

'Not everyone has your courage,' Masha said gently. Since receiving Dorothea's letter in Cobh, Masha knew that Rachel had been deeply unhappy. Her raillery had become bitter; her repartee had turned to spite. 'You're upset about Dorothea. I wish you would talk to me, instead of bottling it up inside.'

'What is there to talk about?' Rachel demanded harshly. 'I am going my way and she is going hers. It's finished.'

'Are you angry with her?'

'It doesn't matter what I feel.'

'But you said yourself she has no choice.'

'Women never have a choice.'

'Under the Nazis, perhaps not. But we're going to a country where women are free.'

'If you believe that, then you're even more of a soft-headed idiot than I took you for,' Rachel snapped. Then, seeing the wounded look on Masha's face, she deliberately dug her nails into her own cheeks. 'I hate myself.'

Masha grabbed her cousin's hands to stop her hurting herself further. 'Don't do that!' Rachel's sharp nails had made red marks on her delicate skin.

'Forgive me, forgive me.'

'I don't mind what you say to me. Only, I can't bear to see you so wretched.'

'She will suffer with Vogelfänger. He's a Nazi and a brute.' Rachel's eyes were full of angry tears. 'Of all the professors, we hated him most. He's killed one wife already. When I think of her having to submit to him—'

'Don't think of that. Think that she'll be saved from something worse.'

'I try to. But I'm full of bile and gall. I want to tear my hair out sometimes. Leave me alone, Masha. I'm not fit company for someone as decent as you.'

But Masha refused to be shaken off. She hurried Rachel to their cabin to apply a cold compress to the scratches her cousin had inflicted on herself. The Hungarian girl, silently gnawing on a dried kielbasa sausage, watched them with large eyes. 'You'll meet someone else,' Masha said, trying to be encouraging. 'That's what I said to myself after Rudi, and I believe it.'

'I would rather you told me to despair than offered me platitudes.'

'At least don't scratch your own eyes out.'

'If I don't, I may scratch out someone else's instead.'

Finding Rachel unresponsive to her consolations, and remembering that they were arriving in New York in four days, Masha left her cousin with her face turned to the wall and set about transcribing the Stravinsky manuscript.

With Masha engrossed in the Stravinsky manuscript, and Thomas keeping out of her way, Rachel was thrown back on her own unhappiness. Despite all the horrors of the past years, she had clung to the dream that, once the war was over, Dorothea would come to her, and they would make a life together. Dorothea's marriage to Heinrich Vogelfänger would make that impossible. And as for the war, which had begun so violently, it seemed less and less likely that it would end in a year, or ten years.

She wandered the ship, alone in the crowds, observing silently. As Mr Nightingale had told Stravinsky, the SS *Manhattan* was making swift progress. Unhindered at last by political borders or human delays of any kind, she sped across the Atlantic at a steady twenty-two nautical miles per hour, night and day.

Since she was sailing west, she was losing time constantly. Every so many hundred miles, as the ship entered a new time zone, passengers were advised to turn their watches and clocks back an hour. This meant, according to some, that they had all been given an extra hour of their lives to re-live. Whether this was true or not, it became a celebration each time, and Rachel noted ironically that the complimentary hour of life was given over in most cases to drinking and partying.

Altogether, there would be six of these hours by the time they reached New York. They became more and more animated as the Manhattan approached closer to the United States coast. Passengers crowded the public areas to drink and dance. The little refugee jazz orchestra was able to earn generous tips by taking requests. Hoffman's Midget Marvels took to sitting on the bar in the Cocktail Lounge, all in a line, a very popular spectacle. Passengers competed for the privilege of buying them a round of drinks, and it was surprising how much they could put away, even the littlest and oldest of the Marvels, who accepted only twelve-year-old single malt.

Everyone was impressed with the speed the Manhattan was making. But one afternoon, an airliner was spotted in the sky above the ship.

The arrival of this fellow traveller in the midst of the vast and empty Atlantic was somehow portentous. Passengers craned their necks at it, waving their hats and handkerchiefs in case anyone could see them from up there. The plane overtook them swiftly. In a matter of ten minutes, it had disappeared again. It would be in New York by nightfall. 'And that,' Commodore Randall commented to Rachel, 'signals the end of the ocean liner business.'

There were other entertainments, which Rachel attended, longing for distraction from her dark thoughts. Madame Quo gave a talk on the history of Chinese sculpture, illustrated with a number of valuable jade figurines which she was taking with her to America.

The Reverend Ezekiel Perkins offered several of his short lectures on a variety of important subjects, including the threat of masculine women, the lies of anthropology, the evil of psychoanalysis, the menace of Negro blood, getting right with God, fighting Bolshevism, strengthening the Mann Act, abolishing dance halls, censoring the cinema, and the foundations of the Republic. There were bigots and Nazis in America too, Rachel saw.

Other than these lectures, the passengers passed the time on the overcrowded ship by playing shuffleboard, quoits or deck tennis in the few free places that were available. The gymnasiums were among the rooms that had been given over to the additional passengers, so a brisk walk around the deck was also a choice made by many, though this involved weaving a circuitous path to avoid others on the same exercise, as Rachel did.

And so the ship, containing as many people as a small town, and at least as much diversity, sailed on towards New York.

HMS Tisiphone

Rudi Hufnagel and the other survivors of *U-113* had now spent two days on HMS *Tisiphone*. Lieutenant-Commander Cottrell was eager to get them off his submarine. He was already back on his patrol, and the five captured enemy sailors to be fed, berthed and watched were causing him a headache. There was also the question of Hufnagel's health, which was deteriorating rapidly. The left shoulder was very swollen. He had not stopped losing blood from the injury to his right forearm, and was growing very weak. The petty officer who had tried to stitch him up was unable to stop the flow.

'To tell you the truth,' he said to his skipper, 'I think I've done more harm than good.'

'You're not a doctor, Terry,' Cottrell said consolingly. 'But I don't want him to die on us. And *Warspite*'s let us down.'

The rendezvous with HMS *Warspite*, the destroyer which was meant to pick up the Germans, hadn't come off; she had been diverted on urgent business elsewhere. There was, however, a second destroyer about to pass within range of *Tisiphone*. She was HMS *Amphitrite*, and as luck would have it, she was equipped with an operating theatre and had a surgeon on board. There was only one drawback, which Cottrell explained to Hufnagel.

'She's in a convoy, bound for New York. Thanks to the endeavours of chaps like you, merchant ships aren't crossing the Atlantic on their own any more. The doctor on board will fix you up, but you're going to be at sea for quite a while longer. Probably several weeks.'

Hufnagel gave Cottrell a hollow smile. 'That may be preferable to a prisoner-of-war camp on land.'

'It's certainly preferable to you dying on my submarine and having to be tipped overboard. You could think of it as a rest cure. So, no objections?'

'None.'

'Right. I'll radio her captain and see if he'll take you on.'

The captain of the *Amphitrite* was not delighted by the request to take on prisoners, one of whom needed urgent surgery. However, Cottrell pressed the issue, describing Hufnagel's part in preventing the *Manhattan* from being torpedoed, a gallant act in the course of which he had received his wound. Also, the young Navy surgeon on board *Amphitrite* said he didn't mind getting a little practice. It might even help, he said, to sort out his station and get everything streamlined, ready for real action.

Accordingly, HMS *Amphitrite* made a brief diversion to intersect with *Tisiphone* the next day. In a high wind and rough seas, Hufnagel and the others were transferred to the destroyer. A line was rigged between the two vessels. *Amphitrite* had no breeches buoy, so they used a bosun's chair to run the Germans across, one by one. The last to go was Hufnagel, with his legs dangling through the canvas harness around his groin. He found the experience only slightly preferable to being shot.

Nor was the welcome on the destroyer a warm one. In contrast to the comradely, even chummy atmosphere on the submarine, the crew of the destroyer greeted the Germans coldly, as enemies. The uninjured members of the crew were sent straight to secure quarters. Two burly able seamen marched Hufnagel to the sickbay, stolidly oblivious to his gasps of pain. The young surgeon inspected him with a keen eye.

'This Jerry's half-dead,' he said with the satisfaction of a man accepting a challenge, as though Hufnagel couldn't understand him. 'Let's get to work.'

While the doctor prepared Hufnagel for surgery, *Amphitrite* put on a spurt of speed to catch up with the rest of the convoy; and in this way, Rudi Hufnagel found himself in the wake of *Manhattan*, on his way to New York.

Ellis Island

Thomas, Masha and Rachel had all made their way up to the Observation Deck to get their first sight of New York. To each of the three of them, Berlin had been a great city. But New York, glimpsed indistinctly across the bay, half-shrouded in the early morning mist, was already immeasurably greater. The forest of towers and spires rose up to the sky in tints of gold and grey, with violet shadows. The tops of the highest buildings, some of which they knew the names of already, reached above the clouds.

'What beautiful buildings!' Masha exclaimed. 'I can almost hear the roar of traffic from here.'

Shortly after passing the Statue of Liberty, the *Manhattan* stopped at Ellis Island, where immigration officers boarded the ship.

All the foreigners – a majority of the passengers – were called on to present their passports and visas for inspection. Long lines of refugees formed on the deck, filtering slowly down the gangplank to the immigrant station, watched by those lucky enough to be United States citizens. Among the latter group were Dr Meese and the Reverend Ezekiel Perkins. The Reverend Perkins took the occasion to deliver some thoughts on the spectacle below him.

'And is our nation ready to discard the costly lessons it learned, and once again open its gates to the refuse of Europe?' he asked rhetorically. 'Look at this trash, most of them with little more than five dollars in their pockets, most unable to speak a word of the English language.' He raised a plump forefinger. 'You will say they are fugitives from tyrannical governments. But when has Europe not had its tyrannical governments? Is that justification for letting them flood our country at the rate of a thousand a day, bringing with them crime, disease, drug addiction and who knows what else?'

As the Reverend Perkins continued apostrophising, the aliens filtered slowly down the gangways towards the immigration station. The addition of incongruous Moorish domes had done little to soften its high red-brick walls, or its prison-like appearance. Once inside, they found themselves in a great, vaulted space where, like human cattle, they were separated into lines and processed at counters. For most, the process was tedious, but accomplished in due course. For a few, it ended unexpectedly.

Almost the first to fall by the wayside was Thomas König. No sooner had he presented himself at a counter with his travel documents when two officers took him off and led him up the stairs, where he vanished.

Masha was one of the few people who noticed this, and she clutched Stravinsky's sleeve.

'Did you see that they arrested Thomas?' she said urgently.

'I don't think they arrested him. They probably just want to check his papers.'

Masha, who was something of an expert on what an arrest looked like, shook her head. 'They arrested him. Something is wrong.'

By the late afternoon, most of the *Manhattan*'s foreign passengers had been processed and had returned to the ship. But Thomas had not reappeared. Masha, by now in a state of acute anxiety over the boy's fate, prevailed on Stravinsky to make an enquiry about his cabin-mate. They went together to the front desks, where crowds of anxious passengers, speaking a variety of languages, were being held in check. At last, they were seen by an immigration officer in a black uniform. He led them to his office, which stank of cigars and sweat, where he faced them across a desk crowded with passports of every colour.

'Thomas König is being detained until his status is clarified,' the man told them.

'What is wrong with his status?' Stravinsky asked.

Clearly weary and overworked, the officer was impatient. 'Are you a relative?'

'He has shared my cabin from Le Havre, and I feel the moral obligation to act as his guardian.'

'Your moral obligations don't have any legal force here.'

'At least tell us what the problem is.'

'Monsieur Stravinsky is a very celebrated composer,' Masha put in.

'I know who Mr Stravinsky is.' The officer, who was an older man named Captain O'Leary, sighed and wiped his nicotine-stained moustache. He opened a folder and took out a passport. 'We believe the boy is attempting to enter the country illegally.'

Stravinsky fixed his glasses on his beaky nose to look at the passport closely. He flipped through the pages. 'I can see nothing wrong with it. It seems fully legal.'

'The passport is legal, but it's not his passport.'

Masha gasped in dismay. 'But – but he's Thomas König. Look at the photograph!'

'The photograph is the problem,' O'Leary said dryly. 'The boy in the photograph looks similar, but he's older. We often see passport photographs that look younger. One that looks older is a problem – unless the passport holder has worked out how to make time run backwards. According to the birthdate in the passport, he would be eighteen years old. But he looks a couple of years younger. There are other details that make us suspicious, too. In our line of work, you get an instinct.'

'What do you intend to do?'

'We don't know who he is, but we're going to find out,' the officer said grimly. 'We'll ask the German consulate to start an enquiry to find out if the passport was stolen.'

'I cannot believe that Thomas would be party to a theft,' Stravinsky said.

'We're not concerned with any crimes committed in the countries of origin, Mr Stravinsky. That doesn't interest us here on Ellis Island. We're concerned with an attempt to enter this country unlawfully. If the kid's papers aren't on the level, this is as close as he's ever going to get to the United States.'

'What do you mean?'

'I mean that he'll be shipped straight back to where he came from. If the Germans ask for him to be deported, they'll pay his fare. If not, Uncle Sam will foot the bill.'

Masha was trembling with anxiety, but Stravinsky remained calm and polite. 'May we speak to young Thomas? There is probably a misunderstanding at the bottom of all this which can be cleared up with a few gentle words.'

'He'll be in the holding cells already by now,' O'Leary said, looking at his fob watch.

'I would take it as a very great personal favour if you would let me see my young friend for a few moments,' Stravinsky said quietly. 'You said you intend to find out who he is. Well, I may be able to get that information far more easily than any interrogation will.'

The officer snapped his fob watch shut and glanced at Stravinsky with heavy-lidded eyes. 'We've processed over a thousand people today.

And we're about to shut the building. But you may have a point. You can see him for five minutes.'

Thomas looked very small in the holding cell, which was also occupied by three adult men, including a heavily tattooed Finnish stowaway and two Central Europeans who wore tickets announcing that they had infectious diseases.

He looked up as the visitors came in; and then he and Masha burst simultaneously into tears. 'Thomas, Thomas,' she choked, 'what's all this?'

The boy seemed unable to answer. Stravinsky spoke quietly. 'Thomas is not who he says he is, Masha. His family were Lutherans who objected to Nazi thuggery. For this they were sent to a camp. Thomas's mother managed to help him escape, using a borrowed passport. He has been sailing, so to speak, under a false flag.'

'Oh, Thomas!' Masha knelt beside him and took him in her arms, hugging him tightly. 'Why didn't you tell us?'

'I couldn't,' he said, his face buried in Masha's soft hair.

'What went wrong, Thomas?' Stravinsky asked.

'They asked me to take off my shirt,' he replied in a low voice. 'They said I was not muscular enough to be eighteen.'

'What did you reply?'

'I said I had been sick.' He raised his head. He was ashen-faced and trembling. 'But they didn't believe me. They looked at the photograph with a magnifying glass, and measured my face with a ruler. They said the picture was of another person. And I am a little taller than it says in the passport.'

'I don't think it will do any good to cling to the lie any longer,' Stravinsky said quietly. 'We have to tell the truth and face what comes.'

Thomas nodded. 'I'm ready. I will go back to Germany.'

'Let's see about that. Be strong, Thomas,' Stravinsky said. 'Come, Masha. We need to see Captain O'Leary again.'

'I knew,' Masha said breathlessly to Stravinsky as they climbed the stairs, 'I knew he was no Hitler Youth. He is too good for that.'

Sitting in Captain O'Leary's office, five minutes later, Stravinsky lit a cigarette. The immigration officer puffed on a cigar. The two men were reflective in their clouds of smoke.

'What seems to have upset the boy most,' Stravinsky said at last, 'was that he saw his mother arrested and led to the van by Gestapo men. He was at an upper window in the house next door, you see, watching everything. She could have looked up at him, but she didn't. This haunts him. I think it will haunt him to his dying day. Now. I invite you to consider the state of mind of a mother who does not look at her child one last time. She has prepared for this day. Dreaded it, but prepared for it. Her husband and his brother have embarked on a course of action, based on conscience, which will inevitably lead to all their deaths. But she believes in her heart that her child, her only son, should not be destroyed because of that. So she has prepared. You follow?'

O'Leary nodded, examining the coal of his cigar.

'As they lead her to her death, she knows that her son is watching. But she does not look up at him. She knows that if she does, she may break down. The child may break down and cry out to her. And all will be lost. So she keeps her eyes on the ground so as not to betray his hiding place. It must have cost her a lot not to look at her child one last time. Don't you think?'

O'Leary swung in his swivel chair and busied himself with some papers. 'I guess so,' he said gruffly.

'His mother has taken his true identity with her to her grave. Her parting gift to him is a theft. A theft that has saved his life. I've thought about this a lot. It's an interesting notion.'

'I guess it is.'

'Now I invite you to consider another mother, a widow who has also lost her son. Perhaps because she needs the money, or perhaps out of pity, she gives her son's passport to her neighbour. It is, at the very least, an action which saves a life. But what happens if you make your enquiry with the German consulate, Captain O'Leary? A message is sent to Berlin. The Gestapo are alerted. They make an arrest. An interrogation, with all the usual refinements. Trial and certain death for Frau König. The boy she saved is sent back to Germany, where he too faces imprisonment and death. Has any of this added to the sum total of human happiness? Or has it simply added to the burden of grief which already weighs this world down too heavily?'

O'Leary cleared his throat. 'I don't deal with the burden of grief, Mr Stravinsky. I deal with rules and regulations.'

'Of course you do,' Stravinsky replied. 'So do I. Music is nothing but rules and regulations. They are the very first thing every musician learns. The lines, the dots, the numbers; so many beats to a bar, so many notes to a stave, the iron laws of key and tonality. Without these rules and regulations, music is impossible. You would just have noise. And yet—' Stravinsky lit another cigarette. 'And yet there is space for human creativity to creep between those iron bars. We bend them, we slip through them from time to time. Without those moments of mercy, all of music would be merely a prison. And so would the world be merely a prison.'

'You're asking me to break the rules.'

'Merely to bend them. If it's of any relevance, Captain, Thomas König is among the more decent human beings I have come across in a long life. I believe he would be an asset to your country. More importantly, his death would impoverish the world to no purpose.'

'I'm not planning to kill him.'

'Others are. You know that.'

'That's not my business.'

'Here,' Masha said. She leaned forward and laid something on O'Leary's desk. It was a string of small, deep-red rubies. They lay like beads of blood among the tarnished gilt and creased leather of the multifarious passports. 'Take these. Let him go.'

'No, Masha!' Stravinsky said urgently. But it was too late to withdraw the gesture.

O'Leary laid down his cigar and picked up the string of rubies. He cupped them in his palm, admiring their colour. 'These look valuable.'

'My father was a jeweller. They are called pigeon's blood rubies. They come from Burma. They're rare. They are all we have left.'

'And this kid – whom you met on board ship – is worth it to you?'

'I have learned the value of a human life,' Masha replied.

'This wasn't a very wise thing to do, young lady. Trying to bribe a public official in this country will get you ten years in jail.' O'Leary spilled the stones back on to the desk. 'Put them away, now.'

Masha took back the necklace with shaking fingers.

O'Leary stretched his arms above his head. They could hear his joints clicking. 'I'm retiring in three weeks' time. I could lose my pension over this.' Masha and Stravinsky said nothing. The officer opened Thomas's file and thumped a stamp into the passport. He rose tiredly to his feet. 'I'm going home to my dinner now. Take the kid home to his.'

Stravinsky put his arm around the boy's shoulders as they walked back up the gangplank. 'Have you eaten today?'

The boy shook his head. 'I can't stop thinking about them. I think they are all dead by now.'

Stravinsky could make no comment on that, except to say, 'But you are alive.'

'Thomas,' Masha said, clinging to his other arm, 'we almost lost you!'

Rachel met them at the top of the gangplank. 'I see you have rescued little Adolf,' she greeted them ironically.

'Really, Rachel,' Masha snapped with unaccustomed fierceness, 'you can be obnoxious sometimes.'

The arrival of *Manhattan* at the Chelsea Piers the next morning was a grand occasion. Mr Nightingale and his staff distributed streamers and confetti for the passengers to throw over the side of the ship; and a tumultuous welcome was waiting on Pier 86 as the liner docked. The large crowd was made up of joyous relations and friends who had been waiting anxiously since the outbreak of the war for their loved ones to return, reporters from all the New York papers eager to interview the many celebrities on board, and hundreds more who had no connection to the *Manhattan*, but who loved spectacles such as this one, and who had come to be swept up in the emotion of the occasion, as autumn leaves are swept up by the wind.

News of the ship's encounter with the German submarine had preceded her arrival. Commodore Randall's coolness was the toast of the harbour. Horns, sirens and hooters praised him in a deafening chorus. Fireboats sprayed high arcs of water, making rainbows dance in the morning air, and altogether the occasion was more reminiscent of the first launch of a great ship than a quiet return to harbour.

In the staterooms and cabins, and in the crowded public areas, all was bustle and preparation to disembark – for some, preparation for a new life. For many, it was also a time for farewells.

Masha and Rachel came to Stravinsky and Thomas's cabin. Masha was carrying Stravinsky's manuscript, together with the fair copy she had made so laboriously.

'I managed to finish it last night,' she said, smiling, 'and there are no mistakes, I promise.' She handed the bundle to him. 'I know that you gave me this work to distract me from my unhappiness during the voyage. It helped me a great deal. I will never forget your kindness.'

Stravinsky took the manuscripts from Masha and uncapped his pen. He wrote something on the original, and then handed it back to her. 'I will keep your fair copy, Fräulein. You may keep this thing of mine as a memento.'

Masha stared at the manuscript, upon which he had written, in his large, sprawling hand, 'To my friend Masha Morgenstern, SS *Manhattan*, September 1939.'

'I cannot accept this,' she said, turning pale. 'I'm not worthy of the honour.'

'In my eyes you are worthy,' he replied. 'It may be useful to you. I hope it does you some good one day.'

Thomas, too, had a gift – for Rachel. He unpinned the little enamel swastika from his lapel, and gave it to her. 'My mother asked me to wear this until I arrived in America,' he said quietly. 'It's the last thing I have of her. I want you to keep it.'

Rachel, who now knew what had been revealed at Ellis Island, accepted the gift awkwardly. 'I wasn't very nice to you during the voyage, was I? But then, I didn't look beneath the surface.' She closed her fingers around the pin. 'I will keep this nasty thing to remind me to take nothing for granted.' She kissed him.

Arturo Toscanini tapped at his wife's stateroom door. He heard her voice from within, and turned the handle.

Carla was lying on her bunk with a black satin sleep mask over her eyes, the curtains drawn across the porthole. The light inside was dull, even though it was a bright winter's afternoon.

'We are about to dock,' he said. 'You should get ready, Carla.'

'There is no hurry.' She didn't remove the mask.

He stood at her bedside, looking down at her. 'I didn't mean you to find those letters.'

'Of course you didn't,' she replied dryly.

'I mean that I would have burned them. I had intended to burn them. But everything happened so quickly. I forgot all about them. I left them behind.' He hesitated. 'It had already ended between me and Ada. When Neppach shot Gretel, the shock was terrible. You were right in what you said. We couldn't go on after that.'

'So it took the death of a young woman to prise you away from her.'

'I am sorry, Carla. Truly sorry. I never wanted to wound you.'

'But you were too selfish to avoid it.'

'I was in love, Carla.'

'Ah,' she said quietly. 'That explains everything.'

He sat on the bed beside her, and took her hand, with its short, unvarnished nails. 'I love you. But I was in love with her. The difference is . . .'

'You need not tell me what the difference is, Artú.'

'But do you understand? You are my life. You are the mother of my children. I could not survive without you. We have spent a lifetime together. But with you, I am an old man. With her, I was young. Time had not passed. The fire had not burned down.' He stared at her masked face. 'Do you understand?'

Her mouth was bitter. 'What are you telling me all this for? Do you think it's going to make me change my mind?'

Tears trickled from the corners of his eyes, sliding along the wrinkles on his face. He bowed his white head down until his forehead was resting on her thigh. 'There is a demon inside me, Carla. I cannot control it. I cannot. Because it is the same demon that gives me my art. It gives me my life.'

At last she pulled off her mask and sat up, pushing him away. 'Do you think I don't have my own demon, Artú? Do you think I don't want my own pleasures, my own life? But I gave everything up for you. So that you could have *your* life, *your* pleasures. I asked very little.'

'I know you did,' he sobbed.

'I asked only for some dignity, some respect—'

'I know, I know.'

'But you wouldn't even give me that.'

'I cannot live without you.' He seized her hand again and covered it with wet kisses. 'Forgive me, Carla, forgive me!'

Carla looked at him with a mixture of disgust and pity. 'You beg me not to leave you, and in the same breath you tell me you will not give up your women.'

'I will give them up. I will give them up. I swear it, Carla. We will start a new life together. Look.' He jumped up and pulled the curtains open. Through the window, the towers of Manhattan could be seen, crowded together in the morning sun. 'Look, my dear. Everything is new today. We're not too old to start again.' He smiled at her tremulously, the light making a halo out of his white hair.

'You are an old fool,' she said. 'But I am even stupider.' She heaved herself off the bunk. 'Let's go.'

Fanny Ward, the Indestructible Ingénue, had prepared for her own interview carefully, starting before dawn. One of the things she most regretted leaving behind in London was her lady's maid of the past twenty years. Lucy had been a treasure. Getting ready to face the flashbulbs and the microphones was terrifying these days. But she had faced it without Lucy to help her dress and put on her make-up, and now she gave the assembled newspapermen her gayest smile.

'I really don't think I can fit any more of you in,' she protested as they crowded her little stateroom. Some of them remained in the doorway, angling their cameras over the heads of the men in front of them.

Miss Ward had positioned herself against the window, as she always did, but there was no escape from the cameras. The popping and sizzling of the flashguns was dazzling, heating up the room as though a miniature battle were being fought in it. Panic rose in her breast. They were too close, too bright. She was going to look ghastly. The best she could hope for was that sub-editors would blue-pencil the photographs as too frightful to publish.

'Please, my dears, have mercy with your flashguns.' She dabbed the sweat that had begun to clog her face powder.

'What can you tell us about London, Miss Ward?'

'Oh, my dear man. Too, too sad. Like a plague city. The streets deserted at night and everything buried in sandbags. No gaiety, no bright lights, so *triste*. I wept to see it like that.'

'And what do you expect to see when you go back to London?' one of the others called.

Miss Ward opened her baby-blue eyes very wide, just in time for the pop of another flashbulb. 'I expect to see everything gay again, those hideous dirigibles gone from the skies, and of course, everything just as it has always been.'

'So you think you'll see the Union Jack still flying over Buckingham Palace?'

'Well, you know, that would mean the King wasn't at home. I would hope to see the Royal Standard. That would mean he was in residence.'

'Do you think Britain can win this war?'

'Oh yes, of course. Britain *must* win this war, mustn't she?'

'Miss Ward,' a man called from the back of the group, 'Walter Winchell has just written in his column that you've inherited two and a half million dollars from your late daughter. Is that true?'

Miss Ward's smile faltered, and for a terrible moment she felt she was going to crumple to the floor, like some creature shot in the heart, in full view of the cameras. She forced herself to remain upright. 'No parent should ever have to inherit anything from a child. It's the saddest thing in all the world. But yes, it's true. My darling Dotty left me everything in her will.' Mentally, she was preparing what she would say to Walter Winchell about revealing that little snippet of news. The man held nothing sacred and everything in contempt.

'Tell us about the submarine, Miss Ward.'

She fixed the smile back on her face. 'I wasn't going to let any German submarine catch me *déshabillé*, gentlemen. I slept in a flying suit all the way.'

There was laughter, and another volley of photographs. She managed to get the reporters out of her cabin and shut the door on the last of them, sagging wearily. She was ready to leave the ship.

HMS Amphitrite

They let Hufnagel out of the sickbay to get some fresh air. The two burly sailors who went with him everywhere, as though he were a wild beast who might at any moment lash out or leap overboard, had finally relaxed their vigilance. Weakened as he was, he presented little danger to anyone. One of the sailors even solicitously draped a blanket over his shivering shoulders.

'There you go, Fritz. Don't catch a chill.'

He nodded his thanks. Clutching the blanket around himself, he went to the rail and looked across the bay at the distant towers of Manhattan. He was remembering his last visit here as a midshipman. The precise phrase which formed in his mind was 'in my youth'. It was an odd phrase, considering he was not yet twenty-five. But he felt old. Much of himself had gone down with *U-113*. He was no longer what he had been.

He glanced down at his right arm, which now ended in a bandaged stump, just above the elbow. It was a pity to lose the arm. And the other arm, thanks to Todt's first shot, still had a doubtful future. He knew the British naval surgeon had done his best, but he was inexperienced and over-eager with the knife. Anyway, there was no use crying over spilled milk. What was done was done. He had saved the *Manhattan*, and perhaps hundreds of lives. That was something. He had no idea who those passengers were, whose lives had been in his hands for a trembling moment. And they would never know who he was. But that was war. *Where ignorant armies clash by night.*

He looked again at the New York skyline, thinking of the teeming streets his younger self had once walked, so long ago. It would surely not be long before the might of America joined with Britain against the Axis powers. Then – for all Hitler's contemptuous dismissal of a 'mongrel nation' – the war would take a very different turn.

It made little difference to him now. He would be spending the rest of it, however it turned out, as a POW. He would see the world from behind a fence for years to come, perhaps a decade. Nobody could tell. And after that, he would have to face his life as an amputee, a wounded bird pecking crumbs on windowsills.

He wondered what sort of Germany he would be returning to after it was all over. There was sometimes a vision in his mind of endless fields of smoking rubble, where scarecrow figures huddled. Among the scarecrows in this vision he could see members of his own family. Perhaps that was overly pessimistic. Yet the first month of the war had already shown him that the dream of glory was in reality a nightmare of folly, slaughter and devastation.

'Don't upset yourself,' one of his guards said. 'We're all a shower of bastards.'

Hufnagel realised that the remark was meant to be comforting. He realised, too, that the warmth on his cheeks was from tears that were trickling from his eyes. He wiped them away with the rough wool of the blanket. They led him below again.

Flushing Meadows, 1940

It was the biggest machine Thomas had seen since disembarking from the *Manhattan* ten months earlier. Pennsylvania Railroad's S-1 locomotive towered over the crowd, more like a space rocket than a train, three hundred tons of gleaming blue steel, sculpted into flowing, aerodynamic lines. Even here at the World's Fair, where everything was the biggest, the fastest, the latest, it was overwhelming: the most powerful train ever built, the Locomotive of Tomorrow.

It had been mounted on enormous rollers so that it could be run at full speed for the excited crowd. As the behemoth got into its stride, its wheels, each one taller than a man, churned into silvery blurs. Dense, hot steam poured over the spectators, drenching them. At peak power the howl of its whistle pierced the thunder of its pistons.

Thomas felt his identity erased by that noise and might. He ceased to be himself; one could not think one's own thoughts. It was not until the great wheels slowed and the thunder sank back into the earth that he could be Thomas König again. Half-deafened, he looked at his wristwatch and saw that it was time to leave.

He walked towards the Theme Centre along one of the paths that converged there. On this Fourth of July of 1940, the World's Fair was thronged with visitors in holiday mood. Ahead of him, over the heads of the crowd, the Trylon and the Perisphere glowed as though in a dream, brilliantly white. They were supernatural, the spire piercing the blue vault of heaven like the steeple of some mechanistic god, the sphere pregnant with infinite possibilities.

All around him rolled the noise of the World's Fair, multitudinous, multifarious. Music of all kinds clashed and mingled with the bawling of amplified announcements, the sound of children playing, the drone of engines. Over in the distance he could hear the roar of the Goodrich pavilion, where Jimmy Lynch and his Death Dodgers raced around the track, performing stunts to thrill the crowd. And from Frank Buck's Jungleland, where visitors could ride camels and elephants, a rich zoo smell emanated.

There had been grave doubts about whether the Fair would reopen in 1940. The prospect of American involvement in the war loomed ever closer. The huge Soviet pavilion had been dismantled and shipped home. So had the pavilions of several smaller countries which had now been overrun by the Nazis. In sympathy, others were flying their flags at half-mast. Slightly anxious patriotic slogans and American flags were everywhere. But these undercurrents were overlaid with sunshine and festivity today.

Thomas reached the Theme Centre and sat on the grass under a tree. The Perisphere in front of him seemed to float weightlessly on the fountains beneath it, light as a ping-pong ball for all its huge size. He watched the visitors taking their photographs, remembering how he had longed to see this sight. In his darkest moments, when grief had taken him by the throat and wouldn't let him breathe, the dream of being here had saved him from despair.

At last he saw a familiar figure approaching across the lawn. He got to his feet.

Masha Morgenstern was wearing a white summer frock and a wide-brimmed straw hat. On this hot summer's day, she looked as cool as an ice-cream cone. When she saw him, she paused for a moment, taking off her dark glasses. Then she ran to him and flung her arms around him.

'Thomas! I almost didn't recognise you at first. You've grown so much.'

'I'm seventeen now,' he said awkwardly.

'And I've had a birthday too. I'm twenty-one, imagine.' She held him at arm's length to study him. 'You're so tall. You must be almost six foot now.'

'Almost,' he said. Where formerly they had conversed in Berlinerisch German, they now automatically spoke American English.

She held up the stub of her entrance ticket. 'See? I used the ticket you gave me.'

A smile flickered across his grave, narrow face. 'I'm glad.'

'So am I.' She read the stub. '*The World of Tomorrow – Admit One*. I remember the night you came into my cabin with this. It was an act of great kindness.'

'I'm sure I got on your nerves.'

'Never once. How you pulled the wool over all our eyes, Thomas! You gave a very good impersonation of a Nazi, quoting Hitler verbatim. You must have been laughing up your sleeve all the time!'

Thomas grimaced. 'Not laughing.'

'Oh, forgive me. That was insensitive of me. Do you have news of your parents?'

'Only that they were sent to a place called Dachau. The Red Cross told me that. But of course they aren't allowed to write. And you?'

'I received a postcard a few weeks ago, saying that they were well. But it wasn't in their writing, and it seemed like something that had been printed on a machine.'

'We must have hope,' he said quietly.

She nodded. 'Yes, we must have hope. You're at school?'

'My uncle and aunt have been very kind. They put me in a private school in Connecticut. It was difficult at first, but I'm working hard.'

'I'm sure you are. Your English is very good.'

'So is yours.' He had been too shy to look her in the face, but now he raised his eyes to hers. 'Are you happy in America?'

'Very happy. I'm studying the piano again at a music academy. I never thought I would. I've lost many years, but—' She spread her hands. 'There's still something left in these.'

'And Rachel?'

Masha laughed. 'Oh, Rachel! Rachel is always the same. She's working as a switchboard operator but I don't think it'll last. She keeps connecting the wrong parties, and then gets angry when they complain.' Her brown eyes sparkled. 'But tell me: have you seen Elektro the talking robot yet?'

'Yes, I saw him this morning. He has a dog now, Sparko.'

She cocked her head on one side. 'You don't sound very excited.'

'I expected a real robot. Elektro is just a big toy.'

'I'm sorry you were disappointed.'

'Nothing can disappoint me today.'

'You're very gallant,' she said solemnly. She hooked her arm through his. 'Now – you're the expert. Show me around.'

With Masha close beside him, he showed her the things he thought would amuse her. They visited Little Miracle City, and were able to pick out some of Hoffman's Midget Marvels, performing among the other little people. They watched nylon stockings being made, and a big Fourth of July parade of soldiers, followed by a demonstration of American military hardware. Ironically, that took place on the Court of Peace, against the backdrop of the Trylon.

There were other grim notes. One of the pavilions was collecting money for medical aid to China, with a display of tragic photographs. The France pavilion was flying its flag at half-mast; and this year's show of the Fair was *Streets of Paris*, with Abbott and Costello, a painful reminder that the actual streets of Paris were now echoing under German jackboots. At the Great Britain pavilion there were displays of gas masks, German bombs, photographs of the Blitz, and even the tail of a German bomber that had been shot down.

'I don't want to see these things,' Masha said with a shudder. 'Are you hungry?'

'A little.'

'When I was your age I was always starving.' She linked her arm through his. 'Come on, I'll buy you lunch.'

The vulgar smell of the fried onions in the hot dog elbowed its way between them. He quietly discarded the garnish, not wanting to lose the intimacy of Masha's scent, which was of lilies and vanilla. But she did not seem to mind the onions, and ate with the relish of a healthy young animal, swigging her vivid red soda from the bottle. She caught him watching her, and laughed.

'Have I got ketchup all over my face?'

'Only a little, on your lips.'

She dabbed her mouth with the paper napkin, and leaned back luxuriously on the concrete bench, stifling a belch. 'I love America. I feel so free here. Don't you? Berlin was a prison. I thought it was just being a Jew that made it feel like that, but now I think that to be a German is itself to be a prisoner. Do you know what I mean?'

'I think so.'

'Where else can you eat sausages on a bench and drink from a bottle, and nobody frowns at you?' She waved the remaining half of her hot dog at the extraordinary buildings all around them. 'Where else can you see this?'

'Nowhere.'

'Nowhere. It's—' She couldn't find the words. 'Well, it's *America.*'

While she ate the rest of her hot dog, Thomas quietly got rid of his in the trashcan nearby. He understood her enthusiasm and wished he could share it more fully. This America was garish and brash and bursting with energy. The women flaunted their bodies in tight clothes and laughed with lipsticked mouths, the men showed their muscles and wrestled each other on the sidewalks. It would take him time to assimilate it and be assimilated by it.

Masha had polished off her hot dog. She pulled her skirt up over her thighs to expose her legs to the late afternoon sunlight. 'I'm sick of being so white,' she complained. 'American girls are always tanned. It looks much nicer.'

Thomas glanced at her bare legs and then looked quickly away. 'You look fine.'

She drank from her soda bottle and held it to him, still a quarter-full. 'Do you want to finish it?'

He took it from her and laid the neck against his lips. There was a momentary trace of her perfume, a slippery suspicion of her saliva. He tilted the bottle up and the strawberry soda, warm and slightly flat, sluiced them away. He swallowed the moment – the nearness of Masha, the sweetness of the soda, the warm sun on his skin.

As he took the bottle from his lips, the air compressed around them, squeezing their eardrums. There was a deep thump that shook the concrete bench they were sitting on. A few leaves scattered off the nearby trees, spinning in the shocked air. Suddenly, people everywhere were running and screaming. Over behind the Perisphere a cloud of black smoke was rolling into the sky.

'What was that?' Masha asked anxiously.

'I don't know. But we should leave.'

People were streaming to the exits, and they joined the crush. There was still some laughter among the crowd. They could hear people around them speculating that it had been Fourth of July fireworks, or a prank, or just another display of some kind. But nobody wanted to stay to find out; and as they left the Fair down the ramp to the Brooklyn-Manhattan Transit, they heard a policeman telling a colleague, 'There's been a bomb at the British pavilion. Two cops got it out of the building, but it went off. Killed the both of them and dug a damn great hole in the dirt.'

'We were there an hour ago,' Masha gasped. Thomas nodded, feeling sick.

The transit back to Manhattan was crowded. They managed to find seats next to one another. Masha was pale and silent. For a while she slept with her head propped against Thomas's shoulder. He closed his eyes, concentrating on the feel of her soft hair tickling his cheek. Why did the day have to end like this? The war had followed them all the way to Flushing Meadows, all the way to his dream, with its senseless cruelty and violence.

The sun was setting by the time they reached Penn Station. Golden-red light streamed through the glass roof, flooding the huge concourse below with fiery shadows. He had to get back to Hartford to be in school by nine. He offered to walk her to her platform.

'It's okay,' she said, 'a friend is coming to pick me up.'

'Then I'll wait with you.'

'Oh, you needn't. You go and get your train.' But then she saw his expression and relented. They made their way to the great clock that hung in the archway, and stood under it to wait. 'Thank you for today, Thomas. It was lovely to see you again. It was a lovely day all round.'

'I'm sorry it ended like that.'

'So am I.' She looked suddenly tearful. 'I don't want America to join the war.'

'If they don't, the Nazis may take over Europe.'

Masha looked at the crowds around them. 'These people came here to escape all that, the same as we did. They don't deserve to be dragged back into it. I want America to be somewhere wars don't happen.'

'I don't think there's anywhere wars don't happen.'

'What are you going to do with your life, Thomas? Engineer? Rocket scientist?'

'Something like that, I suppose.'

'Just don't become a watchmaker.'

'Why not?'

'I don't know. I just don't want to think of you in some little room, tinkering with little things, like a prisoner. Don't end up like that. Be free. Be big.'

'I will try.'

'You'd better. Or I'll come and find you one day, and drag you out, and embarrass you in front of all the other watchmakers.' She turned her head, her eyes lighting up. 'My friend is here.'

Masha's friend was a good-looking young man in a double-breasted suit, wearing a trilby hat. He greeted Masha affectionately. The arm he put around her was casually proprietorial. He smiled cheerfully at Thomas as they shook hands.

'Thomas, this is Dale Gordon,' Masha said. And there was something in the shy, proud way she said the name that opened a door in Thomas's mind. Through the door, he seemed to be looking down the years, as though looking down a hall of mirrors. He could see at once that Masha was going to become Mrs Dale Gordon, that she would live a happy life with him in a happy house, and have his children, and grow old with him. And in that hall of mirrors, his own reflection appeared only once, in the wrong place, at the wrong time.

Far away, he heard Dale asking if they'd had a good time at the Fair, and Masha telling Dale about the bomb, and Dale's voice growing serious as he asked if she were all right. And then Dale said his car was parked on a yellow line and he would probably be getting a ticket right about now; and it was time to say goodbye.

Masha hugged Thomas and kissed him on the mouth. He could smell the onions on her breath, and he wondered whether Dale Gordon would mind that. He thought Dale probably wouldn't mind the smell of onions, wouldn't mind anything that Masha did.

As she walked away, she turned to look over her shoulder, and called to him, 'Remember what I said. Don't be a prisoner!'

But before the hall of mirrors closed in his mind, Thomas knew that he would always be a prisoner, because he would love her forever.

Washington, D.C.

The room was cold and bare. It had whitewashed walls and a tile floor that smashed anything you dropped on it. There was a plain wooden cross hanging over the bed, but no Jesus nailed on it. Rosemary sometimes imagined that Jesus had quietly departed, taking the nails with him. It was hard to imagine that Jesus would have enjoyed this room, or indeed the gloomy convent chapel where mass was said every day and the long benches had no padding and were hard enough to make your backside ache and leave deep furrows in your knees.

Rosemary hated this place. She hated the Clorox smell of the nuns. She hated their hard hands and cold eyes. She had never been lonelier in her life. No matter how bad things had been before, there had always been smiling faces around her, the laughter of children, the sound of music. Not here.

Here there were no games. No children. There were endless lessons, stony tutors who told her she wasn't working hard enough, didn't apply herself enough, wasn't devout enough. There were endless prayers, and a sharp tap on the shoulder if she fell asleep before they were done. And there was endless isolation.

She hadn't been happy since coming back to the States, not one hour of one day. She missed Belmont House terribly. She missed the children she'd been in charge of, and her friends and the fun that had filled every day.

It was all so different here. The hours and the days were empty. And nothing came to fill the emptiness except bad things. Even when she was allowed to go home for a day, nothing worked out. Mother seemed to detest the sight of her. Her brothers and sisters were always busy. They had no time for her. Jack had his graduation and his book and all his classmates from Harvard. Eunice had her tennis and Kick had her English friends, and she wasn't invited to their parties any more. They said she embarrassed them, even though she tried so hard not to.

Even Joe Junior was impatient with her. He didn't want to wrestle with her or cuddle her any more, or listen to her read *Winnie-the-Pooh*. So she'd been pushed in with the younger ones, and that was no good because they made her angry, and then she would lose her temper, and she wouldn't know what she was doing until there were screams and tears and being locked in her room. They'd said if she hurt her little brothers and sisters again, she wouldn't be allowed to see them any more. And she hated to see them shrink away from her after she had been angry.

She missed Daddy terribly.

She had seen so little of him since they'd come back from England. He'd never really explained why they'd had to come back, right when everything was so fine for her. When she'd asked him, he'd got angry and said the damn British had shown their true colours, and blind people didn't have eyes to see, and stupid people didn't like to face facts. He'd said they would be going back to England when the Germans were in charge there, which would be pretty damn soon. In the meantime he was being replaced by someone who was happy to see young men die, which sounded just awful to Rosemary.

Then there had been the Democratic National Something in Chicago, and after that he was always on the phone, sometimes shouting, saying he was too old to start over again. He'd said his career was in ruins, and that old goat Roosevelt had stabbed him in the back at last, just as he'd always known he would.

Rosemary hated Roosevelt for hurting Daddy.

There were a lot of things she hated.

She lay straight in the bed, the way Sister Katherine had left her, with her arms out of the blankets and stretched straight on either side of her, despite the autumn chill in the room. Hands that wandered under the blankets were strictly forbidden. Because you would play with your you-know-what down there, and the chromo of Mother Mary was watching from the opposite wall, ready to snitch on you if you did. And that would earn you the cane on your wicked fingers until they swelled up red and tears spurted out of your eyes.

She was twenty-two, and she had never been so unhappy in her life.

The sounds of the convent slowly stilled. Doors banged, bells chimed. Voices faded. Even when there was complete silence, Rosemary didn't put her hands under the blanket. She had a better plan.

She slipped out of her bed and went to her closet. The dark-red dress was one of her favourites. The nuns had tried to forbid it, but she'd got Daddy to explain that she needed at least some nice things to wear. She couldn't go around in brown or grey all day. She put it on and peered at herself in the dim mirror. Of course there was no makeup allowed, not even face powder; but a friend in England had taught her to slap her own cheeks, which she did smartly, closing her eyes against the sting, and bite her own lips until they looked pink and fresh. That helped things a lot. She practised her smile a couple of times. It was her best feature, they always said, her brilliant smile. They said it lit up the room. It didn't light up this sombre cell, but it did gleam back at her from the mirror. She brushed her hair and clipped on the pearls Mother had bought her in London. She pulled on a raincoat because it looked like being a drizzly night.

Then, with the silent skill of long practice, she climbed out of the window.

Her favourite place was a bar called The Shamrock, but there were only a handful of old men in it tonight. It was a Wednesday night and most of the bars were half-empty. But getting out of the convent on a Friday was almost impossible. So she walked around the corner to Mac's. Mac's was always busy, but it was also a little seedier. Still, sometimes that suited her.

The jukebox was playing Glen Miller at a nickel a shot and the air was blue with tobacco smoke. Rosemary took off her raincoat and hoisted herself on to a stool at the bar. There was a battered cigarette in the pocket of her raincoat. She straightened it as best she could and put it in her mouth. She waited. It never took very long.

A Zippo appeared in front of her eyes. A hand thumbed it open and flicked it alight. She half-turned to check the owner of the hand and the lighter. He was middle-aged but pleasant-looking, so she accepted the light, tasting the gasoline fumes of the Zippo as she sucked.

She expelled the smoke upward. 'Why, thank you, kind sir.' She'd learned to say that from a movie she'd seen.

'Can I buy you a drink?' the man offered.

'Sure.'

'What'll it be?'

Rosemary looked at the rows and rows of bottles behind the bar. A tall, yellow one caught her eye. She pointed. 'I'll have that.'

'Galliano? You Italian?'

'Irish.'

'Ah well, nobody's perfect.'

'What do you mean?'

'It's just a joke.'

'Oh.' She laughed to show him she got the joke, though she didn't.

His face changed. 'You're beautiful when you laugh. Say, have we met before?'

'No,' Rosemary said, 'we haven't.'

'I could swear I know you from somewhere.'

'Maybe,' she replied with a wink, 'I'm just the girl of your dreams.'

He moved closer to her. 'Damn if you might just be the answer to a prayer.'

His name was Lou. He didn't ask for her surname, which was good, because she knew she had to be careful about that, and he didn't tell her his, though she saw the wedding ring on his hand.

The Galliano turned out to be a good choice. The stuff was delicious. It tasted of liquorice and vanilla and it made her feel floaty and gay. Lou was funny and knew lots of jokes. He kept starting them with, 'Have you heard this one?' And he kept buying her drinks.

At two a.m. the bar closed. They spilled out on to the sidewalk, where it was drizzling a bit, and the asphalt was shiny under the streetlamps. Lou suggested they go to his boarding house for a nightcap. Rosemary asked him why he'd taken so long to get around to suggesting that.

They had to creep up the stairs with their shoes in their hands, so as not to wake the landlady, but Rosemary was used to that. In his room, they said nothing to each other. Lou had run out of jokes.

He wasn't rough, the way some men were, but his kisses were infinitely sad. There was no pleasure in this, and much sorrow; but it was better than the empty loneliness. For these moments, which were usually so soon over, she felt part of the world, desired by someone, needed by someone for something. Not a nobody offering empty prayers to a God who had long ago departed.

She tried to think of Cubby, of what it had been like with him. But she couldn't really remember his face any more, only the way he had made her feel. And remembering a happy feeling when you were sad was the worst thing of all. After a while she stopped trying to see his face in her mind.

The nuns were waiting for her when she got back to the convent at dawn. At the sight of them, Rosemary was sick, spewing out the sour liquorice and curdled vanilla of all the Galliano she had drunk.

'I'm sorry,' she said. 'I'm so sorry, I'm so sorry. Please don't tell Daddy. Please don't.'

But she knew they would. The sick puddled around her feet and they had to step through it as they took her arms and led her to the shower.

Santa Barbara

The guest cottage at Santa Barbara was their weekend refuge, and they relished the drive up from the sprawling, grimy tangle of Los Angeles. The Sachses had provided a good piano in the living room, and Stravinsky could compose here, which was what he usually did every Saturday and Sunday morning. But Sundays at noon were reserved for Mother Russia.

Stravinsky closed the lid of the piano, and with his cigarette-holder clamped in his teeth, searched for the fresh box of pins which he had brought up from Los Angeles. He found it in his briefcase, and went with it into the next room.

The large-scale map of Russia had been fastened to a cork board. Coloured pins and lengths of tape marked the progress of the German invasion, which was now in its second month.

That Hitler had suddenly turned on his erstwhile partner in crime, Stalin, had come as a surprise only to the naïve. Between the two nations there was not only a political gulf, with fascism on one side and communism on the other; there were also decades of ancient enmity. The Führer had clearly stated his belief that Russia must be conquered to provide the German people with the living space they required.

It was a campaign being fought with unusual viciousness. The Nazis were waging a rapacious war of extermination and obliteration which would leave nothing behind but naked Russian soil for Germans to repopulate. The Russians were fighting desperately for their very existence.

Stravinsky's map showed the huge gains which the Nazis had made. If it were the map of a human body, it would show an apparently unstoppable cancer invading the healthy flesh in great swathes; or perhaps a savage beast devouring its prey in gulps, tearing off and swallowing limbs and organs each day.

The German armies had Leningrad, Moscow and Kiev in their sights already, although von Runstedt had encountered fierce resistance in the south. Guderian's panzers had captured Ostrov, and were almost at the great gates of Kiev. Russia was succumbing to the Blitzkrieg tactics which had annihilated France; and it seemed that nothing could stop Hitler.

Stravinsky switched on the radio and fiddled with the dials until the announcer's voice faded in. Then, sucking on his cigarette-holder, he sat back to listen to the latest news.

Hearing the radio, Vera came in from the garden and sat on the arm of the chair beside him. She had been sitting in the garden, watching the sea, and he caught the sun-warmed smell of her skin as she leaned on his shoulder.

They had been married for four months. Tumultuous as those months had been, Stravinsky was aware that he had never been happier, might never be so happy again. Vera, his mistress of so many years, was at last his wife. She had brought to his life her stability, her beauty, her magic. Above all, she had brought her healing.

The announcer's voice drifted in and out of the static, dryly cataloguing the progress of the war in Europe. Stravinsky trusted only the BBC Overseas Service, but reception was sketchy at best. He listened intently. When the news turned to Russia, he got up with his box of pins and went to the map. Yet again, he was forced to push new pins deeper into the bleeding body of the motherland. The Germans had made new advances, conquering almost incredible stretches of territory. Cities, towns, villages, lakes and farmland were now behind German lines.

He moved the coloured ribbons into their new places, watched by Vera's large and lustrous hazel eyes. His scowl deepened minute by minute. Then something that the announcer said caught his attention. He peered over his long nose at the map and stabbed a point with his finger.

'Did you hear that?'

'I heard the usual catalogue of disasters.'

'No, no, Vera. They have been checked here, at Novgorod, near the lake. The announcer says their troops are exhausted.' He turned to her, his spectacles flashing triumphantly. 'They've gone too far, too fast. It's the mistake Napoleon made before them. Now they are depleted, far from their supply lines, overwhelmed by the vastness of the country. Here they will sit to recover; and then the rains will come. And then the snow.'

She was a beautiful, stately woman with a dancer's fluidity of movement. She slipped down into the armchair he had vacated, crossing her ankles on the arm. She inspected him over her peep-toe wedges. 'The snow is months away yet, Igor.'

'But it will come.' He laid down the box of pins and smacked his fist into the palm of the other hand. 'By God, it will come. And then we will show these Nazis how Russians can fight.'

She smiled her soft, voluptuous smile. '*We*, Igor? Who is this *we*? For years you've been telling everyone you are French. Then you said America was your home. Now you are suddenly Russian again?'

'I am French,' he said, 'and America is my home.' He struck his chest. 'But *this* is Russian.'

'Your very nice Argyll sweater? As I recall, it came from Bloomingdales.'

'My heart. My soul. Why do you mock me?'

'Only because you have been abusing Russia for the past thirty years. You have been telling everyone it was bad to start with, and the Revolution has made it even worse.'

'All that is true.' He came back to her, and they lit the cigarettes which they tried to restrict to five a day. 'But a man can have only one birthplace, one motherland. And the motherland is the most important circumstance in his life.' He exhaled a cloud of smoke into the sunlight that streamed through the window. 'The right to abuse Russia is mine, and mine alone, because Russia is mine and I love it. I give nobody else the right to abuse Russia. Especially not the Nazi swine.'

'So you *are* Russian again.'

He gestured at the map, festooned with pins and lines. 'While this is happening, I am fully Russian again.' He puffed at his cigarette. 'I am going to start on a new work.'

'But, darling, you've just finished something very important. You need to rest.'

'I've never felt fitter,' he retorted. 'I'm going to write a symphony to celebrate the defeat of Hitler.'

They had a late lunch with their hosts, the banker Arthur Sachs and his charming French wife Georgette, and then were joined by some visitors, including Robert and Mildred Bliss, for whom Stravinsky had written the Dumbarton Oaks Concerto, and Katharine Wolff. By common consent, seeing it was such a lovely afternoon, they drove down to the beach, and walked along the sand in two groups. Stravinsky strolled ahead with the Sachses and the Blisses, while Vera followed with Katharine at a distance.

'How is he?' Katharine asked.

'Very engaged with the war,' Vera replied. 'This morning he made quite a speech about being fully Russian.'

'Is that a good sign?'

'I think so. It shows that he is becoming sure of his identity again. He is not so—' She groped for the English word. '*Épars*.'

'Fragmented.'

'Yes, exactly. He has been broken in pieces for a long time, I think. And the pieces were all scattered. Now he's starting to find these pieces of himself in strange places.'

'Like the war news?'

'The German invasion of Russia fills him with passion. It enthuses him. It's almost like a novel or a film to him. You saw the maps, the coloured pins?'

'I did. It's very impressive.'

She laughed. 'You know how methodical he is.'

'I think he should offer his services to the Allied High Command.'

'He says he has never felt better. He's talking about writing a Victory Symphony.'

'So he's composing again?'

'Not only composing, but composing with great facility.' Vera lowered her voice. 'Don't say anything, but he finished the Symphony in C yesterday.'

Katharine threw up her hands. 'But that's wonderful. I thought he might never get back to it.'

'It came like an easy childbirth. Few pangs, few alarms, few hesitations or second thoughts. The music is sad. But he was sad when he conceived it. It's one of his great works. I see it as his farewell to Europe.'

'I can't wait to hear it. Do you know, he gave the original manuscript of the second movement to a young Jewish refugee we met on the boat.'

'An attractive woman?' Vera guessed.

'Not even especially attractive. A nobody whom we will never hear from again.'

'He is prone to these impulsive acts of generosity. Let us hope she looks after it . . .' They walked in silence for a while, the gulls wheeling over their heads. The laughter of the others drifted to them on the breeze. Robert and Georgette Sachs were the centre of a cultured, elegant circle which adored Stravinsky. 'This place has been a godsend to us,' Vera went on. 'Los Angeles is hellish in the summer. But up here we can breathe. Igor wants to buy a house here.'

'If you need any help or advice, let me know.'

'Thank you, Katharine.'

'And what of the Disney film, *Fantasia*?'

'They're still working on it. It's taking longer than they expected. They say it's the most ambitious animated film ever attempted. They're hoping to release it by the end of the year.'

'Is he still upset about the *Rite*?'

'I think he's dreading what they will do with it. You know how the music was mocked when it was first performed. He doesn't want to go through anything like that again.'

'I hope they show it the respect it deserves.'

'Hollywood is unpredictable. There's no telling how it will be. He has no control whatsoever.'

Ahead of them, Stravinsky paused and turned. 'What are you two gossiping about?' he called.

'Not about you,' Vera replied, 'you can be sure of that.'

'Then come along,' he commanded, 'and don't dawdle.'

'You see what I mean?' Vera said in an undertone. 'Quite masterful.'

The two women caught up with the rest of the group, and they continued across the beach, over the rocks.

Washington, D.C.

Rosemary hadn't been frightened at all because they'd told her how easy it would be, and because Daddy was going to be with her. So even when they arrived at the hospital, and a whole bunch of doctors came out to look at her, and smile in that way doctors smiled, which wasn't really smiling at all, she kept her nerve. That was what Mother always told her: keep your nerve, Rosemary. You're a Kennedy.

Being with Daddy was a treat, though.

There was only Daddy who cared about her any more.

Rosemary pressed close to him, holding on to his arm with both hands, loving the smell of him and the strength of him, which always made her feel soothed and loved. She loved the rumble of his voice and it didn't really matter what he said, she could just lose herself in the sound of it.

He was saying, 'I've been having a lot of second thoughts about this lately. I'm not sure I'm ready to go through with it.'

'Has something happened to change your mind?' Dr Freeman asked.

'Well, yes. Somebody told me that the American Medical Association is warning against this operation.'

'The AMA is a very conservative organisation, Senator Kennedy. It generally takes them twenty years to catch up with leading practices in the field. I wouldn't be too concerned.'

'Easy for you to say. Rosemary's not your daughter.'

Dr Freeman kept smiling. 'What is it exactly that concerns you?'

'Well, I guess it's the uncertainty of it all. This is a very new procedure.'

'Very new, yes. But the results we've been getting have been astounding. There's no other word for it. As medical people, we don't like to use terms like "miracle cure". But if there's any such thing, then psychosurgery comes close to it.'

'Are you saying she'll be' – Daddy glanced at Rosemary – 'restored?'

'We prefer to think of it as clearing the way for a better life. We believe that once we remove all the obstacles that are holding Rosemary back, she'll immediately start to grow.'

'Can you give me a guarantee that will happen?'

Dr Freeman laughed, as though Daddy had made a good joke. He had a neatly trimmed little beard and glasses, and he looked like a happy version of the devil. 'There are no guarantees in medicine, Senator. What we can promise you is that we'll do the very best we can. I'll be directing. The operation itself will be performed by my partner, Dr Watts, who is currently the leading practitioner in the United States – if I may say so, in the world.'

Dr Watts edged forward. He didn't smile as much as Dr Freeman. He was also shorter, and clean-shaven, and he didn't have any laughter in his voice, as Dr Freeman did. 'As we discussed in our previous conversation, the most egregious problems will be solved almost instantly. I'm speaking of the convulsions, the violence, the nymphomania—'

'She's not a nymphomaniac,' Daddy said sharply.

'You've told us yourself about the sexual liaisons,' Dr Watts said, frowning. 'I don't need to tell you how dangerous these drives can be, Senator, especially in such—' He looked at Rosemary with his small, hard eyes. '—such a buxom young woman. The risks of an unwanted pregnancy, of contracting a venereal disease—'

'I know all that,' Daddy growled.

'Then you'll know that Rosemary can't continue like this. Female psychosexual aberrations are among the conditions which respond most favourably to this procedure, in our experience. The abnormal drives disappear, along with the indecent speech, the absence of modesty, the readiness to copulate with every male.'

Rosemary didn't understand all these words, but she knew what they were talking about, and she felt her face flush hotly. Only the fact that she could tell that Daddy really didn't like Dr Watts allowed her to keep her nerve.

Dr Freeman butted in, perhaps because he could also tell that Daddy was getting annoyed. 'The Freeman-Watts technique is the procedure of the future, Senator Kennedy. We call it the "precision method". It's quick and it's painless. Above all, it's been proven to be highly effective.'

Not to be outdone, Dr Watts tried again. 'The technique, put very simply, transects the white fibrous matter connecting the cortical tissue of the prefrontal cortex to the thalamus. There is almost no bleeding.'

'And only a local anaesthetic is necessary,' Dr Freeman added. He smiled at Rosemary. 'In fact, we need Rosemary to be wide awake, so she can tell us how it's going. The operation is performed through small incisions, which will soon heal, leaving almost no scarring. It's no worse than going to the dentist. She'll be a much happier young woman, less frustrated, calmer. Have no fears, Senator. This is going to change her life – and yours.'

Everybody fell silent when he said that, and they all stood around without saying anything, looking at Daddy, waiting. Daddy was looking at the ground. Rosemary felt so proud of him at that moment. He was so tall, and handsome, and important. Everybody treated him like the President. To her, he was far more important than the President, and she'd got into trouble with the nuns for saying he was more important than God, but that was how she felt. The nuns had told her to trust in God, but God had let her down too many times. She only trusted Daddy.

At last Daddy turned to look at her. He looked into her eyes and smiled in that way that always made her heart sing with joy. 'It's going to be all right,' he said.

'Yes, Daddy,' she replied happily.

And then she realised that he was going away, and was going to leave her there, and she didn't think it was going to be all right after all.

They came for her early the next morning. She was still sleepy, and she hadn't had her breakfast yet, but they said there was no breakfast today. She was hungry and thirsty and starting to lose her nerve. She wanted badly to see Daddy but they said Daddy would come along later in the day.

She had to lie on a trolley and be pushed along the corridor, so she couldn't see where they were taking her. All she could see was the rows of lights in the ceiling above her. The way they swept slowly overhead was queer, and made her feel sleepy again.

She was woken up when they reached a bright, white room where they told her to get off the trolley and sit in a chair. The nurse there had a real smile, not a doctor smile. She was kind. She said, 'I'll just cut your hair now.'

Rosemary said she'd already had her hair cut short, which was true. They'd taken her to have it bobbed the week before, because they said bobbed hair was in, and now it curled just below her ears.

'Didn't they explain?' the nurse asked. 'We'll need to shave the front of your head completely for the operation.'

'You mean, bald?' Rosemary asked in astonishment.

'They can't very well work through all that hair, can they?' the nurse said reasonably, draping a sheet around Rosemary, like at the hairdresser's. 'But it'll grow back in no time. You're very lucky. You have such lovely thick hair.'

Rosemary didn't feel very lucky. She started crying as the nurse switched on the electric clipping machine. The hard steel teeth buzzed over her head. Dark locks fell into her lap. She tried to get her hand out of the sheet to pick up the silky strands that were falling, falling into her lap, but the nurse said she had to sit still.

Dr Freeman and Dr Watts came in to see her. They were wearing very strange clothes, like gardeners' overalls, except that their arms were bare right to the shoulder. Dr Freeman had bruises on his arms, as though he'd been wrestling, and someone had grabbed him really hard. You could see the finger marks.

'Don't cry, Rosemary,' Dr Freeman said. 'This is all worth it. You're never going to be angry or sad again. You're going to be a much calmer, happier person.'

They gave her a pill to swallow. They said it would make her feel more relaxed. She took it, hoping it would work fast.

Dr Watts didn't say anything, but he put his hand on Rosemary's forehead and tilted her head this way and that, as though she wasn't even a person, just maybe a melon he was thinking of buying. He had a grease pencil and he wrote something on either side of her head, but she didn't know what it was.

Someone held her head tight. She felt the sharp sting of needles going into her temples, first on one side, then on the other. It hurt so much that she started crying again. But then her face went numb. It felt like they were still holding her head, except they had let go now. She just couldn't feel anything. She asked them if that was it. They laughed and said, just a little bit longer, Rosemary. Just a little bit longer.

She got on the table as they asked her and lay back. She hadn't noticed, but there were leather straps fastened on the table, and now they started to buckle them over her wrists and ankles, pulling them tight so she couldn't move.

Before they started to operate, the nurse tilted her head right back, so she was almost looking at the people standing behind her. She could smell disinfectant and alcohol and the man-smell of Dr Watts's skin as he bent over her. She could feel them cutting into her temples with the knife. It didn't hurt, though she could feel the blade scraping on bone, and the tug of the skin being pulled back. There was sizzling and flashing and the smell of barbecue. They told her they were cauterising the incision to stop the bleeding, and that she was being very brave. That helped her not to lose her nerve. She had never been a fraidy-cat. Her brothers had taken care of that.

And then the worst started. The drilling into her skull with the machine that was so terribly loud and pressed so terribly hard. The grinding of the steel against the bone that rattled her teeth and made her cry out in terror, 'Daddy. Daddy!'

First the left side. Then the right.

It stopped at last. She lay trembling in her bonds, listening to the murmur of strangers' voices and the rattle of instruments, feeling like doors had been cut into where her soul lived, and that it was in danger of flying out, never to return, like the nuns said happened when you died.

Then Dr Freeman's happy-devil face hovered over her, smiling.

'We're ready to start the operation now, Rosemary. We'll need you to help us with this part, okay? And then it will all be over. Can you help us?'

'Yes,' she whispered.

'Good girl.' He looked away from her at the other people standing around the table. 'Dr Watts is going into the brain now. You can see the dura exposed through the access holes. We'll need to penetrate that to get to the frontal lobes. The patient herself will guide us as to how much we need to cut.'

There was a sudden pain, much worse than any of the other pains, worse than the worst headaches she'd ever had. She felt dizzy and weak, and she started to pant like a dog in the sun.

'Rosemary,' Dr Freeman said, 'can you say your Hail Mary for us?'

'Hail Mary,' she panted, 'the Lord is with thee. Blessed – blessed art thou among women and blessed – blessed – blessed is the fruit of thy womb—'

'Go on Rosemary. Don't stop.'

She could feel Dr Watts twisting something into her head, something that scraped and sliced. '—the fruit of thy womb, Jesus. Holy Mary, Mother of God, pray for us sinners now – now and at the hour of our death. Amen.'

'Very good,' Dr Freeman said, as though she'd done something really clever. 'What's your favourite book?'

'*Winnie-the-Pooh*,' she whispered.

'Can you tell us what it's about?'

The twisting and scraping was going deeper and deeper. She could hear Dr Watts breathing through his nose, close to her ear, in that way men did when they were concentrating on something, or when they lay on top of her in the grass. 'It's about a teddy bear.'

'And what happens to him?'

'He doesn't have a brain.'

'What else?'

'He likes honey.'

'Go on.'

'He lives in the Hundred Acre Wood. It rained a lot, and he had to float in an umbrella to rescue Piglet. And he wanted to give Eeyore a pot of honey, but he ate it all, and so he – he just gave him the empty pot instead—'

'That's very good, Rosemary.' His voice lost its purring tone as he spoke to the others. 'We're separating the frontal lobes from the rest of the brain now. As you can see, the patient is conscious and lucid through the procedure. She feels no pain, and only minimal discomfort. She will emerge from this free of depression or other negative moods, her emotions under her own control, and able to resume a normal life within a few weeks.' The instrument was twisting and slicing deep inside her head now. 'Rosemary, can you count backwards from twenty for us?'

'Twenty,' she said. 'Nineteen. Eighteen. Seventeen. Fifteen.'

'You left out sixteen,' Dr Freeman chuckled.

'Sixteen. Fifteen.'

But she couldn't remember what came after fifteen. There was flashing in her eyes, and she couldn't see anything past the flashing. Sounds were coming out of her mouth, but they weren't numbers, or even words. They were just sounds. Nor could she understand what Dr Freeman was saying to her now. She tried to push herself to say the numbers out loud, but it was like there wasn't a Rosemary there to say anything any more. Rosemary was being switched off, like a radio going into silence, like a light going into darkness. She knew that something terrible was happening, but she didn't know what.

Los Angeles

Stravinsky sat transfixed in the darkness of the movie theatre. The music was his, but there was no virgin dancing herself to death. The images were new and extraordinary.

As the familiar movements of *The Rite of Spring* rolled from the speakers, he watched volcanoes erupting, the molten lava pouring and swirling, rolling into the sea with fantastic eruptions of steam and foam. In the depths of the oceans, tiny protozoa and amoebas coalesced, growing eyes and legs, becoming fish, crawling on to the land.

The fish became lizards that nibbled on the lush vegetation, then evolved into mighty dinosaurs that roared and lumbered through the swamps. Tyrannosaurus rex and Stegosaurus battled to the death in primeval rain. Spikes and claws and teeth tore at one another. Pterodactyls soared into a lurid sky.

The rain ceased. The climate changed. Now he was seeing herds of dying dinosaurs trudging across a desert landscape, searching hopelessly for water, their pools and rivers drying up, their mighty limbs becoming trapped in mud. Despairing, skeletal, dying, they raised their monstrous heads to an orange sky, where a fatal sun bloomed.

And then, whirling from the depths of outer space, a meteorite collided with the earth. The movie theatre shook with the rumble of the impact. Eyes were dazzled by the blinding flash which destroyed all life, levelling mountains and emptying seas.

Stravinsky's mouth was open. His fingers gripped the arms of his seat. It had taken a great deal to get him to come here to see *Fantasia* today, but he was experiencing a revelation.

This music – *his* music – had worked on the minds of others to produce images that were very different from the ones he himself had had half a century ago, when he'd written the *Rite*; but they were extraordinary images, images shot through with fire and brilliance and – yes, with genius.

It was a new kind of genius, flickering and evanescent. But was not all art flickering and evanescent? Did not music itself appear from the depths of darkness, flash like a comet across the brain, and then vanish into silence? Was that not the fate of every human soul?

Sitting beside him, Vera put her lips close to his ear.

'Do you forgive them, Igor?'

'It is extraordinary,' he replied, so loudly that people in the audience turned to hush him. 'It is extraordinary,' he repeated in a lowered voice. 'They have reinvented the *Rite*.'

'So you approve?'

'It doesn't matter whether I approve or not,' he replied, his round spectacles reflecting the restless shimmering of the screen. 'They have reinvented me, too.'

He heard her soft laughter.

New York

Arturo Toscanini said goodbye to his wife, Carla, at the door of their apartment. It was a chilly New York day, the wind whistling down the canyons of Broadway, bringing with it the cold smell of the Hudson River. She fussed over him with wifely solicitude, tucking his scarf around his throat, making sure his fur-trimmed coat was properly buttoned, adjusting his kid-leather gloves.

'Don't get yourself into a temper today,' she admonished him, 'and start screaming like a madman. You know what the American doctor said about your blood pressure.'

'I know what the doctor said,' he agreed, patting her cheek fondly. 'Don't worry about me, *carissima*.'

'And don't be late for supper. I'm making one of your favourites.'

'*Mozzarella in carozza*?'

'Something else.'

'*Cozze e vongole*?'

'Stop guessing. Just come early.'

'Tell me,' he implored. 'It will give me something to look forward to while I deal with those idiots.'

Carla relented. '*Zitoni toscani*.'

His eyes gleamed. The long pasta tubes garnished with spicy Tuscan sausage and biting, salty pecorino were indeed among his favourite dishes. 'You are an angel. I love you with my whole heart and stomach.'

She beamed at him. He kissed her hand, put on his fedora hat and hurried down the stairs. Her gaze followed him fondly.

In the street outside, the Cadillac was waiting to take him to the afternoon rehearsal of the New York Philharmonic. There was also a little group of admirers who had braved the cold in the hopes of seeing the maestro emerge. A ragged cheer rose up as he appeared. The bolder members of the group rushed forward now, holding out autograph albums and record covers for him to sign. Since appearing on the cover of *LIFE* magazine (he had been on the cover of *Time* twice) his adoring public had been even more enraptured with him. The series of photographs of him playing with his little granddaughter had done much to counteract his professional reputation as a foul-mouthed and filthy-tempered old tyrant dreaded by orchestras and soloists alike.

He paused to scribble his autograph a few times, nodding and smiling, then hurried to the waiting limousine. He hopped in briskly. It pulled away from the kerb. He looked up out of the window at the building he had just left, his whiskers and dark eyes giving him something of the appearance of a raccoon peering from its burrow. He had always been happy in New York, but now he had an added reason to love the city where he had enjoyed so much success.

A few blocks from his apartment, he leaned forward and tapped the driver on the shoulder. 'Let me out here.'

The driver, who was familiar with the maestro's habits by now, pulled over. 'Pick you up in an hour?' he asked.

Toscanini checked his watch. The rehearsal was not due to start until four. 'One hour and a quarter.'

'Hold on to your hat, maestro. It's breezy.'

He got out of the limousine and trotted down West 69th Street. His nimble gait defied his approaching eightieth birthday; he was almost skipping. Separation from Ada had been cruel, but now there was Elsa. Little Elsa Kurzbauer, sweet and tempting as a Viennese pastry, right on his doorstep! If only his declining virility would support him this afternoon. It was touch and go sometimes, for all her tender ministrations. What was it Shakespeare said? How desire doth outrun performance. Something of the sort. If God took away the little that was left him, what misery! What despair!

Thinking of her naked body in the bed, tipped with pink, lined with pink, waiting for him, he felt his heart leap up in his breast. His blood was rushing hotly along his hardening arteries; the old light of battle was burning in his weakening eyes. He could hardly wait to bury his muzzle between her plump, blonde thighs, grasp her full bosoms in his hands. And the stirring in his loins promised that he would be able to discharge his fervour satisfactorily today.

He reached her apartment and pressed the buzzer with a trembling finger.

Her voice reached him through the speaker.

'Who is it?'

'Your lover,' he hissed into the grille.

He heard her mischievous laugh. The door clicked open. Checking swiftly up and down the street for observers, and seeing none, he darted into the marble lobby and made for the golden portal of the elevator.

Beacon

The sanatorium was not an easy place for a visitor to get into. It had helped greatly that Cubby was in uniform, and that there were ribbons on his breast. A Navy uniform and a Silver Star got you into most places these days without too many questions asked.

The mansion was Victorian Gothic, red brick and stone, with spires and mullioned windows. Ivy hugged the walls. The grounds were all rolling lawns and woods, more reminiscent of a country club than a psychiatric hospital. There was a golf course and a swimming pool and charming views of the Hudson River, like a nineteenth-century oil painting.

The talkative nurse, who made no attempt to hide the fact that Cubby was the most interesting visitor she'd had in a long time, told him that there was a gymnasium for the patients, not to mention rooms for painting or other creative endeavours, and a large library. She also confided that there were a lot of famous patients here. You had to be very wealthy to get your relations into Craig House. The fees ran to over a thousand dollars a month, a staggering amount, especially in wartime. Henry Fonda and F. Scott Fitzgerald had both brought their crazy wives here, although the story of Mrs Fonda had ended badly. Nurse Olsen, lowering her voice to a whisper, had pointed out the turret where Mrs Fonda had cut her throat with a razor.

And then, of course, there was Rosemary Kennedy.

'She'll be so glad to see you,' Nurse Olsen assured Cubby. 'She gets very lonely. She needs stimulation. The family don't come for months at a time, and they've given strict orders that nobody else is to see her either. That's not really fair, is it?'

'No,' Cubby replied, 'it's not.'

'But you're not really family, are you?' The question was half-flirtatious, half-professional.

'Miss Kennedy and I were engaged to be married. It didn't work out.'

'Is that right? That's too bad.' She eyed him speculatively, but didn't ask why it hadn't worked out. 'How long are you on leave, Lieutenant?'

'I have just forty-eight hours. Then I have to re-join my ship.'

'What ship is that?'

Cubby smiled. 'I'm not supposed to say. Loose lips sink ships, as they say.'

'Do I look like a Nazi spy?'

'You're pretty enough to be one,' he said gallantly.

Nurse Olsen giggled. She was a freckled redhead with a buoyant bust which her starched pinafore could not quite subdue. 'You never know, do you?'

'Well, I guess I can trust you. She's the *Saratoga*.'

Her eyes opened very wide. 'The *Saratoga*! Wasn't she torpedoed?'

'That's right.'

'That must have been terrible.'

'It was interesting.'

She laid a stubby finger on his Silver Star ribbon. 'Was that when you got this?'

'Kind of.' He was impatient to see Rosemary, but the nurse was hesitating, and he needed her good graces to get to Rosemary. 'We all had to look out for each other. I don't know why they gave me this. I accepted it for all the other guys.'

She seemed to make up her mind at last. 'I'll give you a private room. It'll be quieter.'

'That's great. Thank you.'

She led him to a room overlooking a rose garden. It was a masculine sort of den, the furniture upholstered in tobacco-coloured leather and the panelled bookcases holding rows of bound medical journals with dates in the eighteen-hundreds. 'This is Dr Slocum's study, but he's delivering a lecture in Baltimore today. Take a seat. I'll bring Rosemary down.'

Cubby sat in a hard armchair to wait. It was getting to be late in the year. Through the diamond-paned window, he watched the heavy yellow heads of the autumn roses nodding in the breeze outside. He wasn't sure what he was going to say to Rosemary. It was four years since he had last seen her, and in all that time he had not received a single letter from her, though he had written – in spite of Mrs Kennedy's warning – many times.

When he looked back on that Cubby of four years ago, he hardly recognised himself. He had been a different person then, untouched by life, though he'd fancied that his heart had been broken.

In the years of war that had followed his enlisting in the Navy, he had been through fire and blood. He had witnessed the death of friends, the loss of innocence, all the terror and boredom and fury of war. He knew he would never play music again.

He looked now upon his earlier self as a man might look upon a younger brother, pitying his naiveté, wanting to protect him from harm, yet knowing that nothing could protect anyone from harm in this life. Sometimes the gulf that separated this Lieutenant Hubbard from that earlier Cubby was so deep and wide that he felt he must inevitably fall into two pieces, fractured beyond repair. Those moments usually happened when he was ashore, and he survived them by going into a kind of somnambulistic trance, sleepwalking his way through everything he was asked to do with eyes wide open, yet feeling nothing.

He heard a footstep outside the door and rose to his feet. Nurse Olsen came into the study, leading a woman; but to Cubby's acute disappointment, it was not Rosemary. It was someone much older, someone who had evidently suffered a terrible accident, for she walked with painful slowness, her head hanging down to one side, her shoulders crooked, with one arm twisted awkwardly in front of her.

'Here she is,' Nurse Olsen said cheerfully. 'She's been quite perky today. Haven't you, Rosemary? Look who's come to see you. Isn't that a lovely surprise?'

Cubby felt as though he had been plunged into an ice bath. He could not speak. As Nurse Olsen steered the shuffling figure to a chair, he saw that this human wreck was indeed Rosemary – or rather, what was left of her, because Rosemary had departed the twisted body, leaving it empty. The dull eyes that met his from under the crudely cropped hair were incurious and did not linger on him. Although the lips were moving, they did not frame any words of greeting. It was no more than a tremor.

'I'll just put this under her, in case of accidents.' The nurse laid the folded towel on the chair, and then carefully helped Rosemary to lower her body down. When Rosemary was seated, the nurse propped a pillow under her head to keep her from sliding over. 'Do you want me to stay?' She smiled at Cubby. 'Of course you don't. You have a lot of private things to talk about. I'll leave you in peace. There's a buzzer on the desk. Just press that when you need me.' She left the room.

Cubby couldn't see Rosemary's face clearly, since her chin was resting on her collarbone. He knelt on the carpet in front of her chair, looking up at her.

'Rosemary,' he whispered. 'Do you know who I am?'

The dull eyes drifted across his face indifferently for a moment, then slid away. He studied her, hardly able to believe what he saw. The beauty of her face, so much of which had come from the vivacity of her expressions, was completely gone. What had once been plump was now drooping. The once-rounded cheeks were pouchy, the once-full lips thin and cracked. Her skin, which had bloomed with youth, was sallow. He saw that even her hands were prematurely aged, their grace gone, the nails cut short. They lay in her lap like two dead birds.

'It's me. Cubby. Don't you remember me?'

He thought he saw her nodding at that, though it might have been just part of the tremors which now and then moved her body. He was appalled at the change in her.

'Do you know why I came to see you today? Do you know what day it is?'

She was unresponsive.

'Oh, Rosemary. What happened to you?'

He sat back in the hard armchair, and rested his head in his hands. He hadn't known what to expect today. Perhaps Rosemary screaming, Rosemary raging, but at least Rosemary alive. Not this. Not Rosemary dead. Rosemary dead was not something he could accept or understand. He sat hunched over in misery for a long time, remembering the intense joy he had once held in his arms, now gone forever.

He heard a wet sound from her mouth, and took his hands away from his face. She had raised her head off her chest. The effort made her neck quiver. But she was looking at him. Her lips were moving, straining to form a word.

'Ca . . .'

'Yes,' he said. 'I'm Cubby. Do you remember me, darling?'

She peered at him searchingly for a while, as though trying to recall something. He was not sure whether she recognised him, or whether she remembered anything about him at all. Then he noticed the wetness that was darkening the brown fabric of her slacks, soaking into the towel she sat on. That was what the nurse had meant by 'in case of accidents'.

He saw her expression change, showing the first emotion he'd seen in her – a rush of embarrassment or shame. Her head drooped down on to her breast again. He thought she might be crying.

Cubby turned away and pressed the buzzer. In a short while, Nurse Olsen came back.

'Ah, I hoped that wouldn't happen,' she said regretfully. 'I took her to the commode before I brought her down, but she didn't do anything. I guess she was too excited to see you.'

'Excited?' he echoed incredulously. 'What the hell have they done to her?'

She turned to look at him. 'Didn't you know about the operation?'

'What operation?'

'I thought you knew. You said you were her fiancé.'

'I was. That was four years ago. I had no idea she was like this.'

Nurse Olsen parted the hair at the front of Rosemary's head to show him the curved scars on her white scalp. 'They lobotomised her.'

'What does that mean?'

'They took out part of her brain. It's a very new medical procedure. It was supposed to make her calmer. It wasn't a success.'

'A success?' Cubby was trembling. 'They've destroyed her!'

Nurse Olsen took him to the window and lowered her voice. 'Watch what you say in front of her, Lieutenant. You don't know what she hears and understands.'

'Whose idea was it to do this to her?'

'Her parents took the decision.'

He felt sick to his heart. 'What did she do that was so terribly wrong? What did she do to deserve *this*?'

'They told us she was out of control. Sexually hyperactive.'

'Sexually hyperactive?'

'I guess this will upset you, having been engaged to her and all, but she was running around with a lot of men.'

'Do you know how her brothers behave?' Cubby demanded.

'There's one rule for men,' Nurse Olsen replied primly, 'and another for women.'

'There certainly is in that family,' he replied bitterly. 'The men do as they please and the women do as they're told.'

'She was a danger to herself. There were incidents. And there was more than that. She had seizures, learning difficulties—'

'You never knew her as she was,' Cubby snapped. 'Whatever problems she had, she's a thousand times worse now!'

Nurse Olsen straightened her uniform. 'Look, we didn't do this to her. We just take care of her now. Okay? So there's no use yelling at me. People bring their problems to us and dump them here, and we just make sure there's no more scandal. I'm sorry you weren't prepared for this. I would have explained if I'd known. I just assumed you were familiar with her condition.'

He couldn't bear to look at Rosemary any longer. He was staring at the wind-battered yellow roses outside, which were drooping their heads like Rosemary. 'No, I wasn't.'

'Well, now you know.'

'Today is her birthday.'

Nurse Olsen looked surprised. 'Why, yes. Of course it is. I'd almost forgotten.'

'She's twenty-five.'

'Well, she has the mental age of a two-year-old now.' There was a silence after this brutal assessment. Then the nurse sighed. 'You'll have to excuse us, Lieutenant. I need to change her. I think it's best if you leave.'

'Yes.' He was sleepwalking now, his feelings numbed. There was nothing more to be said or done.

Nurse Olsen's expression softened. 'She may make progress. Come back in a year.'

He wondered if she meant that to be consoling. He forced himself to look at the hunched figure of Rosemary, her head hanging down. 'A year?'

'It's going to be slow. But you never know. Come back in a year.'

Idlewild

Rachel Morgenstern stood in front of the huge glass window at Idlewild airport. The sinuous lines of the building flowed around her in convolutions of steel and concrete, but she was oblivious to the neo-futurist architecture. She had eyes only for the gleaming silver Pan American DC-7 which had just landed on the far runway. It caught the watery sunlight as it turned to approach the terminal building, its four great propellers blurring.

Rachel felt that she was hardly breathing. Time had ground to a halt. Out on the airfield, the airliner lumbered slowly along the maze of pathways, though airborne it was capable of three hundred and sixty knots. The heavy drone of its engines shook the ground, even through the plate glass and concrete. Spray kicked up from rain puddles on the tarmac, along with stray pages of newspaper, whirled into the air.

At last, the DC-7 stopped in its bay. The propellers feathered and slowed to a standstill. Ground crew in blue-and-tan uniforms pushed the rolling staircase to the single door aft of the wing. It opened. And after a minute, passengers began to emerge.

Rachel let out her breath at last, feeling dizzy. She'd been in the grip of an unreasoning fear that the airliner would crash, catch fire, vanish before it could release its precious cargo. But it was here at last.

She moved closer to the glass, watching the procession of passengers intently. They clutched at their coats and hats as they came out into the windy New York afternoon, many of them pausing to wave joyfully as they caught sight of those who had come to greet them.

The figure in the long English coat was unmistakable. Rachel waved, but the distant woman did not lift her head to search the windows of the terminal for a familiar face, as the others did, partly because she was short-sightedly peering her way down the aluminium stairs, and partly because she was leading a little girl, who clung sleepily to her hand.

Rachel felt an electric current seize her heart. She tried to hold back her tears. Eight years, she thought. Eight years stolen from us, and here we are again.

Dorothea kept her eyes on the ground as she and her child plodded towards the terminal building, but that didn't stop them from walking through a puddle. Rachel heard herself laugh abruptly. Still blind as a bat. Probably worse, now.

Rachel felt the hot hugeness of her love swelling in her heart.

Rachel waited on the crimson suede banquette, her handbag on her knee, her kid gloves growing damp as she clutched them. She had dressed as smartly as she could today. Working at Niemann Marcus had given her the choice of the best couture clothing.

When she'd started as a store assistant during the war, she'd felt it was only a step up from the switchboard, and hardly the life she would have chosen for herself, were it not for Hitler. The years had taught her to be grateful. She had risen quickly, and now managed one of the most prestigious ladies' wear lines in Niemann Marcus.

The years had also taught her that clothes made the woman. And her job enabled her to live in a world of women, surrounded by her own sex, her eyes filled each day with refinement and beauty.

The clothes she had chosen today were expensive and stylish. She didn't want Dorothea to think she had grown dowdy, now that she was past thirty. She hadn't anticipated that Dorothea would choose to wear the old houndstooth coat which had captured her heart all those years ago. That had been a master stroke.

Finally, she saw them coming through the doors, carrying their suitcases.

Rachel got to her feet, her knees shaky, and hurried to meet them.

Dorothea didn't see her until the last minute; but Rachel had time to notice that the years of war, hunger and hardship had made the houndstooth coat threadbare, the woman inside it thin and careworn. The child, too, was shabby, a black mourning band for her father around the arm of her jacket, which was too thin, even for this mild autumn day. She was sweet-faced, but looked undernourished, her blonde pigtails lank, her cheeks hollow. American food and a few trips to Niemann Marcus, Rachel thought, would cure all that. She had the means to make their lives beautiful again.

Dorothea looked up with a start as Rachel confronted her. Behind the round lenses, her eyes were still the grey-green of Saxony rain. She'd touched her lips with pink to make herself more attractive. But nothing could make that face more lovely to Rachel.

'I've waited for you,' Rachel said, her throat dry.

'And I for you,' Dorothea replied, almost inaudibly.

'We don't have to wait any longer.' She held out her arms. 'Welcome.'

The tired child stared up at the two women as they clung to one another. After a while, they drew her into their embrace.

Wisconsin

Cubby reached St Coletta at mid-morning. He'd started making his travel plans the moment he'd heard about the assassination on Friday. He'd wanted to be with Rosemary as soon as possible. During his long journey from California to the Midwest over this weekend, he had seen the grim faces, the women who still cried in public, the huddled groups who talked in hushed voices and occasionally glanced up at the sky. People were still saying the killing of the president was the prelude to a Russian attack. Some were waiting for the nuclear missiles to begin raining down.

Out here in rural Wisconsin, that horror seemed less likely. The November skies were cold sapphire, scattered with fleecy clouds that caught the sun. The last of the autumn leaves were clinging to the woods, red and frail. He saw a flock of wild turkeys scrambling across the road, and once a solitary whitetail buck, looking at him over its shoulder.

He turned off County Road Y towards the school, which was set among trees on a rise of land. As he drove slowly between the school buildings, several people waved to him. He was well-known here.

It had been called many things: 'St Coletta Institute for Backward Youth' had been pretty blunt. 'St Coletta Feeble-Minded School' had been well-meaning but discouraging. Finally, the Catholic Church had hit on the brilliant idea of renaming it 'St Coletta School for Exceptional Children.'

It had been called many things, and it was many things: a school where the young were given hope, a farm, an orchard, a haven where the irreparably damaged were sheltered, a housing programme where the vulnerable could live with dignity. And it was now Rosemary Kennedy's home.

Rosemary had her own cottage, a little white unit that was screened off from prying eyes by tall firs and cypresses that were always dark green at any time of the year. There were borders of geraniums and a patch of lawn, all kept neat by the gardeners. Compared to the residences of her surviving siblings, it wasn't much to look at, but it was sufficient for her simple needs.

He pulled the rental car up in front of the cottage and got out, his ears singing in the silence. There was nobody in the little garden, so he entered the house. The television was on. Rosemary sat in front of it, flanked by two of the sisters. The sisters were both in tears. Rosemary, whom they'd dressed in black, was watching the images on the screen intently but with no outward show of emotion.

'Oh, Mr Bigelow,' Sister Ursula said, rising and coming to Cubby, 'isn't it terrible?' She was pressing a handkerchief to her mouth so that Cubby could barely understand what she was saying.

'How is Rosemary taking it?' Cubby asked.

'She was watching the television on Friday when the news came through. I don't think she really understood. We've been trying to explain to her, but—' Sister Ursula blew her nose. Her eyes were swollen and red. 'Perhaps it's a mercy if she doesn't quite get it.'

Cubby sat on the sofa next to Rosemary. Her hands were lying open in her lap, as they so often did. He took one of them. 'Hello, Rosie.'

She drew her eyes away from the screen and glanced at him. 'Jack is dead,' she said.

So she understood that much, at least. 'Yes. I'm so sorry, Rosemary.'

She squeezed his hand briefly, then returned to watching the television. Jack Kennedy's funeral was underway in Washington.

They watched the widow emerging from the White House, draped in black lace, leading her two small children by the hand. The coffin, covered with the Stars and Stripes, was laid on a gun carriage, pulled by six white horses. They began the long, slow march up Pennsylvania Avenue to the Capitol.

As the funeral cortege passed the blocks, the television cameras panned across faces in the crowd, the soldiers immaculate and expressionless, the civilians stunned, grieving. Many of the women wore headscarves, as though in church. A young girl looked on with tears streaming down her cheeks. Mostly, people were silent and motionless.

Cubby was remembering his meeting with Jack, twenty-four years earlier, in Southampton. He'd liked the young man, despite everything. Everyone liked Jack. He was luminous, persuasive, disarming. His murder in a public street in Dallas had changed America. A light had gone out and nobody knew how to reignite it. The nation was groping blindly.

The nuns brought cups of tea as they continued to watch the long-drawn funeral on the small TV that stood on a shelf next to a brightly glazed tortoise made by Rosemary in pottery class.

'Is he the president now?' Rosemary asked, pointing. Her words were slurred. You had to get used to the way she spoke before you could understand her.

'Yes,' Cubby answered. Johnson looked worn, already overburdened by the office he had once sought, and which had fallen to him so shockingly.

Rosemary hardly said another word after that. In St Matthew's Cathedral in Washington, the requiem mass began. The cameras focused on a statue of Jesus while a tenor sang *Ave Maria*. The voice of the priest was disembodied, intoning words which meant nothing to Cubby, though the nuns crossed themselves from time to time. He wondered how much of this Rosemary was following. He'd raced to be here with her in case she needed him, but it seemed as though the death of her brother, the third of her siblings to die – and all of them violent deaths – had left her unmoved.

Suddenly, however, Rosemary yelled, making them all start.

'Lollie! Get off the chair!'

Rosemary's poodle had jumped on to an armchair with a ball in its mouth. 'Hush, Rosemary,' Sister Ursula said in dismay.

But Rosemary was furious. 'Get off! Get *off!*' Her yelling made the dog roll its expressive brown eyes, wriggling its stump of a tail. Rosemary got to her feet, still a tall and daunting figure. The dog leaped off the chair, dropped its ball to bark, and then picked it up again. 'Taking her for a walk,' Rosemary said, stamping after the animal, which was already making for the door.

'But the funeral—' Sister Ursula protested.

Cubby also rose. 'I'll go with her.'

They walked among the trees, the poodle frisking around them. After a while, Rosemary took Cubby's hand. Her fingers clutched his tightly, like a child. 'They're crying all the time,' she said. 'Getting on my nerves.'

'They're sad because your brother was a great man.'

She nodded. 'I can't cry any more. Don't know how to.' She touched her head. 'After they did this.'

'I understand,' Cubby said gently.

'Used to cry a lot. Before.' She stopped at the sound of a distant shot.

'It's just a hunter in the woods, a mile or two off.'

She resumed walking. 'I cried all the time when you went away.'

'I know you did.'

'Why didn't we ever get married?' she asked.

He was always stuck for an adequate answer to that, though she asked it almost every time he came. 'Well, the war started. I had to go and fight.'

'Can't have children now.' She laid her hand on her belly. 'All gone. Operation.'

'I know.' They'd given her the hysterectomy some years earlier, but it was still fresh in her mind, even though she'd been through an early menopause as a result. She was forty-five now. 'I'm so sorry.'

'Wish I could cry now. But I can't.' Abruptly, she kicked at the dead leaves, her face red with anger. The fragile brown things flew into the air, then settled around her shoes. 'I get so mad. So goddamn mad.' She put her arms clumsily around him and held him tight, her cropped head on his shoulder. Cubby wanted to cry for both of them, but like Rosemary herself, he didn't know how to any more.

They stood like that, leaning on one another among the stark trees, for a long while. At last, she kissed him clumsily on the mouth. There was nothing sexual in the kiss. It was almost a blow, her lips dry and hard. 'Love,' she said, looking into his eyes.

'Love,' he agreed.

They walked back to the cottage.

The funeral took all day. It ended in Arlington, in the dusk. The soldiers fired three volleys into the air. A bugler played 'The Last Post'. The setting sun streaked the sorrowful faces of the crowd who stood among a sea of fallen leaves. Jackie and Bobby lit the flame that would burn for evermore. The coffin sank into the earth at last. Evening came swiftly, and the flame was left flickering in the darkness, alone and restless.

By now Rosemary was tired and irritable. He knew it was time to leave. He said goodbye to her, and then set off on the long journey home.

Kennedy Space Centre, Florida

It had been a particularly nerve-racking three days. The first launch had been aborted at the last second – literally. With seven seconds to go before ignition, Columbia's hazardous gas detection system had suddenly reported high levels of hydrogen in the orbiter's aft engine compartment. With vivid memories of the 1986 Challenger fireball, in which all seven crew members had died, Thomas König and the other system engineers in Kennedy Space Centre's Firing Room No. 1 had had to take a decision. The launch had been aborted less than half a second before the three main engines were due to ignite.

Columbia's five crew members had emerged from the spacecraft in their orange flight suits, disappointed but philosophical. The STS-93 mission was historic in being the first in space shuttle history to be commanded by a woman, Eileen Collins, with a second woman among the five-person crew, Cady Coleman.

On inspection, the hydrogen concentration indication had turned out to be a false reading.

'We took the right decision,' Thomas said to his dejected team, his German accent still noticeable after a lifetime in the United States. 'Better safe than sorry. We'll reinitiate countdown shortly.'

After recalibrating the gas detectors, they'd scheduled a second launch for two days later.

This time, the weather had closed in, with storms and high winds. The second launch had also been scrubbed. They'd initiated a twenty-four-hour turnaround, hoping the weather would improve, as the meteorologists were predicting.

While the shuttle crew tried to relax, Thomas and the rest of the team worked round the clock on preparations for the third countdown. Third time lucky, everybody said. The mission would be a short one, five days in orbit; but every minute of every day would be filled with work for the astronauts. There were several secondary payloads to be deployed, including the Chandra X-ray Observatory, an orbiting X-ray telescope fifty times more powerful than anything yet used, capable of reading the letters on a stop sign from twelve miles away.

On the space station, the astronauts would monitor several ongoing biological experiments, and would all take turns on the treadmill to collect valuable data on how exercise in space affected the microgravity of the space station. Routine stuff; but even after all these years, there was nothing routine about space exploration. Every day brought new wonders and new challenges.

'You're going to miss all this, Tom,' a colleague said to Thomas.

He nodded. 'Yes, I am.'

It was his last launch. Now into his seventies, he was ten years older than NASA's official retirement age. His lifetime with the Agency, and his deep involvement with the Space Shuttle Program, had kept him working, sharing his experience and wisdom. But by the time Mission STS-93 returned to Florida, he would be in retirement. A tall, spare figure in white shirt-sleeves and dark tie, he would in his turn be missed by all those he had worked with. His reputation for brilliance and reserve, tempered with kindness, was legendary.

The day of the launch dawned clear. The meteorologists had prophesied correctly. The Firing Room system engineers were all at their desks by midday. The huge screens on the wall in front of them showed the space shuttle, aimed at the heavens, waiting to be unleashed from earth's sullen bonds. Steam rose tranquilly around it into the pellucid afternoon sky.

Reflected in the lagoon that extended beside the launch pad, Columbia appeared pristine, though the shuttle was now ten years old. Unlike other spacecraft, which took on the appearance of turkeys left too long in the oven, Columbia returned from space relatively unscathed each time. Her tiled surfaces were carefully designed to withstand the heat generated by ploughing into the earth's atmosphere at orbital speed during re-entry. Only a close look revealed the scuffs and burns left by twenty-five previous missions.

STS-93 was to be a night launch, taking off shortly after midnight. The astronauts began to take their seats in the shuttle again during the late afternoon.

The humid Florida night fell. In the darkness, loud with the voices of frogs and night birds, Columbia glowed like a beacon. She had become as iconic a sight to a generation of Americans as the Statue of Liberty herself. The intense light from the floods glanced off her sleek fuselage, streaming up into the sky, as though – or so Thomas thought – she were illuminating a path for herself to the stars.

Commander Collins's voice came through the communications link a few minutes after midnight: 'Great working with you guys, see you in five days.' And then the launch sequence was underway.

A night launch was a spectacle which Thomas always enjoyed. Ignition of the three main engines was reminiscent of a volcanic eruption. Huge glowing clouds billowed around the launch vehicle. Then it began to lift cleanly, jets of fire spitting from the three gaping nozzles.

The thunder of her engines made the earth vibrate under the feet of the watchers. Outside, it was deafening. Like a midnight sun, the rocket lit up the night as it climbed the sky. For a while, it was too bright to watch. Then the dazzling fireball dwindled swiftly. Within a few minutes, it was no more than a spark in the blackness. With burnout and separation complete, Columbia had consumed two million pounds of fuel, half of her launch weight, within ten minutes of her departure.

An appearance of cool professionalism was the norm in the launch centre these days. The days of ecstatic cheers and high-fives had passed. Everybody tried to look as though this was just part of a normal day, a result that had been planned for and expected. But as Columbia ascended on her fiery tail, the mood was elated.

Thomas left the centre sometime around two a.m., his eyes aching, his back weary. He knew that farewell parties and award ceremonies awaited him during what remained of the week, but this was effectively his last working day.

He had never been a sentimental man – he had cut extraneous emotions out of his life as far as he possibly could – but the aftermath of a launch always left him somehow saddened.

The departure of that gleaming white thing left a sense of loss, of something wonderful and magical that would never come again; of moments of glory and wonder that had illuminated the darkness for a while and then had left him bereft and alone.

He had lived with that sense of loss all his life.

He had never heard from his mother and his father again, nor from anyone else in his immediate family. After the war, the Red Cross had informed him that they had all perished in the camps. Though he had made two pilgrimages back to the places where they had died, there had been no graves, no markers, no place to lay flowers. All he was left with were the memorials in various public sites, where their names figured along with the countless millions of others whose lives had been consumed.

There had been other losses, too. He had never married, never had children of his own. There simply hadn't been time. His life had been study and work, work and study. He had given his best years to the space program. There had been nobody else to give them to.

He entered his house, finding it air-conditioned to his specifications, softly lit just the way he liked it. He'd programmed computers to regulate most of the functions of the house. They switched things on and off, paid the bills, kept the pool pristine. They even controlled the large tank in which brilliant tropical fish drifted, the only living things with which he shared his life.

Lined on the wall were photographs of the people he'd worked with over the years: John Glenn, Alan Shepard, Neil Armstrong, Sally Ride, others who had been places he would never go, while he watched from his desk. Smiling in their sky-blue space suits were the seven Challenger astronauts who had died in 1986, two women, a black man, an Asian, two white men, a cross-section of America.

He ate a breakfast of cereal standing in the kitchen. He was thinking of that remark, almost a cliché: *You're going to miss all this, Tom.*

It opened the question which, strange to say, he hadn't considered until this moment – what he was going to do with the rest of his life. He was healthy, fit, active. The question was going to become pressing.

But it was time to sleep now. He would start thinking about that when he was rested.

He cleared away the tiny disruption he had caused in the kitchen and went to his computer to check his messages before going to bed. He'd been using email for over ten years. Now, in the era of AOL, Prodigy, CompuServe and Hotmail, it was becoming the norm for millions of Americans.

Most of his mail was work-related. Already, messages of appreciation for his lifetime's service to the space program were starting to flood in. But one message stood out because it contained a name he hadn't heard for decades.

He opened the email, and read it. Then he clicked on the attachment, and found himself looking at a face that for over half a century he had only seen in dreams.

New York

The ceremony at Juilliard had been a heady occasion. The mediaeval splendour of so many colourful academic gowns, blue and red predominating, had been a feast for the eyes. There had been wonderful music, inspiring words that had brought tears to her eyes, the joy of seeing her granddaughter graduate among the flower of her generation.

At her age, Masha was inevitably reminded of another generation, which had been cut down in full flower; but now was not the time to dwell on the past. Now was a time for rejoicing, for new beginnings. The past could wait until later.

She'd taken her daughter and granddaughter to lunch, and had bathed in the light shed by youth and hope. Mariam was a gift to the world, as beautiful within as she was on the outside. Her musical talent had shown itself almost from infancy. If it was a genetic inheritance, it had skipped a generation, because her mother, Masha's daughter Judith, had never been particularly musical.

So it had fallen to Masha, the devoted grandmother, to nurture the flame and fan it into a blaze that would endure a lifetime. It had been a labour of love. After Dale's death in 1973, at the age of only fifty-seven, it had turned from a labour of love into a sacred duty. Today was the culmination of all that hope and devotion. There was no more she could do for Mariam now except watch her soar.

Lunch ended late. Judith and Mariam had shopping to do with Mariam's partner, Kevin. Then they would be meeting Mariam's father – amicably separated from Judith for two decades and more – and continuing their celebrations into the early hours.

'Sure you don't want to come along, Granma?' Mariam asked, tugging on her grandmother's arm the way she'd done ever since infancy.

'I'll only slow you down,' Masha said.

'Take that back. None of this would have happened without you.'

Masha smiled. 'Okay, I take it back.'

'What are you going to do now?'

'I'll just rest, I think.'

'You've never rested a day in your life,' Judith scoffed.

'Well, maybe now's a good time to start.'

'You're up to something,' Judith said, eyeing her mother keenly. 'What is it?'

'Nothing.'

'I don't believe you.'

'Well, if there *is* something, it's my business. Now go on, enjoy yourselves.'

Loud with city noise, the air was mild. She felt buoyant, like a woman who had discharged her duty and had time to burn. There was still warmth in the day, still sunlight in the afternoon. It slanted across the green spaces of Central Park, between the towers and down the canyons of Columbus Avenue. She enjoyed the energy of the city. Walking the streets of New York had never lost its thrill for her. She had spent much of her life in a small, leafy, upstate town, where such things as the quality of life and the cleanness of the air were treasured; but she was a Berliner born, and had always considered herself a city girl. Grime, noise and seething energy were her natural habitat.

She walked briskly, reached the sprawling complex of the Lincoln Centre and climbed the steps into the main plaza. The great space, surrounded by the palaces of the new American Renaissance, never failed to inspire Masha. She sat on the wall of the fountain in front of the high arches of the Metropolitan Opera. To one side of her was the New York Ballet, to the other the New York Philharmonic. She watched the people who passed by – visitors, artists, lovers; those who had come to dance or sing, and those who had come to be part of the performance.

So many lives, intersecting through the power of art. Sometimes the intersections were momentary, lasting no longer than a single performance; other intersections lasted a lifetime, becoming partnerships, enshrined in memory, perpetuated in beauty, never dying or fading away. At the heart of it all was art, that strange endeavour of the human species, which had no other end than itself, but which brought out the best in a race of beings all too prone to dark deeds.

She was lost in her own thoughts when she heard her name spoken. She looked up. Thomas König was standing in front of her, a tall, slim, grey-haired man in a seersucker suit.

'Thomas!' Masha got up and hugged him. 'How wonderful to see you.'

'It's been a long time,' he said formally. He drew back and studied her with grave, grey-blue eyes. Then the dry landscape of his face was lit by a smile. 'You never change.'

'Oh, such nonsense.' Masha laughed a little breathlessly. 'You needn't flatter me. Change comes to us all.'

'Some change is natural and therefore pleasing,' he replied.

'Ah, what tact. I'm so glad you came.'

He looked around. 'So am I. I've never been here before. This place is amazing.'

'You must be used to amazing sights, Thomas.'

'True. But this is different.'

'Yes, I imagine this is different. You didn't become a watchmaker, after all.'

'No. I took your advice and went big.'

She took his arm. 'Will you come with me? I want you to see something.'

The Stravinsky exhibition was well-attended. Masha had taken the precaution of getting two tickets well in advance. They made their way through the crowds who surrounded the collection of photographs, paintings, scores and other original documents from the period of Stravinsky's association with the New York Philharmonic.

She led him to a glass case, where several pages of a musical manuscript were laid out under soft lighting. At first he wasn't sure what he was looking at, and then he saw the museum card:

> Original Manuscript, Igor Stravinsky 'Symphony in C' (1939/1940)
>
> On loan from Masha J. Morgenstern

'You kept it all these years,' he said quietly, bending to get a closer look.

'What should I have done, sell it? No, no. It was a gift, a treasure. A mitzvah. I've kept it safe, all my life. It will go to my granddaughter when I am gone. She can trade it for a really good violin.'

'Is she that talented?'

'She's that talented.'

Thomas stared at the scrawled and blotted pages. 'I remember running to get this from your cabin, the night of the submarine.'

'Oh, I remember that, too. I will never forget it. There are so many things about that voyage that I will never forget. They're as fresh in my memory as though they happened yesterday.'

He nodded. 'For me, too.'

'There's something else I've treasured all these years. The ticket you gave me to the World's Fair.'

Thomas laughed. 'Masha, that's not quite on the same scale as an original Stravinsky manuscript.'

Her face stayed serious. 'To me it is. It was also a mitzvah. A gift from the heart that gave me strength when I didn't want to go on.'

'To tell you the truth, I was amazed when you showed up at Flushing Meadows.'

'I would never have failed you. That is another occasion that stands out in my memory as though it happened yesterday.'

'I remember the smell of onions on your breath,' he said, almost to himself.

'What!'

He looked embarrassed. 'From the hotdog. When you kissed me goodbye.'

'There are some memories that ought to be suppressed,' she exclaimed. But she was also touched that he had recalled something so personal and intimate. 'I always had the feeling that your visit to the World's Fair didn't quite live up to your expectations. In more ways than one.'

'What do you mean?'

'I guess I felt you were disappointed in it.' She hesitated. 'And in me.'

'You couldn't have been kinder to me.'

'Oh, I think I could. I could have spared your feelings more.'

He didn't ask what she meant. 'I was very sorry to hear that your husband died so young. You never remarried?'

Masha shook her head. 'I never wanted to. And I had my hands full with Mariam.'

'Your granddaughter?'

'Yes. Judith wasn't really into the whole stay-at-home-Mom thing. She was more interested in self-exploration. She and Mariam's father separated when Mariam was around five. Judith followed her own course in life for years – ashrams, religious retreats, Buddhist monasteries, artists' colonies, you name it. She was away in India for nearly two years. Then she went to a commune in New Mexico for another three.'

'So you were more mother than grandmother?'

'Effectively.' Masha held up a slim hand. 'I don't want to make Judith sound crazy or anything. They're a lot closer now. And I loved being there for Mariam, especially after Dale died. He died of a work-related illness, so there was compensation. That meant I could quit my job to be there for Mariam.'

'That was a big sacrifice.'

'I never begrudged one moment. Talking of souvenirs, you'll never guess what Rachel kept all these years: the swastika pin you gave her.'

'Really?'

'Really. Her partner Dorothea recently asked her why she kept such an ugly thing. She said it was to remind her not to jump to conclusions about anybody.'

Thomas smiled slightly. 'That's a good lesson. To answer your question, I wasn't disappointed in the World's Fair. That visit helped me distinguish between fantasy and reality – what was impossible and what could really be achieved. My ideas about technology had come out of comic books. After the World's Fair, I knew that wonderful things were going to be done, and that I could be part of them. They were just going to be different from what I had dreamed.'

'But you were disappointed in me.'

He thought for a moment. 'I would say you also showed me the difference between fantasy and reality. What was a dream and what could really be attained.'

'That must have been a hard lesson,' Masha said gently.

'It needed to be learned.'

'It's funny,' she said, as they moved away from the glass case, 'the age difference between us now seems irrelevant. Back then, it was unbridgeable.'

'Yes.'

'In fact, you've gained authority now. I feel humble next to you.'

His features, refined by age and self-discipline, expressed surprise. 'Why should you feel that?'

'You've achieved such amazing things. The whole nation has watched them on TV. All I've been is a quiet little music teacher in a quiet little town.'

'We've both launched others on their life's voyages. There's nothing more valuable. We can both be proud of that.'

'That's a very nice thing to say.'

'It's true.'

She hesitated. 'You never married, Thomas?'

'You know I didn't.'

'Was that my fault?'

He smiled slightly. 'You had something to do with it. I wouldn't say it was your fault, exactly.'

'I would hate to think it was. Was there never – somebody?'

'Oh yes. There were a couple of somebodies along the way. Just never anybody I wanted to make a life with. Besides, I was married to NASA. None of the possible incumbents were prepared to play second string to a space agency.'

'But you finally left the space agency.'

'I did.'

'So there's hope for some lucky somebody?'

'The age of saints has passed, my dear Masha.'

'I'm going to sign you up for a dating agency.'

'Please don't.'

'A *seniors'* dating agency.'

'*Was Hänschen nicht lernt, lernt Hans nimmermehr.*'

It was the first German he had spoken, and Masha snorted with laughter. 'You can't teach an old dog new tricks? I wouldn't count on that.'

Twilight had fallen by the time they left the building. The plaza was a spectacular sight. The fountains were illuminated, the great halls on three sides blazed with light. Laughter and music were everywhere. They stood together, enjoying the evening and its magic.

'Thank you for bringing me here,' Thomas said. 'I might never have come.'

'Next time we're here we'll do a concert or a ballet.'

'That's a deal.'

'Good. I owe you that.'

'You don't owe me anything, Masha.'

Her face, still heart-shaped and pretty, was sad for a moment. 'Over the years I've become more and more conscious of the debts I owe to others. To my family, who gave up everything to save me. To Rachel, who kept me strong. To Stravinsky, who was so generous to us all. And to you. Your kindness stands out as one of the defining moments of my youth. I revisit it often, and each time it means more to me.'

'I've been thinking,' Thomas said. 'About what to do next. I sat at my desk for a lot of years and watched a lot of people leave for exciting places. Maybe it's my turn now.'

'You want to travel?'

'I thought I might see a bit of the world. Paris. London. Rome. And yes, Berlin. Maybe even Tokyo, Singapore.'

'That sounds wonderful, Thomas. I've always been a city girl, myself. I'd like to do that too.'

He was watching the fountains, the dancing lights reflected in his eyes. 'There's no reason why you shouldn't.' He paused. Was it too late for him to have these feelings? Was he making a fool of himself – an old fool, this time? He decided to go ahead. 'We could go together.'

'No reason why not,' she said quietly.

He felt his heart soar. 'No reason in the world.'

She took his arm. 'How about a hotdog? I promise to skip the onions.'

'I think we can do better than a hotdog these days.' He looked down into her face. The soft glow had given her back her youth and beauty, or perhaps his own eyes were blurring, because she didn't look a day over twenty. 'And you have no idea how I long to smell onions on your breath again.'

'Let me see what I can do about that. Shall we go then, you and I?'

They walked down the stairs, which sparkled with lights, and out into the glittering tide of noise and life in Columbus Avenue.

Wisconsin

Cubby Hubbard had to plan his visits with more care these days. After the decades of near-isolation, people had dredged Rosemary's name out of their memories and had started calling to see her. Her family had begun to drift back around her. Or at least some of her family. She had already outlived her parents. Her father, devastated by a stroke a few years after Rosemary's lobotomy, had ended up in a worse condition than she, unable to talk or walk. Her mother, once so sharp and ambitious, had declined into dementia. From what the nuns had told Cubby, Rosemary had never forgiven either of them, despite the irony of their fates. Of Rosemary's siblings, four had already died, in accidents or at the hands of assassins, giving the family name, which had once been so proud, the ring of tragedy.

Those who remained had begun to show an interest in the recluse at St Coletta of Wisconsin. They came to see her and sometimes they took her on outings, to revisit the places of her youth, or to see new ones. There was even a tendency to turn her into a cause célèbre, and make her suffering an emblem of compassion – she who had received so little compassion in her life, except from strangers.

So Cubby had to plan his visits with a little foresight so as not to coincide with other visitors, or find Rosemary not there. It wasn't too difficult, because Rosemary's visitors and outings were not so common – she still spent most of her time alone – and with the help of the nuns, something could always be arranged. But it was a long journey to make, and he didn't like to make it in vain.

He drove the car he'd rented through the Midwestern cornfields of bronze and gold, now almost ready for the harvest. Along County Road Y, the strips on either side of the tarmac, which they called berms here in Wisconsin, were speckled with pale-blue forget-me-nots. He was remembering a time when he hadn't needed to check in advance, because he had always found Rosemary alone, and St Coletta had been the middle of nowhere.

He had been coming to St Coletta twice a year for half a century. This was his hundredth visit.

It was eight months since he'd last seen Rosemary. He wasn't able to travel as easily as he had done in the past. Everything was more effort, more of a challenge these days. The passing of the years was something he'd learned to accept; yet it struck him to the heart to see Rosemary huddled in her wheelchair now, in front of the porch. She had been robust through her middle age, retaining some of her physical vigour, though her movements had always been clumsy. She had loved to walk. But in recent years he had seen her shrinking, fading, becoming immobile. The nuns had told him she would inevitably be wheelchair-bound one day, and during the past eight months, that day had come.

He got out of the car. She raised her head, and he saw her face light up. In her eighties, she still retained that magic, that ability to make your heart sing with a smile.

'She's not talking a lot any more,' Sister Hedwig murmured to Cubby. 'So don't expect too much.'

'Okay. She looks awfully frail.'

'She's quiet. At least her temper's better lately.'

'Glad to hear it.'

'I'll leave you two to get some privacy. The buzzer's round her neck if you need me.'

Cubby sat beside Rosemary in the chair the nun had vacated. He saw that the call button was indeed hanging around her neck, along with the rosary, which pretty much covered all spiritual and temporal emergencies.

'Hello, Rosemary,' he said.

She didn't reply, but held her hand out to him, still smiling her lop-sided smile. He took it. They sat in silence for a while, holding hands, as in the old days.

'Your garden's very pretty,' he said at last. He pretended to examine her fingers closely. 'Aha. There it is. Your green thumb.'

He saw a spark of amusement in her dark eyes. 'Cubby,' she whispered.

'That's me.' It was warm in the sun. He felt his skin flushing, and unbuttoned his collar. 'I didn't think it would be so hot. I wouldn't have worn a flannel shirt.'

'Love – sun.'

'Yeah, I know you do. You're a sun-lizard, aren't you?'

'Tortoise.'

Cubby laughed. She could still surprise you with the things she came out with. He stretched out his arms, with their patterns of discoloration. 'The doctors say I have to watch my skin. I take medicine that – well, never mind.'

'Medicine?'

'Nothing to worry about. I brought you some stuff. Want to see?'

Rosemary nodded. He disengaged his fingers gently from hers and went to the car, returning with the holdall he'd packed in California.

'These are candies, fudge and whatnot. The stuff you like. I'd better put it in the house. It'll spoil in the sun.'

The cottage was spotless, almost clinically so. He stood at her little dining table in the cool interior, looking at the painting of Jesus on the wall, one finger indicating the thorns that bound his sacred heart. Seeing Rosemary always changed him. The even tenor of his life was disrupted, like a pond into which someone had heaved a rock. The ripples spread, squeezing and stretching his emotions until he didn't know whether he wanted to laugh or cry.

When he went back out again, she had picked the photograph album out of the holdall and was paging through it. 'Children,' she said. It was one of her favourite words.

'Yet more photos of the grandchildren,' he said apologetically.

'Beautiful.'

'Yeah, they're okay. A pain in the ass sometimes. At least they go home when you've had enough of them.'

'Love.' He thought she meant the grandchildren, but she was smiling directly at him. 'Cubby,' she said again. 'Love.'

'I love you too.' She nodded a few times. Her lips tried to frame some further words. He waited, but she didn't manage to get them out. She didn't seem able to string a complete sentence together any longer. 'I brought you something else. A poem I came across a couple of weeks ago. I thought you might like it. Should I read it to you?'

'Yep.'

He took the book out of the bag and opened it to the page he had marked.

'When you are old and grey and full of sleep,
And nodding by the fire, take down this book,
And slowly read, and dream of the soft look
Your eyes had once, and of their shadows deep;

How many loved your moments of glad grace,
And loved your beauty with love false or true,
But one man loved the pilgrim soul in you,
And loved the sorrows of your changing face—'

Her hand touched his, stopping him. He saw that tears were spilling down her cheeks. He closed the book. 'I didn't mean to upset you, honey.'

She shook her head. 'No more.'

'Okay, no more. I'll leave you the book if you want to go back to it. There's a marker in the page. Maybe one of the nuns can read it to you.' He didn't know whether she'd understood the words, or whether just the cadence of the poetry had moved her. 'He was an Irish poet.'

'Mmm.' She fumbled for a handkerchief and blew her nose.

'I just loved that line, *the sorrows of your changing face*. It reminded me of the first time I saw you, in London. I've been thinking about that a lot lately. About your face. Of course, you were the most beautiful woman I'd ever seen. But it wasn't just that. It was the way your expressions changed, all the time, never staying the same from one moment to the next. Your face was so alive, compared to other girls. It was restless. It was luminous and dark at the same time. Once you saw that, you could never un-see it.'

'Mmm.' He wasn't sure if she was listening to him. She was staring at the geraniums that nodded in the sun. They'd prettied her up for his visit, with some lipstick and eyeshadow, and her nails done nicely. They kept her hair dyed black, her original colour, but it was cropped short these days, easier to manage, he supposed. There was a safety-belt clipped round her waist to keep her in the chair.

'You looked scared a lot of the time. But there was something dangerous about you.'

This time he got a reaction. She seemed amused. 'Still dangerous.'

'Oh, I believe you. You're still a bomb waiting to go off, aren't you?'

She tilted her head and glanced at him from under her eyelashes. For a fleeting moment, it was there again, the captivating mischief of long ago.

'Yep,' he said, 'you'll always be the best Kennedy Girl.'

Slowly, the smile faded and the light went out of her eyes. Her eyelids drooped, and she was asleep. He picked up her hat, which was lying next to her chair, and laid it gently on her head to shade her face. Then he lay back in his chair and folded his hands on his chest. The air smelled sweet, of new-mown hay and the ripening fruit in the orchards. He closed his eyes.

He was awoken by Sister Hedwig's hand on his shoulder.

'Sorry to wake you, Mr Hubbard, but I think you may be burning.'

Cubby looked down at his arms, which had turned a dull red. 'You're right, Sister.'

'We'll have tea indoors.'

Afternoon tea was one of the rituals Rosemary most loved. She'd picked up the habit in England, at Belmont House, during the happiest period of her life. It was a proper English tea, with dainty little cakes and finger sandwiches. The two nuns who looked after Rosemary set everything out in a cheerful display, with flowered china and Irish linen. Cubby accepted a cup of Oolong and a plate of petits fours, though he didn't touch the latter.

'How's your health, Mr Hubbard?' Sister Gertrude asked, eyeing him keenly.

'About what can be expected,' he replied.

'What does that mean?' Sister Gertrude was always a bit sharp.

'Means I can't complain.' He changed the subject. 'Does Rosemary go everywhere in the wheelchair now?'

'She had a couple of falls. Nothing too serious, thanks be to God. But we don't want to take chances with her.'

He looked at Rosemary, who was eating cake with great concentration. 'You care for her wonderfully.'

'And you, Mr Hubbard – you've been her most constant visitor. You've been coming to St Coletta as long as I can remember.'

'Well, she means a lot to me.'

'It's a rare quality, fidelity. Devotion. We admire you for it.'

'I can't claim to have done anything special,' he said wryly. 'I never felt I had much choice.'

'But you do have a choice,' Sister Hedwig chimed in. 'God always gives us a choice.'

'I never felt that. I loved her from the moment I saw her. I couldn't help it.' The nuns said nothing. Rosemary was intent on her food, apparently not listening to the conversation. Then her lids drooped and she fell into one of her sudden dozes.

'It was a terrible shame,' Sister Gertrude said in her abrupt way. 'What was done to her. It was cruel.'

'Now, now,' Sister Hedwig said. 'Nobody expected the operation to go so terribly wrong.'

'They knew what they were doing,' Sister Gertrude said grimly. 'They wanted her out of the way. No embarrassment, no breath of scandal. Well, they've paid for what they did. Four of her brothers and sisters dead, all violently. Her parents struck down—'

'The family had the best intentions, Sister Gertrude. Rosemary was a danger to herself. Going with strange men. Who knows what might have happened.'

Sister Gertrude sniffed. 'Look at the girls today. Look how they carry on. They let their sex drives run free. *They* don't get locked up or lobotomised.'

'In the Thirties,' Cubby said quietly, 'a woman with a strong sex drive was in danger of being called insane. Especially if she didn't try to hide it. And Rosie couldn't hide her feelings. She didn't know how. That's why she was so vulnerable, and so terribly fragile. She loved life and fun, and didn't care too much about the consequences. I loved her for her spontaneity. We never got a chance to see what she would have grown into. What they did to her didn't change my feelings,' he went on. 'But it froze them. She vanished, but she was still there. It might have been easier if she'd—' He didn't finish the sentence. 'I don't think there was ever much chance that we could have had a life together, but after the operation, I had to give up whatever hope I still had left. I still love her. I always will. I'm a grandfather, and I have my own life at home, but deep inside, it's always me and Rosemary. Frozen a lifetime ago. Just waiting for something that will never come.'

Rosemary had woken up. Her eyes were on his, dark and warm. Her lips moved, framing words, but without a sound, as though only he could hear and understand.

He took her hands as they were saying goodbye.

'Rosie, I don't know when I'll be able to see you again. They want to do an operation in a couple of weeks' time, and after that – well, I don't know how things will be. So if I don't come for a while, I hope you'll understand.'

She nodded.

He kissed her. 'If I don't see you through the week, I'll see you through the window.'

He left her sitting in front of her little house, huddled in the wheelchair, flanked by the nuns.

He had plenty of time to get to the airport for his flight, so he drove slowly, the windows down, enjoying the balmy evening air and the sunlight on the cornfields. He found it soothing. The ripples in his life were flattening out. He was returning to his customary calm. Or was it numbness?

A long time had passed. A long, long time. And yet it had gone by in the blinking of an eye. How did you explain that, the way the years and the decades sped past so slow, so fast? It was a mystery.

County Road Y was deserted. There was not so much as a car coming either way, just farmland and crops. The pain in his chest, which had been there all afternoon, was swelling so much that he found it difficult to drive any further. It seemed to occupy the whole of his body.

He pulled over and stopped the car beside a field of grain that rolled down between clumps of trees and lost itself in the haze of twilight. He tried to breathe.

The last verse of the poem came to him; the verse Rosemary wouldn't let him read to her:

> And bending down beside the glowing bars,
> Murmur, a little sadly, how Love fled
> And paced upon the mountains overhead
> And hid his face amid a crowd of stars.

AUTHOR'S NOTE

In September 1939, the United States Lines ship SS *Manhattan* left Europe for New York with a passenger list very much as I have described. However, this book is a work of the imagination, not a historical account, and should be regarded as fiction from start to finish. The thoughts, words and actions of all the characters in this book were invented by the author.

Most readers will have no difficulty disentangling the historical passengers from the ones I put on the ship, but a few notes may help.

Leaving Europe at the lowest ebb of his personal and professional life on the *Manhattan*, Igor Stravinsky made a new start on his arrival in the United States, immersing himself in American music, including a number of Hollywood projects. He and his second wife Vera took American citizenship in 1945. At the time of his death in 1971 he was among the most celebrated of composers, having left an indelible stamp on twentieth-century music.

Carla Toscanini died in Milan in 1951. Her husband Arturo was left broken-hearted and in poor health. He died in 1957. More than any other conductor, he defined the interpretation of classical music in the twentieth century. His recordings bear testimony to his fiery genius.

Fanny Ward, the Girl Who Wouldn't Grow Old, did not return to London after the war, but remained a fixture on the East Coast high society scene until her death in 1952 at the age of eighty.

Elektro the talking robot is still in existence, passing a peaceful retirement in a museum in Mansfield, Ohio.

Commodore Albert 'Rescue' Randall received a citation from President Roosevelt on his retirement in September 1939, praising his service and heroism. He died in 1945.

The encounter with the German submarine which I have described actually took place in 1940. The vessel involved was *Manhattan*'s sister-ship, SS *Washington*, commanded by Captain Harry Manning, whose cool-headedness helped to save the day.

The character of Rudi Hufnagel is very loosely based on the U-boat ace Reinhard 'Teddy' Suhren (1916–1984).

Joseph P. Kennedy was withdrawn as ambassador to Great Britain in October 1940. His political career ended shortly thereafter. He suffered a stroke in 1961 that left him unable to talk or walk. His wife Rose also suffered a stroke in 1984, which together with advancing dementia, placed her in care for the last eleven years of her life.

Rosemary Kennedy died in a Wisconsin hospital in 2005 at the age of eighty-six, having outlived most of her siblings. Her lobotomy was one of over three thousand performed in the 1940s and 1950s by Doctors Freeman and Watts, who promised happier (and more docile) patients, but delivered irreparably damaged brains. The procedure, which destroyed so many lives, is now very rarely performed. While nobody could have foreseen the shocking results of the botched operation, it was clearly a last resort. Her adolescent 'slowness' had been an embarrassment; but her unrestrained adult sexuality presented much more serious problems to the Kennedys. She fell victim to a fatal combination of her family's political ambitions, repressive attitudes towards sex and mental health, and her own tragic vulnerability as a young woman with educational disabilities.

Cubby is an imaginary character. The poem quoted by him is 'When You Are Old' by W. B. Yeats, which appeared in 1892.

Racial attitudes underlay and partly caused the Second World War. Derogatory terms used in the novel reflect the language prevalent at the time and are not intended to offend any reader.

In 1941, with America's involvement in the war imminent, *Manhattan*, along with the *Washington* and the newly-built *America*, were all seized by the US Navy on the orders of President Roosevelt. They were fitted out as troop carriers, *Manhattan* being renamed USS *Wakefield*.

Having served throughout the war, she was decommissioned in 1946. But she never re-entered passenger service. She was mothballed for over a decade. The glory days of ocean liners were coming to an end and the United States Lines was heading for bankruptcy. The *Manhattan* was eventually sold for scrap and broken up in 1964.

ABOUT THE AUTHOR

Photo © Marius Gabriel, 2015

Marius Gabriel has been accused by *Cosmopolitan* magazine of 'keeping you reading while your dinner burns'. He served his author apprenticeship as a student at Newcastle University, where, to finance his postgraduate research, he wrote thirty-three steamy romances under a pseudonym. Gabriel is the author of several historical novels, including the bestsellers *The Seventh Moon*, *The Original Sin* and the Redcliffe Sisters series, *Wish Me Luck as You Wave Me Goodbye, Take Me to Your Heart Again.* His most recent novel is *The Designer.* Born in South Africa, he has lived and worked in many countries, and now divides his time between London and Cairo. He has three grown-up children.